Packs

D. T. Kizis

This is a work of fiction. Names, events, and locations are either the products of the author's imagination or have been used fictitiously for literary purpose. Any resemblance to genuine or actual persons, events, or places is wholly coincidental and beyond the intent of the author and publisher.

Stone Ring Press
www.stoneringpress.com

Copyright © 2011 by D. T. Kizis
Published by arrangement with the author
Cover art by Maria Talasz

Library of Congress Cataloging in Publication Data
Kizis, D. T.
Packs / by D. T. Kizis
p.   cm.
ISBN 978-0-9829712-3-9
1. Wolves – Alaska – Fiction. I. Title
PS3600.O666   2011
813'.57-dc20   2010940093

For Sidra and Orca and Sterling,
of course

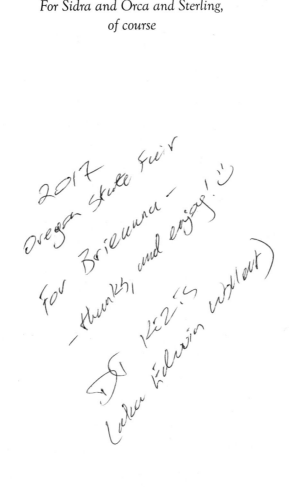

Prologue:

We have not always been enemies.

You eager humans once admired us.

Oh, always from afar, of course. Even then, through your admiration, lauding us with noble traits instead of demonic ones, you remained fearful to get close. At least, you would not stay close. You could hunt us, even capture us, and after thousands of years find yourselves questioning just how you managed to create so many "breeds" of these domestic animals which, strangely, do not fear you the way we do. So be it. Inbreeding always has strange results; no one knows that better than humans.

You studied our ways. You listened to our music and learned to harmonize. You watched us on our own hunts and learned the advantages of stealth, planning, ambush, and strength in numbers. You sneaked as close to our dens as your fear and comfort would permit you, and then marveled at how dedicated such creatures could be to their own. Of all the primates, you alone mimicked our societies, creating your own in their wake, but you misunderstood the need for wise and egalitarian leadership, and decided that the only true right was might. How many billions of your kind throughout history could fairly be described as "omega" because of this confusion? We did not impart cruelty to you. You developed that on your own. We did not cause unnecessary suffering. We took what we needed to live, and wasted next to nothing. Now you cry out for what has been lost, looking to us once again from entire wastelands you have created. We have to live on this planet, too, so perhaps there is time for one more alliance.

It might help to glimpse, even if just briefly, how it was, where we diverged. Perhaps we could both benefit from a history lesson, if for no other reason than to give an idea of symbolism run wild. We have always been that, more than anything else: a symbol of some artificial human projection into this world. We have been the Wild Hunters, the Admired Packs, the Ancestors of Dogs, your greatest allies, your most hated enemies. We occupy prime positions in the cultural mythologies of every human group which has lived near us, appearing as shape-shifters, tricksters, teachers, lesser deities, and, as you would have it, monsters, devourers, seducers, murderers. Return with us there now. Take a look at a piece of our mutual pasts.

We are wolves. And this is our story as well as yours.

* * *

Scenario One: 12000 years ago, wooded and escarped hills near the River Danube, in what will be called the Black Forest.

Germany looks a bit different back then, does it not? Absent are the well-built cars, the factories which made them, and the toxins which flow from industrialization. Here, then, so many centuries past, the only waste is what even the insects will not eat. Just the bones, really, and of course, you have already fashioned them into more of your tools, demonstrating talent for recycling which exists side by side with your predisposition for wasting. For now, though, there is simply forest in this region, an immense creature in its own right, engulfing rivers and hills, and only stopping when it reaches shoreline or too high upon the mountains; it knows not the sound of the axe or the chainsaw or the bulldozer. It is no meager green stage for your dramas; it is alive, and in turn offers life to innumerable creatures who rely upon it, as do you, for food and shelter. This is still before the time when your kind vainly wondered whether a tree would make a sound when it fell in the forest and no one was there to hear it. Your wandering philosophizing can wait; in the meantime, know that there are always those around to hear those falling trees, but you have acquired difficulty considering their presence. This vast forest is an easy place for our kind to hide within. Perhaps that was some part of your motive in destroying so much of it.

Look closely now. Remember that we are quite talented at concealment. Remain quiet, crouched to the earth, and maybe you'll catch a glance of one of...was that one? No...keep scanning the vastness; you shall find it trying to see one of us if we wish to remain hidden. Wait! There, atop on of the hills. Let us take a closer look.

Have you noticed the golden eyes yet? Or perhaps the footprints in the soft cool earth? These tracks have always been there, since you first grew such sizable cerebrums and started walking upright. Those amber globes watch you curiously and attentively; the stare of such a creature is disarming, making one wonder just what the intentions are of the brain behind them.

This first specimen is noteworthy: the alpha female. A good description, that. It bespeaks both a sense of primacy, as well as a reminder that your attempt to understand us is ancient, as the denotation appears in the old tongue of your early philosophers. She sits alone for now, gazing down at the landscape unfolding beneath her. This has been a beneficial location for some time: a good water source in a nearby river; plenty of food to feed one's pack; places in which to dig a den for one's pups.

There are six of them this year. It has been a healthy time for this pack. Sometimes life can prove so bountiful for the wolves that even some of the betas might have litters of their own. That requires a tremendous territory, perhaps as much as 1200 square kilometers, with enough food for the extra mouths. Just marking the terrain against interlopers in such a region is a major task involving all adult pack members. But this female has never known such a domain. She finds herself content with less, and has aggressively ensured that, among the females, only she mates.

She scans the land, sitting upon a rocky outcropping which affords views in all directions: the winding and rushing river to the north and east, with water still cold from the recent ongoing melting of the terminal European glaciers; the chuttering, buzzing forest to the south and west. This would be an ideal vantage point for a human, or an eagle, or any other primarily visual species. The wolves have excellent vision, too, even if it remains forever in black, white, and shades of grey. But this high point also proves useful for picking up scents and sounds. This alpha female has smelled deer from some kilometers away merely by perching atop these rocks, and attuning her senses to the awaiting world.

Her senses return to her comrades now, passing half a kilometer upwind, and in the less dense part of the forest. There walks her mate, the alpha male, all grey and tan and black and weighing a full eight stone. Hefty for a wolf, yet he earned his position not through brute strength, but with cunning. Two leaders, this couple: two distinct hierarchies, one for each gender. This hunt, like all those before and since, will be the result of teamwork. The large male does not betray anyone's position; there will be time for socializing later. Food comes first, then relaxation and contentment.

The alpha male merely looks at the three betas trotting up behind him, all four wolves keeping to their uniform jog. Efficient biological machines, all of them, able to maintain this regular eight kilometer-per-hour pace for most of a day, all days. A pair of twins, one of each gender, and another male who has survived an additional two winters, have joined the alpha male. The old male omega remains back at the rendezvous site with the half dozen scampering, eager, and perpetually curious and playful pups.

The four grey shadows continue their hike. Over these roots, under those branches, their padded feet leaving shallow tracks and mere whispers in the cool ground. They know they are being surveyed by the other pack leader, who will alert them with a quick but projective bark if their quarry is lost. They just need a close location, a place to observe, to study their prey and check for weaknesses which might prove exploitable. The adult hunters know this exercise, even the younger twins: the most difficult part of hunting is the waiting, the steely patience. All three of the lower-ranking pack members acknowledge their male leader with their own quick glances, and then it is back to waiting, then moving, then waiting more, for they are still learning the art of observing which individuals can be had with the least work. They have faith in their leaders; they must. Pack survival depends on this mutual trust.

This deceptively simple exercise is nothing less than a biological arms race, to use the human phrasing which will emerge millennia from the day of this hunt. A predator evolves its cunning, its speed, its brain, its natural weapons. Prey species simultaneously develop their keen hearing, sharp noses, agile legs. It is always a contest, part instinct, part desire, part adrenaline-rushing adventure. The roe deer near the meandering Danube are familiar with the wolves, indeed prefer to know their precise whereabouts. The forests make them nervous: too many places for predators to hide. Yet the forests can conceal deer as well, and there is no shortage of food. These deer must be cautious, as always; drinking from the river itself is both risky and necessary, and this day has been warm. This warmth has made them lethargic and careless.

No more than a glance is necessary from the alpha male to his three underlings to begin the contest of survival anew. The three betas leave their secure positions, spacing themselves out so that twenty body lengths separate each of them. They demonstrate the discipline of soldiers on a live training exercise, again masking the sounds of their large feet. They must get closer to have a chance; otherwise, they return to the waiting game with their ungulate ambitions too far away to serve as dinner.

The alpha female surveys all of this with those haunting eyes. If eyes are truly windows offering glimpses of souls, then a lively spirit indeed must dwell behind this pair of small but shiny piercing orbs. She stands at last, and at once begins to navigate down from her rocky observatory into the perpetual dusk of the forest. She can faintly smell her comrades even from here, and her presence in the rear will enable her to cut off any of the deer which might outmaneuver her companions in this direction. She has noticed her mate's shrewdness: the river is on two sides of the deer, the thicker forest on another. The wolves occupy the final dimension, thereby making escape quite trying.

The other wolves can see the deer much closer. A good herd, this: several bucks and dozens of does with a few fawns, some drinking, the others nibbling grass or looking warily around. It is not *easy for them, either; constant vigilance must accompany their speed and reflexes for them to live. Prey species never evolve as intelligently as predators, but they are nonetheless well-equipped to survive. The predators are nothing without them.*

An eager male beta wolf, one of the twins, can hardly contain himself. He wants so truly to charge, even though he realizes the others will chastise him if he ruins the hunt. So close now! The thick old trees provide plenty of visual cover, but unlike human hunters, the deer and the wolves can locate each other so easily by noticing scents and sounds. This drooling young beta allows his hunger to get the best of him. He steps carelessly.

Such a delicate sound: a paw plunging into a mud puddle. But it is distinct, and enough. The deer simultaneously prick up their oval ears, aiming them towards the beta. He has already frozen, hoping yet for a positive outcome. His breathing makes not a sound now, after he clamps his hot mouth shut, and his companions have similarly stopped all discernible motion. The beta licks the outside of his muzzle. Even the alpha male, twenty meters behind now, has crouched and become invisible, hoping the ruse might still work.

And then the group behavior of survival, common to so many social species which live under threat of predation: first one deer, then a second, then dozens, flail hooves and kick up loose, loamy soil, and the chase begins. The younger wolves are close enough that they might yet succeed. Their footing must prove surer, since the deer are actually faster: their prime advantage in the genetic arms race.

But now there is a more observable race. Gone for now is the stealth and planning and patience. Only pursuit remains. The wolves know they are slower, which is precisely why they must be smarter. For all their tactics and skill with an ambush, roughly one hunt in ten will actually manage to feed them. They sprint with iron muscle and coursing adrenaline, mouths agape and tongues tasting the air and the dirt raised by hooves. The female twin gets close enough to a younger deer to snap once at a hind leg, but no, the quarry leaps easily over the exposed roots of an ancient tree; the attempted bite leaves the wolf top-heavy for an instant, and she must spend a moment navigating over the same woody extension. It costs her some precious proximity, but she will not yet quit.

Her twin runs with the alpha male, eager to atone for his mistake; it was a good trap they set, and he would be shamed to have ruined it. This desire to both please and apologize grants him an edge, as he remains focused utterly on a single animal. That is the trick, when the patience can finally be abandoned: to keep all senses locked on an individual, so that the group is forgotten. The dance of death is thus reducible to just two partners. The alpha male observes this focus and tries to cut off both animals, the other wolf and the deer. If he can do so, the other pack members can encircle the single prey animal, which would transform this exercise into a question of time.

Tired and panting, knowing his sprinting speed cannot last long, though it can reach fifty kilometers an hour, the alpha male still grunts and extends his stride just a touch further, and when the lone deer notices him, it panics.

It turns away from the alpha. In so doing, it has turned away from the herd, away from escape. Perhaps it already knows it is surrounded, doomed. But life never quits, and nor does this deer, its seemingly fragile representative. Life struggles.

And perhaps this is the first behavior which made the humans so nervous. They do not generally tolerate this sort of thing in domestic dogs; to people, it seems so unforgiving and frightening. It is the growling and the exposing of so many teeth that elicits the flight, fight, or fright response. But it is merely part of the way for the predators. Baring teeth and snarling might be related to the hunt, or it might establish or reinforce the pack hierarchy, or it might simply be done for fun. But it always has meaning, despite the trepidation of humans. Now, of course, it is part of the hunt, and the betas keep their spacing, offering no escape to this young buck. It darts behind another tree, dashes clean over another shrub. The alpha male is already there to intercept it. From then it is over in seconds, the young female catching up to tackle the deer, as the alpha male reaches its exposed neck and ending its life almost instantly.

And this is the ritual, the dance of survival. Even with a less impressive-looking kill like this, the smaller creatures will benefit still: scavenging foxes, rodents, birds, insects, all the way down to bacteria. This is part of the sacred cycle: violent, yes; dangerous, absolutely; and also wholly essential to what humans will eventually call an ecosystem. The wolves will rest well this night, bellies full for another day. The young pups will also receive portions of this feast, the adults taking food back to them.

Yet for all their sensory apparatus and intelligence, for all the fear they engender in some of the species which live near them, these wolf pack members have yet to learn that someone else has located their rendezvous. Busy at the kill site, the adults remain unaware of the several creatures flattened onto their bellies, inching their cautious way towards another, smaller hill. The alpha female dug the nearby den, not needing to evict any prior tenants. As the soil here proved soft enough to mask sounds, it was an easy and secure place to dig. And this rendezvous location is the first chance the pups have to interact with a larger world, as they run and jump and nip playfully at the older omega, who displays endless patience with the energetic and rambunctious brood. These seven wolves enjoy the shade of the surrounding trees, granting a safe view of the neighboring terrain. The pack recognized its advantages, determined the site to be quite safe, but never considered this new type of interloper.

Though their twenty-first century descendants might register shock at the sight of them, these are nonetheless humans: one of the five remaining great apes, the only survivor among the various branches of the hominid tree. The other proto-humans are already gone from the world, leaving this creature, Homo Sapiens, in their wake. There are two females and a male here, dressed in skins and hides and simple coverings passing as shoes. Each carries a long wooden spear, not straight enough for accurate throwing, with a carved granite tip. Primitive tools, these; the humans at this stage, when the ice is finally *receding and agriculture has yet to permit overwhelming specialization of tasks, still seem much the same as their so-called "cavepeople" ancestors, right down to the animal images this group has painted on stone walls. Still, those advanced cerebrums allow for rapid learning and quick dissemination of sensory data. Thus the interest in the wolves' rendezvous site.*

The omega notices them at last, his faithful snout alerting him. The humans have been careful, and while their noses might be superior to those of the billions of more "civilized" members of their kind which will follow them, they are mere appendages compared to the olfactory receptors the wolves possess. Hundreds of times more sensitive, the omega's nasal passage has registered something it knows only as foreign, and therefore to be treated with caution, especially considering his responsibility. The pups notice it too, of course, but have not learned sufficient discrimination among competing scents, and so choose to ignore it.

The omega quickly weighs each option available to him. He can try and escort the half-dozen squirming pups to shelter back at the den. He can bark, snarl, and growl at the interlopers, hoping to scare them off. Or he can howl until his lungs burn, hoping that the rest of the pack members are still within range of his vocal abilities. He selects the latter.

The pups join him, still thinking it all just a game, but it works. The humans freeze, thankful for their own partial shelter amidst the rocks and trees, and listen to this eerie, piercing, haunted sound. No other noise in the world comes close to replicating a wolf's howl. Whether done for sorrow or celebration, to signal a gathering or a warning, the music of the wolves is absolutely distinct, rising into the sky and carrying for kilometers. Even the pups, in their limited experience with wolf song, already provide a natural harmony. The effect makes these seven sound like dozens, an impressive canid choir.

The people are now the anxious ones, unable to resist glancing about for the other animals which surely must be responsible for this much noise. The baying encourages shivers, and is felt in the very spines of the humans. They will have to return and try to observe the wolves another time. Indeed, already the rest of the pack is scrambling towards the rendezvous site, even with the slowness resulting from sated bellies; "meat drunk," the human trappers will one day call this. But they come anyway; they know the sounds of their own relatives, distinguishable from other wolves. To the people, it is all so much howling.

But as the humans retreat, they cast glances back at the site, already unable to see the now hiding elder and the pups in his care. The women and man will remember: they have seen the wary animals and how they behave, and wonder what it could be like to live with such creatures. In these forested hills in the future Deutschland, it is still centuries before the sweeping domestication which will forever alter so many plant and animal species into variants more adapted for human utilization.

And yes, the long-term descendants of these animals will be known as German Shepherds, Siberian Huskies, Irish Setters, Pekingeses and Dalmatians: different breeds from different lands selectively created by human interference for different purposes. So what went wrong? If the wolves and the humans were close enough to create such a myriad of domesticated forms in places around the globe, then why did the wild wolves and the domestic humans part ways, learning to distrust each other as they did on this day? Why were some of these dog breeds even created to hunt wolves, in a genuinely ironic turn? There was no overt hostility here in the Black Forest this day, only wariness. No violence, just curiosity expressed by two intelligent species. But if the dog is descended from the wolf, and the dog is the man's best friend, but the man yet loathes the wolf, then something has gone awry. Yet this is only one small region of the Earth, an early chapter in their relations with one another. Time to explore other possibilities shall come later.

For these are wolves. And this is their story as well as ours.

PART ONE: DISTANT HOWLS

"The soul is the same in all living creatures, although the body of each is different."
    - Hippocrates

"Universal compassion is the only guarantee of morality."
    - Arthur Schopenhauer, *Über die Freiheit des menschlichen Willens*

The view from this perspective is always entertaining. I thrill in watching the whole room, the faces of my training colleagues, revolve completely up, over, and around me, too fast to pick out facial details, yet still slow enough for identification and the noting of smiles. This is an odd sensation at first, even scary, but also exhilarating. That may be the main reason why I keep coming back here. And then, if I've timed things like I should, and if I've kept up with my partner for this little exercise, my landing should prove, if not wholly graceful, at least gentle and fluid enough to keep injury at bay. Relative lack of noise is a good indicator of successful *ukemi*, this art of falling and rolling; but I've landed this time a bit hard, wondering how many of my colleagues heard me slapping the padded mat an instant after impact to absorb some of my energy. When I first saw this motion, it seemed like a mere somersault, but it's actually a way of redirecting life's own force into something less violent.

That's perhaps the commonest misperception of this art called *aikido*: the person getting tossed about actually has a more difficult job to do. For now I am *uke*, the person committed to what onlookers perceive as an assault, as I threw a punch at Tony three seconds ago, using my whole body, with the punch extending from my hips instead of my hand and arm. I liken this sweaty living philosophy to a dance: two partners locked together, one leading, the other following. Not to hurt, but to harmonize, until the leader decides for separation to occur. If the dance analogy holds, then I currently act in the woman's traditional role: that of follower. I do some formalized dancing, too, and maybe my simplest love of *aikido* is that in this room I get to dance both parts, rather than just follow all the time.

I should offer something more of an introduction, I suppose. Maybe my sweating and jumping about, wearing what looks like a bulky off-white pajama top and a navy blue skirt which is actually baggy pleated pants, isn't the most ideal way to meet me, but this exact time seems most appropriate. This is where this odd little story seemed to begin, in hindsight. Good old hindsight; it never lets me down. Foresight, though? I have to wonder. We all do, from time to time, whether we'd have done this differently, or said that instead, but like a friend of mine used to like to say, playing the "what if?" game is a useless exercise, except as perhaps a sort of philosophical mental training. And right now, I'm too damned tired and hot to bother much with formal philosophy.

My birth certificate back in Salem reads, "Morgan Greene." That's it. No middle name, no needless decoration, nice and simple, like this spartan concrete edifice. What else should I mention now, when so much lies ahead? The usual, I suppose: 180 centimeters tall, or an inch shy of six feet if you prefer, with the coloring of an Irish goddess, to use the phrase my father liked to use to tease me. He said I would be like the dreaded *Morrigan*, the feminine Celtic triple deity who could appear as a raven or an old hag and who decided the fates of the ancient warriors. Great image, that: I wonder what my fellow *aikidoists* would think of it. There aren't many freckled redheads in this city, so I do tend to stand out, from my coloring along with my height. I'd always hoped for green eyes to match this short-cropped rusty mop of hair, but I've had to content myself with that generic shade of brown that so many people have. Chocolate, I call it, to be different: chocolate eyes.

I don't recall thinking much about this at that moment, though. What I do remember is our *sensei* clapping her hands once to signal that our time with that particular technique was done, and we were about to move on to something different. That was when I started thinking about our upcoming trip, right then. I'd not given it much consideration before, since the journey wasn't my idea initially. It had crossed my mind, of course, but now that it had almost arrived, it finally sank in while I knelt on the side of our training mat. Dave, Jack, and Mariska were waiting for me. I'd insisted on working out once more this morning before finally packing up for this trek into the wilderness.

Time now, however, to sit in *seiza*, on my knees, which have toughened up considerably since I began this exercise more than eight years ago. I barely hear *Sensei* Rogers briefly discussing what she intends to have us do next, as she demonstrates what we'll all be performing in another minute or two. I love this next one; it looks even more violent than what we just left behind, but again, the goal is peace, not brutalizing an enemy. I hear Tony and the others breathing hard and heavy on either side of me. *Good.* At least I'm not the only one feeling the workout.

Felicity Rogers is wondrous to watch. She's been at this *aikido* stuff for most of her life now, and damn her, she makes it look so easy. This practice is simple, yes, always simple. But never easy. That's the part some onlookers misunderstand right from the start, and some of them who try it become quickly discouraged and quit. Maybe the likes of *karate* and *judo* are easier, though I don't know enough for comparison. Maybe I'll ask Jack later.

The elegant Miss Rogers glides and slides through her demonstration, using poor Richard as *uke*. Like the rest of us, he's already tired, but he gallantly keeps going, partly because it would be disrespectful not to keep up, and partly because there's just enough instinctive male chauvinist within him to want to look good for the rest of us as a woman tosses him about the room.

That's it for now. Another clap of her hands and Felicity beckons the rest of us to select new partners and give this a go. We all simultaneously bow towards our now kneeling teacher, then glance about quickly for someone with whom to train. Most of the others have paired off by the time my eyes meet Richard's, so he and I offer each other another bow and we both stand and then jog a few steps to find some space on this mat to move.

At least it's cool in here this morning. There's not much of a view inside this industrial little building, with its windowless walls and rather minimalist décor. A few paper scrolls of Japanese calligraphy adorn the walls in evenly spaced locations, there are a couple of simple racks with wooden practice weapons along the north wall, and overlooking the middle of the mat along the eastern side hangs a photo of an ancient looking man. The one who created this art, Morihei Ueshiba, or O-Sensei: a small person who used to send multiple men up to two meters in height soaring across a floor without even touching them. I often wonder what he was thinking right as that photo was taken of him. His eyes look serious and somehow serene all at once. And yet, if you look at them again later, it's like he's the only one who understands the punchline to some grand joke.

I'm of course not quite as proficient as he was, and accept that I never shall be, but I need this. That's why I harp on it so. This is the activity which keeps me even vaguely rational, especially in light of both my messed-up background, and what happened the few days after I left the dojo that morning. Well, what's about to happen, if that makes sense. See? That weird hindsight again, or maybe it's foresight, or maybe I should just focus on the technique at hand.

Sure, this workout offers some great aerobics, and yes, there are some intriguing self-defense aspects to what we do in this place, but the reason I keep coming back is, well...

Mariska and Jack at least try and empathize, but their vision in this regard is limited to seeing it as either sport or combat, especially Jack, who's done a fair amount of *karate*. He used to compete in tournaments, sparring with hand and foot pads and performing short form demonstrations known as *kata* with old weapons, but he doesn't really see martial arts in philosophical tones; he grew up more interested in learning how, if the need arose, to kick someone's ass. I don't know if it's something in the testosterone, or if he was bullied, or something like that. Dave, meanwhile, comes closest to understanding, which I thought surprising, given his outlook on life, but he does know some of the philosophy behind this. So damn it, I just have to say it: I think this effort makes me a better person.

That sounds both trite and vain. I'm sure not about to share this with Richard, even though I like him and enjoy training with him, mostly because he's funny while off the mat and sincere with his attacks while on. Maybe it's because he doesn't want to go easy on another chick who can mop the floor with him.

That's right: this chick here, doing the narration, the one pivoting and turning and rotating her hips to get this lower-ranking student into position so specifically that he actually has no choice but to throw himself, leaving me in such a state of physical calm that I don't need to open my mouth to breathe.

Yes, I'm physical. I'm a good hiker and cyclist, too, all part of that growing need to keep some semblance of a fit body without catering to those dipshit magazine ads of what women are supposed to look like, and simultaneously starting to fight off osteoporosis now that I'm old enough to no longer be acquiring new bone mass. That would put me in my early to mid-thirties, if you're up to speed with that sort of thing; you likely already know to never ask a woman her true age. And I'm working on a new job: a field reporter for the Anchorage *Daily News*. It's more of a freelance sort of gig for now, but the exposure helps, and it's good practice for an aspiring writer. Dave asks me about writing regularly, and I keep asking what it is that he wants to write, but he remains so secretive about it all. Like there's some big manuscript lurking in the nether-regions of his brain waiting to be born. Maybe he's just anxious. After all, the publishing world is a tough mistress, many would say. I think it's more of an evil two-headed bitch demon myself, probably more than a match for the old *Morrigan*, but there you have it.

That's enough for the moment. Back now to my other training: the more physical kind. Richard has already obtained a hard cherry wood *jo* from the side wall, bowing towards the black and white photo to show respect for both the school and the weapon. Then he steps back from me and simultaneously raises the *jo* above his head menacingly, exhales and tries to bash the thing over my head. I step gingerly off the straight line of his incoming attack, taking much smaller steps than might seem reasonable, and my arm meets his as the staff cuts downward, finding only air for a target. Without stopping, which would both give Richard his balance back and interrupt our energy flow, I finish positioning myself so that I'm next to him, right at his side, even looking in the same direction. This feels so alien at first, but it's really an application of good physics and body mechanics. The hard part is focusing your own center of gravity as the source of your movements. That center is just below your navel: nothing metaphysical, just a different way of looking at human kinetic energy. In an instant, my step has been followed by a pivot with my left arm just under his right. From here, all

I have to do is rotate my own arm over while stepping forward from the side adjacent to his body, and a mix of the motion, Richard's forward momentum, and my raising my arm slightly to inhibit his balance just a touch further, compels him forward until his options consist of stampeding into the wall or aiming lower and rolling into the mat. He takes a smooth roll and stands at once, pivoting in place to face me again, still gripping the *jo* in one hand. His other hand is what led his forward roll. Then he attacks me again.

I feel both elated and disappointed by what I've just done. Our mutual motion was fluid and the technique I performed worked, but what I did was a technique more appropriate for our regular unarmed practice. And, of course, Richard still seems rather threatening with that length of wood in his hands. He smiles just slightly, aware of my mistake, and raises the *jo* once more to assault.

This time I can better picture Felicity's prior movements. Now I'm in the opposite stance, so I step forward with the right foot and pivot fully on it, which brings me into Richard's personal space, to use the trendy terminology. It looks the same so far, just done from the other side, and disturbingly vulnerable, but this time I've met his hands, and even taken a light grip on the *jo* myself. I rotate more than last time, and now when I step forward, Richard is almost rolling over me on his way down to the mat.

To protect himself from the fall, he has to release his own grip. So now I clutch the staff, feeling the firm but light mass of it. I bow slightly to my partner as he stands, offering the weapon back to him. We continue this way for six more attacks, and then switch roles, so I get to pretend to bash his head instead, and then gently fall where he leads me.

Weapon disarming intrigues me. It's a reminder that the dummy staves and swords and knives we train with are just extensions of the people holding them, the same as their more lethal counterparts. It is scary looking at a raised sword for the first time, or a rubber knife that appears possibly sharp at a distance, ready to try and run you through. But it's empowering, really. Not in a macho, destructive, pummel-your-enemies-and-make-the-world-safe sort of way like Jack might admire, but more in a holy-crap-I-can-actually-do-this manner instead. The *bokken*, *jo*, and *tanto* might look like a sword, a quarterstaff, and a dagger, and they're indeed the traditional weapons of the feudal Japanese warrior code of *Bushido*. But I occasionally wonder: what would it be like to be assailed by something more modern? Like a gun, perhaps. Most of the historical *samurai* were known to loathe firearms, considering them dishonorable for their ability to dispatch someone from great distances, without having to look into an adversary's face and thereby assume responsibility for one's lethal actions.

As I intimated, it's extremely difficult to have linear thought take place while you're actually doing this sort of thing. Indeed, the masters of this art, of any physical art I suppose, do not really think at all while doing it. *Aikido*, writing, riding a horse, painting, anything, I suspect: the artist simply performs the motion, and it appears effortless. Here there's no planning of a technique, no bodily tension, there is simply an encounter of two beings, who ignore everything else that exists for these brief moments. Yeah, I know: it sounds weird. And yes, there's a sort of Zen thing going on with this approach, that "no-mind" that I always picture the Asian monks in their orange robes trying to achieve, never mind that the harder one tries to achieve focus without thought, the more elusive it becomes. Try, as an experiment, to spend the next thirty seconds *not* thinking of a blue-eyed polar bear; you probably can't do it, can you? It's almost like you have to rationalize the irrationality of it.

Okay, okay, I'm getting ahead of myself here. I said there'd be time for this philosophy stuff later, which is true. Gods, but spending a few days in the middle of freaking nowhere with three friends will likely either lead to multiple fights or to far more philosophical thought than may be healthy. Dave and Jack and Mariska. That morning in the *dojo*, I started wondering how the four of us would fare out in the great Alaskan bush. And I thought, for the first time in reference to this trip, whether or not the four of us would make a successful backpacking team.

It wasn't until the end of the *aikido* class that I could focus more on this planned excursion. Yes, all four of us have extensive wilderness experience, else we wouldn't be trying such a trip in the first place, especially not this late in the year. In much of the world, mid- to late September is no big deal, but in Alaska, in any part of Alaska, September is a time of reckoning. If you're a plant, you've already shed your leaves or held onto your precious water supply or done whatever else plants do to prepare for months of freezing. If you're a bird, you might opt to get the hell out of the region entirely; it amazes me how smart some birds are in this respect, getting off to warmer climes. Only the birds who can still find food among snow can remain. And if you're a mammal, you might have to store a lot of food somewhere safe, or gorge yourself silly to prepare for months of winter rest when dietary necessities become all but unattainable.

I guess I hadn't mentioned much of the Alaska part yet, had I? This is my home, though I'm not from here originally. I asked Richard here in the *dojo* once where he was from initially, and he replied, "I began as a speck of space dust, and everything after that is just a blur." I made the mistake of encouraging him that day, so he added, "You know, Einstein once said that, 'I feel the insignificance of the individual, and it makes me happy.'" A smartass, yes, but I recall laughing at his answer anyway. I remember hearing somewhere, shortly after moving up here, that a bit more than half of Alaska's resident humans were actually born elsewhere. All I can do is hope that the state doesn't fill up with so many people that the wilderness here becomes more like that in my home state of Oregon. Down south in that latter state, the wilderness certainly exists, of course, and you can still escape not just from the cities but from all other people as well, it's just that down there you have to look more for the wilderness. Up here, it's awaiting you, right outside your front door. I learned that the day I stepped out of my building to find a moose staring at me, nonchalant as could be. Like it owned the damn place. Anchorage has over two thousand of those hoofed critters, and they're more lackadaisical than most ungulates, content with exploring the city for food, only showing annoyance at the dogs who run off their leashes, and they're among the luckier mammals who can still find food during winter.

As for these friends of mine, Mariska is the only one actually from here: born and raised. She's of Athabascan descent, one of the many local cultures, with some European thrown in, German I think. Her coloring is magnificent: naturally bronzed skin which makes her appear something like American Indian mixed with Polynesian. She smiles easily and with flawless teeth, which also shows off the dimples her parents have always been proud of. She's several centimeters shorter than me, with luscious dark locks that curve and taper a bit at the ends, and those hazel eyes which for some reason remind me of dark opals, an unusual color mix for an indigenous North American. Her face is slightly rounded, which is part of her genetic background, and she keeps herself in outstanding shape, which is no meager feat for a professional academic. Suffice it to say she's a knockout, and she has bones I could die for. She's never quite understood the way men sort of get goofy at the sight of her, her students included.

Jack and Dave? Both tall, Dave slightly more so. He also has what might be called dirty blonde hair, which he keeps short enough that it sometimes spikes on its own. Jack keeps his hair longer, down part of his neck, and he has eyes the color of a cloudless bright sky, very attention-getting. Dave has the look of someone who is incapable of genuine inner peace: that constantly animated gaze which makes you wonder either what he's thinking or whether he's really pissed off by something. Jack's face is a bit more playful: he still gets "carded" in shops and restaurants for buying booze, even though he's well into his thirties, and he's the sort you'd always want to have as a big brother. He laughs as though he's found some huge gag that the rest of us aren't yet privy to, though he's fanatically loyal to his small circle of loved ones. Beyond that in appearance, both men are like me, "white" through and through. Of northern descent: ancestors enslaved, killed, poisoned, cheated, and otherwise kicked the crap out of everyone they encountered, you know the story. Dave doesn't get hung up on this racial kind of stuff, but Jack's curiously embarrassed about it. He's traveled all over the world, maybe as a way of making peace with his own European identity. Or maybe it's because of his on-again, off-again relationship with Mariska, who walks that line of feeling proud of her Native background without lording it over anyone else.

Hell, I don't understand those two. Jack and Mariska do seem to adore each other, sometimes anyway. Maybe they're just bullshitting one another, both guilty of that curious social disease, fear of closeness. Taking a leisurely and planned break from romantic entanglements myself, I still hold out hope that love stories can be simple. But I guess the *aikido* analogy carries over to here as well: simple, yet never easy.

And such were the various thoughts parading about my head while I stood in the women's small dressing room in the *Alaska Aikikai Dojo*, now cooling from the workout, unable to resist a quick glance at Felicity's lithe and sculpted body. Don't get your juvenile hopes up: I'm not fantasizing, just admiring. It takes years to get a body like that, and she's so matter-of-fact about her physical form I could cry. I feel like I have to work so damned hard at my own, but I'm still proud of it.

That's part of the appeal of backpacking, too: tremendous exercise, and the ability to justify the ingestion of unholy amounts of food while on the trail. This comes with the additional benefit of knowing that when you're so hungry, and so far removed from what we call civilization, that just about everything you shovel into your gullet tastes fabulous. Even now I'm a bit hungry; with a Saturday morning class starting at eight, I don't really have time to munch on anything before coming in here, so it's hitting me while I finish dressing. Sometimes I join the training crew here for breakfast out somewhere in town, but there's no time today. I promised the others I'd be ready for the drive out of Anchorage by ten o'clock at the latest, and it's after nine now.

At least I can pack in a hurry. My dad used to give me a hard time about that. "Why can't you pack the night before?" I can still hear him shout, but it was always light-hearted, since he knew I would invariably be ready right on time. I just put off packing until the last moment; somehow it makes me ironically less likely to leave important items behind. And like I said, the four of us going on this little outing are experienced. I know where each piece of my gear is, and how much it all weighs when dropped into my pack. All I need to replenish is food and water supplies.

Damn! I utterly forgot to get food for this trip. That's the problem. There's not really time to do a full supermarket run, with the gang picking me up soon. But I know just where to go. I'm picturing a brief shopping trip as I utter my goodbyes to my training colleagues while heading for the door. Then I pause, as always, offering one final glance at the wall where the archaic image of a Japanese master hangs, as though he's surveying each of our classes. I bow at the door, picking up my shoes which have been respectfully left outside, Japanese fashion, then back out of the grey building, and head for the car.

Driving in full winter in a Volkswagen Beetle is not my usual idea of fun, though on this warm and slightly windy autumn day, winter itself still feels months away. It'll be sooner, of course, at least in a place like this. Living here, you quickly learn to savor the briefer summers, with their shorter growing seasons and longer periods of daylight, both of which amuse and annoy the tourists. Part of the appeal for heading out now for our trip is that first, the middle of September marks the official end of cruise ship season for this state, and consequently a huge drop in the number of visitors; and second, all four of us love the fall.

The old Bug obediently starts on the first try, which continues to impress me, since this is its original '72 engine, with over 200,000 miles on it. You may have noticed I prefer metric, since that's what the rest of the world uses, but this car was made for the American market. It dates to about the time I was born, so I take that as somewhat of an omen, and my dad maintained it quite well over the years, enabling me to inherit it as an undergraduate back in the nineties. You hardly have to be a car enthusiast to instantly recognize the distinctive purring of an older Volkswagen engine: rattling but light-hearted sounding, like it's eager to please. I pull out of the small parking lot from my martial arts school and head for midtown.

Anchorage still looks pleasing this time of year. It's come a long way from being a tent city just a century gone, existing mostly to fulfill the material needs of those who came up to pursue their mad dream of gold. The whole region was still "Seward's Folly" then, an apparently foolish purchase engineered by the former Secretary of State right after our civil war. People thought it was just a damn polar bear-infested ice box. Anchorage's creation helped enable others to learn what a varied place this really is. We do get our share of fall colors, even within the city, though not quite what you'd expect from, say, New England. The city itself reminds me a bit of the *dojo*: simple, functional, not very ornate. Some of our tax funds pay for the planting of many thousands of attractive annuals, which the tourists rave about, and the city does look well manicured during the four-month travel season, starting in mid-May. If only they could see this place in the winter: slush, dirty snow, and the trash has a way of getting buried beneath it, leaving us a nasty visual surprise with the spring thaw.

I'm on the east side at the moment, on a hellishly busy street called Tudor, and I opt to cut north just northwest of the Native Medical Center. I did a story about that place for the *Daily News* once: it's an immaculate and large modern hospital, and while anyone can receive treatment there, you don't really have to pay for the service if you can verify the presence of Native Alaskan or other indigenous American blood in your veins. I asked Mariska about it once, and I remember her looking almost embarrassed. She's proud of her heritage, sure, but she doesn't like the thought of anything resembling entitlements. She said she'd support a national health care system like the European Union countries have, based on how the Native Center here was performing. I still have trouble imagining it even with recent reforms, which was part of my interest in writing the piece.

The real reason for my turn here, though, is to head past the universities. We have two of them, adjacent to each other. Alaska Pacific is smaller and prettier, and I pass it quickly on the right, then turn west again to head for the University of Alaska at Anchorage campus. I just wanted to enjoy more of those annual plantings, the city-wide flower show, before they all die off for another winter, and the median along this stretch is overflowing with this floral spectacle. I pass Providence Medical Center on the left, briefly wondering why we have two universities and two large hospitals all so close to one another; perhaps it's so the more accident-prone but wealthy undergraduates can be close to places where their physical mistakes can be remedied. I drive west, cruising into the heart of the city.

My destination this hurried morning is my favorite shopping section of town. Within a couple of blocks of each other, we have a variety of shops catering to the likes of my three hiking companions and myself. REI is the biggest and most impressive looking, but there are local folks here, too: Alaska Mountaineering and Hiking, Barney's Sports Chalet, Gary's Sporting Goods. Sixth Avenue Outfitters is also good, though it's downtown past my home, by our acoustically-excellent-yet-visually-questionable Performing Arts Center, and there are others as well like Sunshine Sports which was nearby but moved, while REI and Sixth are my favorites. This town has anything you could ever dream of when it comes to facing the wilderness, so much so that we often laugh at some of the crap that gets invented to try and convince impulse buyers that they're capable of becoming survivalists overnight. My destination this morning is REI. I ease into the parking lot they share with Dave's favorite bookshop, Title Wave, where I once worked myself. Then I leave the Bug at a lucky space in front of the store. They've just opened for the day when I lock the car.

There's way too much stuff even in here, though at least they do a plausible job of rotating stock, depending on what the primary activities of the day are likely to be. Dave used to work here, once upon a time, and he always hated what he complained of as the hypocrisy of retail stores: "moving the same shit around to different parts of the floor to confuse idiotic shoppers into thinking that some of it's new." Or something along those lines, I think. And people think *I'm* cynical. No, this story isn't really about me. It's about my friends, and about

the wild world we were about to go explore. I'm only telling it
to work it all out, to understand its results.

Entering the two-story shop, I at once notice that the
kayaks and canoes and mountain bikes have gone into storage,
and the staff here are preparing this weekend for winter as
well: out to the shelves are coming scores of snowshoes, skis
for cross-country and alpine styles, thicker jackets, heavily
insulated boots. I bypass all that, and head right for the center,
finding a shelf which always has the same items displayed on it:
dehydrated and freeze-dried foods.

I have to be quick, of course, and no, this is not my
preferred method of eating while backpacking, but remember
what I said earlier: when you're hungry after a long day of
hauling a pack on- or off trail, damn near anything goes down
quite easily. I stare at the expensive foil and paper pouches
hanging about the shelf. There are six companies represented
here. Imagine that: at least six manufacturers of dehydrated
food aimed specifically at those of us who consider our tents
second homes. I do like fresher more, but this is easier. Most
of these just involve the addition of boiling water. Let's see...

I hurriedly choose five different entrée packs, two
dessert items, while remembering that Mariska promised to
bring sandwiches for this first day, along with some fresh fruit,
which is unfortunately difficult to keep non-bruised inside a
backpack. I've still got some trail mix at home with my gear,
so this should be fine. I jump into the thankfully short line,
simultaneously grabbing my own impulse item (half a kilo of
imported gummy bears, my favorite sugar source), and wait to
pay. For a three- or perhaps four-night trek, this is more than
adequate, though I always keep a reserve of food, even when it
means cinching the hell out of my bear-resistant food bag.

Because this is, after all, Alaska. Also known as the Last
Frontier (Dave says outer space is actually the Last Frontier, but

that's a Star Trek fan for you). And you don't dick around and take stupid chances with such an environment.

My shopping done, I can hightail it out of here. I like this place, but it does feel oppressively corporate sometimes, and I'm in a hurry anyway. Tossing the brown paper bag of dehydrated delectables onto the passenger seat, I vacate the lot to head home. My apartment is downtown, a few minutes from REI, so I cruise north on Spenard to reach I Street and 13th Avenue. The former was apparently Anchorage's red light district, way back when, and still has a reputation bordering on the unsavory, but I've always delighted in seeing it. The hilarious and time-tested but now gone Fly By Night Club's comedy show, the bicep-crazed bouncers at Chilkoot Charlie's huge bar (actually several bars and dance clubs), the Bear Tooth Theater, (and Pub and Grill), the curious little head shop which continually gets a legalize-pot-measure on our election ballots, to no avail... I mean, what's not to love about Spenard? Something here for everyone, methinks.

I once again savor the view of downtown, with its large hotels and huge oil company office buildings, as I cross over one of the city's many bike and jogging trails and head uphill to get to I Street. Turning west onto 14th, I'm right at my building, just a block and a half stroll from New Sagaya, a restaurant and grocer which imports foods from all over Asia and the Americas. If I'd had more time, I'd've shopped there today instead, but I really wanted to train on the mat once more before we left.

And of course, my damned phone can be heard while I engage in a physical dispute with my keys. I'm only through the outer security door, which naturally takes a different key than my apartment. I prefer living on the ground floor like this, though the views from the upper story of this building do offer better glimpses of Cook Inlet and Mount Susitna across the water to the west. This is a quad building, looking a bit cheap compared to the lovely Park Place complex which occupies the block between me and my favorite international market, but it's quite homey, really. I finish switching keys one-handed while holding my new merchandise in the off hand, and then I'm finally in, hearing my own voice finish its electronic greeting.

"...-1268. The wittier your message, the likelier I am to call you back. Thanks." And then comes a beep, the sound of my recorded voice fading. During the few extra seconds, I drop the bag onto my throw pillow-infested couch, and go straight for the pets. My children, I call them. Since I'm hurrying, I want to hear who's calling first. I let Angus out of his connected cages, and he at once starts bounding through the apartment. I love watching how ferrets run, like a fast furry Slinky, that metal spring toy from the 1970s which would go end over end down a staircase, and I can just hear Dad's voice cut in on the answering machine as I reach with extended fingers to gently stroke the plumage of my backtalker, Cozy. The bright cockatoo hops onto my shoulder from his artificial tree while I'm still debating how quickly I can have my father off the phone.

"Hi! Hello? I'm here, Dad." Cozy tries to grab the phone cord in his beak. I offer him an index finger in its stead and hear the man's voice.

"Oh, hi, honey. You are there. Did I just wake you up or something?"

"No, of course not. I just got back from class, is all."

"Hi, Dad," Cozy pipes up, not really content with my bony digit. Talking birds are usually only fun when you have time to enjoy them. Living with one can be different. I'll never forget the look on Dad's face when he came to visit me after my last breakup and was promptly called "asshole" by my extroverted avian. At least Dad understood when I explained that it was the last word Cozy had heard me say prior to his arrival, as Charlie walked out with a dreary sense of completion that day.

"Still with the martial arts madness, eh?" Dad's never quite understood my interest in the arcane disciplines, either.

"Yeah, and still loving every minute of it. Listen, I'm in a bit of a rush here."

"Oh? Where to today?" I knew his tone. He was genuinely just curious, and not nosey like Mom used to be. Growing up, he always respected my independence more, but this was hardly the time to dwell on Mom.

"We're going packing south of Denali Park. Me and Mariska and the guys." Dad knew exactly who the guys were, indeed could never quite get that I was never that attracted to Dave or Jack. Sure, they're both good-looking and I love them both, but we were friends first. I seem to have an unwritten policy of only shacking up with men I hardly know. Something about not wanting to lose a friend if things go sour, although lovers always seem to say that their best friends are the people they're waking up beside. I told you it was never easy.

Dad wasn't fazed today. "That sounds good. Be careful, my dear."

"As always. Hey, what's behind this call, anyways?"

"We just haven't spoken for a week or so, is all."

"Are you feeling lonely still?" I hated asking, regularly thinking it was only fifteen months since Mom died, but at least I no longer heard the sadness in his voice as often. They truly adored each other, those two. I found myself looking at where a picture of Charlie and me, with Angus in my lap, used to sit on one of the kitchen shelves. Then I remembered getting rid of it, though I kept the frame. It's good pewter, that frame; I'll find something else to fill it eventually.

"Actually, I'm doing quite well. Chris has invited me again for tennis this afternoon. And Lila and I caught a performance of *The Lion King* up in Portland."

Good. He sounds good. I'm struggling to balance bird and phone while simultaneously beginning the mental rummaging of my hall closet. That's where the outdoor gear is, all of it. "So, what's the latest with you two?"

I could hear him sigh, hesitating. "We're still good friends, if that's what you're after."

"Hey, I should talk, right? I'm just happy for you. I'm glad you're having fun. And how the hell did *Lion King* get to Portland?" I remembered the day Mom and I went to see the original animated version, when I was down visiting Oregon for part of the summer. It was right after I'd opted to return to school to pursue writing, hoping for a Master of Fine Arts from my alma mater (a "Magnificent Farts" degree, to use Jack's lingo). I realize journalism's different, but at least for the *Daily News*, I know that something I've written will actually be published.

Why on earth was I feeling sentimental that day? I was eager to get going. "The show is still on tour, and we just got lucky, so to speak. Listen, you're probably still getting ready, so I'll let you get to it. Tell the gang I said howdy," I heard Dad say.

"Yes, I'm still a professional procrastinator, which is fun to say, I might add. I love you, Dad. I'll call you after we get back next week."

"I love you too, my Morrigan. Be safe."

And I hang up the phone, refusing to glance at a clock or my watch. Time to hit that closet. I pull my sweaty *gi* from training out of its small duffel bag and toss it into my cantankerous dryer, so it will be sort of fresh for more martial arts classes when we arrive back in Anchorage. I stride down the hallway and eagerly fling open the closet door, proud of my organizing skill. Staring into it, I look from the top shelf downward, which holds the winter gear: aluminum-framed snowshoes and waterproof boots which resist temperatures quite far below freezing. The snow clothes hang to the right of these shelves. Down at the bottom lurks my trusty, dirty, beloved backpack, with extra-wide hip straps designed for a female frame (one advantage we have over the guys is those wider hips to take pack weight). I pull it out first, at once glad that I emptied it after the last trip, back in mid-August. I did a solo overnighter just northeast in the Eagle River Nature Center, overlooking the namesake river and contentedly watching the mountains and trees.

The pack's light metal frame feels cool and at home in my grasp, and I lift it from the closet effortlessly, knowing how much room is to either side of it and not wanting to knock any of my other stuff out onto the hallway floor. It weighs just a few pounds, and has gone from its original red and black to some perpetual dusty earth-tone, evidence of its dozens of trips and many hundreds of hiked kilometers. Its very appearance makes me smile, like I'm greeting an old friend.

The boots are next, the most important piece of gear other than my own warm grey matter, and they too have weathered the trails superbly. I sigh in relief as I notice the results of my maintenance after my last trip out: the boots are dirty, sure, but there's no mud caked on, and they still have the unmistakable oily smell of waterproofing solution. These are leather ankle boots, with an interior steel shank for support. They've been re-soled once and are currently sporting their third pair of laces. Even an early mild snow would not likely justify my hard-core winter boots, which are better protected against water and insulated with so much recycled fiber that the rest of me could potentially freeze rock-solid before my feet even began to shiver. The leather ones will be warm enough, I decide, especially with the sock liners.

Then come the other accoutrements of a successful trip. I briefly open the drawstring sack for my down sleeping bag, content again that there's no musty smell coming from it. Into the bottom of the top-loading pack it goes, fitting snugly. It'll stay dry down there, even if the pack gets submerged. I love the goose down inside the sleeping bag, but it won't insulate a bit when wet. Then comes my stove. Dave introduced me to outdoor stoves when we first met. Full fires are no longer allowed in many wild locations, throughout dozens of countries, and the stoves work far better anyway (campfires heat unevenly, and the soot they leave on cookware will get all over the other items in your pack). This little Dragonfly stove even has a flame control, and has proven very difficult to damage, not to say I've actually tried to bruise it. I'm more concerned for its tank. I pick up the separate red metal half-liter tank of white gas for fuel and shake it. It sounds almost full, and I remember I barely used it in Eagle River a few weeks back. I check the detachable pump to make sure it will still build up pressure to the gas line once attached, convince myself that all is well with my heat source, and then it goes in separately, vertical atop the sleeping bag.

My first aid kit goes in next. I did some emergency medical technician training five years ago and kept my certification current up until last year, upon deciding that I would never use many of those skills, and have since just kept up with first aid and CPR training. Still, the EMT work taught me how to better equip a kit, since first aid kits never seem to have barriers for rescue breathing or even gloves to work on emergency victims. I put this kit together myself: a dozen flat sterile gauze pads of various sizes, smaller fabric bandages, medical tape, scissors, tweezers, Betadine for disinfecting, a tiny plastic bottle of Advil for pain, another with Immodium for diarrhea, Spenco Second Skin for burns, some moleskin to cover around blisters, a metal Ace finger splint, an Ace bandage wrapping for sprains, safety pins, needles and sutures (Dave's a paramedic, and in addition to teaching me to cook in the outdoors, also taught me to sew wounds, even though he's not actually allowed to do it for his job). This sounds like a truckload, I know, but it's quite compact, actually, fitting into one of the side pockets of my pack.

Related to this is my emergency kit, with the last-resort survival items: water purification tablets (I have to check these to make sure they're still within their expiration dates), a coiled-up wire saw in its own aluminum compartment, an assortment of fishhooks and sinkers with some twenty-pound fish line, one of those shiny foil "space blankets" for warmth, a signaling mirror to reflect sunlight, extra matches, an allegedly windproof candle (the only piece of gear I pack which I've never field-tested), and an extra, small compass. This is all compartmentalized into a small plastic tackle box.

I can't wait any longer, and sneak a peek at my watch. I've still got a few minutes. This is one of the rare times when I almost wish my friends were less punctual. Very rude, I've always thought that: people who couldn't bother to be on time when you needed or wanted them. I've been called anal retentive for usually arriving fifteen minutes early for things. Even Charlie once chided me for that, saying I was the only woman he'd known who usually reached orgasm earlier than he did. I still wonder whether he meant that as an insult, and if so, then to whom.

My time-worn Camelbak gets pulled down from a hanger in the closet. I thought it strange when these things started appearing in the equipment shops: basically miniature backpacks with a couple of small pockets next to a main compartment designed to hold a sizable water bladder. It seemed they would be just another stupid trendy device at first, and I wondered if they'd really replace canteens and plastic water bottles, but now there are several makers of similar items. My own model is the Mule, and not even a day hike goes by without my having this thing strapped on. A slender blue hose extends out of the collapsible water bag and attaches to one of the shoulder straps, so you can suck water out of it without breaking stride. With my full pack on, I've even carried the Mule on my chest, which took some getting used to, and requires a bit more dexterity to put on, but it's convenient. For this trip, though, I'm saving space in the top of the main pack for the whole Mule, and then I can take the smaller pack with me for shorter hikes from wherever we make our base camp.

I consider the various methods of cleaning water, since there's very little "wild water" that can be fully trusted. Yet some folks are content to take their chances, especially with small streams, and there are countless thousands of water sources in Alaska. I have a smaller plastic water bottle with a carbon filter cartridge that fits into the top to clean water. All I have to do is lift off the top, remove the filter, then plunge the whole bottle into a clear water source. Then, with the equipment replaced, I can drink through the bottle top as the water runs through the filter, and I don't have to worry about giardia and the other nasty little bugs which live in streams, rivers, and ponds. My friends poke fun at me for having so many ways of treating water: filtration, chemical additives, boiling with the stove. And I have to remind them that while I've never had "beaver fever," we've all heard enough horror stories of excessive diarrhea and vicious cramping to want nothing to do with it. The nastier forms of hepatitis can also be transferred through contaminated water, as can dysentery, so I always have a way to deal with water sources, even if it's another example of being anal retentive (in this case, far better than being anal explosive).

I habitually grab the smaller of my two tents, one designed for just a single person and some equipment. The other's big enough that it won't quite fit into my pack. We've not yet discussed who's bringing which tents, always a consideration in a group outing, so I'll just throw the small one into Jack's vehicle and we can decide later whether it's needed.

The most important items now secured into their various compartments in the pack, I can start adding the slightly less essential things. Attached to the bottom of the pack's frame is a rolled-up grey foam mattress. I've tried the inflatable ones, too, which in fairness are truly more comfortable, but they're harder than hell to roll back up tightly enough for their protective cases, and it's quite difficult to find the tiny leaks which will eventually plague them, usually caused by pebbles or twigs at a campsite. Mariska swears by the inflatables, though, and the duct tape covering the several holes in her mattress has always held, to my knowledge.

Bedding considerations complete, I can toss in some extra clothes. I check the topmost pack section, which is a small zippered space in the flap which folds over to close the pack. I keep nothing but cold clothes in there: a long underwear top and pants, and two pairs of sock liners. I'm a cold-sleeper, always needing to bundle more stuff on. The undergarments are still there and still smell clean, so I can consider other clothing. Alaska is a land of layered outfits, and I fold up a second nylon blouse, two changes of cotton panties, and a second pair of convertible nylon slacks. The first blouse and pants will of course be worn today. I often take just a single set of clothes, but there's something emotionally satisfying about changing into dry, clean clothing, and even though the nylon is quick to dry and slow to absorb odors, you can never judge accurately just how much you might stink to the people who are hiking with you.

I consider my Tevas, those ultimate walking sandals with the tire-quality soles, then decide they'll be extra weight. I only use them while backpacking for crossing streams, and we're not going to encounter big enough streams on our chosen trail. It would be too damned cold this time of year, anyway, and I've never felt thrilled about voluntarily making my feet turn blue.

That's almost it. You're likely wondering how big a motorized vehicle is needed to haul all of this, but my inventory for this outing comes to approximately twelve kilos, with almost all of that weight to rest squarely on my hips, thanks to the pack design. I recall reading that you should only carry a maximum of a quarter of your body weight in a pack, so this works well (no, I will not confess my actual weight; after all, I didn't even offer a precise age). Only a few things remain: a waterproofed jacket, insulated lightly for fall but not enough for a hard winter; my knife and sheath; a small vinyl kit with some toiletries like a toothbrush, paste, aloe gel, a hairbrush, and dental floss; the Ursack for food; and United States Geological Survey quad maps for the Talkeetna series for the area we're heading toward. This entails a pair of the 1: 63,000 scale quadrangle maps: Talkeetna Series B-2 and C-2, with an inch equaling a mile, and sufficient detail by which to navigate. I'm sneaking another glance over the USGS maps, some of them inside their water-resistant case, when the pounding on the door commences, sounding like the Anchorage Police are about to raid.

"Morgan! You ready, or what?" Dave's voice, eager and playful. When he's in a good mood he sounds like an excited kid.

"Door's open. Get your ass in here and help." In he stumbles, sending Angus scurrying for his dignity, and eliciting a squawk from Cozy. Cozy likes Dave, though Angus has shown some reservations.

"Hi, Coz," he begins, extending an arm towards the bird's artificial tree. Cozy hops onto the proffered limb, yells "Dave!" while turning his head about.

"God, I love this bird. I should really get one like him. I love how you can leave him relatively free and he doesn't crap all over everything. So, are you all set?"

It amuses me to watch my friend with my feathered child. "Yeah. Oh, hey, one question: what's everyone doing about sleeping?"

"What, you mean with the tents?" Dave asks.

"Yes. What did the others bring?"

"You know, I think Jack and Mariska are sharing this time. I've got my little burrito along."

I can't stifle a giggle. "What's so funny?" he prods.

"Do you remember what Mariska thought the first time you called your tent a 'little burrito'?"

"Ha! She didn't know about the tent, and thought I had a new euphemism for 'penis'!" Dave has a genuine laugh, when he allows himself to smile: all toothy and uncontrolled, again like a kid.

"Here. Take this for me." I toss him the yellow Ursack, a Kevlar drawstring bag designed to keep those of the ursine persuasion securely segregated from the contents. "I'll fit it into the pack later. Give me just one more minute."

"Is that a woman's get-ready minute, or a man's football minute?" Still grinning. He's insufferably adorable when in an upbeat mood.

I ignore the crack about feminine and masculine misperceptions of time due to distraction by other interests. "Neither. Just let me feed these guys." I set about searching for Angus, who frights easily but forgives just as quickly. He pokes his head and his perpetually twitching whiskers out from behind my closet door, the same closet from which I just excavated so much gear. "Angus," I offer.

He hops out, a length of fur, looking, one supposes, rather like a burrito himself, albeit one with legs. As I kneel down he's already hopping my way, then he jumps onto my thigh, and I lift him closer to my head. He inspects my face, which always tickles from those whiskers, and I offer him a smooch to the top of his little noggin. "Be good," I admonish him, still convinced that non-humans are better at understanding human language than people are typically willing to give them credit for, even if they can do it just by picking up the nuances and subtleties of tone, pitch, expression, and gesture. Still, the first two criteria are enough for blind people, and the latter two enable the deaf to have full comprehension. So why not ferrets, too?

Angus is already hopping from one shoulder to the next, and I'm having a difficult time controlling my giggling from the sensations. I have to grab him and set him down, hoping he'll be content with me gone for a bit. At least he'll be out of the cage, I remind myself, and even that isn't as much of a hardship as it is for some pets: I connected two larger cages to each other, and then extended about twenty total meters of that hard plastic rodent-run tubing so that it meanders all about the apartment. It's quite a conversation piece, Angus' trail system, but I want him to have room to run and play, too. He spends more time exploring that than he does with his toys and diversions, like those little rubber balls and rodent wheels which line the shelves of the world's pet shops.

Hoping Cozy's not too jealous, I walk away from my ferret, and stroke the bird's neck several times while he still sits perched on Dave's tiring arm. "You too, Cozy; try to keep each other out of trouble this time, okay?"

"Do I even want to know of the event to which you just obliquely referred?"

"Hell, no. Let's just say it took half a roll of paper towels and half a can of Lysol to set it right again."

"Okay, Coz," Dave begins. "Let me set you down so we can leave. I'll see you soon." He likes talking to animals, too, one of his more endearing qualities. Like me, he doesn't feel foolish doing so. Besides, people make fools of themselves for talking to very young children, and I for one have gotten far more satisfying results from conversing with a pet than from trying to chat up someone's baby.

Quickly refreshing the supply of food and water for my beloved non-human companions to last them several days, and more or less forcing a hug onto each of them (it's difficult to truly embrace a bird), I fold up the additional maps into their case, grab the backpack and loose tent, and we head out the door.

On my way out, I see Dave gazing towards my kitchen, but don't stop to wonder why. I glance again at the telephone, and the pewter frame which still sits empty.

But this is no time to dwell on the past. There's a gorgeous fall day awaiting us, and Dave is already bounding for the door, almost skipping towards Jack's car, while I lock the front door and shoulder my pack.

* * *

Days previously, Dog-chaser had not been able to remember such a level of exhaustion. His tongue merely dangled from his hot mouth, his feet sore enough that even his soft pads were starting to hurt, and all four of his long, lean legs begged for a rest.

No rest, though. Not yet. Safety first, then maybe, just maybe, all the rest wanted and needed. Dog-chaser just wanted that precious safety, along with his companions.

But there were only three of those now. Two days earlier their pack had numbered eleven, and the sudden plethora of fatalities had shrunk their ranks dreadfully. The survivors would mourn those deaths when time permitted. But for now they had to distance themselves from the booming and cracking man-thunder. A wrenching noise to canid ears, it had kept the four remaining members of the Fire Creek wolf pack motivated to drive themselves into such high fatigue.

Dog-chaser thought they were free of men here. This region was just not well-traveled by the humans, not even by their aircraft or snowmachines, and the closest settlement was the village of Nikolai; even that lay some hundred kilometers to the south, where Dog-chaser had once experienced his first glimpses of humans. The topography here was harsh for people, ideal for wolves and their prey. The wolves' territory nestled in between the wind barrier of the Sunshine Mountains to the west, and the Mystery Mountains to the east. These were all small peaks compared to what lay to the southeast: the legendary Denali and its innumerable granite partners comprising the tremendous Alaska Range. Accordingly, with none more than 1200 meters in height, the Sunshine and Mystery ranges were regarded as drab by comparison, at least by the humans.

But the non-humans thrived here: moose, caribou, black and brown bears, squirrels, hares, wolverines, lynx, dozens of types of birds. The wolves made a living primarily on moose and caribou, and being opportunistic, would also occasionally opt for smaller prey, like the squirrels and hares. This was good, healthy land: hilly and rocky but checkered with hiding places, including useful denning sites. All the present members of the Fire Creek pack had lived their whole lives here.

Only Dog-chaser had seen humans before, back when he had briefly made a living on his own, always much more difficult and risky for one of his kind. But that was some time ago now, and he was perpetually grateful for his position with the other pack members. Being an *omega* was a thankless job, but it still meant companionship and food and support, even if he was the low rung of the pack ladder and so had to eat last.

That would all change now, with the four of them just trying to stay alive. Almost two full days had elapsed since their actually seeing the men. These humans on their trail had slowed down, or perhaps even stopped, thankfully. There were no roads in this region, and travel was actually slower for humans in the absence of snow, since a dogsled or snowmachine could be used during the winter. And besides, the men were trying to augment their livelihood; wolf pelts were still valuable, even after a recent drop in demand, and the deceased members of Fire Creek would eventually have their remains sold at a handsome profit in the shops in Anchorage or Fairbanks.

But the fact that the wielders of the man-thunder were hunting legally made no difference to Dog-chaser, Oak, Paddler, and Trap-dasher. Paddler was the only surviving female member of the pack, so she would automatically change her status from *beta* to *alpha*. Oak already was an *alpha*, a sizable black male, who had wisely coerced the three others to not howl their mourning to the mountains. Indeed, Oak missed his dead mate; Midnight was sleek and companionable and smart, an ideal pack leader. But Oak's nose had recoiled in horror at the smell near her body; gunpowder was a potent odor, even worse than the traces of poison noticed on the other bodies, and the cordite had made his eyes water. Even at a distance, the wolves learned to associate that nauseating scent with the deafening sound of the man-thunder. They could not believe that there was a noise even louder than their own howls, which could be heard far away if conditions were favorable. So Oak let them know that howling would have to wait, since it betrayed their latest hiding places.

The big male led them, knowing they would be at the end of their territory within a few more hours. Oak also knew the others might balk at leaving their own home behind; the domains between wolf territories were the canid equivalent of what humans called no-man's land. Neutral land was generally not contested, but wolves caught venturing into the homelands of other wolves tended to be ruthlessly hunted down and eliminated as competitors. Oak recalled when they readmitted Dog-chaser to the pack; it took months for them to trust him again, and he was always at the bottom of the pack hierarchy, knowing they might have killed him outright as an interloper. But there'd been plenty of game, and safety from other animals, so he was accepted. Oak realized that the four of them likewise being adopted into another pack was quite unlikely, since it did not often happen at all, and when it did, was usually an act reserved for just single wolves. Four of them still constituted a pack, and would rightly be viewed as a threat.

Oak stopped then, near a stream running south of the small Mystery range. They sometimes had fished in here, even watched the bears with their cubs play near the water. But that could not be anymore. Oak was a leader; he would not give up on his packmates, but also recognized they were facing more than one danger. Men behind, unknown land in front. The other three wolves caught up to him. Paddler looked devastated, her eyes drooping and tail held low. She stopped briefly to lick at a small gash on a hind leg, not remembering which low branch inflicted it. She was more typically colored for an Alaskan wolf, black down the spine and at her points, with tan and ivory shades marking up her flanks, belly, and legs. She was smaller than Midnight, but was also in her third year now, and sexually mature to perpetuate the pack's members when the time came. Trap-dasher lay down briefly, catching his breath as best he could. Perhaps the cleverest member of the pack, he was the one who first spotted the humans, after they had done most of their work. Fortunately, he had kept quiet, and was able to warn the others, and they only returned to the rendezvous site when the men had left for a time. But they'd returned, and the surviving wolves had no chance to confront what had befallen them all.

The survivors did not chastise themselves for guilt, as humans might, but they were crushed by the loss. The four of them were hunting by themselves, the other wolves left behind at the site. Their hunt had gone unsuccessfully; caribou were often easy to find in their territory, but the wild deer had noticed their presence too early and managed to elude them that day. These remaining adult wolves had been already tired, returning from an aborted hunt, when they found the bodies.

Trap-dasher, too, was almost entirely black, earning his name as a rambunctious pup when he figured out how to set off the man-traps without getting ensnared himself, after one of the rare occasions when humans actually came this way, even though Trap-dasher had not seen the bipeds. It had been an old track, forgotten, and no longer smelled like men, so the curious young pup had gotten closer. Wolves like him were the bane of human trappers, the latter of which had to grudgingly admit that their targets were intelligent enough to not only avoid traps, but to teach their pack members how to avoid them as well. The type of trap that the young wolf had dodged was illegal in this area, as was the use of poison, and had not been set by the pair of men who now tailed them.

Paddler derived her name from her otter-like ways in any body of water. Stream or pond or river, she was always at home in aquatic environments, content to play even when her packmates thought she was just acting foolishly. She was dual-skilled, though; her swimming ability also resulted in her being the best fish-catcher of the group. And Dog-chaser, the one who had come closest to men of them all. Living alone for a brief period, he had gotten just enough into Nikolai to annoy and scare some of the local dogs, and then there'd been his odd subsequent encounter in Kantishna. But he wasn't afraid of them; domestic dogs were usually more pesky than threatening, and he had even befriended one of the local strays in Nikolai, though he noted that this dog was a clumsy and sloppy and wasteful hunter, and knew little about surviving away from the comforts that men provided for dogs.

The only sounds now, thankfully, were their own breathing, and the trickle of the stream. Oak was postponing the inevitable: when they would have to cross, and shortly later be beyond their borders. They could all swim well enough when necessary, and the creek's current was always fairly gentle, even during the spring thaw, when every body of water in Alaska would swell with the additional depth of recently melted snow. The creek was hardly the problem.

The wolves sat watching lazy raindrops collapse into the stream, their coats thick enough already at this time of year to not feel any water less than a full submersion. It should have been a peaceful day, but now they pricked up their ears at the slightest noises, knowing that even a light rain could disguise sound. A vole trotting beneath the shrubs, usually a source of amusement for pups. A sudden increase in wind velocity, eliciting rustling from the short trees. What other sounds could they trust? Their nerves were stretched perilously thin, and all four continued their alertness, rotating their heads about to let their senses do their work.

Oak glanced above the stream, facing southeast. On clear days from this area, they could see the High One, which humans called McKinley or Denali, but it was hidden in the mists this day. Yet that was where they would head, to the most difficult terrain the humans could possibly face, all the better to hide wolves within. But Oak did not know how far it really was, indeed was unaware even of what lay beyond the much smaller hills and rocky peaks that were now just several kilometers away from them. Fortunately the snows had not yet emerged. The wolves could smell the seasonal change that was imminent now, and knew how much easier it could be to track other animals through snow. Hopefully the winter would hinder the humans as much as it would slow the wolves.

Oak missed his dead mates' judgment. Humans spoke of *alpha* male or *alpha* female, though a pack had two members making the important decisions, maintaining pack order and discipline. But he knew Midnight would have agreed with him; they had to head southeast. The terrain north and west of the Sunshine Mountains was beautiful and filled with game and delightful to explore. But the north also marked the far boundaries of another pack, while the west was where they usually encountered the brown bears. The latter were few in number, to be sure, and while wolves and bears generally co-existed peacefully, too many of both in the same territory was begging for trouble. No, those directions were not viable options. Only towards the huge mountains seemed safe, so they would follow that route, come what may. These mere hills overshadowing them now were simple obstacles, but Oak kept staring at them, seeing them as a marker. No one in his pack had ever ventured past them. Not even several generations of his ancestors had known what the topography was like on their far side.

But they had to rest, at least for a few minutes. Oak stood, and strode over to Trap-dasher. The latter wolf wagged his tail, then collapsed onto his side, offering his vulnerable belly to his higher-ranking relative. Oak accepted Trap-dashers' licking of his muzzle, appreciating the act of subordinance but also savoring the simple feel of physical contact with a packmate. Wolves were very affectionate, bodily speaking. Trap-dasher whined briefly, but it was more of a question than a sign of bad spirits. He wanted to know what Oak's decision would be, though he already had his suspicions.

Paddler was next, and Oak could sense her anxiety. True, mating season was several months away yet, if they all lived long enough to see it, but Paddler was acutely aware of the huge responsibility she'd inherited. She'd once expressed a passing interest in Oak, and while the latter may have considered reciprocating the sentiment, Midnight had been there to intercept Paddler. Wolves maintained their numbers naturally; even the human scientists still debated just how, exactly. Did they somehow know whether any of their numbers other than the *alphas* could mate in a profitable season? Did inter-wolf competition help keep numbers down? Or did available resources adjust their numbers, as was taught to elementary school children? Some scientists thought it was a mix of all these factors and perhaps others. And the adage that wolves were somehow oversexed was simple fabrication: despite the mythological association with lust, this was a species which was lucky to have sex once a year. So whatever the motivation, maybe even simple jealousy, Midnight kept the other females away from her partner, while Oak had always fended off the periodic advances of the other males towards Midnight.

That was all different now. If they survived four more months, then Oak and Paddler would become the new mated *alpha* pair. But it was so much to even take in right then, so Oak contented himself with another oral greeting. Paddler remained standing, but kept her tail held low, almost between her hind legs, as another sign of submission.

That just left Dog-chaser. Oak valued this subordinate wolf, understood that the lowest member of a pack was ironically the pack's cheerleader, and Oak wanted to howl his appreciation over the fact the Dog-chaser had been the last to lie down to rest for the past dreadful days of running, always making sure that his higher-ranking packmates were secure. At Oak's approach, Dog-chaser sat, then went prone, and looked up into Oak's golden eyes. The leader did not enforce his position again, knew that Dog-chaser was not one to question the order. He simply laid a forepaw onto the *omega's* muzzle, hoping Dog-chaser could feel the strength that was needed to get them all through this.

The Fire Creek pack members would never know, but their assailants had already given up on them. They had bodies to transport, and these had to be kept fresh for their pelts, lest too much decomposure set in. And it had been a profitable trip. They could hardly believe their luck, and their timing had been meticulous as well as fortunate.

* * *

John Graydon knew that this particular pack had acquired some skill with evading the conventional traps, and as a lifelong distance hunter, he hardly considered traps sporting, anyway. That sort of issue came up in Alaskan politics periodically: whether it was acceptable to trap certain species but not others, and how that would alter bag limits, and whether bait could be used for the larger, more difficult species like bears.

His brother, Benjamin, was less experienced, but likewise understood how fortuitous their results were. He still questioned his brother sometimes about trying to actually capture very young wolf pups, but was always rebuffed on that score. There was virtually no demand for that anymore; almost all captive wolves around the world were born to captivity, and newly introduced wild ones could be too aggressive with their slightly tamer zoo companions. And besides, zoos were about controlling species; John explained that more than once. Nobody wanted to go to a zoo to watch wolves snarling at each other, even though it was usually for play or to just test and keep testing the established pack order. No, folks visited zoos to see how cute the residents were.

Benjamin still marveled at how easily the pair of sleek adults had been taken. John had told him about this pack being able to avoid traps, which he had heard about through the rumor mill in Nikolai, and Benjamin generally shared his brother's attitudes on trapping, but no wolf or bear or moose or caribou could outrun bullets. Indeed, aside from firearms, the two men were outfitted rather similarly to four other humans who were just leaving Anchorage that same day. The former preferred more rugged clothing: combinations of natural and synthetic fibers to insulate and maintain relative body dryness, along with color schemes that could offer visual camouflage from all but the keenest of eyes. Cabela's mail catalogs were the men's mainstay for this equipment, from their camo outer layers to their long underwear to their knee-length rubber-shelled boots. Besides that, they likewise had specialty backpacks, MREs (the military acronym for "meals-ready-to-eat"), water filters, basic packaged first aid kits; they lacked the meticulousness of, say, a Morgan Greene. Still, they felt quite prepared, and had only planned on a few days afield, anyway.

Part of the Graydon's sense of comfort remained clutched in each man's hands. Benjamin liked to copy his elder brother's habits, a holdover trend from childhood, which currently extended into wanting the same outdoor gear as John. Accordingly, each man carried at his side a walnut firearm from Northwestern Hunting Rifles; both guns were identical. They were bolt-action at the core, each built around a Czech action model which had been developed from the older German Mauser 98 models: the working mechanism of *Wehrmacht* sniper rifles dating to the Second World War. They were lightweight, expertly oiled for water resistance and wood longevity, and had dovetail scope mounts for their telescopic sights; the brother's own chosen optic devices had better magnification than most of the world's zoom camera lenses. Their twenty-five inch stainless steel barrels propelled a bullet from a .380 ammunition cartridge, each of which measured over three inches unfired, and delivered their soft point rounded nose bullets at approximately 2700 feet or more than 800 meters per second until they ran out of proverbial steam. Needless to say, there existed few species on the planet with any genuine chance of getting back up after taking one of these rounds, which were advertised partly for their ability to penetrate dense tissue. For about a thousand dollars apiece, the brothers felt very safe with these items close by, even though they suffered the same fate of all bolt-action rifles: a slow rate of fire, since the bolt had to be cleared and reset after each discharge, to allow the next bullet to enter the firing chamber.

The catch, of course, for men opting to hunt animals for their usable pelts, who resorted to firearms since their targets were adept at avoiding traps that the men wished not to utilize anyway, was in attempting to avoid having "deeper penetration in compact tissue" translate practically into something more like "blowing large craters into flesh and thereby making the eventual pelts less valuable." The Graydons had to rely on patience and rifle skill; John was proud of saying how much attention he paid to avoiding the unnecessary suffering of the creatures he hunted, since these .380s induced enough damage, cavitation, shock, and blood loss that death was quick indeed. Mercy could be granted while still minimizing profit loss; and besides, the Graydons were not really in this for the money, seeing that as a mere bonus when available.

The men had tracked the pack for some days. The wolves knew they were close; one even went out of its way to be spotted by John and Benjamin, like it wanted to know more about them. That was an almost all-white female, whose pelt would likely fetch the greatest price in a fur shop in a few months' time. The men knew the exact count of the pack members, even what they looked like, and were actually glad that they'd not killed the whole pack outright; the survivors would have a chance to make more wolves, and the human brothers would be able to periodically come up here again to reap the benefits, so to speak.

Plus, hunting was just so damned much fun. That was the real attraction. John and his younger brother understood that other species hunted to eat, and they both sometimes did the same thing themselves, twice proudly bagging hefty and delicious bull moose, and also venturing closer to the southern coasts each year with their tackle to take advantage of the salmon runs. But this was different: just being out in this incredible wilderness, this unspoiled landscape so removed from human interference. Little wonder they'd gotten close to a whole wolf pack; the wolves were instinctively anxious of humans, yes, but had yet to learn what the purpose of the man-thunder really was.

Nikolai was days ago now, and John and Benjamin
were just about out of food supplies by this point anyway. They
were about three miles north of their camp site, which was also
the location of their all-terrain vehicles, meaning that one of
them would have to remain by the old wolf den while the other
fetched an ATV so the wolf carcasses could be hauled out of
here. They had too much weight to carry now. These vehicles
were rather more costly than the guns, and here again Benjamin
aped his elder, selecting the same model and only differing on
the color. They each had a Honda FourTrax Recon model,
John's in glowing candy red, Benjamin's in olive drab like an
army vehicle. They weighed in at slightly over four hundred
pounds, and while they had tiny couple-gallon fuel tanks, they
nonetheless maintained excellent mileage. Benjamin was still
paying his off in monthly installments, but both men remained
excited just by seeing these open air machines, looking like
wide motorcycle bodies with four wide knobby tires protruding
from them. John had seen other drivers get careless with such
vehicles, so he picked up the bill for helmets for both of them.
The only question was how far he could bring one of them to
the wolves' rendezvous site, since the terrain here was much
more forbidding than the topography they'd ridden through
since leaving the main trail out of the Medfra camp site where
their friend's boat was also parked. He'd try and navigate
back, and then see if they would simply have to prepare the
wolves out here, and then take them back to Nikolai; both men
preferred to do their messier work closer to home, since the
carcasses would attract scavengers, perhaps bears, and they'd
been more successful hunting than they'd thought. Not that
wolves had much meat on them; indeed, no human group in
history had ever relied on such gamey flesh. Fortunately, they
were still close to an old game trail, used by the wolves as well as
the various other residents, including moose and a few caribou,
which should make ATV access that much easier. Indeed, the

original game trail had been expanded and largely maintained, heading out of the camp site which lay on the South Fork of the Kuskokwim River. This was no place for cars, or even trucks, but the little rugged Hondas did admirably here.

Two healthy adults: that was their take, though they'd hoped for more. They had been distance snipers that day. Benjamin yet had trouble keeping his rifle still enough for the longer-ranged shots, but he nonetheless took down one of the adults. And indeed, the invasion of deep tissue advertised by their ammunition manufacturer had lived up to its promise, while simultaneously allowing for relatively small holes bored into the coats of the wolves: the nearly white curious wolf, and another which was almost completely black, making a tremendous bold contrast. She'd bring a good price, too, now that Benjamin considered it again.

But both brothers were disgusted by the flagrant waste of the other wolves, as they found the poisoning victims half a mile from the wolves they'd shot. John was not one to mince his words over this.

"Assholes. Damned poachers. At least when we kill, we do it quick and efficient. These poor things went badly."

Benjamin nodded his agreement. "John, I know how much you hate trapping, but do you think we should try and take them?"

"Take them?" The elder brother was confused at first, still seething about what he regarded as a lack of sportsmanship. At this point, he was hoping the pack still had surviving members, as neither man had witnessed four wolves making their escape.

"You know. Maybe we can use these pelts as well. I know they stink like hell, but they're probably still worth something."

John decided this was at least plausible, and he kept with his earlier decision to have Benjamin remain at the rendezvous site while he began the hike back to their camp. And though the younger man would never admit it aloud, he was often anxious while he waited the several hours for John to return for him. This was such a wild place, he kept thinking, and like the wolves, his senses alerted him to the slightest sounds his less refined ears could detect. John would have called him jumpy, but being out here brought out shades of an instinctive anxiety living deeply in Benjamin's bones: fear of the utter vastness of this place, and its accompanying isolation from other humans; fear of the occasional curious bear, or charging moose, or strolling wolf. It was almost like a genetic agoraphobia; small wonder that human ancestors were so often described as "cavemen," seeking shelter in natural hollows. He knew how some of those damned liberal-minded Alaskans kept spewing off about how no wild species was out to get you, and that you had to just be in the wrong place at the wrong time to get assaulted by something big and furry, but those same people never really came out here, did they? No, this hunting trip was elation. Some part of Benjamin was cognizant of the fact that this solitude-bred anxiety was the counterpart to the patience and feeling of control that came from putting a target into one's crosshairs.

He likely would not verbalize it in such a way, but Benjamin felt the cities were just too much, which was why he lived in a town sufficiently sized to be almost a village. Small Town America was a dream very much alive and well for this man, the elusive and illusive notion that people in smaller settlements just cared more, and looked out for one another, and had simpler values, and that the towns themselves were intrinsically safer. And even Talkeetna hardly felt big, but it was about the right size for a pair of outdoorsmen like him and his brother. He had an inherent mistrust of those "city slickers," with their expensive suits and cars, hectic schedules, and lack of appreciation for the wild lands.

And yet his anxiety remained. There was safety in numbers, to be sure, and that applied to humans as much as it did to countless other species, and Benjamin would never quite learn to voice this irony: he felt safe and secure in town, at home, so he needed the social net of human groups, and yet that crowded feeling which accompanied the town's security was precisely what he wished to escape by hunting. What he and John actually brought down or caught on one of their trips was almost immaterial, really; the point was just to escape, and that was always how the two of them phrased it: escaping from town and getting out to hunt and fish and live wildly. Just for a while.

Benjamin eventually relaxed more, but he never stopped looking around that afternoon, wondering just how many of the bigger species were out here, or what they might be planning and thinking. Sometimes he could swear that whenever in such a remote locale, he could almost feel the eyes upon him. Then, when he allowed himself to relax again, he would laugh at his apprehension.

And yet, there was something he regarded as nerve-wracking during those rare times when he'd made eye contact with one of the larger creatures out here. Then it became a mix of fear and curiosity, to be met with a gaze that revealed...what? Intelligence? Emotion? Benjamin shoved those feelings aside; they were incompatible with hunting. Still, the face of a bear or wolf, or even a moose or caribou, could prove disarming. He would never forget how that female wolf, now dead just a few feet from him, had glanced his way, briefly connecting with him and his brother.

What did it mean, that gaze of a wild animal?

Benjamin Graydon stood and paced, warding off potential chill, and awaited his brother's return. Eventually, he relaxed more, and savored the isolation their trip had brought.

He remained wholly unaware of the proximity of the pair of human poachers.

* * *

Curiously enough, just west of the region that Morgan and her companions were heading towards was another pack of wolves, and this one, unlike their Fire Creek counterparts, had been thriving recently.

There were an even dozen in all, large for a pack of wild wolves, though the Alaskan wolf population could more often be found in greater territorial numbers like this. Indeed, Alaska was the only place on Earth in which wolf packs had even been known to top out at thirty members! The Chelatna pack had never attained such an unprecedented size, but had always managed quite well in this terrain nonetheless.

Bear Heart and Owl Eyes constituted the indomitable *alpha* pair of the Chelatna pack. Owl Eyes weighed in at a solid thirty-six kilos, big and intimidating for a female, and her vision was so refined that she sometimes spotted prey the size of mice a kilometer distant. Her face exhibited a pattern of white, tan, and black stripes, almost tiger-like, and she relished the physical presence of her mate even more than the privilege of helping to lead the pack. Bear Heart was black and grey, not the biggest member of the pack but indeed the quickest, even with six winters behind him now. His ascension to *alpha* was almost inherited; the other adults clearly remembered his *beta* days, and indeed, his tendency to dominate and boss the others about dated clear to his first weeks out of the den as a pup. His glossy coat was interspersed with flecks of lighter fur, and from a distance he looked like he would match the darkest Alaskan winter night. His subordinate relatives had yet to see the creature which could stand him down or frighten him away; even as a *beta* he once single-handedly defended the then-pregnant and now long dead former *alpha* female from a brown bear who had exhibited too much curiosity in their territory, only leaving when the other members of the pack arrived. No injuries were taken by either partner in that standoff; bear and wolf had just stared at each other, moving slightly to and fro, neither wanting to commit to an actual attack. The bear could have killed Bear Heart with a single swing of its foreleg, but would have had to catch him first, and wolves were more agile than bears, even though both species could reach similar top speeds. The same bear could hardly believe that a single wolf was that fearless.

One only had to glance at how these two *alpha* wolves carried themselves to realize very quickly who was in charge. Bear Heart and Owl Eyes were open and compassionate, yet their tails habitually stood rigid and erect, their heads were always held high as they walked, and they commanded such respect that they rarely had to display anger towards other pack members.

They stood now as well, feeling the light wind dart about them, moving rippling patterns down their fur. Most wolves were content to lie down after feasting, but these two stood together, slightly apart from the others, listening appreciatively to the ongoing crunching and gnawing that accompanied feeding wolves. Owl Eyes glanced back briefly at the scene, noting the bright glossy shade evident on every muzzle in the pack. Satisfied, she turned back to her partner.

The young moose had been a good kill, with a minimum of work and a total lack of wolf injuries. So many mouths continued working at the carcass of the moose, which had been in its second year, so that it was big enough to feed the pack to their contentment, but young enough and still just slightly small enough to offer an easier hunt. They had left its mother alone, since she would have proven feistier. Actually, the cow had birthed two calves the previous year, and moose, like bears, did not enjoy the benefits of larger family groups as did wolves and caribou. That made them more vulnerable, but a moose could be fearfully lethal. If one stood its ground, wolves would ignore it; vulnerability only revealed itself when the moose gave in to fear and began to run. But if it stayed to fight, its kicks were powerful enough to shatter a wolf's skull, and were also so fast that they barely telegraphed, so it was difficult indeed to see the big legs and hooves coming.

But not so, this younger specimen. It had opted to run, and therefore sealed its own doom. Tornado and Swifter had lunged at it first, a brother and sister in their third year who had also been first to spot their prey and its family earlier in the day. Cabal, Wave, Tracer, and Fisher had emerged from the tundra almost instantly when they realized that Tornado had sunk his jaws into the moose's neck to get a solid grip, while Swifter went for the front legs, further immobilizing the animal. By the time the others had arrived, the moose's life expectancy was already measurable in seconds.

It was only a few kilometers from the pack's rendezvous site, which was used less and less these days, anyway. The pups from the spring litter had almost all survived so far; only one had died, too small and weak at birth to make it more than a couple of weeks. Wolves had high mortality rates: typically only half were likely to survive their first year. The remaining young generation included Puddles, Foxtrot, and Sterling, of which only the last was female. Puddles loved playing in mud and dirt, and remained perpetually filthy, so he always seemed browner than he actually was. Foxtrot walked close to the ground, like a cat or a fox or a naturally low-ranking wolf, and was good at quickly skulking about, able to move even more stealthily than his family on his long bony legs. And Sterling was always curious, her coat glowingly silver, eager to explore every hole in the ground, every insect moving in the low brush, every bird chirping and flying overhead, and even the berries that she knew wolves could eat if they had sufficient trouble locating and bringing down prey. She loved exploring, but was also quite focused on maintaining her dignity.

That just left Rendezvous, the pack *omega*, who had eagerly participated in the hunt once it looked like they had a good chance of success. She had more grey in her coat, alternating with black points and almost no tan nor white. She and the others no longer had to guard the pups as much as they had to in prior months; indeed, the pups had already reached most of their adult size, weight, and strength, and had to be growled down by Bear Heart himself to avoid the hunt. Their survival skills were still developing, and even a younger inexperienced moose could have proved too much for them.

The cacophony of alarming table manners continued, the wolves gorging themselves, not so much from selfish gluttony as a simple instinctive knowledge that one could never guess for sure just when one's next meal might arrive. Since this had proven a year of relative contentment, there was no fighting over portions, though some occasional growling would always emerge whenever more than one wolf took a liking to a choice bit of the kill. Tongue and viscera were preferred, followed by the musculature so prized by humans, and these canid jaws could also chop up antlers, hooves, bones, any part of the kill which could offer sustenance. It was a frightening enough scene that the local scavengers, while already visible within a half kilometer or so of the carcass, nonetheless knew enough to hold their positions until the hunters left the remains. A red fox was among these, as was a small murder of ravens. The tiny carnivorous mammals were present, too: a young marten, a mink further away. No coyotes or wolverines were yet on hand, but if any were nearby, they would come calling soon enough. A wolf kill was too good an opportunity to pass up, especially for carnivores who were both small and solitary.

To the side, Bear Heart and Owl Eyes watched their pack with pride. They had a grand territory. This was the region just south-center of the world-renowned Denali National Park and Preserve. The Pack's namesake, Chelatna Lake, was an eleven kilometer-long narrow body, more reminiscent of a Scottish loch in appearance, though not nearly as deep. It lay nestled between the icy but smaller peaks of the southern portions of the Alaska Range, with Kahiltna Glacier to the east and Dall Glacier to the west. These glaciers and accompanying mountains fed into a flatter valley, west of the small town of Talkeetna, and as it was only visited by humans when they flew by during their flightseeing tours, it was a safe haven. Some parts were wooded, a few more exhibited the low scrub, shrub, and bush that marked the tundra, and many were often quite muddy from the ongoing runoff from the mountains. But like the Fire Creek area, it had abundant prey.

The Chelatna *alpha* pair continued watching their comrades, not knowing that the frantic survivors of another wolf pack had embarked on a course which would lead them towards their territory.

* * *

Scenario Two:

So what went wrong? we asked earlier. Let us leave the Black Forest behind now, and follow the wolves and the humans as they migrate, and we shall look ahead a few years as well.

We can glance this time towards a much larger region, beginning in east Africa and heading further northeast. Thus we begin at the cradle of humankind, and extend outwards until we reach the region now known as the "Middle East" for its lying between Europe and the rest of Asia. Strange, this is, too: how many modern people even realize this unusual common factor to Israel, Saudi Arabia, Syria, Egypt, and Ethiopia?

Each of these nations still contains a wolf population.

Oh, not so many that you would really notice them often, of course. Indeed, there are likely no more than a few score in Israel or in Ethiopia. But it makes one wonder. Today there is a Western stereotype of much of this region being inhospitable desert, but two details are worth noting: first, that here is where the Great Divide between wolves and humans occurred, and second, that even now, in the early twenty-first century of human reckoning, the wolves still struggle to survive here.

Sometimes they do get noticed, and then possibly for strange reasons. Take the case of Lieutenant Commander Daniel Collins, USMC. A helicopter pilot, graduated from Annapolis with a degree in aviation technology, he's even considered trying his hand in the wilds of Alaska as a bush pilot when his duty obligations come to an end. His Naval Academy days over a decade past, the professional departure time was supposed to be in seven months, but in his current posting, he figures he'll get out whenever the Corps decides to let him go. He hopes it is soon. Loyalty notwithstanding, Collins has already had his first shell-shocked nightmares regarding his recent experiences. He knows enough military history to realize how dreadful such experiences can become.

He has a knack for positive thinking, however, even up here where his altimeter reads 2000 feet and he and his partner are keeping sharp eyes out for threats from the Iraqi desert. Lieutenant Michael (Mickey) O'Malley occupies the other seat, in front of Collins, rather like those old two-seat biplanes from the 1920s and 30s, with the pilot in the rear. O'Malley acts as the weapons man while Collins flies this rotary bird, and his field of vision is widened by being in front, just behind the swivel gun.

Bell brand helicopters make distinctive sounds, even apart from other rotary aircraft, and that applies to the more famous UH-1N Huey model as well as to this version of the Cobra, the AH-1W, specifically designed for the Marines. Collins and O'Malley cruise along with a single additional aircraft, another Cobra, at an even speed of 135 knots, just on a routine patrol. Or so they hope. The early versions of both the Cobra and Huey go back to the war in Vietnam, so both models are instantly recognizable to most Americans, though they've been repeatedly updated to keep with the technological times.

At present, it's been three months since Camp Commando was finished, construction starting in October of 2002, as a forward base in Kuwait for what Collins cynically refers to as "Gulf War Two." He's a dedicated marine, loves his country, his girlfriend, his weapons officer, his chopper, and the Corps, in that order, but has some reservations about being over here. Lt.C. Collins is no coward, and believes strongly in duty, but wonders why the Iraq question wasn't resolved over a dozen years earlier, when there was an even larger coalition of military forces, from many more nations, bent on liberating Kuwait from the Iraqis. But ours is not to wonder why, he reminds himself, thinking of his girlfriend back in San Diego, and the night before he'd shipped out. He couldn't wait to get back to Camp Pendleton; he once thought that part of southern California was hot and dry, but that was before he was introduced to the Basra and Muthanna regions. Out here, during the summer months, it's actually fucking hot enough to sizzle an egg on the hood of one of the Corps' Humvees. It's difficult to believe humans wanting to settle in such an area; even Phoenix and Las Vegas aren't quite like this, and they don't suffer from nearly as many sandstorms, either. It's an impressive logistical feat just to keep up with Camp Commando's water demands.

"Amazing, isn't it, Mick?" he says forward, looking at the drab olive back of O'Malley's helmeted head. Even with the flight visors from their helmets currently shading their eyes, the desert still looks bright. Fortunately, it's getting late in the day, so the temperatures are almost tolerable.

"What's that, Dan? The only amazing things out here are the rocks and sand."

"That we're actually in the middle of the oldest known civilization. Do you ever think about that?"

Silence, and then the head which looks huge because of its protective casing shakes to and fro. "Shit, no. I can't believe that civilized people came from here."

Collins shakes his own head. He regards his younger subordinate as a friend, and usually an intellectual equal, but when their unit was called up back in Pendleton, O'Malley was far more gung ho about the prospects than he was. It just seemed so futile, going back into Iraq again, and for vaguer reasons than those offered back in '90 and '91. There was no country to liberate this time, despite Collins' loyalty, and he recalled how his government had left the Iraqis to their own devices those years back, calling on them to just take matters into their own hands and shake off their dictator, as the dozens of countries in the coalition almost all went home. Collins was still in flight school then, and had missed it all.

He wants to keep talking; it's how he deals with the stress of his posting. "This is part of the ancient Babylonian Empire, Mick. In between these bone-dry rivers, the Tigris and Euphrates, people built the first ziggurats, and invented writing, and developed agriculture. This place used to be really fertile, too; elephants and rhinos and giraffes used to live right below us."

"Yeah, fuck, whatever, Dan. We're not on an African safari here, okay? That was then. And besides, when was that? Five thousand years ago, give or take? It's too old to be relevant."

Collins alters the chopper's heading by ten degrees to the northeast, his wingman following obligingly. The Cobras are flying a standard two-aircraft combat air patrol, or CAP. Collins then gazes at the phosphorescent radar display, showing nothing but the two machines. Then he returns his point of view to the inside of his helmet, which contains the heads-up-display. The HUD gives instant readouts of tactical information like airspeed, threat warnings, weapon locks, without him having to glance about. The missile age had made the old dogfights deadlier; in aircraft dominated so heavily by computer technology, the fastest pilot to process incoming data would likely be the survivor.

The chopper levels out again. "It's not too old to be relevant."

"Yes, it damn well is," comes O'Malley's terse answer. "And what the crap is a ziggurat, anyway?"

Collins knows that his partner dabbles more creatively in profanity when nervous, and that changing a subject is usually a refusal to acknowledge defeat. Or ignorance, or both. "A ziggurat was just one of their old temples, dedicated to the gods. They looked like pyramids, kind of, but more like the Central American ones rather than the Egyptian ones." He hopes that one day he may return to this land and check out more of it on foot, and in civilian clothing, and unarmed. Needless to say, Iraq's borders have been rather sealed to many travelers for some time.

In Collins' mind lurks a group of images of the fabled Hanging Gardens of Babylon, the result of a simple love gesture of King Nebuchadnezzar II for his wife Amytius, though the implementation of the gardens was so superb that modern techniques had never managed to duplicate them. Somehow these gardens were built on terraces, with tremendous architectural attention paid to irrigation (how do you construct multi-story buildings and get water to a large city in the middle of a desert which lacks good materials and which hides its liquid life source from you?) There were flowers and fruit and exotic trees in the hanging gardens, with a head botanist allegedly from Judea, and all of it constructed basically as a wedding gift. God bless cable TV channels, thinks Collins; he has learned more about the Middle East from pay television than his Academy instructors in Maryland ever imparted. He is entranced by the knowledge that one of the seven wonders of the ancient world lay just a few miles northwest of them.

"Look, Dan," O'Malley says. "I was just asking. And all traces of Babylon are buried down in that desert for good. I mean, even if we could locate some more of the ruins, how the hell do you think anyone would ever get them exposed? This is one of the worst-off countries in the world."

"I know, Mick, I know. But don't you think it's sad that we could be learning from this place, when all we're supposed to be doing is feebly trying to help the people who live here now?"

"That's part of my point," he counters. "We're here to bring the Iraqis just a little bit closer to freedom and rights and elections."

"*But what if they don't want those things yet? You can't change a culture overnight. Do we have the patience to really stick around and help, or will we just abandon them again?*" Collins remains frustrated by the overall war plan. He's no more thrilled by the idea of this regime possessing weapons of mass destruction than anyone else is, but even if that could be verified, then so what? A half dozen countries possessed nukes, even more had chemical and biological weapons, and nobody was really policing them about it. What would the United States do next? Invade Britain, France, China, India, and Russia, in the name of finding another media cliché, the dreaded "WMDs?" If that was truly the logic behind invading this country, then the United States had an inescapable logical obligation to invade those other countries and take away their nuclear weapons as well. It was thus either irrational, or based on dishonesty. And only the United States had ever used those same WMDs offensively anyway; who was policing such a nation?

"*You know what your problem is, Commander?*" Collins dreads whenever his partner refers to him by rank.

"*Tell me. What?*" Collins feels his hands tighten slightly on both of the pitch control sticks, as he gives his basic instrumentation another cursory glance, satisfied that all is well outside the confines of their lethal machine.

O'Malley says, "*Some people are just violent. Some are just hateful. What do you expect from a country that has some wealth but squanders most of it on a useless military? Where was their infrastructure during their nine-year war against Iran? Both countries went broke over that, and neither of them gained a damn thing from it, and maybe we didn't either, since we've supported both of them in the past. But how do you deal with people who follow a religion that condones mass murder?*"

"*What?! There's nothing inherently violent about Islam! Where do you get this shit, Mick?*"

"*It's in the Koran: you're supposed to make holy war against the infidels. Try reading it sometime. It's a scary-ass book.*"

"*Hardly any more so than the Bible. Have you really read yours?*" That was likely a pointless question; O'Malley was descended from migratory Irish Catholics, and could probably quote significant passages from his own well-worn copy of the Revised Standard Version, the Ignatius Bible.

"*Hey, all I know is, Jesus offered a message of peace, and Muhammad was a warrior with four wives.*"

Collins is getting frustrated now. "*God damn it, it's not that simple, or even that accurate. Part of the problem with this region is our inability to understand it. And besides, if you're talking about religious differences, the Crusades were begun by the Popes, not the Caliphs.*" He doesn't mention the latest historical evidence about Jesus and his apparently sizable ego, or that it was his brother who may have been more of a messenger of peace anyway.

O'Malley wishes he could see this man he usually respected. He tries to do God's will, he truly does. He prays, and obeys, and wants to reach heaven and have a brotherly chat with Christ himself. "*The Crusades are also ancient history, you know.*"

"*Not around here, they're not. The people who taught medicine and math and philosophy and literature to the medieval Europeans were Muslims. And the followers of Allah, whom you seem to think are just naturally violence-prone, used to let the Jews and Christians living in the Holy Land worship as they pleased. And then the Church decided it couldn't stand the thought of infidels living where Jesus once walked and preached, and we're still feeling the aftershocks, even now, after nine centuries.*" Christ, thinks Collins. If I recited the likes of that in front of my commanders, I'd likely be out of the Corps that much sooner, only for a court-martial instead. Still, it is part of what he's been thinking for some time. Enemies are easier to kill when they're described as vicious, or evil, or greedy, or simply as "enemies" at all. But he had the twisted thought, as he watched the helicopter burn that he'd plowed a missile into, that the bastards on board were somebody's sons. He'd never thought that before, not even of the guys in the enemy tank. Maybe it was because he could see traces of bodies in the chopper wreckage, the images which were starting to haunt his dreams, leaving him feeling guilty for hoping it will not yield the emotionally crippling yet sterilely named post-traumatic-stress-disorder.

And O'Malley is having none of this sympathy. That wasn't how wars got won, or how evil dictators were removed from power. "Listen, Dan. You know I regard you as a friend, but watch some of this shit, will you. I know you want to think the best of everyone, but does that really apply to the scumbags who engineered the takeovers of the planes that crashed into the World Trade Center and the Pentagon? And besides, we're here now to set things right in Iraq. And don't give me that crap about whether or not it's our place to do so, either."

Collins can only sigh. That is the problem: he questions every day the merits of American involvement over here (and British, and Polish, and Italian, though the other nations who'd played a part back in '91 seem to have better things to do this time around). "I'm just so tired of the conflicts. The 'scumbags' you mention, I hate them too. But according to their own religion, they're consigned to the Flames. You're not allowed to commit suicide as a Muslim any more than you're allowed to as a Christian. God doesn't like us giving up, especially on ourselves. You pray to the same god that these people do, just in a different manner, using a different language, in a building which exhibits a different style of architecture."

"You don't hate them all, do you?" O'Malley asks, himself exasperated, but no less convinced of the rightness of American involvement than he has been all along.

"No, I don't. I can't. I thought I'd be able to once we got over here, thought that would make this job easier, but I was never able to pull it off. Now I'm just interested in learning more about the area, and its people."

It has occurred to Lt.C. Collins on previous flight patrols that beneath their bird, amongst the endless rocky debris and trackless sands and dunes, lay priceless ancient artifacts, even remains, and perhaps the last thing he wants is to become part of the destruction of such.

He wants to see the remnants of the Beit al-Hikmah, *the House of Wisdom in Baghdad, whose 9th-century founder, Al-Maamun, along with his followers, had taken pains to translate the Classical texts written in Greek and Latin into Arabic. That was the gesture which allowed Plato and Homer and scores of other famous writers from the past to have their works survive into modern times. They had to be translated back out of Arabic for the Europeans to study them.*

But it is so difficult to try reasoning in the face of flag-waving. Collins has heard that back in the States, dissent is still being interpreted as tantamount to treason, never mind that freedom of speech and press were not only guaranteed by law, but also that dissension and the ability to question were what created the United States in the first place. Strangely, he sometimes feels more socially at ease in Kuwait, although it is generally far more conservative: at least back home he can drink, his girlfriend can vote, they can kiss in public and not have to wear certain clothing, and they can both enter a mosque or a church if the mood takes them.

Lt.C. Collins has yet to even try discussing what he regards as the most curious episode of the human history of this region. He remains hugely fascinated by a historic figure, one of the ancient Sumerian kings: Urukagina. Somewhere around forty-four centuries earlier, this young king of the city-state of Lagash, the ruins of which are a short flight from Collin's Cobra, actually took it upon himself to utilize his power for something revolutionary. He revised the tax schedule to accommodate the poor, he separated the secular authorities from the religious, and he intended a union of the other local city-states. This was still long before the advent of the actual Kingdom of Persia begun by Cyrus the Great; and what we might admire in Urukagina as noble traits also became his downfall, since reformers are so often perceived as weak and too compromising.

At any rate, the part which sticks with Collins is the reference to Urukagina establishing "amagi," which translates roughly as freedom, but in this case, not in a general negative sense, but more specifically as freedom from fear. The ancient king apparently believed no one should have to live in fear. *The idea amazed Collins when he read about it: here he was, fighting a war on "terror," or fear allegedly incarnate, against some of the descendents of Urukagina. The irony seemed compounded by the fact that one can hardly use an army to destroy an emotion; fear and terror must be removed by other, more subtle means. But for now, the Marine pilot and confused idealist focuses anew on the drab landscape beyond the helicopter's canopy, and tries to forget the political differences which seem to force behaviors from members of different groups. Collins tries not to wince at the ironic absurdity that is the ongoing shifting of attitudes taking place so constantly amongst humans.*

The cyclic pitch control remains so comfortable in his right hand he barely notices it, permitting fingertip and wrist alterations to both airspeed and banking of the aircraft. His left hand remains securely on the collective pitch control, by which he guides altitude and power to the engines. This collective control mechanism adjusts torque, which requires compensation gently applied to the pedals from his booted feet, which would control the rudder in a fixed-wing airplane. Collins enjoys the quirks of helicopters, making them quite unusual compared to their winged counterparts: they display dissymmetry of lift, and a tendency to spin to the right while hovering, but he loves how maneuverable this rotary bird is, and of course, helicopters can hover for marvelous observations.

Both these general control sticks in Collins' gloved hands seem akin to traditional video game joysticks, though the left one also contains a variety of button controls for the release of additional weapons. Lt. O'Malley might handle the 20mm rotating cannons in the forward turret, but Lt.C. Collins retains autonomy over such key features as the forward-looking-infrared radar system, and the switches which can release either of the Sidewinder antiaircraft missiles, or the Hellfire missiles to use against vehicles as difficult to destroy as tanks. It is this remembrance of tanks which has him again pondering the integrated features of his machine.

The idea of sitting in an armored, treaded ground vehicle makes Collins claustrophobic just to think of it, especially after seeing his first aforementioned fried egg demonstration, though there are tank drivers who would say the same about him, loitering over the heads of "pissed-off enemy troops just waiting to put your sorry ass into a fatal tail-spin," or something to that effect. Maybe it's the fact that he and his weapons man have eliminated a Russian-built T-72 tank, and they hate the thought of burning to death inside of a huge steel can. They've also knocked down a pair of aircraft, both of them likewise Russian-built: a Mi-8T transport helicopter, and a Su-24 ground attack plane, both crashing earthward compliments of the Sidewinders. The plane's pilot bailed out, and appeared to have landed safely, but the helo was a complete wreck, falling out of the sky as a twisted and flaming pile of metal shit. While the tank gave Collins some pause, the aircraft let him know what he was really capable of, since combat pilots just seem to want to get into dogfights. Neither of these was much of a dogfight; the Cobra is more agile than the air machines it has blown out of the air, and so far Collins and O'Malley haven't really been shot at very much. Just some light ground fire, none of it which has hit their trusty bird.

And the point of the helicopter's tale is that during this patrol, on April 1st, the day of the fools of 2003, ten days before the famed Beit al-Hikmah was assaulted by looters, Collins and O'Malley had a curious sighting while finishing their CAP. They were nervous, and tried to be extra attentive. Perhaps that was part of why they noticed what they did. On March 24th, an Army Apache AH-64 attack chopper was shot down, and while the two-member crew survived, they were paraded about and shown on Iraqi television, so of course, CNN and the other American media got hold of the video. Collins hopes Americans will see it regularly, while O'Malley feels images like that should be subjected to military censor stamps. But they both hoped like hell that the crewmembers from that Apache were holding up well, though little other news about them had been forthcoming.

The "helo" business in this part of the world was proving dangerous all around: just three days prior to that, on the 21st, a CH-46 Sea Knight carrying both American and British troops crashed just south of the Kuwaiti border, apparently killing all on board. And they weren't even shot down. Additionally, March 29th was not such a banner day for combat helicopters either, as two more AH-64s reportedly went down, and Collins and O'Malley weren't sure yet what had become of either of those crews, but they tended to pay close attention to anything to do with Allied aircraft, especially the rotary kind. So here now were their current orders: patrol and destroy, particularly anti-aircraft units that might be found. And so far, nothing. Scanning the rugged and dry landscape was what permitted them their sighting, still in the Basra region, quite close to the border with Iran.

Usually when pilots have "sightings," people at once begin thinking of UFOs, and Collins himself would admit to a strange curiosity regarding such incidents. He tries to be open-minded, knowing that, by definition, a "UFO" is unidentified, so it could be damn near anything. Accordingly, there's no logical reason to automatically start imagining extra-terrestrials and flying saucers and Star Trek reruns. Indeed, nothing so melodramatic is needed to explain what follows, and the sighted objects weren't flying, anyway.

Collins, as a pilot, has slightly superior vision than O'Malley, and notices the tiny dust cloud first. A sandstorm can often be seen for dozens of miles, and this is just a trickle by comparison. "Mick, check out two o'clock."

"What have you got? I don't see anything out there."

The Cobras are still averaging a mere 2000 feet, an altitude low enough to give many jet pilots some concern, but these craft can operate at far slower speeds. "Wait. Maybe we'll see it again. It was just a little dust cloud, and then it was gone."

"Troops?" says the gunner, expressing a logical first assumption.

"I couldn't say, but we're going to take a look." Collins clicks on his microphone so he can address the other helicopter. "Scorpion Three to Scorpion Four."

A new voice fills his ears. "Copy, Three. Whaddya got?" *Apparently they've not seen anything out of the ordinary yet, either.*

"We're making a course correction, fifty-five degrees east. We need to check out some motion on the ground."

That is enough for the other unit. "Roger, Three. We're right on your tail, though we've never seen anything suspicious in this sector."

That much is true. This area is allegedly devoid of human settlement, to their knowledge. There is little vegetation, including almost no trees, and the fauna consists of ibex, which are kind of like wild goats, along with sand rats, desert foxes, hares, a humble assortment of snakes. And most of these species are nocturnal, though Collins supposes a number of ibex could at least make a decent dust cloud if agitated. He has a responsibility to verify possible troop presences, and it would be a refreshing break to actually see signs of wildlife anyway, so with his two reasons in mind, Collins finishes redirecting the course of his vehicle and hopes for signs.

"Aren't you getting a bit close, Dan?" *comes the familiar voice.*

"Yeah, I know," *Collins answers his weapons officer,* "but radar's negative, and intel says there's nothing around here we should be worried about." *Collins is actually suspicious of military intelligence, has often posed the riddle about the phrase being an oxymoron, since good " intel" was not only hard to come by, but subject to alter at a moment's notice. Indeed, often there was no notice; those downed Apaches from the past week were part of a warning that the relevant data had changed.*

"Come in, Four. Do you guys see anything noteworthy down there?" *Collins figures they are right above the dust cloud's source by now.*

"That's a negative, Three. And you're close to hovering. We need to keep moving." *That was a dictum of helos: hovering was a nifty ability for such an aircraft, but it did leave one an easier target, despite Collins' love of loitering over the same spot and rotating in place for the best views.*

Collins ignores the protocol, indeed letting the Cobra rotate slowly in a couple of circles, easing slightly off the foot pedal which would compensate for the right translating tendency, thereby offering a chance to inspect the ground beneath them. "Wait! I see now. Scorpion Four, follow my leader." The Cobra finishes its first clockwise circle.

"What the hell is out there, Commander?" comes a slightly anxious sounding reply, but the second machine obediently gives chase.

"Dan?" O'Malley says.

But Collins is wholly focused now. Because down below, not half a mile to the east, is a pack of wolves. Actual, living, breathing wolves.

He draws cautiously closer, guessing correctly that the heart-vibrating thumping sound of helicopter rotors will terrify most wildlife, including anything as skittish as wolves. Closer, closer. The Cobra edges forward, just 20 knots now, its pilot craving another peek, knowing he will never get close enough to satisfy his curiosity, not even on foot. Those same cable television channels have informed him that these are extremely elusive and shy creatures, at least when it comes to the presence of not just humans, but their accompanying technology.

"Holy crap," O'Malley says, himself seeing one of the canids now.

"Yes. Do you see them, Mick?"

"See what?" demands Scorpion Four's pilot.

O'Malley is breathing faster and shallower, Collins can hear it. He knows now that he was not suffering some stereotypical desert mirage, and he raises his helmet's protective visor to take what feels like a more direct, personal look. Taking shelter among a cluster of large boulders they can see two wolves now. "They're not just somebody's dogs, are they?" Collins says.

"Dogs?! What in shit do you two monkeys see down there?" barks a voice from the adjacent helo, but it goes ignored by the other two men. O'Malley shakes his head. "No. I mean, how could they be? We're too far from any settlements, and just look at those legs.

They're so long! And skinny. I don't know of any dogs that look like that."

"Me, neither," adds Collins. *The wolves are already gone, hiding in the crevices amongst the mineral haven they've found. Perhaps there is a denning site nearby, or maybe this is just the safest place to find refuge from the loud flying machines.*

But they looked right at me, *puzzles Collins.* Right into my eyes, like they knew me. *He feels emotional, not understanding why such a reaction should occur, but he nonetheless suspects he's just received a rare treat. There are wolves in Iraq. Close to the Iranian border. Holy shit!*

"Come in, Three." *Collins looks around from his revelry, taking in his immediate surroundings, consisting mostly of eleven million dollars of high technology which the American taxpayers believe they control.*

"Three here. Did you guys see them?"

"We still don't know what the hell you two meatheads are talking about, but we're almost at the end of our patrol. It's time to head back."

Collins checks his basic gauges. Fuel status indicates that his wingman is correct, and it's time to head for Kuwait, where the other elements of the Third Marine Aircraft Wing await a report as to why two of their units veered off course to chase dust clouds and phantom wildlife.

But Collins and O'Malley did see wolves. Struggling to keep existing, few in number, but alive and healthy regardless.

* * *

Like the rotors of the helicopters, the wheels of sunlight and shadow continue their infinite revolutions, often seeming quicker or slower than they truly are. The wolves we saw previously in the Black Forest and the humans who wanted to capture and attempt to domesticate or to hunt them are many millennia dead now. Yet in order to understand the distribution of humans and wolves alike in this region, we have to go much further back, as well as further south.

"Cephalization" is the scientific name for the evolutionary growth and development of the upper portion of an animal, particularly its head. In humans, this eon-consuming process has yielded the cerebrum, with its twin hemispheres, which permit reason and language and creativity on a scale never previously witnessed by the planet. Current consensus has this initially taking place from half a million to two million years or so in the past, and additionally that these early humans started spending less time in trees and more time on their hindquarters and that this all really got going in the general region of the Rift Valley, part of what is presently called Kenya and Tanzania.

There are no wolves in either of those countries, indeed no known evidence that they ever lived that close to the Equator, nor south of the Equator, anywhere on Earth. So how did the two species encounter each other, and how might it have affected this cephalization among the humans?

As the upright primates became slightly more domesticated, as well as simply smarter, they undertook tremendous migrations, covering distances matched only by the annual treks of certain birds and aquatic mammals. "Humanness" was still embryonic; Cro-magnon and Neanderthal and Australopithecus managed to escape or at least to further explore the African homeland, only to die out elsewhere. The true humans followed, struggled with, and outsmarted these fellow hominid competitors until only they remained, and by then they had unwittingly embarked on an unplanned mission of planetary invasion and occupation. Some went north into Europe. Others remained behind in Africa. Some went east and engulfed all of Asia. And only very late in the game would any of them reach the Americas or Oceania.

And in the earliest recorded human civilizations, the wolves were already there, in so many of these locales, wondering who the interlopers were, and what might become of their territories.

Of course, no one knows precisely what happened during those early encounters. Did humans and wolves curiously gawk at each other, wondering about motives and potential threats? Did they make moves to attack each other, isolating the weaker, sicker, slower members of groups to make them easier prey? Or might they have kept safe distances? Whichever the case, one detail remains essential to consider: intelligent species are perpetually curious, easily bored, and in physiological and emotional need of regular physical and mental stimulation when not resting. This applies to humans, wolves, elephants, dolphins, whales, other canines, all felines, other primates, and an assortment of avians, at a minimum. So whatever motivations might have lurked in the heads of those earlier humans and wolves, they would have undoubtedly wondered deeply about each other.

An additional crucial detail is that all those impeccably-groomed, lovingly kept, and expensively-maintained creatures who win such accolades from modern humans at the innumerable dog shows have ancestors. They're known as breeds: not really separate species so much, but actual breeds. This implies being bred for something, for specific purposes. The technical scientific designation for domestic dogs is "canis lupus familiaris," which applies equally to Malamutes, Corgis, and Poodles.

But that seems odd. There are well over a hundred dog breeds officially recognized by the various international agencies which adopt the job of classifying "man's best friends" into task-based groups, like Toy, Hound, Worker, and others. So if there are so many breeds, each with its own purpose, why are they all classified identically? The wolf is "canis lupus," though it also has undergone a long variety of subspecies classifications, at one point totaling eight "Old World" and twenty-six "New World" types. Clearly the biologists and taxonomists are cognizant of the genetic similarities; indeed, dogs are closer zoologically to wolves than are humans to chimpanzees, our own closest genetic relatives.

And millennia in the past, wolves and humans first met in northeastern Africa and the Middle Eastern lands, as their descendents still but rarely do into the present. Some of the wolves were captured, countless were killed, and the very rare others who were willing to brave the smells and the fires of the people were eventually tamed. Humans knew a good thing when they had it: these animals were bright, loyal, brave, and very hardy survivors. It only took a few centuries for the original dog breeds to be identifiable as such, and some of these indeed joined people in their migrations outward to the rest of the world.

And interestingly, there is absolutely no known evidence of wolves, tame or otherwise, having killed any of these earlier humans. Our modern protagonists will take up that point later, but for now, we can rejoin them on the speedy blacktop outside Anchorage.

PART TWO: TRACKS

"Do you know the meaning of the word Goodness? It is, first, to avoid hurting any thing; and then, to contrive to give as much pleasure as you can."
- Mary Wollstonecraft, *Original Stories from Real Life with Conversations, calculated to Regulate the Affections, and Form the Mind to Truth and Goodness*

"Love the animals. God has given them the rudiments of thought and joy untroubled. Don't trouble it, don't harass them, don't deprive them of their happiness, don't work against God's intent."
- Fyodor Dostoevsky, *Братья Карамазовы*

"Hey, let me see that other map this time," prods Jack from the back seat.

I continue poring over the highway map, taking it all in. And as you no doubt noticed earlier, I love inspecting maps. This particular one is DeLorme Mapping's *Alaska Atlas and Gazetteer*, which I still have opened to show the Glenn Highway heading out of Anchorage, where it passes the Army compound at Fort Richardson as well as Elmendorf Air Force Base, then the town of Eagle River, and then northward into the Matanuska-Susitna Valley. "The Valley" is where we'll head past the towns of Wasilla and Willow and Houston, and then enjoy the view clear up towards Denali. "I hope we can see the mountain today," I say to whoever might be listening. Denali is *the* mountain, of course, never merely *a* mountain. And it's also, as Mariska and I together insist, *Denali*, and not *Mount McKinley*.

"Me too, Morgan. The map, if you please."

"Hmm? Oh, right. Here you go." The Gazetteer is extended over my headrest, flapping madly in the incoming wind. It's a great map, but the damn thing has the length and width of a coffee-table tome, so it's not really conducive to backpacks. "Sorry. Here, I'll put the window up." I know Jack isn't thrilled with getting a head full of wind like that; whenever I'm not driving myself, I love feeling just a bit of the outside air. The contents of cars and trucks feel so much like airplane air otherwise, the views through the windows of safety glass just another type of television: passive acceptance rather than active involvement.

I've thus far been stymied by the relative quiet of my companions. It doesn't feel tense, exactly, but still. "Hey, you two in back. Are you making out, or what? Somebody say something."

Mariska's laugh answers me. "Ha! You wish. Like I would ever waste myself on this freak." I hear a sound oddly similar to the atlas pages flapping in the wind, realizing the Gazetteer is temporarily finding utility as a weapon.

"Ow!" cries Mariska this time, but it sounds obviously faked. She knows how to flirt, that one, though she'd never admit to it. "Lay off with the map, you."

Jack might have not heard her. "Who's a freak?" he says, in the same playful tone. This air between them, I don't know, it's not really traditional sexual tension, it's... What is it that makes adults behave like youthful idiots when in the presence of the opposed gender?

"Do I have to separate you back there?" I say, imitating my late mother's nagging tone. Dad and I agreed we actually missed that tone after she died.

But by now both friends are deaf to me; the Epic Tickling War has begun. "Hey! Watch the hair," comes Mariska's protest, answered by: "Then watch the nails."

They might as well be six-year-olds. Dave, stoic and focused on the pavement and its shoulders, steals a quick glance my way, just enough to roll his eyes and shake his head, but like the rest of us, he's also smiling. This is what I'd hoped for: a few days away with no bullshit, just fun and amusement and old friends. Jack's laughing again in that carefree manner I tried describing earlier, and Mariska's loosening up a bit from her hectic work schedule. Although I recall she's pretty casual with her students, too, though I don't believe she's resorted to tickling any of them. Hopefully not. Pesky undergrads. They're so impressionable. Sometimes.

I decide to continue the role-playing, deepening my voice like before. "Well, honey, whatever shall we do with those damned kids in the back seat?"

Dave tries not to smile too openly, feigning gravity and similarly choosing more of a bass tone. "Gosh, er, sweetums, we may just have to abandon the pair of ingrates out here somewhere." And the funny part is that only the two of us laugh at that; the others are still giggling and struggling in the back seat. Dave and I are mildly annoyed by the periodic thumping of knees into the backs of our own seats, but we're likely just jealous of the random fun taking place behind us.

I think it's time to segue. "Where are we, anyway?"

Dave tries to get Jack's attention. "Yeah, 'Mr. Navigator,' what's coming up next?" Actually, we all have a good idea of every kilometer of this stretch, each having spent many hours over the years on this very length of asphalt. I'm just interested in talking.

Jack speaks through slightly labored breaths. "Can't you fools read? We just passed Eagle River. We're a few miles southwest of Eklutna."

"*Eydlytnu*," corrects Mariska. "Eklutna is just an Anglicized corruption." I can almost feel Jack wince.

"I know. I remember," he says sheepishly. "But I still can't pronounce its old name. And the old Russian Orthodox church up there is one of the oldest wooden buildings still standing in the state. And we're going to remain in traditional Athabascan territory this whole trip."

"That sounds more encouraging," Mariska says. "My grandmother grew up in that little village, you know."

That makes my eyebrows raise automatically. "Really? I didn't know." Actually, I barely know a damn thing about her cultural background. She's such a good, honest friend, I've never really felt the need to push. I'm the sort of tag-along visitor to the Alaska Native Heritage Center on the outskirts of Anchorage, which we've already passed, quietly wondering what it is that makes these people tick. And then I remember: "these people" is already a bigoted phrase, and to even wonder seems to treat them like Martians or something. They're simply people, just with different histories. Still, I hope Mariska takes my lead.

She does, feeling comfortable with the subject. "Sure. I used to spend most of my summers with them at fish camp down in the Peninsula. They were always great storytellers, too. My grandmother is often visiting the Heritage Center to talk with the visitors, maybe teach them a few words of Athabascan. *Dena'inaq'e qadak'dinesh du?*"

The syllables roll off her precise tongue, each sound clipped and full of energy, though a bit heavy sounding compared to other Americans. Usually I take huge offense by someone who goes out of his or her way to speak in a language that I don't know, since it's a way of leaving someone out of a conversation, but for some reason I love hearing Mariska. "*Naqeli htaydlan. Nutalghatl kiq'u,*" she adds. Sometimes it's good to listen without necessarily understanding. I have a vague sense she's making small talk: asking if we speak the language and describing the weather, which I know from experience are among the more typical methods for starting conversations in alternate dialects.

And fish camp. I can almost smell salmon guts just from that reference: there are still quite a few folks around here who devote a chunk of their precious and short Alaskan summers to harvesting the larger rivers during the fish runs, and drying or smoking the flesh. The locals have done it for many centuries as a way to store plenty of protein supplies for the long winters. And the Peninsula is the Kenai Peninsula, the stunning land mass which juts into the Pacific south of Anchorage. There are idyllic little towns dotting various parts of the mountains and tundra and coastline, the kind from the cruise ship passenger's dreams: Homer, Seward, even tiny Whittier. And the Peninsula is legendary for its fabulous long-distance hiking trails, all of which we've each done on other outings, often with one another.

Not wanting to discuss the imagery of hundreds of salmon husks drying in the summer sun, I opt to dare another tactic instead. "Mariska, does she ever really teach anyone?"

"Teach them what?"

"You know...the language. I love languages. So does Jack. He's been so many places, he's probably closer to fluency in some of these other dialects than he readily lets on."

"Right, Morgan. I speak decent enough Russian, and know probably enough of a few others to get by, but I'm hardly a professional translator or linguist." Jack's actually being modest; I've heard him speak in several languages, with what I thought were quite plausible national accents. His thick rolling Russian and Scottish brogues are rather sexy; I wonder if Mariska appreciates them.

I don't want to get off track of Alaskan culture, but I offer Jack a chance to shine, though he's usually shy about that talent. "Like which ones?"

He looks at me from the backseat, since I've turned about to face them both. "Well, I can order a pint of beer and tell you to fuck off in about a dozen languages total."

So much for the alleged shyness. Dave has to force his hands to remain on the wheel at that one, already struggling to keep his laughter non-violent. "Well, what else do you really need to communicate?" Jack says. The rest of us are cackling at him; usually only Dave and I are quite so risqué.

"And that's probably my most marketable skill," Jack adds, making us laugh that much harder, although I briefly consider what subtext might lie in his comments; he is the most seasoned traveler of us all, but he's also trying to decide what to do with the rest of his life. Mariska's grinning, yet still looking contemplative. She shifts her glance to the Eklutna exit sign as we speed past it. The exit leads to a variety of intriguing stops: a short neighborhood hike to gorgeous Thunderbird Falls, a campground and mountain bike trail down the north side of Lake Eklutna, which also acts as something of a water reservoir for Anchorage. And, of course, the town of my friend's grandmother.

By now we've finally calmed down, mostly. Mariska resumes where she left off, a receding image of the tiny village with the oldest building in the Anchorage vicinity not quite reflected in her eyes, now facing out the car's rear window. "Morgan, you asked about my grandmother." At once I wonder if I've pushed. Since I've never raised the subject with her, I don't know if this is off-limits. How can I be a friend of hers and not know her own linguistic preferences?

"She is amazing, really. She has always tried to keep parts of the culture alive, probably more so since my grandfather died a few years back. The tourists only see the quaint, obvious stuff: the dances at the Heritage Center, the occasional syllable of a language they have trouble deciphering, even that church up on the hill." I follow her lead, though the hand-hewn twin cottonwood domes in that "onion" shape unique to Orthodox Christian architecture cannot be seen from the highway.

Jack chimes in, trying to be gallant; he doesn't seem as concerned about tiptoeing around people's cultures as I am. It's probably because of how many semi-blurry ink stamps are in his passport. "Mariska, do you remember the first time you took me up there, to the village?"

She nods, smiling. "That was shortly after Grandfather died, actually. I remember you asked me about the spirit houses."

"Yeah. I'd never seen a tradition quite like that."

I'm growing ever more embarrassed over my own ignorance, but immediately want to know more. "Spirit houses?"

Mariska responds. "They are just additions to grave sites. Jack asked me at the time what was with all the brightly painted dog houses, which almost earned him a slap or two." Jack shrugs and hangs his head, obviously recalling his discomfiture, if a bit exaggerated. "These are for more personal memorials. People can leave offerings in them for their loved ones, like flowers or food. But they remain quite well-kept, and brightly painted, so I suppose they do look like glorified dog houses."

I briefly picture myself placing carnations at Mom's grave in Anchorage, feeling like an idiot because I wasn't sure whether the flowers were for me or for her or for just making the cemetery look a bit more pleasant for everyone else. I've never really understood the nature of how people interact with the dead. An involuntary shiver begins at my lower vertebrae and rockets north to the nape of my neck.

As though knowing my thoughts, Mariska says, "The spirit houses link this world to the spirit world. They are sort of shelters for the spirits of the deceased to visit. My grandfather is one of the last people who shall be buried in there."

"I remember there was a tiny picket fence around his site, which the others didn't really have, and I meant to ask you about it then," says Jack.

Mariska now seems to enjoy conversing about her family. "The fence means he was not really Athabascan. He was well liked by the community, but was also always an outsider, too. He emigrated to the States from Germany, back in the 30s. I can tell you about him sometime." It seems clear she doesn't want to give away too much just yet.

As we keep driving, Mariska murmurs, barely audible, "*Itaghidzes.*"

"What?" prompts Jack.

"Oh, something my grandfather used to tell me, whenever I would leave him. It means, 'You will be safe.'" Jack just nods.

"But look, you guys," Mariska says now. "This trip of ours is not a downer. It is supposed to be a major upper instead. This area has been inhabited consecutively by my ancestors since at least the middle of the seventeenth century, at least 120 years before Cook first sailed from England."

Dave snickers a bit at that. "Leave it to you to put everything into historical context."

She's not about to be put off by that. "Well, what do you expect, then, from a history prof at UAA?" Mariska is justifiably proud of her academic posting at the university, well into her tenure track by now.

"I know I expected nothing less," quips Jack. "You were my toughest teacher back at Berkeley." I've always been amused by that, I think, looking at them both. Jack was a flaky undergrad working on a biology degree in California when he met Mariska, who was already finishing her doctorate, specializing in twentieth-century world history. I think that's part of their attraction: Mariska tries to learn everything about the world, while Jack keeps traveling to so many parts of it.

He's backpacked and gotten his hands dirty and feet blistered in six continents. A few days on a small trail in Alaska is child's play for him.

Mariska's no slouch when it comes to the wilds, either, hardly the stereotypical image of a university lecturer and researcher. You know: the sort who perpetually views the world from over the rims of her reading glasses, and knows everything there is about one subject, yet has no idea how to actually interact with the larger realm of everyday existence. That's what makes her intriguing. She's totally different from that traditional image, and can teach as well as relate to her students, and they adore her. She's been known to host student-only dinners at her own home, giving the undergraduates a place to hang out and be themselves, with no pressure. "You know, Jack, I once might have taken that as almost an insult, but I am glad I was your most difficult instructor. Hopefully it means you got something out of the course."

"I did," he says. "The section about social and economic causes of modern war has always stuck with me, but like you said, this is about having a good time."

"Damn right," Dave says.

"When was the last time we were all together like this, anyhow?" Jack asks.

I suppose I'm about the best with personal instead of historical dates: "All four of us? That would've been the weekend of the 4th." I take in their simultaneous grins. That had been a good couple of days: a July fishing trip down in the Peninsula outside Seward, then a hike just south of town, which was crowded for the annual Mount Marathon race. Only Jack reeled in a salmon that day, and we all rummaged through the low bush hoping for ripe wild berries, but it was a bit early for them. The silver salmon that night was outstanding, especially since I wasn't the one who'd cleaned it. I can never remember the best angles for cutting, and you need a hell of a sharp knife for such work, too.

"Good thing we are finally not so busy all at once," Mariska says. "I had a full load for summer school."

"And I've been busier with the paper, for a change," I add. I always feel insecure discussing the contents of my résumé around this group, even though I've also done postgraduate work. "Dave, how's the career with AFD going these days? What's it been now, three years?"

"Fortunately, the tourists largely behaved themselves this season, and as we start to lose daylight, we'll start to see more traffic accidents." David Thomas is presently employed as a paramedic by Anchorage's fire service, so his discussions about work focus more on people than on building and property damage, like with his firefighter colleagues. It's a strange turn for a guy with a degree in forestry, though he once applied to become one of those parachuting "smoke-jumpers" who leap out of perfectly good aircraft right near forest fires. He's wearing my favorite one of his t-shirts today, in deference to his job, a blue cotton with the following emblazoned on the chest:

"Feed the bears.
Walk on the glaciers.
Lean over the boat railings.
We thank you for your support:
Alaska Paramedics."

Okay, so it's aimed more or less at tourists, but plenty of folks behave hopelessly the world over, including here, and stupid human tricks represent a sizable chunk of Dave's business; he once confided to feeling uncertain whether to be extremely glad or extremely annoyed that paramedics don't work on a commission basis.

"So you can sort of predict what sorts of things you'll see in the field just by the season?" I say.

"Yeah, to some extent. I mean, some things can't be predicted of course, like falls and vehicular crashes and a lot of diseases. But some things I swear you can almost set a clock by."

"Like what?"

"First snow of the season: lots of X-rays of hips, legs, and arms. Major holidays: lacerations from tools or fights, and head and neck CT scans from traffic incidents. Summertime: more injuries from water activities, and more cardiac and respiratory stuff from people over-exerting. It just makes sense. The unpredictable stuff is more fun."

"But how do you 'set a clock' from those?" I prod.

"Oh, I meant more with gastrointestinal issues, and a lot of cardiovascular problems. You know: the stress-related things, and the bad-eating conditions, along with the diabetics and the chronic smokers. If you find out the dietary, alcohol, and smoking history of someone, and then note their condition when they call 911 along with their age and gender, then you can get a feel for how much time they've got left."

"Creepy," observes Jack.

"Hey, the entire insurance industry makes prices based on those kinds of data. And if you think I'm jaded, you should hear the ER staffs in hospitals. You guys know what 'TSTL' stands for?" Dave senses, rather than sees, us shake our heads. "'Too stupid to live'," he says. "It's an honorarium of sorts that we reserve for future Darwin Award recipients, the ones who never quite learn that stupidity is the most dangerous of sexually transmitted diseases, as well as incurable."

Okay, I confess here, I think that one's pretty funny, and it matches Dave's temperament perfectly. And the already legendary "Darwin Awards" are receiving more attention each year, it seems: stories told via the news media of those souls who have removed themselves from the human gene pool through often dazzling acts of incomprehensible idiocy. Like the guys up here who do their snowmobiling up the most vertical mountainsides they can find, only to start avalanches which often bury them. The woman who compiles the pseudo-awards even visited Title Wave a couple of years back. And Dave has warned me in the past that working in emergency health care at any level requires a flexible and mostly dark sense of humor, kind of Monty Python meets Stephen King, with a dose of the older and more physical Saturday Night Live skits thrown in for flavor.

I once asked Dave if he felt guilty for finding the humor in people's conditions, and he said he was sympathetic for accidents that resulted from events other than idiocy, and for those suffering from afflictions which struck randomly or genetically. He genuinely feels for someone with Down Syndrome, or a person who gets lung disease from inhaling smoke second-hand, or one who survives an accident that someone else caused. He's done volunteer work with special needs persons, and even tried his hand (no pun intended) at sign language to be able to at least get some basic ideas across to deaf patients. But a relative lack of street smarts in people with functional brains he regards as grist for the comedic mill.

"I take it back," says Jack. "Glad to hear work's still going well." Dave's not cynical to the point of not caring; indeed, I can tell from personal experience that bitching about work indicates caring about it, and not a lack of caring. True antipathy leads to silent acceptance. That's what makes folks who respond to 911 calls burn out.

Mariska decides it's time to throw the spotlight elsewhere. "So long as we are discussing work, guess who will start as a substitute teacher next spring semester?"

Jack blushes, so maybe some of that shyness remains. "Yes, it's true: I'll be gallivanting about with the School District for a year. Apparently some of this love of teaching nonsense has rubbed off on me." I turn towards them; both look proud.

"What do you get to teach?" Dave says.

"Oh, you know, this is just high school, so it's pretty much whatever they need me for each day I get called in."

Mariska enjoys the image of Jack toying with impressionable young minds. "Maybe you will be like the guy in that movie, about the substitute."

Jack considers it. "I think it was called just that. Tom Berenger, I think."

"Yeah," adds Dave. "There was even a sequel, with Treat Williams." I can never keep up with that stuff; Dave loves movies like some people love chocolate, or heroin, or anything else which offers a chemical connection making the partaker continually crave. Even the crappy movies Dave thinks are worth his time, and he's great at pulling film quotes out of nowhere. He probably has a frequent buyer card for greasy popcorn.

Jack continues. "I'd probably need Morgan around to help me kick ass like that, though."

"Why, are there aikidoists in those flicks?"

"Not really, but you never know when I might need help quelling classroom disorder." He almost says it with a straight face.

"Come on, Jack," I keep at him. "You're a third-degree black belt in *goju-ryu*," I remind him, hoping I've pronounced the name of his style of Okinawan *karate* properly. "Surely you don't need my help."

"I suspect *aikido* is more suited to simply keeping trouble-makers in line. Don't the Japanese teach it for law enforcement, since it tries to be gentle while still immobilizing?"

"So I've heard."

"Well," he pauses. "I love what I've done with martial arts, but I don't do that tournament stuff anymore. I just really lost my taste for that crap, even at a sport level. The things I know how to do are pretty destructive, if you really use them on someone, despite the occasional temptation."

"Well, yeah, there are legal ramifications for martial responses: you can only meet force with an approximately equal amount of counter-force, whatever that means."

Jack's thought about this before. "So if someone tries to mug me, I might actually be in trouble with the police if I, say, kick my assailant's kneecaps out of place, or gouge out his eyes, or..."

"Enough of that, then," I say, wanting to keep all four of us in the conversation. "And what about the travel agency?"

Jack offers an expression like that of a cat who's just found some of our fishing leftovers. "Oh, we've reached an agreement, for the most part. They're pretty much willing to keep me on at a part-time basis for whenever I'm in town, so that should leave me with summers largely open. It's a good deal, too, since obviously there's not much demand for secondary-level subs during summer break."

Mariska's openly grinning now. She's been hoping Jack would not just come closer to a so-called "real job," but it also seems like this is closer to what Jack really wants. Besides, with his travel experience, the agency should really prize him, even if he finagled his way into them permitting his devoting entire months away from the place.

I smile back at them both. "That sounds cool. Far be it from me to make it sound like you're finally settling down."

Jack laughs. "Never. Once wanderlust really afflicts you, you're done for. It doesn't go away. So if it's an acquired and incurable disease, then maybe Dave can estimate how much time I still have to live."

Mariska smacks him twice on the arm, then says, "Maybe you should turn all these travel stories into a narrative book." Easy for her to claim, in this company: she's part of a business in which "publish or perish" is still the accepted norm, and I write for a living, or at least try to, and Dave asks about writing, so what the hell.

But Jack rolls his eyes. "I'd rather try and sell some of my photos of these places. I know good photographers are a dime a dozen throughout Alaska, but I've got some decent shots from places that most Americans never see. I could organize it by continent, or country, or geographical features, or even wildlife, though that last category's so hard to get good material for."

It's interesting to hear him this fired up about work. Plus, he's the only decent photographer in the car; none of us have the dedication needed to line up shots with timers, or get used to the nuances of over- or under-exposing shots intentionally, or learn what light really does to images, or to stand next to a tripod in the dead of winter freezing your ass off while you try to shoot the aurora borealis or, and this is particular up here, have the patience to sit still for wildlife photos. It's difficult to explain to a busy bear or a jittery caribou that you'd really like it if they held still for a few seconds, or, better yet, looked right into your lens for a portrait.

I turn back around to watch the nearby mountains, semi-listening to the pair in back talk about UAA's art gallery, and where else Jack Godwin might be able to show off some of his photography, just to get a start in what is an extremely competitive market locally. I opt to get Dave back into the discussion. "Can you believe Alaska Global Travel is keeping him on? I thought they'd decided he was too flaky."

"Oh, he's hardly that. I mean, he used to be, and there are still times when he cannot help but have fun with the industry. Remember when he used to call all the cruise ship lines, and keep asking whomever would speak with him how much their companies were fined in the past year for polluting the Sound?"

I laugh at that, noting that Jack and Mariska are ignoring us, Jack with a dreamy countenance that I recognize as the one under which he's imagining and picturing many of the places he's visited. "Yeah," I say. "He kept wanting me to do stories in the *Daily News* about which cruise ship line was the worst offender." I giggle, sure, but that's been an issue with us locally for many years, though the tourists don't hear much about it anymore. Prince William Sound has never really left our ecological news since the April of '89 oil spill. Accordingly, any kind of waste in that area tends to get reported, but usually now just at the local level. After all, would tourism suffer if visitors were told that 45,000 ship passengers arrive in Alaska each day during the May-to-September cruise season, and that they arrive with 4.5 million gallons of wastewater? Or that efforts to introduce a bill to Alaskan voters have been made, which would tax the cruise ships? Or that the cruise companies are sometimes accused of being virtual tourist monopolies here, since they also own their own buses and hotels, and can thereby keep passengers under the umbrella of their own corporate logos for the duration of their visits?

In fairness, there have been recent legislative efforts to improve upon cruise ship dumping, at least, and while pollution in local water, especially Prince William Sound, has gotten better, it still leaves open the question of whether the cruise companies really try and dominate the local travel business. But that's always been a question up here: who should be able to influence the industries associated with non-residents from around the world coming up here and bringing their money with them?

Dave continues. "Or how about when he wore that shirt to work there once that said, 'If it's tourist season, how come we can't shoot 'em?'" We both laugh at that; when Jack told us, we expected to hear that he'd been immediately fired, but he has such a way of exciting others about traveling, that he was just told not to wear the shirt to work again. Naturally, he has occasionally refrained from obeying such a demand, and still hasn't been fired for it.

Jack once suggested another seasonal shirt slogan which mentioned something about how "Wouldn't it be interesting if humans had a mating season?" He'd made us crack up with a description of how easygoing we'd all be for most of the year, only to go completely crazy during that one month or so when suddenly everyone was frantically trying to get laid. Maybe humans really would be less jealous of each other afterwards.

"I wonder what he'll wear to the local high schools next term?" Dave says. I can only shrug.

"Maybe not shirts this time. Maybe he'll get a car just to have something on which to put a bumper sticker that says, 'My kid knocked up your honor student.'"

Dave loves that. "Or maybe, 'Proud parent of the kid who sells drugs to your honor students.'" I can't really see it, actually. Jack once said that people who tried to make slogans on their bumpers were insensitive assholes, since the practice had a way of contributing to road-rage. Anyone not liking one of his shirts could ignore him, or tell him where he could stick his attitudes, but he reasons that motorists are already way too dangerous to have their emotions manipulated so blatantly. And besides, bumper stickers are always products of a "groupthink mentality," and tend for that very reason to be quite socially divisive and less than conducive to individual thought. Still, I suppose almost everyone has some catchy slogan they'd love to see pasted over vehicles, even if they're simplistic and black or white.

The highway continues its seemingly endless meandering. We're well beyond Eagle River, past Chugiak. The topography will flatten a bit on the way into the Valley, at least in the section over which we'll drive. You're never far from mountains around here, and they'll be visible in at least a couple of directions for our entire drive. Dad once asked me what the best part of living in Alaska truly was, since, like most folks from the "Lower 49," he understands the attraction during the summer, but still displays that characteristic prejudice suggesting this land is a giant ice cube in winter. Parts of it surely can be, and I've often admitted to myself that it's a good thing I like winter camping, snowshoeing, and alpine skiing, lest I suffer too much from cabin fever.

"The best part?" I began my answer that day. "The best part of living in Alaska is easy to sum up, Dad: there are mountains here without names." He'd like it up here now, even with summer really over. Traffic's comfortably light today, and the RVs have returned whence they came, waiting for next year's road trips. All the ships from those cruise companies have likewise returned to warmer waters, wintering in Baja or the Caribbean.

"I think your ancestors knew what the hell they were doing, Mariska," I say.

She nods, though I can't see it. "Yes. The people who came through here thousands of years ago must have felt divided. They had no idea where they were, and some wanted to stay while others wanted to keep moving." I love listening to her. She has this way of informing while keeping it interesting. Somewhere around twelve thousand years past, the ancestors of every cultural group throughout the Americas came traipsing through this corridor, having left behind the bleak Bering Land Bridge, which even now almost connects Alaska to Siberia during the winter.

"You know," she says, "the Navajo language is very close to Athabascan, but more different from most other Indian languages from the Lower 49, so one group appears to have settled here, while some of their same members made it to the southwest desert and thrived. Talk about a gap in climate!"

"Does Rebecca share your interest in her heritage?" I wonder aloud. "Where is the little creep, anyway?"

Mariska doesn't mind my jibe. Her daughter, currently ten, lives with her in Anchorage, and tends to view me as the evil aunty with whom she can get away with more mischief. I've sat for her on a number of occasions. Her dad was some guy back in California I've never met, and Mariska doesn't really discuss him. From her early postgraduate days, I think. "She is doing great. She wanted to tell you all 'hi,' and she is staying with a colleague in the department."

"How's the new school year going for her?" says Dave. He has a son, just a bit older, living with his mother in Chicago, and Dave gets to see little of him, though the kid did visit once last year. Apparently, Dennis' stories of bears and fishing really impressed his schoolmates back in the Windy City.

"Rebecca is really enjoying fifth grade. And to answer your question, she has already started drumming. Last month she said she wanted to either play in a rock band or else become a Native storyteller who uses lots of drums."

"Good for her," says Jack. "It must be refreshing to know what you want to do with your life."

Mariska seems initially taken aback by that, as if trying to determine if the remark was insulting, then decides better of it. "Why would you say that?"

"Well, look at us. You guys are the most eclectic bunch of friends I've ever had. And all I meant was some of us are still trying to decide what we want to be. Rebecca herself will likely change her mind a bunch of times, but she's still at an age where people don't pressure her to justify her answers, at least not as much."

Mariska breathes easier. "I thought this was about to turn into some dialogue about raising a kid cross-culturally." I make eye contact with her briefly, wanting to pursue this, hoping she won't think that I'm viewing her as a subject, which I'm not.

Jack must sense my thoughts. "Well, how does that work? Do you want her to learn the language as well?"

She pauses, mulling this over. "Yes, I do, Jack. I want her to learn the ways of her native culture as well as those of Americans as a whole. Does that help answer your question?"

Her interrogator seems to be feeling pushy. "Well, what else, though?"

"Is that not a good enough starting point? What else is there to connect members of a culture, beyond language? Do you know how many indigenous languages are still spoken in Alaska? Twenty. And do you realize how many of them will probably be gone within our own lifetimes? Sixteen. Eighty percent of them. Think about that for a moment: Native cultures are going fast, that is how it has been all over the world for centuries. This is just the latest example. Luckily, a couple of the Athabascan dialects are doing better recently, but we are not nearly as strong as, say, Aleut."

Jack, who admittedly could be thicker emotionally than even Dave at times, was beginning to note the sensitivity of his erstwhile girlfriend with issues that couldn't be just turned on or off like a light switch. Which, in hindsight, actually rather surprised him: through all his journeys he's gone out of his way not to stand out, not to make others feel uncomfortable, especially considering that he was the one visiting their homes and lands. And anyhow, the best way to learn about another's perspective was to clamp down your own cake-hole and just listen.

Unfortunately, Jack was still, even for the wealth of his multi-cultural forays, a product of a society which emphasized talking and making noise, not listening.

"Iska, I'm sorry. I don't mean to be an insensitive asshole. I just know..."

"What?" she says.

Now he's tongue-tied. "Just how much you care about Rebecca, and how smart she is, and Alaska still has a lot of racist shit going on, and, well... Anyway, I'm sorry."

"Forget it. Maybe I worry too much about these kinds of things. But I still wonder what place there is in modern America for its original cultures."

"Why is the language so important to you?" I ask her, gently as possible.

"Pretend you have just recently taken over a tract of land, or even a whole other country. Perhaps you traded for it, or maybe you just decided to conquer it. So there are probably mutually resentful feelings, and now people from two or perhaps more groups have to live near each other."

"All right. Sounds familiar. Americans did buy Alaska for pennies an acre from another group of European descendents who did not really own it to sell in the first place." I wonder after saying this if I'm correct in feeling vaguely guilty about that bit of history.

"The Russians, correct," Mariska says. "They no longer thought this land to be worth exploiting, though that was before the 1898 gold rush, and just before the global addiction to oil. They only thought it was worth timber and hunting, and even then it was too much work. The primary motivation of the Russian government in selling Alaska was that they had decimated the local sea otter population for their pelts. Can you imagine that? They overhunt one species, and then give up on 570,000 square miles, almost one and a half million square kilometers, of land. I mean, I know they were worried about the influence of the European countries on the world stage, especially in the wake of having to fight against several of them in the Crimean War a few years before; they even had a temporary ally in the Americans in that regard. But still: how bad must their economy have become to warrant that decision? Or were they just being short-sighted?"

I think I'm the only one who hears her add, "Like so many Europeans" after her last question, but Mariska can have a gift for understatement: Dave once described the 1867 sale of the Great Land as "the most completely screwed-up real estate deal since the Dutch got Manhattan Island for some damn beads." Even the British acquisition of Hong Kong seemed almost rational by comparison.

Jack is silent now, rapt, though he looks like he has heard this and its implications.

"So now," Mariska says, "what do you do with the people you have recently subjugated? You could just kill them all off, which has certainly been done in some places of the world. Or maybe you could intermarry, and start a mutual cultural exchange, although there will always be the bigots and racists who try and impede that, who try and make the offspring of those marriages feel like half-breeds. That happened up here as well: the early Russian settlers generally had trouble with the notion of intermarriage, and they practiced physical racial separation for much of the period that they controlled their main settlement down in Sitka." A dark cloud passes over Mariska's face, just briefly, and I picture adorable little Rebecca. Whoever her father is, he's probably not of any direct American Indian descent if he's from southern California. "But if you are afraid of the conquered peoples rising up against you later, and if you also feel guilty about the prospect of slaughtering them all, then you have to undermine their culture to weaken them and control them. And the strongest way to do that is to get rid of their language. Having them switch religions is the second strongest method, though they are likelier to resist the latter plan with violence. But either way, you need numbers on your side, which happened more in the Americas than anywhere else in history."

Dave nods. I try to take it all in. Jack looks out the back seat window, pointing out a cow moose with its mostly-grown calf just off the highway, walking easily towards the mix of marsh and forest between us and the mountains.

Moose admiration lasts only a few seconds. The lesson continues. "Look, you all," Mariska says. "When the descendents of those who sold Alaska formed the Soviet Union, they violently insisted that everyone in the Socialist Republics speak Russian, and not Lithuanian, or Kazakh, or Georgian. With the breakup of the USSR, those languages started getting stronger again. When the Europeans settling America thought they were doing the Indian tribes a big favor by putting them in classrooms on reservations, they punished the children for speaking Hopi, or Navajo, or Sioux. And that was only for the children who were strong enough to have survived the attempts to kill them off, with guns or smallpox."

Jack speaks again at last. "When I was in Scotland, I found a bookshop in Edinburgh, in full view of the huge castle there, and I remember how surprised I was at seeing books and CDs in Scots Gaelic. And then I found out later that Irish and Welsh are even stronger, after the English tried so hard to wipe out the Celtic languages."

Mariska nods. "I said language is the strongest cultural link. It is how we identify members of certain groups, more than anything else. So, yes, Rebecca will study it. I cannot tell you how diligently, or whether she will try to hang onto it later in her life, but she will learn it now, and it will always be part of her."

Listening to her, I marvel at how Mariska can charge a conversation by remaining subtle, taking the time to enunciate, which has more effect than yelling or intentionally lilting the voice musically. It's amazing how moving speech becomes when you don't use contractions, like you do when you're in a hurry. Mariska could sound like any of the other three of us when she wanted, but when she was trying to emphasize something, as she did in her university classes, she was slower and more deliberate. I remember reading that during the 19th century, so many white American settlers and conquerors thought that this indicated a certain "slowness" on behalf of the Indians, and it wasn't until later I realized that it made for more direct, honest speech.

And Mariska can make the transition instantly, only occasionally speaking fast like the rest of us: "As for the other elements of being Athabascan, Jack, wait until you've had your first glimpse of my daughter dog mushing. That's an excellent example of local culture, and we've done it for centuries before the world learned of the Iditarod."

"So you're adaptable. I admire that. So what's Athabascan culture, really?"

"I once read that culture is what can be learned or copied from others," she counters.

"Then plenty of non-humans have their own cultures," Dave says.

"Okay, Jack," I intone. "Tell us: what do you want to be when you grow up?"

Jack is grateful for the lightening mood in the car. And like I said earlier, the ability to get along is essential with any small group that's about to spend a few days in very close quarters.

"Are you aware, Morgan, that your very question contains the painful assumption that I actually will 'grow up,' as you call it? What could possibly be my incentive for such misery?"

"Should I be sorry I asked, then?"

"Not at all. But what's my motivation for behaving all 'mature-like?' Surely it can't be to impress the ladies."

"Clearly, that is not the case," Mariska says.

"Truly, my dear. It seems women are impressed by immaturity only at first, saying that the latest man they're attracted to 'knows how to be a kid,' or is 'good at having fun.' But when these same individuals want something else, suddenly the guy's an immature jerk. I got tired of that."

"Maybe people, especially women, would take you more seriously if you grew up more," suggests Dave. The two men have been jibing one another like this for years. I make no claims to understand this male bonding stuff; it always seems like insults.

"Ha!" exclaims Jack. "Serious people are terribly boring. You should know."

"What in hell does that mean?"

"I mean you used to smile more before you became a paramedic. Remember when you used to just ride trains in as many places as possible? And how you wanted to visit every National Park in the country?"

Dave chuckles. "When did I say that?"

"A couple of years ago, although you were a little loaded at the time. Those drink-induced confessionals are a bitch, and that's something I should know." I once thought Jack was a full alcoholic, and sometime after suggesting that possibility to him, he seemed to very quickly lose virtually all interest in booze, like maybe he recognized that he was too close, so to speak.

I know the expression now on Dave's face, like he's close to angry but not wanting to damage our collective mood. It took a lot for him to get out of retail management and go back to school for a very intensive year to become a paramedic, and then to have to spend a few hectic months in Chicago doing his clinical rotations and come back up here to get a job with the AFD. Still, he and Jack are friends. They trust each other. And that time in Chicago was the most Dave's ever spent with his son at a stretch.

What begins as a slightly tense silence grows more companionable as we savor the clear driving weather. Dave's Subaru Outback hugs the pavement smoothly, the car a good compromise for up here between wanting the off-road abilities of those monstrous so-called sport-utilities and wanting to expend a bit less fuel. Our packs are stacked creatively in the hatchback, taking up space clear to the ceiling, so Dave has to rely on the side mirrors to see behind us. The distance starts to slip by this way, and I'm surprised by how quickly we reach the first traffic light we've seen for fifty kilometers. Straight ahead would take us toward Palmer, the State Fairgrounds, and to places like Tok, Valdez, and even Canada if we stayed on it long enough. But we're veering left, onto the Parks Highway. Less than three hours to go now.

"Who wants gummy bears?" I say, remembering my snack from REI, which I've intentionally kept with me up front.

Three hands shoot up. "Pass those around!"

Everyone takes a handful as I offer them. "So how'd we go from booze-inthuced honesthy to food?" Jack says, through a mouthful of the multi-colored miniature bears. They do have a way of sticking to one's teeth, thereby impeding good pronunciation.

"Oh, now you've got it, Jack," Mariska says. "Not only do we women folk love honesty, but the maturity of speaking while eating. Didn't your mother ever teach you not to chew with your maw gaping?"

Jack's trying hard enough not to laugh that I suspect he's almost got a bear or two lodged up his nasal cavity. "Thut up!" is all he can verbalize, which makes Mariska very daintily place one gummy bear at a time into her mouth, taking the extra second necessary to tease Jack with her tongue.

He finally gets the contents of his own mouth under control. "Damn, woman, you know that drives me crazy."

"What's that?" she says, making her voice suddenly half

an octave higher in pitch, as she flutters her eyelids rapidly. She's actually batting her eyelashes at him. I didn't think anyone did that anymore, but Mariska's gorgeous enough to pull it off without it looking hopelessly neurotic. I self-consciously try the same gesture, making sure none of them can see me, and feel like a complete schmuck. So much for womanly wiles. There's no way Mariska could do this in front of her students.

I don't really feel like considering physical relationships these days, so: "So what's everyone hoping to see on our trail?"

"What, is this to be like the backpacking version of 'I spy'?" Dave says.

"Sure. It can be anything: a type of tree or plant, a certain animal. We already saw those moose off the highway, and we'll likely see more in the Park."

"Bears," votes Jack. "Brown or black, either's good for me." Jack's the only one of us who has seen all three types of Alaska's bears in the wilderness. Well, four, if you count the huge Kodiak bears on their namesake island, which are considered a brown subspecies. We've all seen browns, or grizzlies, before, and Jack and Mariska have seen blacks as well, a bit smaller than their lighter-colored relatives, and good climbers to boot. But Jack's been far enough north of the arctic circle to have witnessed polar bears on the prowl.

"You know me," Mariska says. "I am the ornithologist wannabe, so any and all birds are good in my book. This is good country for willow ptarmigan and tundra swans, and if we get lucky maybe we shall get a glimpse of some trumpeters or snowy owls. It's already a bit late for sandhill cranes and Canada geese." This whole state offers good viewing of huge bird species: bald eagles have wingspans longer than my own height, and those trumpeter swans are even bigger.

"Dave?"

He thinks about it. "Me, I'm always hoping to see the most uncommon species up here. I finally saw my first wood frogs just last year, and then there was that pair of coyotes north of Seward the year before." I don't know what he's on about: I've seen plenty of wood frogs, one of our only indigenous amphibians. The little guys literally freeze solid during the winter and then thaw out again, none the worse for wear, amazingly. And coyotes are hardly rare.

"So what about this trip, then?"

Dave looks like a kid contemplating opening the first gift beneath a Christmas tree. "Something really unusual this time. Like a wolverine, or a lynx. Or black bears or wolves."

* * *

When you are within the wilderness, there are two main ways to avoid stupid decisions. The first is to keep properly hydrated, and the second consists in simply obtaining adequate rest. Oak, Paddler, Trap-dasher, and Dog-chaser had little trouble with the former, though the latter was continuing to prove a far more difficult requirement.

The Graydons had already embarked on their trek back to Nikolai, from where they'd shortly fly home to Talkeetna and its tiny airstrip, the ATVs, wolf carcasses, and supplies loaded onto their borrowed friend's flatbed boat at the Medfra campground. The river was not the roaring rapid sort that attracted the adventurous white-water fans, but a far more gentle option for water transport. The riverside had seen its share of trapping, gold panning, and salmon fishing, and was one of two ways to really reach Nikolai at all, the other being flying. This remoteness of so many Alaskan villages held an obvious appeal (Nikolai was eighty percent Athabascan), but transport costs could be distressing; the Graydons could not have afforded this hunting trip without the friends who operated the boat and flew them back home.

The image of a small cargo boat was a bit different from the more common Alaskan roadway sight of four-wheeled flatbed trailers carrying ATVs or motocross bikes during summer, and snowmachines in winter. To the wolves, motorized vehicles on land or water were all so many smelly shells, the paved roads themselves fairly pungent as well, especially the first summer that they were laid down by the human workers: that tarry odor drifted well into the wilds. Even most domesticated creatures turned their noses away from the likes of that, and the non-domesticates kept well away.

And that was what the survivors of the Fire Creek pack wanted more than anything else: distance. The hunters with their man-thunder might have left, along with the bodies of their slain packmates, but the poachers were still pursuing them, with the help of hunting dogs. Dog-chaser alone understood that wolves taking on dogs was typically not even a contest, as the domestics were usually weaker, always clumsier and generally unsure of themselves, even in a fight. But the poachers had more with them than just dogs. Traps could always be evaded if one knew how, but outsmarting a spiraling bullet was another matter.

Brent Muskey had reserved some choice expletives for the Graydons as they had for him, although neither pair of men knew the identities of the others. Nikolai never received much traffic, even with its status as a stop on the Iditarod Trail, and this was Muskey's first visit, coming from his home in Fairbanks. And he certainly did not consider himself, or his friend Trey Stone, to be anything as disgraceful as "poachers." Both these men would have regarded the Graydon brothers as prejudiced and misguided. The former believed they were performing a necessary, though perhaps distasteful task: wolves and certain other species were essentially vermin, and often needed to be eliminated. Muskey was disgusted that thousands of people from around the world had actually boycotted Alaska back in the mid-nineties, all because of these goddamned wolves. The state governor at that time had helped see to it that the practice of "same-day-land-and-shoot" hunting was outlawed for most big game species, wolves included. This involved using aircraft to chase larger game animals to exhaustion, then land close by so they'd be easier targets for guns. Alaska, for all its inherent wealth and natural resources, nonetheless was heavily dependent upon the travel business, and the video footage of planes chasing large furry pests was as damaging to the state's international reputation as the previous footage of the aristocratic snobs in formal outfits riding well-bred horses through parts of Britain, while their dog packs chased a single fox to exhaustion, then tore it to pieces.

People were so easily moved by simple imagery, fumed Muskey for the thousandth time; those dickheads with the cameras should try living up here and get a taste of what was needed. Some damn backbone, for one thing. And never mind that Alaska's voters had decided, legally, twice, to outlaw the dreaded aerial hunting practices for all species. Once again: wolves included.

The two subsequent state governors made it clear that this collective voice of the voters was inconsequential, to the delight of Muskey and Stone. The first new governor appointed hunters and trappers to the state's Department of Fish and Game, and his own daughter to the position of state senator, and both family members were excitedly in favor of the on-again, off-again topic of opening up parts of the Great Land for further economic development, like the proposed usage of a large designated national wildlife refuge in the northeast for more oil. And then the next new governor likewise ignored the voters, convinced that predators could be "controlled." If the wolves and bears and other species that some of the more misguided tourists loved to see got in the way, well, there were ways of circumventing such irksome issues as public opinion, scientific data, and expert testimony; no species could stand in the way of economic development. That was what so infuriated Muskey and Stone, after all.

Of course, politics aside, even with the occasional culling of some species, usually predators, within Alaska, there had been no recent targeting of wolves approved for their current location, but that hardly worried this pair of hunters. This was the eastern portion of Game Management Unit 19, part of a huge grid artificially superimposed upon some maps of the state, delineating types of hunting and fishing, their accompanying seasons, and "bag" or "take" limits determining allowable kills and catches, as well as even which tools of the trade could be utilized for the purpose. Alaska was arranged into 27 such game zones, each with slightly different regulations, and so far as the hunting men could determine, those damned pesky wolves were heading roughly east, towards GMU 20. These two game units actually exhibited equal regulations, though neither of these men was overly concerned with what state law had to say regarding the hunting of particular species.

True, there could be some political or economic fallout from the actions of Muskey and Stone, but the current activities were hell and gone from most of civilization, so none of those damned "lib'rals" would ever have a chance to miss a few more wolves. But Brent and Trey also relished what they were doing. It was easy to get distracted by watching wolves acting cute; even the hardest trappers had trouble eliminating pups, for example, especially since they looked so like the puppies of a number of dog breeds, with their blue eyes and playful whimpers. That was why trapping worked better in the first place. Traps were designed to target larger animals, could in fact be built for specific species, and the poisons they sometimes used could only be transferred to other animals if they ate the flesh of the recently deceased. And since no species larger than ravens or foxes or wolverines would ever likely be caught munching on dead wolf meat, it was hardly a problem. Besides, to Muskey and Stone, the scavengers were just pests as well.

Far better to have dogs, like the assortment trotting along with them now. The men were not breeders, but had their own favorites among the larger breeds. They exclusively loved hunting dogs: black and chocolate and yellow labs, goldens, pointers, wolfhounds, setters, even the occasional terrier, though they both thought terriers were generally too small to make a decent show of things in the bush. These men knew that size mattered, at least in the wilderness.

And with them now marched a pointer, a chocolate Labrador mixed with husky, and one of the so-called Alaskan huskies, which were slightly smaller than their Siberian namesakes and typically looked like a blonde and black blend of not-quite short hair. The canine trio poked and sniffed and generally loved being outdoors for its own sake, and despite what their masters thought, would have been terrified at the sight of actual wolves. Their wild ancestors were more like dreams, and all these dogs had exchanged howls during hunting trips before, but like Dog-chaser's suspicions, realized that they'd be in trouble indeed around actual wolves. That was what Brent and Trey were for, them and their guns and traps.

Muskey and Stone still marveled that the traps were so easily defeated. Stone had once admitted listening to an old report about Alaskan trapping, and someone who'd sounded to Trey like just another old fart sourdough who rambled on about how his own trap was once bested by something he'd ignored during placement.

This old man had allowed a drop, one single, solitary drop of his sweat to fall off his heated forehead and spill onto the well-worn iron of the trap jaws. And it was enough: the wolf pack in the area at that time detected the presence of humans, and while they likely did not realize what humans might do, they nonetheless associated this unknown odor from a drop of sweat with uncertainty, and therefore danger.

In the meantime, Dog-chaser remained cognizant that the dogs were no genuine threat, his packmates maintained their anxiety, which was all the more strange considering that Dog-chaser was, after all, the *omega*. And higher ranking wolves did not, simply put, show fear in the presence of such a low-ranking individual, at least not unless the latter was already terrified as well. Trap-dasher was the only other one who also seemed even remotely relaxed; Oak and Paddler, perhaps because of their dominant positions, perhaps due to the responsibility that those positions entailed, tried diligently to not be short-tempered, but kept failing as they struggled to put safety distance between themselves and their pursuers. Dog-chaser in particular simply tolerated the nips and growls of the others, offering them the chance to vent their frustration and sadness. All four wolves still wanted to howl their mourning clear to the clouds above, but kept their vocal chords largely in check for now; the dogs and humans hardly needed additional clues to their whereabouts.

Dog-chaser had also taken some comfort in the belief that humans rarely strayed far from home, something he understood all the more since the guideline applied as well to his own kind. Wolves were excellent observers of the habits of others; predators generally did tend towards such systematic studies. Dog-chaser also had an additional advantage, since he had made visits closer to human homes. And in his experience, travel for humans was, like travel for wolves, mostly confined to a specific area. The idea of a human vacation, by which the takers simply vanished from their territories, was unknown to wild species, though clearly there existed many which did travel impressive distances along migration routes. But for the most part, the humans stayed close to their stinky homes. They moved in their smelly-shells out of their block-rock homes, and glided along their dark runs to go, well, who could say, really? Dog-chaser, unfamiliar with the human concerns of monetary employment, figured that the work of two-leggers paralleled that of wolfkin: patrolling, hunting, establishing and maintaining territories, with time for eating, playing, and socializing with packmates coming afterward. He had noticed from afar humans playing with their foolish dogs, and knew firsthand that the two-leggers had a capacity for simple, undiluted joy. But they also seemed to frown so often, and it was harder to read the body linguistics of a species that stayed painfully vertical so much of the time. Maybe that was their problem: Dog-chaser could certainly stretch his way into an awkward bipedal stance, and had seen bears do it, too. But why would anyone do it for such prolonged periods? The bears seemed to get a better view, huge as they could be, but Dog-chaser decided quickly that two legs was just a step from lameness. How could the "takers," as they seemed to be to wolves, keep any semblance of balance while on only two feet like that?

None of the four survivors of the Fire Creek pack was familiar with maps, of course, so they had to rely on other means of navigation besides the well-worn and creased blue, green, and brown papers that the Graydons and the likes of Muskey and Stone possessed. The wolves had their species' instinctive ability to know roughly where north was, though in a place like Alaska, the declination from magnetic north, which lay to the northeast in a remote portion of Canada, was quite large, so direction-finding for many northern creatures lay in practice almost as much as sense. At any rate, a northerly course was what these wolves considered their last option. They still had a plan, of sorts, knowing that they couldn't just flee purposelessly: that would either give their position back to the poachers, or else more than likely lead them into other wolves' territories. And none of them were genuinely aware of the extreme geographic obstacles that Alaska often put in front of travel, ones that even the humans had to either go around or fly over: high and jagged mountains with little or no cover, broad glaciers which might or might not support one's weight when stepped upon, and rivers which could vary from pleasant streams to torrential unswimmable rapids. Indeed, the Fire Creek survivors had been fortunate so far to avoid all such, though they still were roughly heading towards the tremendous mountains southeast of their territory, wholly unaware that the park delineated around those same peaks bore witness to millions of biped visitors, perhaps not the most ideal of locales for wolves who only wanted to hide from such creatures.

Dog-chaser remained in the middle of the pack's trot. Oak still led, with some navigational assistance and confirmation provided by Paddler. Indeed, the *alphas* took what precious time they could getting to feel more comfortable being in greater proximity than before. Oak had once considered reciprocating that interest of Paddler not long ago, though Midnight had quickly squelched any possibility of returned sentiment: she had growled Paddler down until she rolled over and exposed her lighter and quite vulnerable belly to the now-deceased former *alpha* female. Still, there was barely any time to consolidate anything resembling a more intimate relationship; survival concerns didn't permit such.

Trap-dasher currently brought up the rear, though that position normally belonged exclusively to Dog-chaser. He didn't mind, though, since he knew that he probably had the best stamina in the pack, and just couldn't be entirely content unless he would pause while the others kept going, long enough to gaze back behind them.

How far had they already trod, these four? Their measurements accrued as hours or days spent traveling, rather than kilometers or minutes. The weather had mostly cleared after the last couple of days of rain, which was near-freezing when the wind-chill was computed into it, and the USGS

survey maps that Morgan Greene so prized would have revealed
the packs' position as roughly following Jones Creek through to
a semi-flat section amongst the taiga which lay nestled roughly
equidistant between Strand Peak and Limestone Mountain.
These peaks were impressive in their own right, surely, but as
part of the ongoing Kuskokwim Range, they were just another
couple of jags. A small settlement, mostly a camping area and
river base with tiny airstrip known as Medfra, lay due south of
the wolves, but they kept up their hopes up of being able to see
their way safely past the rugged terrain.

The problem, noticed by Trap-dasher as he stood
panting and staring back whence they'd come, was that while
taiga offered some natural cover in the form of a mix of shorter
alpine trees and rounded boulders, it nonetheless was steep
enough that if their pursuers still followed them, there was no
way to turn back without being detected. And forward, in front
of Oak and Paddler, lay the mountains which to Trap-dasher
seemed to just get higher and higher. He knew they could keep
their stamina up far better than almost anything living in the
Alaskan bush, but wolves were just not very good mountaineers.
If mountain goats or Dall's sheep were foolish enough to
wander too far off their craggy perches and windswept inclines,
they could indeed become easy wolf meals, but so long as they
stayed on the steep rocks, no wolf could reach them. Trap-
dasher knew that well, having tracked goats in the Sunshine
Mountains before giving in to frustration the previous year.

He turned his look back towards his companions,
noting that Oak had stopped, noticed him lagging, and barked
once, quietly, to get his attention. He kept eye contact with
the *alpha*, a gesture safer at this distance, as though challenging
the higher-ranking wolf to realize the sheer exposure of their
position. There was just no escape going back, and they were
now committed to heading south by southeast; that was the
only opening. Maybe during midsummer they'd have a chance

of overcoming the peaks, but even color-blind creatures like these could see the snow already on the summits.

Trap-dasher plodded on, only stopping when he'd reached the others, who took turns lapping up the crystalline water that defined Jones Creek. He took his fill as well. Paddler strode over, offering him a couple of licks about the muzzle for simple reassurance. Dog-chaser and Oak, their thirsts slaked for the present, merely looked ahead.

Just over a kilometer eastward, another creek, named Medicine, picked up where it was regularly fed by the mountains. It ran south, shortly helping to feed the Kuskokwim River, right at Medfra. The wolves were tempted to follow that route, wholly unaware of the likelihood of more human encounters that way, until Paddler instinctively pulled back just enough of her own muzzle to reveal her unmistakable canines, and let out just enough of a growl to be heard by her packmates.

The bull moose, all seven hundred kilos of him, had certainly not headed this way expecting trouble. In fact, this was a relatively safe watering stop precisely because the topography was a bit less welcoming of wolves than of others. He'd not seen wolves since his own first winter, when a pack, maybe even some of the four now facing him, had caught his sister, while his mother had managed to save him.

Predators stank, the moose remembered. A lifetime of chomping up other animals made for an undeniable scent which could sometimes be detected at impressive distances by herbivorous noses, depending on the wind conditions. Even lamer noses like those of humans could note the sharp differences in piquancy between plant- and meat-eaters, at least up close. But no matter now: the moose had to contend with a cadre of wolves who were in excellent health, as well as being lately short-tempered from loss, and hungry, seemingly always hungry.

So the moose stared at them for a minute or three. The big bull, with his wide antler rack, dark and velvety and perched proudly atop his massive skull, just stood there motionless, hoping these damned wolves would seek other targets. This was one animal who already knew the fateful steps of the dance of death.

The "dance" was first proposed using that particular term some thirty years or so earlier, by a sympathetic but well-read scientific writer. Essentially, the dance consisted of two partners, predator and prey, who, upon encountering one another, would size each other up. The former examined the latter for weakness, while the latter was actually the one in control of the situation, whether this was realized as genuine thought processing or not. In other words, whether this bull moose would be chased was ultimately up to him, or so went the dance logic: if he gave in to anxiety and fled, the wolves would give chase, and the moose did not know that these wolves were hardly prepared to chase a moose for what could be days to reach a successful conclusion.

But if the moose stood his ground, not giving a single step, even if the wolves tried attacking, they'd eventually realize that they would get nowhere. A running moose could be exploited: the neck was bared, the legs each became targets. But a standing moose could offer kicks of tremendous pressure and speed. Not all forms of dance are peaceful partnerings.

This was a genuine Alaskan standoff. Dog-chaser was perfectly content with the smaller prey they'd lived on for the past few days now, and Oak understood best of all of them that with such depleted pack strength, this moose was likely to prove far more trouble than his tasty and succulent flesh and viscera were actually worth. Accordingly, the two *alphas*, without taking eyes from their potential prey, used the soft barks of their kind to give basic commands: Dog-chaser and Trap-dasher were to come up to Oak and Paddler, and the four of them would simply go around the stubborn moose and resume their way. Let the humans tangle with this big brown thing, with their man-thunder.

Eye contact was maintained by all parties, the wolves crossing the chilled waters of Jones Creek, still insisting on heading south by southeast through the pass. But turning brought them necessarily slightly closer to the moose, and the cantankerous bull was having none of that.

He charged. Most creatures would hardly believe a prey species chasing multiple members of a predator species, but it did happen. Wisdom with a charge from a bear suggested that you generally stood your ground, but for a charging moose, you simply ran like mad and hoped the creature's confidence would resume as it watched you take flight. And the wolves were completely startled. Not one of them had ever been chased by anything besides other wolves, except of course for Oak and his history with a bear.

What started as panic quickly degenerated into a comedy of errors. Trap-dasher lost footing and slipped on some of the rocks lining the creek, hitting his behind on yet another rock. He could have been trampled, but the moose had opted to focus his main attention on Oak.

Paddler simply leapt over a narrower part of the creek, possessing supreme agility herself, with the moose in close pursuit since she was still with Oak. That left Dog-chaser, who quickly wondered why he was the only wolf now actually trying to chase this heavy moose, while his companions all ran from it. The hooves and deceptively thin lanky legs of the bull splashed water all over Trap-dasher as it, too, ran through the creek, and it indeed lowered its thick skull and sizable rack to take half-hearted aim at Oak, then Paddler, who could turn faster and with a smaller radius than the moose could.

And the moose demonstrated supreme control of will. The charge had lasted seven or eight seconds, and then the bull stood there again, motionless, daring the wolves to try anything. Trap-dasher took a few seconds to shake the excess water from his coat. Oak and Paddler looked quickly at each other and then at their quarry, as though questioning just what kind of animal this really was. And Dog-chaser was in the moose's blind spot, almost directly behind, not making a sound in case the *alphas* decided to really go after this ungainly-looking fighter.

Though they wouldn't. It could easily take a dozen-member pack to pose a true threat to an ornery moose like this, and even then the likelihood of canid casualties remained. Awkwardly and uncertainly, the four wolves made their way back across the creek, looking behind them after a short distance, and noticed the moose still watching them impassively. They headed deeper into the mountain range.

* * *

While the Fire Creek members had thus far managed to avoid further injuries, the Chelatna pack had a new incident of their own with which to contend. Foxtrot, one of the pups, had managed to find some mischief of his own.

Pups were notoriously curious, as dedicated in that regard as any feline kittens, and Foxtrot, along with his littermates Puddles and Sterling, tried their utmost to experience the best adventures they could find, while apparently believing themselves more or less indestructible. The adult wolves generally tolerated such behavior: perhaps because they knew they had little choice in the matter, or maybe because young intelligent animals had an annoying tendency to have to learn certain lessons the hard way. Whatever the case, whichever wolf remained on guard duty during a hunt might have been able to fairly complain that he or she exerted as much energy just babysitting the pups as the other adults did hunting some prey creature.

Fortunately for Alaskan wolves, there were no indigenous snakes or naturally venomous creatures with which to tangle, but there remained plenty of other potential hazards nonetheless, including, in the case of Foxtrot's recent cries for help, the bane of young predators throughout North America.

This, of course, could be none other than that most fearsome of wild beasts, a creature clearly devilish in design, such that just getting too close could cause agony, blindness, infection, and perhaps even death for the unwary or careless. It might have been another mammal, endothermic and able to survive Alaska's extreme environments, but that hardly made it less dangerous. Indeed, poor Foxtrot would always remember the musky smell of this nasty animal, the way it just lackadaisically meandered through the tundra, inflicting suffering on all who might oppose it, and the curious lack of expression on its black and sinister-looking face as it went about its destructive business. What, indeed, could have caused the existence of such a vile thing with which to plague wolfkind?

The porcupine: menace to tender noses and paws throughout the North American continent. Foxtrot would have gladly brought the others over to kill it out of simple spite if not for two details: he was already terrified of seeing it again, and he could think of no way to initiate such an assault in the first place. He simply ran screeching back to the pack rendezvous site, white Sterling and grey Puddles in anxious tow, the adults immediately sprinting towards the sound of such commotion.

It was Cabal's turn at watch near the rendezvous. The other adults had actually been out exploring: Bear Heart and Owl Eyes jogging in the shadow of Mount Kliskon, playful but also remarking their territory at its northern edges; Tornado, Swifter, and Wave returning from the Midway Lakes, three small but permanent watering holes where some of the local caribou could often be found, even if not today; old Fisher checking out the base of Rich Creek where it fed into the quicker Yentna River; and Tracer just reclining on a hill near the base site. Tracer arrived at the scene of chaos first, looking to Cabal, who wisely hung his head shamefully, and then to the three pups, who were now all making too much noise, as though by howling Foxtrot's siblings could somehow alleviate his suffering.

If the wolves could have counted, Tracer and Cabal would have found no fewer than five quills protruding from the nose and muzzle of Foxtrot, who initially tried to back up from the adults. It had been some time since anyone in the pack had a run-in with the creature that would now occasionally haunt Foxtrot's canine dreams, but Tracer could still recall over a year earlier when she and the others had to coax Wave into stillness while they pulled the painfully sharp quills loose. By the time the others arrived, the pups had largely quieted down, and Cabal gently but firmly kept his forepaws around Foxtrot, to try and keep him from moving. They had to get back in position again when Owl Eyes returned, *alpha* female and mother of the pup trio, and she personally helped keep the injured pup's movements to a minimum by displacing Cabal.

Strange it would be to watch this concerted group effort. The pup continued to yelp as each quill was forcibly removed, Tracer yanking each in turn. Wave just watched sympathetically; his own porcupine run-in had yielded just three quills, and he still remembered that it took weeks for the pain to fully depart, the scabs to finally heal over, and his sense of smell to return to its original degree of perception. And of course Bear Heart himself was back now also, growlingly chastising Cabal. The younger male skulked away, continually hounded by the *alpha*, keeping his tail tucked in an arch between his hind quarters, until Bear Heart tackled him completely. Cabal rolled over to expose his soft and unprotected belly, the most submissive act members of their kind were capably of exhibiting. Bear Heart growled once or twice more, then clamped down on Cabal's own muzzle with his own, until he elicited another yelp, which sounded every bit as juvenile as those coming from Foxtrot. This was both punishment for what the alphas perceived as dereliction of duty for not noticing the offending porcupine, as well as demonstrating yet again that Bear Heart would remain the dominant male.

Two quills into his ordeal, young Foxtrot felt he might go blind from pain, though some part of him remained glad that he had, after all, not taken any of the quills into an eye. Contrary to a common misperception, "porkies" could not shoot their quills like so many darts or arrows; they simply came loose from the skin easily once snagged in something, and what made them so dicey were the barbs on the other end which, like tiny fishing hooks, embedded themselves readily into soft flesh. As the other old adage went, however, porcupines indeed had to mate carefully, and their craving of sodium had proven the bane of more than one pair of human hiking boots, salted from sweat and then chewed by surprisingly sharp beaver-like teeth into little more than sandals with shredded laces.

Three down, two remaining, and Foxtrot could smell his own blood. His mother continued to hold him, knowing she could not safely lick his muzzle to comfort and clean him until the quills were removed, else they might even become lodged in her tongue and mouth. Just another moment or two, they all hoped.

What made it even more curious to any creature who might have observed such a scene was that none of the wolves, young or old, remained aloof. When one suffered, part of each of them did. This was not mere emotional consideration, but came also from a practical concern, which was actually the basis of sympathy in every creature which was capable of feeling it: the suffering of any member of the pack weakened that member, which in turn weakened the pack as a whole. And for a species which relied so heavily on group strength and community ties, this was hardly a trifling concern.

Foxtrot sensed the final quill get torn from his ravaged flesh between Tracer's front teeth and felt he had been in this position for days. Gone was any memory of life without pain. He whimpered again, but then quieted as he noticed both Tracer slipping silently away from him, and the warm sensation of his mother's tongue around his muzzle. Wolves, like all canids domestic and wild, were extremely oral: muzzle greetings were common every time pack members reunited, even if they'd only been apart for a few hours, like rambunctious dogs leaping all over their humans as they returned home from wherever it was humans went during the day and sometimes night. And in this most recent case, canid saliva had also recently been shown to contain several enzymes to encourage healing of wounds, so there was more to this behavior than maternal concern. From Bear Heart's correction of Cabal to the way pups licked at the mouths of adults returning from the hunt to get them to regurgitate food for their own meals, wolves communicated quite extensively with those fearsome-looking long snouts with the rows of very capable teeth within. This included the patience of Tracer's invasive care; Wave's treatment had taken longer, since it was based more on trial and error, until Tracer got the hang of placing the thick quills into her own mouth. Quills varied in diameter, and fortunately Foxtrot's encounter was with an adult animal; a juvenile would have likely had quills too small to be gripped by the front teeth of a wolf.

Foxtrot quieted quickly, wanting to keep licking the more tender spots of his muzzle where the quills had been embedded, but could only reach a few. The small wounds still stung, but he was already jealous of his two siblings as they bounded off into the bush, wanting to resume their games. The adults, too, had begun wandering back to their previous activities. It remained a lovely day, and even young Foxtrot was hardly about to let it slip by without further adventure. Still, pain always had an exhausting effect, and he would not make it far from the rendezvous site before falling asleep.

* * *

"How much further is the Talkeetna junction?" pipes up Jack from the rear seat. I can't help smiling, since he manages to make it sound like a progressively whinier child on a trip, asking the ubiquitous "are we there yet?" until we almost have to threaten him with ever worse forms of violence.

Dave appears not to have heard this time. He seems mesmerized by the scenery. Outside the windows, only the mountains seem immovable, while the closer trees and signs fly past us. Who was it said that driving and looking through car windows is just another type of television? I think I read that in *Zen and the Art of Motorcycle Maintenance*, or somewhere like that. A good traveling book, at any rate.

"A few more miles," Mariska says, who probably gives more attention to highway signs than the rest of us. "Why, did you want to stop in town?"

That would likely be lovely, given the time of year. Talkeetna's a fun little town, and I've really only seen it from the perspective of a single night. That was four years ago now, when Mom and Dad came up to visit and we rode the train from Anchorage to Denali Park. The only privately owned rail system left in the States, and rumor holds that you can just flag it down in the middle of nowhere, hop on, then pay your passage from one of the conductors. And of course, no trip on the Alaska Railroad would ever be complete without a mass mooning outside one of the smaller settlements: nine men there had been on that prior occasion, with clearly too much time on their hands, lined up to make sure my parents and I would always have pasty pink and white butt cracks as part of our trip memories. Grinning, I recall that Talkeetna remains outside our plans, and we've already been driving about three hours.

"No," Jack says slowly. We've reached that part of the drive when questions and answers are allowed to take longer, as if it'll help pass the time. Strange how even in the most picturesque of locales, drives can still become boring. The television metaphor seems to hold in that regard, and we can't really change the channel here.

"Actually, gang," Dave says, "we've plenty of gas still, and I'd just as soon get hiking. It's already afternoon, and I'd like to see if we can do maybe a half dozen miles on the trail yet today." He grins at me, knowing I still prefer metric, and I know either way that it means over two hours of hard trail, but we do have plenty of light left for it. It's more a matter of how tired we are after the drive. Fortunately, the gummy bears haven't quite worn off yet, but they're hardly a protein source, so they'll be hiked off in no time.

The side road does not get mentioned again as we veer west of it and remain on the main highway, passing the handful of small businesses that cater to the mix of highway traffic and Talkeetna residents. Then we're quickly over the Chulitna River and I officially start to feel more excited by our prospects. This is what we've been needing, been waiting for! A few days away from work stress and schedule commitments and distracting technology. "Just remember to hit the Peters Creek turn," I tell Dave. He glares at me like I'm being stupid, but for some reason it's easier to miss a turn when you only really have one of them to make.

I wonder again, like I always do in Alaska's backcountry, what it would really be like to have more of a homestead than a home, and supplement your groceries with things that you gather or grow or catch. Or maybe not even be able to buy groceries at all, or have some supplemental items flown in at ghastly prices; it is possible to come to regard eight dollars for a jug of milk as a fair price in communities not far from here.

Our present locale has us well past the rough cutoff where Anchorage becomes a viable option for work commuters, though I know there are employees in huge cities who actually do two hours each way. I can barely imagine it; I'd have to have a laptop computer or plenty of books along to ward off madness, which of course would mean I'd then have to not be driving. I wonder if the Alaska Railroad could ever be used as a form of public commuter transit.

At any rate, it's easy to imagine the romantic appeal of living from the land, when your immediate neighbors are gleefully undomesticated, and the closest human neighbors might be some distance away. Some of the homes we pass even on the highway make me think in those terms. I do love city life: museums and libraries and live performances, and Anchorage has such, but it would be quite something to see the aurora borealis unaffected by urban light pollution, and to be completely out of range of the noises of twenty-first century civilization. I used to fantasize about having a place with at least a few acres around it, but the price of land in the Anchorage region is frightening: I know people who have paid $100,000 for a single acre with no home to speak of yet on it.

That recalls another chat I've had with Mariska on some occasions: the term "subsistence" is a big word for Alaska, and it doesn't really refer to its usual usage, which suggests life at an absolute poverty line and just barely scraping by financially. Up here, it instead reflects an entire lifestyle, largely indicative of the indigenous traditions, but also incorporating more modern elements. Subsistence is just the ability to "live off the land," so to speak, which is often just a cliché, but here it takes on stronger meaning. It might indicate farming, though of course there's not nearly as much arable land in a place this far north, and the soil can be quite hard, although Alaskans do still produce gigantic cabbages in this long growing season. It also can include hunting and fishing, maybe supplemented by some gardening, and harvesting of other food and medicinal offerings in terms of plants, especially the many species of berries and herbs which grow wild. I know Mariska's extended family includes folks who have actually tanned wild leather, and sewn with wild fur, and even made stone-age tools out of bones using traditions that date back to the last ice age. It's not supposed to be about exploitation, yet subsistence is nonetheless an extremely sensitive issue for Alaskans. We have the attitude shared by all people, everywhere, to not want to be told what to do and what not to do by "outsiders," never mind that I've been one myself. We also have varying degrees of interest and proficiency with subsistence skills, which often conflict with attitudes that are more exploitative in nature, like drilling for oil, mining for gold and other metals, creating regular fisheries, or hunting for trophies instead of for food. It can get ugly up here, and it's all too easy to let reason and science get ignored for the sake of what seems a temporary bonus or convenience. These considerations are cultural as well as economic, and therefore rather complex.

But now I'm merely focused on the most noticeable aspect of the Great Land: its simple beauty. I'd rather avoid politics for a while, if I could, and savor my friends. "That looks like the turn just up there, Dave."

He adds an "uh-huh," and releases the vehicle's cruise control. I am amused by how, simultaneously, Jack and Mariska and I begin stretching our legs and arms within the confines of this machine.

The road turns west at Trapper Creek and heads to Peters Creek and Petersville, and I briefly wonder who the hell Peter was to get all this immortalized credit. Maybe one of the gold-rushers from 1898 or something. Most of this road is still paved, and it's only a few more kilometers and minutes before

I sigh at the soothing sound of a large engine being shut off, surprisingly quieter than the tamer engine inside my adored Beetle. "Let's get moving, people," Jack says.

The packs come out of the hatchback door of the "sport-yoot," as I call it, not liking the asinine sport-utility wagon description, since I don't know what it means. I mean, no one races these things, do they? And don't all motor vehicles have some particular utility in the first place? Damn logic; this is what it does to you.

We each dedicate several final minutes going through our backpacks and accompanying gear, and it takes longer for me, since I was the one they had to wait on this morning, finally cramming the last items and newly bought things into the hatchback. Now that the proverbial moment of truth has actually come upon us, I feel just slightly edgy, and glance about at our environs. My companions think I'm just taking in the scenery again.

"Morgan, come on; we need to get going," Jack says, and I notice that all three of them are indeed just about ready to start the trail: retying of boots, reorganizing of food, ensuring that favorite items are in place, have all been done. I quickly reorganize my beloved Ursack with its assorted dried nutritional contents, and then close my eyes and breathe deeply of the surrounding air. Recalling the prior ambiguity with tents, I opt for my own counterpoint to Dave's "burrito." Better to just grab it now than deal with awkwardness later.

There's nothing that smells out of place out here: no smokiness, no artificial scents, no muskiness of wildlife. Yet there is nonetheless a certain tang to the air. I feel almost no wind against my face, but there is still that crisp sense which reminds one of weather about to turn cold. Can you smell snow, or fall? Science says no, of course not, but to live here will change your view on that. We're all well prepared in terms of warmth, but if we actually got snow up here now, we'd have to just trudge through the terrain as best we could. I open my eyes, can tell that my friends are not quite impatient but not quite tolerant, either, and decide to cast the potential warning away. It's still September, not November, and the climate should be on our side. Besides, who the hell wants to carry snowshoes on a trail if they go unused? And we decided not to bring any, regardless.

So what time of year was it a few years back when Dad and I got snowed out of the National Park because the Mountain decided it was time for an early snow? August? I can't remember for sure, but what I can ascertain is that Denali is so stunningly high that if it decides there'll be snow, then snow's what you get. A dim view from the science corner on that as well: you can't *personify* or *anthropomorphize* a mountain, of all things.

I quickly reorganize the various items I'd pulled out of my pack closet earlier today, keeping heavier things more on top to help with weight distribution once the pack is on me, and then I sit on the hatchback floor and pull it on me, feeling more of a hug than a strain, so comforting and comfortable is the old pack. Hip straps and cross-chest strap snitched in snugly, I stand, feeling the mass of my stuff settle about my waist where it should be, with very little actual pull on my shoulders. These things should really be called hippacks, not backpacks; the whole idea is to get most of the weight around your middle, not your shoulders. And then we lock the car and leave.

One of the lovelier signs of summer and fall evenings in the North gets noticed first by Jack, as our boots continue to scuff their way along the trail. "Check out the full moon, guys." He loves full moons, is piqued by their mythology. Dave hates them; as a paramedic, he agrees with the old conventional "wisdom" which suggests the crazies really do come out more on such nights. He's assured me that the firefighters and police and hospital people he knows feel the same way, and that anyone even remotely associated with emergency work often will try and change shifts once they become aware of the completion of lunar waxing. Some of them apparently buy those night calendars for this purpose, enabling them to plan work schedules a full year in advance in their efforts at wacko-evasion.

Dave is initially on "point," though none of us really use military terms, with Mariska and I spaced in between the men, and Jack pulling up the rear. After following the trail for a while, the front three of us stop at once when we hear the howling, then turn around to see Jack, who can no longer keep a straight face. "Are you actually attempting to frighten off the local wildlife, Jack?" Dave says.

Jack is still giggling, having taken his hands from the sides of his face, which had helped accentuate the volume of his howl, and which I admit probably sounded as much like a dying crow as anything else, even though for just a moment I permitted myself to almost believe that it was from a non-domesticated species. "Hey, I'm just having fun. You guys should've seen Mariska jump when I first did it."

Mariska's inherent dignity leads to an immediate and firm denial, and she sets about reaching Jack's more ticklish regions; the man simply cannot tolerate a rib tickling, and we all know it. Soon he's laughing so hard I wonder if he'll yet have the energy to keep up with us. This is like being in the car: are these two goofs still in the seventh grade, or something? I wonder if I even still have hormones like that. But when she ends his torment, he honestly wonders aloud if his howl had sounded anything like a wolf's.

Dave just shakes his head. "Shit, no. That was more like a coyote having a tooth pulled." That gets me laughing, and the four of us realize that we're now taking an impromptu break. I glance at my watch; we've only been hiking twenty minutes. I doubt we'll keep to Jack's semi-rational schedule at this rate. We're energetic, but also very relaxed, probably just insufficiently stretched after the long drive.

Jack hardly minds the crack, but he really wants to know. "Well, how do they sound, then?"

"You mean wolves?" Dave considers it a moment, wondering to grant a request which may or may not be that of an overgrown juvenile delinquent. But once he notices all three of us eyeing him expectantly, he takes two deep, full breaths, cups his own hands around his mouth, and offers a howl of his own.

It probably lasts just eight or nine seconds, yet something about this sound has a timeless quality, and I close my eyes one more time, like I do whenever I wish to savor non-visual sensory data. And I swear, for the last few moments, I can mentally picture a wolf. Gods, Dave's actually good. Either that, or I'm just good myself at imagining mind's-eye pictures. I don't recall ever seeing a live wolf up here, but I can really see it in my head now: grey fur tinged with black and tan streaks, long and thin legs, teeth exposed from breathing orally, in a perpetual trot, like it can never seem to reach wherever it might be going. And I'm still relishing the image when the answer comes from the west of us, which I believe is still on our tiny trail.

I open my eyes to find my friends staring sheepishly in that direction. "Do you think someone else is out here?" Jack wonders, the quickness of his speech betraying some other emotion besides curiosity.

"I doubt it," Dave says. "This is really just a winter track. I've hiked it once before. Even the locals don't use it much, and usually then only as kind of a winter getaway. At least, that's what I've heard. It appears as a 'winter trail' on the maps." That's true, I recall: my beloved Gazetteer displays this path in tiny red dashes, with the relevant fine print nearby. I know that sounds counterintuitive: it would seem a "winter trail" would either not be marked at all, or else known only by the locals, to discourage use by ignorant tourists, since they're the ones who usually get into trouble, and...

Mariska interrupts my haphazard thinking, and asks the question we all want to know, but refuse to pose, since it probably sounds too goofy. "So what, then? You think that might have been a real wolf?"

This is followed by the obvious objection, compliments of Jack: "Nah. Probably a coyote." But even I know that's not the case, and tell them.

"No. Coyotes are higher-pitched. And they're loners. That sounded like there might have been two or three of them." Granted, I'm guessing at this point, at least with the latter detail. I try to remember where I might have read that just a few wolves can somehow sound like dozens when they howl, as though to ward off competitors, but I can't conceive of the source now. If there was one. Maybe I'm just excited by the prospects. Like Dad has reminded me so many damned times: people believe what they want to, and disregard the rest. Like that old Simon and Garfunkel song he used to sing, which Mom would claim to hate, but then she'd join in and harmonize, just like wolves may or may not do.

"Morgan, what does a coyote sound like, then?" Jack says.

"Let's just get hiking again, you guys."

But that won't do; they'll have their howl. I can sense this is already some wilderness version of *karaoke*. Indeed, my favorite memory of *Sensei* Felicity Rogers from my *aikido* school is of her entertaining a bunch of us during happy hour at the local Benihana restaurant, while she terrorized the staff with a *sake*-induced rendering of that old Wings song, *Live and Let Die*. Paul McCartney would've had conniptions, especially with several of the other *dojo* crew squealing their falsified falsetto backups of the chorus.

Fine. Let these goofy friends have their coyote. I don't know why humans seem to instinctively cup their mouths with their hands while howling, but I jump on that bandwagon as well, and almost try mimicking Dave before remembering what I said about coyotes. My own howl emerges shorter, with clipped notes and, as promised, a notably higher pitch, and not just because my voice is an alto compared to Dave's baritone. It has a "yipping" effect, almost like a dog frantic over getting its tail shut in a car door. But that's closer to what coyotes sound like, even during their good days. Maybe that's how a solitary life plays with a voice.

I decide the subsequent applause of my friends is false and inform them so, though I receive assurances to the contrary. Whatever; I've always hated being in the spotlight like that. I'd rather observe: write for the paper, attend the theatre, sleep in the wilderness, go to concerts and movies, but that focused attention is unwelcome when landing on me.

"Alas, I can offer no encores," I admonish them. "Now let us move, lest we remain forever bonded to the lovely landscape." Gods, what is it about being watched that makes you want to speak more formally? I could almost hurl up the surely colorful remains of gummy bears and a late breakfast.

Crunch, scuff, slide. Crunch, scuff, slide. Eight leather boots with their steel-strengthened heels and bouncy laces reinforce the often subtlely marked trail, paying homage to the trillions of footsteps made around the Earth since our species became upright. Just keeping one's balance as a biped is no mean feat, and this ability came right along with massive cephalization. Witness other creatures which walk, or try to, on two legs: the only ones who can make a decent go of it are birds, and they've turned out to be fliers or exceptional swimmers to compensate for their precarious two-legged talent.

Crunch, scuff, slide. A reduction in ambient noise, I have decided, is fundamentally good for the human condition. Not even the airplanes bother us here. And I'm often intrigued by how long the oral silence lasts in situations such as this, since we all come from a culture in which you're supposed to constantly be saying something, anything. It's like having a staring contest, or some other mild clash of wills. Some would say there is no competition here, though I remain curious as to which of us will destroy the near-silence first. For the half hour following my yelping, there are only the sounds of boots, birds, and the brushing of branches as our legs pass through and by them from the low tundra, higher trees, and even residual but quickly wilting cow parsnip and devil's club plants leftover from summer. Our ears tell us that this is what the world has been reduced to: *crunch, scuff, slide.* Dave pauses briefly, looking vaguely westward, as though his ears might have picked up something else, but then he shakes his head. Nothing, apparently.

Dave opts to wreck the serenity this time; I'd expected it to be Jack instead. "I spy, with my little eye," he says, which is immediately met with Jack's "Yeah!" and my groan. I don't mind that the game is immature. I mind that I'm here for the tranquility, and the "I Spy" game should've been already played in the car, when there were far more objects categorizable by their starting letters. "Something starting with 'a'," he adds.

Asshole? No, too easy. And what's with the attitude, Morgan? These are your closest friends. Maybe I should report "attitude." No, that won't do, either; an attitude is hardly visible, right? "A bush? A cloud?" I offer.

Jack alone accepts that as funny. "Anything goes, eh, Morgan? Let's try a little harder, shall we?"

Mariska is taken aback at first. "I thought it was supposed to start with an 'a,' no, wait, I see it now." I can't help grinning at that.

And leave it to Jack to save the woman further embarrassment. "But there's nothing out here that starts with an 'a,' Dave."

"You'll have to keep thinking, then. The game can hardly proceed unless you guys get past the first letter of our alphabet. And there're three of you to work this out."

"How does anybody ever 'win' this alleged game, anyway?" I wonder aloud, partly to be more of a smartass, and partly because I strangely, actually, suddenly want to know. Who decides such a grand fate as the victor of "I Spy?" And what are the rewards likely to be? Is there some accepted standard, or will a democracy of four manage to resolve this?

Dave looks over his shoulder as best he can, though without losing stride or speed. The top of his pack has a fleece jacket tied to it, so it overlaps part of his titanium pack frame. I've seen him do this with his cold clothes before, though I don't understand it: he always informs me that he overheats quickly while hiking with a full load. Maybe I just don't sweat as much as he does. "Morgan, it's not a matter of scoring points like in a lot of thinking or drinking games. It's more an issue of one party eventually conceding defeat."

"What, you mean if none of us can think of your clue, it's like you get a point anyway, right?" Jack says.

"Well, not unless you anal retentives wish to literally keep a score. It's more like how something such as politics or philosophy works: when you don't have much of a leg to stand on any more, so to speak, you're supposed to more or less graciously admit that your opponent has gained the upper hand with his or her argument, and that settles it."

Yet Jack is having none of this. After a ridiculing snort, he adds, "Are you asking us to believe that politicians and philosophers are expected to behave graciously?" And phrased like that, it proves difficult for Mariska and I to likewise refrain from doing that semi-laugh, the kind always done at someone else's expense, which sounds like you're either trying to clear your throat or hock up a big sticky loogey. And I'm sufficiently amused by the image that for a few seconds I actually ponder how "loogey" is truly supposed to be spelled.

"Look, people," Dave begins, and I at once recognize *that* tone in his voice. "This is really how it works. Back in college, I had politics and philosophy profs who kept emphasizing this, but you'll note I never claimed that this is really how such people really behave. There's not much graciousness in politics, or in academia, either, from what I've come to understand."

"What's with this interest in philosophy then, Dave?" Jack says. "I mean, your degree is in forestry, right? And isn't it 'political science'?"

Mariska can't help but contribute. "Political science is an oxymoron, Jack. There's very little that can be said to be scientific about the art of bullshitting."

Now I'm smiling, my feisty attitude receiving a necessary boost; I love conversations like this, even if we killed the silence. Then again, none of the local creatures seem to mind our voices. Even Dave is trying not to grin, though I'm the only one who really notices. I know that face a touch better than the others.

"Good point, Mariska, certainly. If you all grow sufficiently tired of playing 'I Spy,' then perhaps we can play another verbal game, whereby we take turns thinking of mutually exclusive terms."

"'Oxymoron' sounds better, though, you have to admit. I always imagine a slow-witted musk ox."

"Yeah, thanks for the input, Jack. But at any rate, back to my original point: the rules of logic are pretty fixed. You work your way through the topic or argument at hand, but when you either can't get any further, or you create a fallacy, then you're obligated to concede. Otherwise, you're just whining and holding onto some unjustified dogmatic position, and it's hardly worth talking further with you at that point."

"My, oh my, what smart talk this is," quips Jack, though with much less sarcasm than the phrase could've contained. "Now I'll admit that uttering the word 'fallacy' is even more entertaining than saying 'oxymoron,' but what's this crap about holding out for some unjustified...unjustified what? 'Dogmatic position?' Jesus, that sounds patronizing. Or possibly like a weird reference to robotic canines humping."

But interestingly, Dave seems prepared for this: both a response, as well as a certain comfort level with Jack's juvenile ideas of the humorous. "It's not, though, not at all, but plenty of people seem to think it is. I remember my intro philosophy professor, well, actually, just never mind." He even winces at this, like he's committed some grievous and unpardonable blunder, or, dare I say it, a *fallacy*. Fat chance, in this crowd.

And, like God saying, "You can do anything in this Garden of Paradise you might possibly please, but stay away from *this* tree," the rest of us begin to demand a reckoning from Dave and the words of his long-lost would-be mentor, just as Adam and Eve sought out the sweet crispy fruit; we cannot *not* demand a reckoning.

"All right, but you're not going to like it, okay?" And naturally, that only serves to whet our intellectual appetites yet further.

"Spill it!" Jack barks, who, truth be told, doesn't much care for formal philosophy, gets pissed off in the face of logic which he regards as a tool for the enslavement of weaker minds, like the academic version of the Jedi mind trick from *Star Wars*. But his curiosity remains intact, the perpetual dream-chaser. He might have academic hang-ups, though he's probably the most open-minded of us all.

Dave sighs, makes a falsified motion of adjusting his pack straps while continuing to hike. "He said that a lot of the world's more painful issues could be dismissed out of hand as pseudo-problems if more people realized that no one automatically is entitled to an opinion."

Forget my words about open-mindedness. Jack's immediate response comes from somewhere deep and generally inaccessible: "What kind of shit is that?! Of course people are entitled to their opinions. Do you know what happens when people aren't free to have opinions?"

Dave will not offer a centimeter, however. "Have them, or express them?"

"Both, of course. Don't you remember my stories from my trips to Russia and China? How I had to hold my tongue on so many issues, and just observe, and occasionally beg for permission just to use my camera, and all because the powers that be in those countries don't trust free opinions, either? Dave, for God's sake, it's when I'm abroad that I realize how free our own country is, even with its own bass-ackwards issues, but at least we're free to be having this conversation."

And after the initial wincing, I can sense Dave smiling now, not condescendingly like the academics that Jack's always despised, but more like the teacher who's finally seeing the gears click into place for a troublesome pupil. "Finished yet?" he says.

"I haven't even started yet, especially since I still don't know what the hell you see out here which might start with the letter 'a.' What about freedom of expression, or religious belief, or freedom of employment, or freedom of the printed word?" Jack glances briefly and knowingly at me during this last phrase. "Aren't these all based on people's opinions?"

"Freedom of religious belief and the press and perhaps even job-seeking are forms of expression, so listing these freedoms separately is a bit redundant. But yes, they are based on opinions."

Jack senses he is missing something. "And?!"

"Let me ask you this: do you genuinely believe you have the right to your own opinions?"

Now Jack shakes his head, grunting as his boots scuff their way over some scree. I halfway follow the conversation, still just mildly annoyed at the intrusion of human noise in the medium of speech like we were mere interlopers, and keep my intrigue at how we never slow our pace during this exchange. I would rather focus on the Peters Hills on our right or the gradually descending path in front of us which would eventually take us to the Kahiltna River, but I also hear Jack say, "Well, no shit. Of course I do."

"Great. Now tell me what you gave up in order to have such a right."

Not even a pause: "I didn't give up anything. This is a fundamental right I have simply by having been born."

"But you weren't born just anywhere, as you almost implied; you were born in California, within the United States, just the sort of place where people tend to feel they have certain rights which are all but sacrosanct." Dave is really taking his time, like the smooth and flowing manner of speaking Mariska uses constantly. I feel puzzled by how thoroughly he's put all of this together. But then, I've often found him poring through obscure tomes concerning history, philosophy, science... and then, weirdly, taking notes on the inside covers, like he'd eventually write some huge academic work of his own about them all. I once questioned him about such practices. He simply told me he was intellectually promiscuous, a genuine book whore. Or, as he put it so elegantly on another occasion, "I've yet to find a book I won't take to bed with me." But I wondered then, as now, what he might have been hiding with such a response.

"What does that matter to the debate, though?" Jack says.

Dave continues. "It has everything to do with our debate. You're the one who already mentioned Russia and China. Now to my knowledge, both those nations are presently easier for the likes of us to enter than they were just fifteen or twenty years ago, yes? So even there, it seems there's a growing, if not fully acknowledged recognition that maybe people should have certain freedoms, certain liberties, certain rights."

"Absolutely," Mariska says, who, compliments of her career as an historian, has often spoken at length about the breakup of something which was haphazardly labeled "communism" and what future history books might have to say about such a revolutionary development for the rest of the world. "Fundamental human rights are, albeit more slowly than I would like, reaching more and more people all the time."

"That's true, Mariska, and I agree that it's encouraging news. But my question remains: what did Jack, or I, or you, give up in exchange for any of these rights? Or shall we keep the discussion limited to this one specific right of holding whatever opinions we wish?"

"Either is fine," she replies, with another tone I recognize, especially since it's one I've been guilty of utilizing myself on some occasions: the lowering of one's voice mixed with deliberate intonation to suggest that one is quite confident of one's answers. Mariska likely thinks Dave is lacking a proverbial pot to piss in with this subject, and I wonder as well how he can justify all of this. Maybe he's just having us all on, like with the previous game.

"Ants," I offer, thinking maybe it'll disrupt the group, or give David a way out if he needs one. I actually have noted a few ants here and there on the trail. Alaska's are mostly tiny and black: no red ones to my knowledge, nor the super ant-armies like in Africa or South America that might carry off whole villages if the ants happen to head in that direction.

But Dave needs not my insect reference as a way out: "Thanks, Morgan, but let's see this through if we can. Now, what is so surprising about the notion that you have to give something up in order to have protections like rights, or any other type of liberties? This is what the social contract is all about."

"That sounds familiar," Jack admits.

"Yes," Mariska says. "Rousseau and the French *Philosophes* and all their revolutionary talk in the coffee shops of the eighteenth century: they chatted about how in the wilds, there exists perfect and complete liberty, but no safeguards or protections. They also said that we want to return to this freedom, at least sometimes, which is likely why the four of us are out here right now anyway. The part I find fascinating about that period is that it led right into the American and French Revolutions, as well as being the first known period in history when people starting seeing walking as leisure, or as inherently philosophical, and they started to prize the wilderness like the more ancient cultures did."

I like the sound of that, and of course had to read the likes of Rousseau, Voltaire, and Montaigne for high school history and social studies classes. I remember still my favorite quote from Montaigne: *the only thing I know for certain is that nothing is certain.* I wonder what that would do to Dave's hold on logic.

Jack catches on now, too, and wants to keep this from becoming a history lesson. "So some species, humans usually, elect to give up some of that liberty in order to be safer and exist in organized societies."

Dave nods. "Precisely. Now, how about those pesky opinions?"

And the three of us ponder it, really mull this over. I for one am really awaiting the punchline now. "By the way," Dave says, "it really was 'ants,' so it's someone else's turn now."

Maybe I'm the only one cynical enough to wonder if Dave's offered that answer to mollify us, like he's taken things far enough already, or something. Then again, he really has worked out an argument about this. I have to be careful to use that term appropriately, too; he once informed me, rather diplomatically, that an actual *argument* does not consist of screaming, threatening, throwing objects, or utilizing weapons, and that it is actually a rational, logically-based form of social intercourse. When I questioned Jack on this later, he of course assured me there was only one form of human "intercourse," and it already caused more than its fair share of trouble.

And now Jack still doesn't see a way out. "I really haven't given anything up. Part of what Mariska referred to in the eighteenth-century revolutions was the notion of societies guaranteeing specific rights and freedoms to their citizens. And it feels like it's done now, like we don't have to keep sacrificing."

Jack presently hikes next to Dave, with Mariska and I bringing up the rear. I don't like to think that Jack has unconsciously moved ahead to disguise some instinctive male insecurity, like he needs to be around other males when he's afraid of coming off as a schmuck, and his voice suggests he's really trying to understand this. He doesn't always believe Dave, but their friendship is pretty close, and I know trust binds them. Still, it feels kind of like the guys have to be up front, which somehow represents being in charge, or some ancient symbolic crap like that.

"But you do have to keep 'sacrificing,' as you suggest, Jack," Dave says calmly. "In this case, it might no longer need to be violent, or part of a political uprising, and you surely don't need to shoot at the Redcoats, but now the obligation is to reason itself."

Jack sighs, sounding serious. He does offer a quick laugh when Mariska says, "I spy, with my little eye, something that starts with 'b.'"

"I give up," he concedes. "I just don't understand."

"Jack," Dave says, "we're only entitled to our opinions when we've thought them out, and attempted to arrive at reasons for holding them. Then logic has a chance to have a say, rather than our just relying on emotion, or tradition, or anything else which tends to be irrational. Holding an opinion is thus a privilege, not a right. Does that make more sense?"

"Yes, but I still have to consider it some more, Mister Spock."

"Come on, people: something with a 'b' now."

And for the first time, I feel suddenly pulled to this debate. "So, Dave, this means we actually have to consider these opinions before we just start spewing them about; is that it?" I was almost amused by Jack's *Star Trek* reference, but Dave is far too sensitive and emotional a soul to ever be confused for a Vulcan. Plus his ears are much cuter.

"Yes. Otherwise, like I said before, all we have is a collection of 'unjustified dogmatic positions,' and the whining and self-righteousness that tend to accompany these are often extremely dangerous. That's my concern. That's why I took that teacher's words to heart. I still remember what he said the first day of class."

"I can't wait to hear this."

"He said, 'philosophy is an attempt at a set of beliefs which are coherent and rationally defensible.'"

"Okay," Jack quips. "No more for now."

"That's fine, but I want to pick up on this again tomorrow."

"Why is this so important to you?" I ask him, wondering if maybe Jack was onto something before, and Dave should really have studied philosophy. Maybe he's spent such time in the wilderness by now that he's turning into another Rousseau, or Thoreau, or anyone who's had too many deep thoughts by walking amongst trees and mountains for too long.

"Well, Morgan, you're the writer. Let's just say I'm working on something, too, but I'm not sure if it's academic, or journalistic, or should be just turned into some piece of fiction."

"Cool," Jack says simply, who is always impressed by writing and writers. He once told me there's a storyteller, or at least a bullshit artist, in everyone, but that he lacks the discipline himself to really pursue it (amount of discipline being directly proportionate to amount of bullshit, allegedly). Yeah, I write for the paper, but that's new, and I spend more time dreaming about creating the Great American Novel than the others, although Mariska's a writer, too, albeit by professional necessity. Just not fiction: I wonder if schools realize that not all professors are cut out to be writers, really. For that matter, they're not all made to be teachers, either. But after all, in Mariska's case, she's survived a dissertation, and has had some articles published in magazines, though they tend to be scholarly periodicals read by other historians. Or am I just splitting hairs? Maybe the point is just to have a voice, albeit supported by some semblance of rationality, like Dave's insisting.

So how does one gain that voice? I wonder. And then the notion arrives, like a developing dawn: this is why everyone feels entitled to their goddamned opinions, regardless of whether they have any merit. To miss out on offering one's voice, to not have one's views stated... gods, what a horror that must be. We want so badly for someone to take notice, for someone to listen, for someone to take us, even if just once, seriously. But the old adage yet remains: "opinions are like assholes: everyone's got one, and they all stink." At least Dave's refined such sentiment into something more coherent.

I know it's a terrible cliché, but the thought of each of us craving even temporary idea-acceptance literally stops me, right in my boot tracks. I suddenly feel enveloped by the sunlight to the southwest, smiling gently at the realization that tonight's sunset will be gorgeous, and for a few uninterrupted moments, I *get it*. That fleeting sense that I actually understand something: what Dave was yammering about wasn't some uptight anal logical crap or ego positioning. It was about the need to feel like you might make a difference. Even if this feeling or belief turns out to be totally unfounded, and perhaps it usually is, don't we still have to try? Don't we need to get those views across? Maybe it's selfishness personified, but don't we need to make the attempt? Why write otherwise, or talk, or even live with others of our own kind at all?

And yet Dave insisted we have an obligation to reason, to actually use the extremely complex and little understood grey matter we are each born with for its highest possible purpose: to *think*. But it takes work.

It requires effort, I silently tell myself, standing there, probably for two or three minutes before Mariska and the guys notice I've now fallen behind. They probably think I've paused for one of the innumerable potential distractions which await hikers and backpackers: broken bootlaces, pack straps rubbing too snugly, a requisite water break, a quick taking in of the surrounding vista, sneaking behind a bush to pee.

The sense of emotional and rational security and faith is already starting to dissipate. This must be what the Asian philosophical models speak of, when referring to enlightenment, and the sun's searing imagery drives the point home in a literal sense: to be effused in light, the antidote to ignorance and stupidity. But how does one acquire it as something ongoing? The Asian traditions speak of this, too: Zen practice and meditation, Buddhist ethics that eliminate the self to eliminate suffering, Hindu recognition that divisions are illusory and that there are no subjects and objects. These are difficult to reach, probably even tougher to speak of, so some of us naturally try and achieve this feeling of contentment artificially, without paying the appropriate admission price:

drugs, adrenaline-based activities, stressful jobs. Is this why Dave's a paramedic, for the rush and the constant newness of much of it? This is the first time I've ever considered it, and I wonder if his work is ironically what's led him into such inquiries; people who go to college to avoid boredom and then work in high-stress jobs rarely seem to read philosophy just for the fun of it. And this connection he's tried to describe, of feeling more in touch with the physical environment and landscapes... most of his colleagues in the fire department are into roughing it and doing adventurous things, so maybe he's started to feel out of place at work in other ways.

And what, then, of hiking off-season to avoid the crowds? Is that another cheap effort? And is my background in *aikido*, and Jack's experience with *karate*, more of the same? If we can't find enlightenment because we're products of a neurotically fast-paced society, then is our studying more traditional and esoteric activities a way of compensating?

I already confessed my belief that *aikido* somehow improves me, but was unable to qualify it further, at least not in any way that might sound appealing for a sales brochure. And yet I cannot shake off such a belief, and now find myself standing here and vaguely wondering what has the same effect, if anything, on my friends. Does such practice even matter? And who's benefiting: me, or someone else? And maybe it's just an ego-trip either way, since I've never quite been able to completely forego bragging rights from having achieved at least some expertise in a difficult path; I still clearly remember the feel of the tightly-woven black canvas as the seams ran beneath my fingertips and I first strapped on that belt, sweaty and exhausted but beaming.

I love these three adventurous souls with me, feel like I belong to them and they to me; one of them even admits in mixed company that he's "on a quest for truth," and manages to say it with a straight unsmiling face. Like it's a penance, this idea of the desire for sincere self-improvement. Yet my thoughts and opinions and beliefs and reasons are my own; they reside in places that Mariska, Jack, and Dave can never access, and nor can I ever become so intimately attuned to any one of them. Funny: I seem to recall Charlie saying something painfully similar the day he dumped me. Those inaccessible non-physical things might get described as part of someone's innate charm and attractiveness from one perspective, or used against you from another, since it's just as easy to accuse someone of holding out on you, rather than facing the simultaneously creepy yet liberating notion that in a very real sense, we really are each alone.

"Hey, Sweetie," Mariska says, having come back after vanishing briefly behind a curve in one of the low hills. "We thought we had lost you. The masculine man-children stopped ahead; Dave asked you a question and you were not there to hear it."

If Dave asks a question in the forest and no one is there to hear it, does the question make any sound? If he crosses a stream along this trail, will he be able to ever cross the same stream again? "Hmm," is all I can offer just then. It takes a few more moments to realize that I must have looked utterly vacant, or stoned, just grooving on the upcoming sunset. I can still hear my mother's old warning from childhood: *don't stare at the sun!* But I let the light wash over me still. In three months, our sun will barely emerge during the day in this part of the world, and in June it will return so forcefully that I might actually complain of all the excess light.

"Berries?" I finally ask Mariska, the word encouraging the trace of a smile.

"What? Oh, right. Yes, you are right." She's walked back to stand beside me now. "It was 'b' for berries, but what kind?"

Looking down at the earth for signs of inspiration finally pulls me back to Mariska's reality: I know from experience that this time of year, the blueberries, salmon berries, and crow berries, to name a few, will be growing wildly along the tundra. This female friend of mine likely knows recipes for each type of Alaskan wild berry; there are about a dozen of the little buggers up here, in a delightful mix of colors. I immediately notice some of the tiny black crow berries, and offer that as my answer, trying not to wince from the realization that Mariska's potential berry wisdom is another of those internal items which I've never accessed in her, and that my assuming she has such knowledge might also be another form of my own bias, since I may be estimating that she knows such things simply from being an Alaskan Indian.

"Close enough," Mariska says, and she throws a knowing arm around me. "Come on, you. The boys are waiting. What has got you so distracted, anyhow?"

How to even begin explaining that, I bemusedly wonder, although at least I have some semblance of where my weird mood is coming from, even if I don't understand it. "Nothing. I was just thinking about part of what Dave said earlier." *And for that matter, just what the hell has he written?*

"Saints preserve us, there is another philosopher among us! Maybe this will become 'Zen and the Art of Backpacking.'"

I grin. "Hardly. It's just been a while since I've heard him talk like that. And the tone has changed; did you notice?"

She nods as we start walking again. "Yeah, he sounded serious. I remember when almost everything academic was a joke with him."

"That was so long ago, Iska," I remind her, trying to avoid recollection of the period when Dave expressed his patronizing concern to Mariska in no uncertain terms that pursuing an advanced collegiate degree was "bullshit," "stupid," and "a waste of a good brain," though not necessarily in that order. And now he's given us the sense of having reversed all that.

"I know, and I am a big girl now, so I got over it. But something is up with him. Jack feels it as well. Maybe he is having a premature midlife crisis."

I have to laugh aloud at that. "I like to think I got my own out of the way when I was in high school." Strange isn't this? Mere seconds ago I was staring at the sun and actually hoping for enlightenment, and I've just down-shifted into colloquial mannerisms again, since there are few if any words to describe what I've just been feeling.

"Yes?" She releases my shoulder and we slowly hike onward. It's impossible to offer true hugs or even partial shoulder embraces when one or more of the parties involved is laden with a real backpack.

"Oh, yes. I was all gangly and too tall for the boys and too good with grades for the girls, and caught up in that popularity head-game stuff. It was all very depressing, really. So I decided that was my own crisis, and have been thankful since that it came early." That's something of a downplaying of facts, actually, and one thing I prize about my current batch of friends is their lack of interrogative attitudes regarding the minutiae of my past. Talk about inaccessible regions of one's psyche: suicidal depression from one's teenage years does not seem to go so well with adult relationships, and like I just reminded Mariska, that, too, was long ago.

"Well, at least Dave has not gone out and bought a Porsche, or some moronic stunt like that."

"Iska, why do men do such weird things for their midlife crises, anyway? I mean, all we're likely to do is get some fake tits, or liposuction, or collagen injections." *Christ. Never. I usually avoid wearing makeup on a first date, just to gauge a guy's openness to bodily honesty. Maybe more women would receive that honesty we claim to crave from our men if we were equally honest with them, right from the get-go. And I don't care if my nipples eventually reach my hips; there'll be no "augmentation" for this chick.*

"The guys get fake tits, too, my dear. They just call them 'pecs.' It is more manly, apparently. And you hardly see many women with hair implants, or transplants, or whatever those are. Where does all that hair come from, anyway?"

Both of us are laughing now. "I'm not sure I want to know. From their legs, or their butts?" More laughter follows, plus a dim recollection of Jack informing me that the Zen practitioners prize humor for its ability to move one beyond the rigidity of logic. The ancient practitioners of more unusual magics preferred simple orgasm for the same purpose. "Okay, so we're all horribly insecure and it gets worse with age. But I'm used to my body now; I'm not neurotic about it like we're all supposed to be." *Sensei* Felicity Roger's ripped abdominal muscles briefly flash before my amused mind's theatre.

"You know, so long as we are on the subject, Dave put a philosophical spin on that one as well."

"How so?"

"He said this 'cult of the body' stuff and the obsession with trying to look perfectly sexy for whatever reason is something we inherited from the ancient Greeks, the same folks who gave us Socrates, Plato, and Aristotle. They, of course, were themselves all rather ugly, but still thought to leave us with some hopelessly confusing ideas about who we are and who we are supposed to be."

"Who the hell studies the Classics from a sense of impending emotional crisis?" I wonder aloud, almost hoping that the surrounding tundra will actually proffer a response. For a moment I'm jealous of the tiny crow berries; they just get to sit there and look pretty, without having to think. Bimbo-berries, they should be called. "B" for bimbo-berries, cruising through life on good looks alone, just like the stereotypical magazine models.

"I know. We came here to get away from all of that. Hey, look up there," Mariska points, roughly northwestward. "Do you see them?"

This woman really has good eyes. If I do have a second, more traditional midlife crisis, I'll be sure and get some kick-ass glasses, with an extra pair in the same prescription but with tinted lenses for bright summer sun and glaring winter snow. In the meantime, it takes me a second to spot an exposed rough side of one of the closer mountains. Sure enough, three-quarters of the way up the slope, are a half-dozen or so white specks, which I likely wouldn't have noticed without my friend's senses. "What do you think: mountain goats, or Dall's sheep?" I say, vaguely proud that I have a good idea of which species would be found there.

"Considering how loose the rock looks in that area, I say mountain goats. I still think they are the slightly better climbers of the two. There is no way we could see the horns from here, though." Indeed, the goats have little horns, while Dall's rams have more impressive curled appendages, like Rocky Mountain Bighorns.

I simply nod, pleased to be feeling more grounded in the amazing majesty of our surroundings, as we come into view of Jack and Dave, who are sitting and smiling at us, and we hike on into the approaching night.

* * *

Dog-chaser decided that the wind was different now. It blew from the northeast, out of the high mountains, and had both a new scent and new feel. The wolf typically loved winter, but that was a feeling reserved for the comforts of home, and home was just a dream now, a series of images he wanted to no longer recall. Clearly, there was not much in the way of permanent shelter for wolves, nor for any of the other larger species in the Alaskan wilds, other than a denning site for pups or cubs. So while exposure to cold and snow were typically not problems, the feeling of safety and security was so long gone as to almost be forgotten now.

And then again, simple cold exposure could be enough to do in even wolves and moose and caribou; there were limits, after all, to what even their tight and insulating fur could repel. Theirs wasn't exactly the incredible hair density possessed by sea otters, and the gangly, thin-looking wolves hardly had anything resembling the insulating blubber of other sea mammals. The guard hairs which they did have, with the color that so intrigued humans, acted as windbreakers, while the undercoat of shorter but denser fur was what really dealt with the cold. And even then pack members would snuggle together to share bodily heat if it was truly cold and windy. The wolves understood and were perhaps envious of the abilities of brown and black bears: but wolves and others lacked that ability to monumentally slow down their metabolic and digestive functions for months at a time. Such species needed to keep eating, whether it was the caribou which could sniff lichens through almost a meter of snow, or moose with their talent for finding edible buds of trees covered with ice, or wolves able to detect the smells of musk and spoor from distances difficult to appreciate.

Oak and Paddler had taken turns physically leading the small pack's ceaseless march, with Dog-chaser and Trap-dasher likewise alternating turns at bringing up the rear, the proverbial tail of the dog. Trap-dasher remained the more visibly anxious of the two lower-ranking animals, expending more effort to glance here and there, to and fro, always alert to the prospects of danger. The huge bull moose had scared him, after all, to say nothing of the near close encounter with the hunting dogs. The young male was perhaps the most emotionally troubled by their lack of a home, and had occasionally stalled deliberately, as though to inform the others that he just wanted to head back and have them take their chances, humans and their deafening man-thunder be damned.

Dog-chaser seemed more practical, and at any rate, Paddler and Oak were having none of this resistance to their forced emigration. Paddler herself had dentally chastised Trapdasher for being a potential detriment to pack morale, so the male was at some risk of becoming relegated to the position of *omega*, in which case Dog-chaser would strangely find himself as the pack's sole *beta*.

And that was odd to Dog-chaser, who had been the Fire Creek *omega* for years, so long that he almost took a perhaps perverse sense of pride in his learned ability to roll with some very sizable punches and still land on his feet, like those small furry things he had witnessed at human habitations. They weren't canids, he felt sure, and they made odd vocalizations and tended to hiss or try and make themselves seem larger than they actually were by turning partly to the side. But they had tremendous balance and adaptability, so far as he could determine, and he admired that. He couldn't know, though, that a housecat's pride would never tolerate the job description of an *omega* wolf; some species just couldn't stand to be picked on by anyone else.

The terrain had been flatter for some while lately. And the wolves did take some comfort in the knowledge that the endless ponds and small lakes they'd passed by, swam through, or forded, would offer that much more concealment of their distinctive scents. The men and their smelly shells and their man-thunder and their dark runs, on which the smelly shells ran on things other than legs, were thankfully absent from this region. Indeed, the wolves might have found it wondrous that Alaska had so few roads per capita in what was the world's mightiest nation, both financially and militarily; in fact, the road linking the Great Land to the outside had been constructed for military purposes, and these four members of a once proud pack might have taken comfort in the knowledge that many

Alaskan human settlements could be reached only by small
aircraft or dogsled. Even with tens of thousands of kilometers
of coastline, there were few ports, making waterborne access
questionable.

The familiar loping of wolves on the move seems almost
instantly recognizable to people from around the globe, as
though some distant collective memory of those early hominid-
canid encounters remains in the deep unconscious, in the
manner of Jung meets Freud. These wolves and their several
subspecies in other lands keep a steady pace of approximately
eight kilometers per hour: quick enough to attend to the
obligations of territory maintenance, relaxed enough to not
require hours of panting and water-seeking afterwards, and
people usually recognize this walk as eminently wolf-like. Dogs
move sloppily by comparison, especially the very large and very
small breeds; wolf tracks instead leave the impression that the
animals might have been attempting to negotiate a tightrope
through the wilds. Not the crunch-scuff-slide of the human
hikers, this motion; even when worried and afraid, the wolves
keep that distinctive bounce to their trot, warm foot pads
making light impacts into the tundra and taiga and earth below.

Truth be told, the going had gotten a bit easier, if wetter.
There existed simply too many lakes and ponds throughout
Alaska for them to ever be completely counted, not that the
cartographers and surveyors had not tried. East of Medfra
and northeast of Nikolai lay a relatively flatter tundra basin.
The Fire Creek wolves were past the Kuskokwim Mountains
now, safely beyond the humans and their dogs and noisy
vehicles, following an assortment of streams south of the East
Fork Hills, much less imposing than the Kuskokwim peaks,
though even their summits already exhibited traces of snow.
The tremendous peaks including and surrounding Denali
itself were now almost due east of them, and certainly easy
enough to follow. Dog-chaser remained yet a bit hesitant to

keep heading there, believing, correctly, that the prior humans were no longer a threat, though Oak and Paddler remained just as steadfastly convinced that the mountains would protect them and were accordingly necessary. Somehow. Maybe it was just a foolish dream, though the same huge land features had likewise proven just as emotionally magnetic to the ancient Athabascans, already many centuries past the time when they'd slowly crossed Beringia.

The East Fork Hills did contain some Dall's sheep, and it was two days now since the four wolves had ventured closer to them and consider their hunting options. They had lived on exclusively smaller prey since their departure from home, plus a few berries here and there, most of which were still in the midst of their short seasons. Dog-chaser and Trap-dasher actually savored the tiny fruits, and while wolves were technically omnivorous like dogs, Paddler and Oak hated the alleged need to supplement their meager and hasty recent hunts with the likes of berries; they seemed to think such fare beneath them, and of course, it literally was, as the berries grew close to the ground among the flatter tundra and mountainous taiga.

A Dall's sheep, though: that would prove quite a prize to enterprising wolves, who were finally beginning to feel slightly more at ease. Their home might be gone, perhaps forever, but the wolves dimly understood that migration was part of life for many other animals, so maybe it could be for them as well. They certainly knew nothing of the famous grey and humpback whales heading from Alaska to Baja California or Hawaii, respectively, but the caribou herds indeed migrated, as the wolves did know, and the huge herds could be identified by their scents, as could some of the long-distance traveling birds, like Canada geese.

Still, these sheep knew the terrain. They understood the basic trade-off of their existence: they were master mountaineers of course, but cliff faces tended to offer little by way of fibrous and herbivorous sustenance, which meant inevitable and necessary forays off the protection of rocky areas into more open ones. Naturally, the flatter areas where the best vegetation grew were also terrain easily navigable by most footed as well as hoofed creatures, wolves included.

Dog-chaser's belly still grumbled periodically, and he could only wonder about the dietary frustrations of his packmates, particularly Oak. The four wolves were thankfully no longer fighting the sheer exhaustion from the earlier days of their forced emigration, but that hardly meant they were no longer struggling with stomach pangs. The Dall's had last been seen in the East Fork Hills, and while there might lurk some in the Slow Fork Hills up ahead, the likelihood of being able to catch any was probably remote. Earlier in the year, Dall's rams would catch up on their male bonding in more difficult mountain patches, including a portion of Polychrome Pass within Denali National Park where the human travelers could easily see them, and then they would brave the flatter regions to make it back to the ewes and youngsters born earlier in the year. Risking such a gauntlet, since the flatlands were likelier to contain predators, was the price to be paid for absentee parenting by male Dall's sheep.

But wolves were simply not the best climbers, when all was said and done. Magnificent jumpers, yes: zookeepers around the world knew that wolves could leap over three-meter fences, and were always quick to learn how door and gate mechanisms and latches operated, being able later to manipulate them with their paws or jaws. They could also climb trees in a pinch, though this required much more effort from them than it would from a black bear or any of the world's felines. And as for rock-climbing like the mountain goats and Dall's sheep: even in summer when the mineral surfaces were dry, this was mostly a hopeless effort for canids.

Thus, smaller prey, for lone wolves and the surviving members of the Fire Creek pack. Trap-dasher had actually managed to secure an unwary beaver in one of the ponds they'd passed, providing lunch for the four hungry mouths. And Oak single-handedly had brought down a moose calf who had wandered too far from its mother, its plaintive cries giving away its position even more accurately than its own scent. But to keep that continuous wolf-pace, especially when no den, no rendezvous site, no home at all was nearby, burned away all the calories the wolves could consume. All four of them had lost weight, never being prone to chubbiness in the first place.

The flatter terrain only really looked so from a distance; attempting to traverse it took much work. The most obvious impediment was the forest itself, and both tundra and taiga contained patchworks of forests rather than huge unending ones. The trees themselves did offer some protection from the rains, and even mammals the size of bears and moose often took their shelter from the elements at the bases of trees, beneath the canopy offered by branches and leaves. Even the evergreen species could keep one dry if their branches were thick enough.

But the land between the trees might be rugged, strewn with small rocks and earth or sand, and thus easily navigated. Or, alternatively, it might be spongy, with countless invisible soft patches and deeper holes where a larger creature could never really risk running. Wolves had a slight advantage here just from being lighter in weight, and while such spongiform plant life offered tasty treats for moose and caribou, both had to remain extra wary of predators while in such an area, since running through it at full speed could become an easy way to get stuck and break a leg, offering the predators an easy meal.

It was this softer terrain, lovelier to behold but more slowing of effort, that the Fire Creek wolves now found themselves wandering through. At times the trees were sufficiently thick that they could see little besides one another and the trees, though at other moments more sunlight could penetrate the cover and they could receive glimpses of the mountains that Oak and Paddler kept heading toward. Mountains meant more cover: that was the basic rule. A territory should indeed contain plenty of flatter topography, but elevation meant better shelter as well as sensory reception, both visual and olfactory.

This particular terrain now followed a whole network of streams, heading to the southeast, eventually diverging into the Tonzona River to the north and Pingston Creek to the south, both of which meandered into the mighty Alaska Mountain Range. At the moment, and for most of the past day, the foursome had been getting soaked in mosses and lichens and the other spongy and bouncy vegetation which followed much of the Tonzona. The likes of devil's club and cow parsnip plants, with their thorns, thickness, and tendency to dominate small areas, were more annoying, but such large plants also offered plenty of room in which to hide. And being wet hardly annoyed the wolves; they were used to sleeping fully exposed to the elements, usually with no additional cover like moose often sought from trees. But they remained aware throughout their trek that they had to find someplace safe. The humans had not been seen, heard, or smelled for some time, but the wolves knew they had already trespassed through the territory of another pack, and had kept going.

Now they were back in neutral land, from the perspective of wolfkind at least, so no other wolves should vex them. But attempting to stake out some of the neutral territory to ensure that it did not border or overlap the homes of other packs would take time that Oak and Paddler did not believe they possessed. True, while territories did not typically coincide with each other, individual wolf activities might and often did venture into another packs' region. But there was no staying, lest the interloper be found by the land's rightful residents; the Fire Creek members had fortuitously avoided encounters within the boundaries of the other pack, and they still behaved as though the fates were genuinely working against them. Dog-chaser and Trap-dasher often expressed their curiosity, and were continually rebuffed by Paddler and mostly Oak, who seemed quite insistent on reaching more mountainous terrain for its greater safety, preferably before the setting in of winter.

Other packs in other regions typically did not venture off on such risky migrations, however. Indeed, some distance to the east within the human boundaries of Denali National Park and Preserve, the world's most famous wild wolves, the Toklat River pack, had the frustrating and often tragic tendency to have its numbers decimated, sometimes year after year. And yet this pack always rebounded; lone wolves were known to have joined it, adding to its strength, and some healthy pups were born into it, also year after year. While nowhere near tame, these wolves had acquired their curious reputation by allowing themselves to be photographed more often than any other known pack on Earth. The best chance people had to see wild wolves was in Denali Park, and the likeliest wolves to be seen were the Toklats.

Nonetheless, there were certainly other packs living and trying to thrive within the Park lines, sometimes venturing beyond the no-hunting restrictions of the Park and being hunted or trapped legally. Kantishna, Bearpaw, East Fork, Grant Creek, Chitsia: some fifteen packs had members involuntarily wearing radio tracking collars which enabled biologists and field researchers to plot the movements of member wolves on graphs of the Park. With dozens of individuals within the Park, perhaps overlapping was inevitable. And the Fire Creek members had no idea that so many wolves could sometimes get so close to humans and yet survive the encounters.

In the meantime, the soggy plodding along the course of the Tonzona would continue. The weather remained cool, and the wolves had been rained on twice since their departure;

the overhead sun would help them dry faster, if they could only escape the wetness offered by their current path. And then, in the late afternoon, with Trap-dasher enjoying a rare and brief stint in the lead place, came the unmistakably pungent and musky odor of one of Alaska's most potentially aggressive animals.

The wolverine was as tired as the wolves, sufficiently so that it had yet to detect them, so busily was it engaged in its current task. The size of a mere beaver, this spunky member of the weasel family was dragging off the remains of a kill left by a black bear: a juvenile caribou calf, left right next to the banks of the Tonzona. The bear had had its fill, at least for the time being, and ventured off into some other part of its territory, believing no one would be stupid enough to interfere with its spoils. It hadn't counted on the cunning and tenacious strength of a wolverine.

Paddler was the first to encounter the smell, dark and sharp, often reminding humans of skunks, though none of those lived in Alaska. The scent hit her so hard that her hackles went right up, a behavior which automatically brought the other wolves to a quick halt, and she retook the lead from Trap-dasher. They each looked around, nostrils flaring while mouths remained closed, to gather the strongest input from the scent while giving the least away themselves. They all knew what it was as they found it, and were surprised that a wolverine had allowed itself to get caught upwind. They still could not see it, however. Perhaps it was asleep.

That initial hypothesis was disproved as the wolves drew closer and felt surprise by the simple loud grunting effort made by the wolverine. Its jaw was utterly clamped around the meatier portion of one of the caribou calf's rear legs, which the bear had left intact so far; the bite pressure of that tiny jaw was almost enough to put wolves to shame, and what made an encounter with such a smaller creature dicey was that a wolverine could hold on with extreme tenacity. Humans had often likened it to either a miniature bear trap, or the bite of a rabid terrier. Still, it was far more often a scavenger than a hunter, and its odoriferous emissions served mainly as a warning to other nearby animals to not disturb its food source, which might be cached or even urinated upon. Oak knew from first-hand experience how awful was the scent of wolverine piss; even by canid standards, it was rather rank. Humans would be brought quickly to tears, nausea, or both.

But the feisty wolverine now lay in the path of the wolves: any deviation from their present course would lead them inevitably to more large streams, which they were by now more loathe to cross, even with the benefit of concealing their own scents. Trap-dasher had gone shrieking down a branch of Pingston Creek for almost a hundred meters before finding a place where he could extricate himself, and then he had to be coaxed, cajoled, and outright threatened to cross right back to where the other three wolves were, just so they could locate the larger but more easily followed Tonzona River. To put it mildly, the wolves were tired of water hazards, and tolerated the soft and chilly river terrain as the lesser of problems.

So they watched, and waited. The wolverine still had not noticed them, which made the wolves even more curious. They had no idea about the local black bear, its scent overpowered and superseded by that of the smaller animal. And they marveled at this smaller animal's strength: this creature, the size of a young wolf pup, was dragging a carcass twice as heavy as itself through rough terrain with countless obstacles just so it could keep the already decomposing meal for itself. The wolves had to respect it, even if they had trouble understanding it. They had all prepared food caches themselves; burying food was a useful way to make it last longer and keep it safe, usually, from the thieves of the wilderness, be they bears, coyotes, other wolves. Or wolverines.

Mere meters from Paddler and Oak, who had taken their dominant frontal stance as *alphas*, the wolverine finally noticed its unwitting company, and immediately dropped its prize, jumped upon it, and hissed at the wolves, actually taking a moment to make eye contact with each of them. He did not wish a fight, but his dead treasure was worth defending, as such a lucky find. Besides, the bear might be back soon.

Oak and Paddler returned eye contact with the creature. Trap-dasher lowered his head and looked away, wondering what would happen next. And Dog-chaser alternated between blinking several times, and looking to the pack leaders for guidance. He likewise wanted no fighting today, though the caribou calf could offer all four of them a good meal, and it did not seem to smell as bad as the wolverine did.

Unlike their prior standoff with the bull moose, this one was interrupted by the wolverine dismounting the kill, and once again getting a tenacious toothy grasp of it. It emitted a low growl which sounded more like a purr, and continued trying to stare down the interlopers. The wolves did not move a muscle, content for the moment to watch the carcass get dragged a few more meters from them.

His packmates had the same thoughts that Dog-chaser did: the remains of the calf might be too rewarding a food source to simply pass up, and they did not know when they might again find something the size of caribou to hunt. None of the gigantic migrating herds came through this region, though smaller herds numbering in the few dozens or less could often be found nearby. But it was tricky and time-consuming to pick out a single individual with an exploitable weakness, and then spend the additional effort in bringing it down. More opportunistic than they ever had been in their lives, the Fire Creek wolves began advancing towards the wolverine.

As soon as their quarry noticed that the gap between himself and the wolves had begun to close, it opted to try and scare them off in a more traditional and direct manner. He actually lunged right at Trap-dasher, since like the wolves, the wolverine, too, knew something about targeting the weakest-appearing animal from among a group.

Trap-dasher backed up, watching the wolverine for the mere instants it took to close the distance once and for all, trying to avoid panicking when his rear abutted a tree he had not otherwise noticed. Oak and Dog-chaser at once closed ranks around the wolverine, as Paddler placed herself deliberately between the scavenger and its kill.

Considering how little wild animals truly wished to fight under almost all circumstances, this one began and resolved very quickly, though it naturally felt longer to the participants. The wolverine lashed out with its left paw at Trap-dasher's muzzle, drawing a yelp and blood as its claws found purchase in the wolf's flesh. Oak tried to bite the wolverine right on its posterior, hoping for a quick and clandestine kill, but was completely surprised by the speed with which his adversary wheeled about, offering a similar strike as the one which hit Trap-dasher, although only Oak's ear was hit. It stung; he ignored it.

Dog-chaser tried to bite down himself, noticing an exposed wolverine leg, but his teeth shut together on empty air as the animal sidestepped out of the way. Only Paddler did not join the combat, mostly since she could not see a way to really get into it: a wolverine surrounded by three wolves was a roiling chaotic tumble of aggression, not permitting entry of other creatures into its midst, at least not without the risk of injury.

Then the wolverine managed to pull itself free of the furry entanglement, refusing to run away as the three male wolves regrouped, ready to face it again as a more cohesive unit.

It looked aside to where Paddler stood, next to its stolen prey, and then it ran directly there, expertly and adroitly dodging the trio of snarling jaws as it did so. Paddler could hardly believe what she was seeing and hearing; this ferocious thing was willing to ignore such danger to its flanks and rear in the simple effort of protecting its newfound property, and she was now the only thing in its way. She did not run, not knowing how fast wolverines might be and not wanting to increase the distance between herself and her packmates who were her sole protection.

The wolverine leaped back onto the calf's body, snarling and snapping, Paddler having safely moved aside while the other wolves joined her. The motion helped to impede theirs, and as the combatants stood there with their mouths open and panting, the standoff resumed itself: a lone wolverine refusing to budge, with several of the world's toughest natural predators unable to think of a way of eliminating it.

How does one end a direct physical confrontation with a lack of violence? When body language has tremendous subtlely and nuance, and spoken words, much less reason itself, are unavailable, then what course of action is wisest? In the case of the wolves, they now understood, as did the wolverine, that they had the potential for a real fight on their paws, the sort which might lead to serious, even fatal, wounds. The wolverine was clearly not about to abandon its catch; the wolves wondered if they would be attacked if they just turned and left, since dislodging this annoying creature for its food seemed likely to prove far more trouble than it was really worth. After all, they might be hungry and anxious, though they were hardly starving yet.

Trap-dasher had already had enough. His muzzle still throbbed, though the pain was beginning to dull into more of an ache, and he could still taste blood as he wiped his tongue near his nose. Dog-chaser felt slightly winded but ready to proceed with whatever decision the *alphas* handed down, and he noticed the *beta* wolf begin to slowly ease away from the calf's body. Oak and Paddler observed this motion as well, and Paddler risked a glance towards Trap-dasher, sending him an accusatory glare which would have had him on his back if not for the danger of the nearby wolverine, who was only a few steps away.

Oak barked once at the creature, and received nothing but disdain in return. He and Paddler then growled at the wolverine, allowing their hackles to show, and again the other animal gave the impression of not caring in the slightest. This was beyond the wolves' experience and knowledge; while each had some familiarity with wolverines, none could truly fathom what might motivate a creature to protect its food unto death. Perhaps it was hungrier than even they were; they could almost feel sorry for it.

Trap-dasher had completed a few more back-steps in the interim, hoping his packmates would take the hint. He was afraid of the wolverine, and was not concerned with showing it. Finally, the other wolves did what he considered the only sensible thing: the trio turned away from the wolverine and continued their way into the shadowy wet tendrils of the moss-infested forest. Only Trap-dasher spared a look back at the wolverine, who met his glare just once for a single knowing moment, before sinking his sharp teeth back into the carcass, ready to continue dragging it back to his lair. He had forgotten completely about the black bear.

* * *

Like all wolves, Owl Eyes and Bear Heart trusted their sensory apparatus; hallucination, in the strict sense, seemed to be unknown to them, so they had opted to explore the source of this new sensory information. The annoying part was that they had not yet managed to pinpoint its origin, which left them slightly anxious. They had chastised the pups initially, though the *alphas*, too, went along with the group consensus; it would be most unlike the pack to get something wrong like this, so what harm could there be in answering one of the calls of the wild?

Howling served a variety of functions for canids, though wolves reigned supreme in the art of long-distance throaty vocalizations. And the howls they had heard earlier this evening had caught all members of the Chelatna pack unawares.

There had been several of them, actually. The first howl pricked up twenty-four ears in total, though it sounded more like a dying large animal than another wolf, so they paid it little heed; if it was truly something in its death throes, then it would likely be scavenged by the time they investigated, considering how far away it had sounded. The pups, still so young and rambunctious, wanted to chase after it, but were prevented by Fisher and Cabal, who had been closest to the rendezvous site at the time. Only Foxtrot, his nose still quite tender and scabby, remained uninterested in the noise, seeming to realize that it was not truly the call of another of his kind anyway.

But then, quite shortly afterward, came more howling: gentle, controlled, and alternating between tones which sounded admittedly wolflike, and then something else resembling a coyote. This was the sound which really got the attention of each packmember. Humans often tried howling in the wilderness, sometimes to try and frighten each other, sometimes to sincerely if feebly and ignorantly attempt to commune with some natural aspect only remembered in the evolutionarily older parts of their brains. Strangely, wolves were never known to respond to recordings of howls, even those made by other wolves, as though they could easily disseminate the falsehood offered by technology; even really good expensive recording equipment failed to fool them. But a genuine howl often brought return howls, even if it was amateurish. Sometimes coyotes would get in on the action, too.

The Chelatna pups: tender and agile Foxtrot, demure and proud Sterling, and goofy and spastic Puddles, all began panting and looking about excitedly as the howl came from almost due east of the rendezvous site. Most of the other adults were still nearby, the pack having killed a young and inexperienced bull moose in the afternoon, so that most of the adults were meat-drunk and feeling lazy; "food coma" this was sometimes colloquially and colorfully called by humans who'd themselves consumed too much in a sitting. Digestion of that much intake was quite energy-intensive, which left little over for doing much other than contemplate the universe and possibly fall asleep. Only Rendezvous, the *omega*, and Swifter, both females, were still out exploring, not having eaten as much and feeling less lethargic than their companions, though they heard the howling as well, and had granted a quick return call to announce their presence to their own pack mates. That was one use of howling: pack members could locate each other at impressive distances this way.

True wolf howls also carried like the roars of lions: for many kilometers, and they could be detected by any creature with sufficiently adept hearing. These howls left the impression that the other wolf pack had to be somewhere near Talkeetna, though the Chelatna members had of course never ventured near the town, indeed had never explored east of the Kahiltna River, which was beyond their territory. So it seemed harmless to offer a return howl; Owl Eyes and Bear Heart led the way, and the wolves offered their own blended if brief song-fest. First came the *alphas* with their lower, bass-like cries, sounding mournful. The *betas* added their own notes next, and brought a crescendo in volume along with an increase of almost a full octave in tone. Finally, the pups contributed as best they could, though their younger voices indeed seemed to mimic the sounds of adult coyotes with higher and sharper yips and yaps. Wolves harmonized, adding coherence; alternatively, a smaller pack could make themselves sound like more, perhaps as a falsified show of force to indicate control of territory. That was the second use of howling: it served as a long-distance version of property establishment and maintenance, warning other creatures which animals dominated in that area.

The Fire Creek wolves, meanwhile, had only howled twice since leaving their home territory, and both of those occasions fulfilled a third purpose of howling. It could be used to signal mourning. Packs, being extended families, bewailed the loss of a member, be it from death or disappearance, the latter case typically resulting from an individual who had ventured off to make its own fortunes as a lone wolf. The Fire Creek members had acted on these occasions like four lone wolves who just happened to be traveling together, such was their sorrow at the loss of their packmates. The notes tended to sound different, too: the plaintive ululation of the Fire Creek wolves contrasted with the multisonous elements comprising an overall group melody of the Chelatna wolves.

And yet a fourth purpose behind howling was still hotly debated among scientists and researchers; wolves often seemed to howl for no discernible practical reason at all, at least none that humans could determine with great accuracy. Accordingly, it was hypothesized by many that they might partake of this activity simply because it was, well, fun. Indeed, wolves and other canids were avid players, and countless wild items might become toys, from bones to sticks to rocks to insects and other small animals. Many bird species used toys, as did felines, primates, and several other larger mammals, both land and sea.

But to engage in something of a communicative nature, like howling, just because it might be entertaining in and of itself? It seemed too much of a stretch for some people to grasp, but that was precisely the major reason why the Chelatna wolves attempted to answer what they heard this night. They were actually slightly disappointed that the song competition did not continue; they received no answering howls, even though their group musical effort had lasted slightly over a minute. That was a fairly long symphonic episode for a wolf pack. And again, the initial howls to which they'd responded indeed sounded sufficiently far away to not be interpreted as threats to Chelatna lands.

And wolves never howled at the moon. Too many writers of fantasy and horror fiction had somehow managed to perpetuate this false notion, likely based on ancient and medieval bestiaries, the latter of which tended to be full of gross and sometimes amusingly false anecdotes about the behaviors of various other species. Wolves howled when they felt like howling, and since the species could be equally active day or night, sometimes the moon just happened to be visible at the time. Wolves might be easier for people to see with a bright full moon overhead, and since that may have been the general time of the most frequent human observations of wolves, perhaps that was how this strange but wrong stereotype developed largely unchecked.

The only snag with this lupine long-distance conversation was that David Thomas, who'd granted the initial howl in the first place, at least the first one of any quality, never heard more than the first two or three notes of it; he and his own companions had been upwind at the time, so that while his howl was easily picked up by the Chelatna wolves, he had no chance to hear their return cacophony. At one point he did think he heard something, but had brushed it aside, not recognizing or appreciating it for what it was. Morgan Greene and Jack Godwin had also heard a brief initial response, as did Mariska Kline. David especially would have been sorely disappointed had he known how close the four hikers were to an excited wolf pack when they established their camp that night.

Since the eastward howling seemed to present no challenge to Chelatna security, the adults returned to their lazy leisure, save for Fisher and Cabal, possibly the pack's most energetic members, who had now taken it upon themselves to engage in some simple play with the pups. Both *beta* males, they endured gregarious nips on their noses and muzzles, as well as tugging and gentle chewing on their tails, as the three perpetually rambunctious pups ran about. Tug-of-war, chasing one's own or another's tail, wrestling and rolling about, and variations of chase which often became as complex as tag, were all preferred activities of the young. Bear Heart and Owl Eyes lay down nearby, heads up and attentive, sphinx-like, full of pride in their latest litter of small trouble-makers. It almost made them both feel old to watch such flagrant and unending displays of unabashed energy; where did the pups get it all?

Still, Cabal and Fisher took it all in stride, and while they occasionally had to make a correcting yip or even full growl to prevent an activity from being injurious to anyone, they delighted in acting like pups themselves. *Betas* and pups hardly had to concern themselves with dignity; these were wolves whose tails remained in a neutral middle position, not the bolt upright posturing evident in the tails of Owl Eyes and Bear Heart. And revealing one's underside to another, aside from being a clear indicator of submission, was also a side effect of canid grappling and tackling.

Puddles insisted on wrestling with Sterling, each taking turns assuming a dominant position. They each had to work to get the best advantage over the other, and the fact that Puddles was male and Sterling female had little effect on the outcomes of these brief matches. Sterling more often tended to stand aside, not from lack of energy but more from a sense of general quietude; had she been born human she would have been described as bookish and contemplative rather than outdoorsy. And Foxtrot kept up as best he could; he was just glad his nose no longer bled whenever he tried to play with the others, as the quill injuries were already healing quickly and smoothly.

Young Sterling seemed to think that her eventual status as another *alpha* was a foregone conclusion, and she tended to act like it. She fought back more aggressively when Puddles tackled her from behind, and she had to decide which was more important: trying to establish dominance and possibly ending up angry, or simply enjoying herself like her brothers. She wanted it both ways, naturally, and wolves usually did begin to struggle for ranking positions this early in their lives. And finally, Foxtrot now set about dancing figure-eights around the two older males, sometimes sneaking a nibble on one of their legs. He possessed more lithe grace of any member of the pack, the balance of a lynx or any other cat, and was as a result the most difficult member to take down in these ongoing wrestling matches.

As often happened, the individual activities morphed into a more chaotic general mêlée, with Cabal and Fisher trying vainly to keep some sense of order, but likely knowing it was futile. While no more howling took place among the pack that night, there was nonetheless plenty of noise emanating from grunting and panting and sometimes barking. Only Bear Heart and Owl Eyes ever looked back towards the east, towards the human settlements, wondering how far away the howls they'd heard truly were, though they remained satisfied in their sense of peace.

The *alphas* mutually decided to close ranks, at least to some extent. They were tired themselves, and it was easier to give orders than to confess to fatigue or show weakness. The wind still gently blowing southwesterly, they emitted a different howl: more of a monotone, constant and deeply sonorous. The pups and *betas* stopped their roughhousing at once, and came trotting over. The others, Rendezvous and the remainder of the *betas*: Fisher, Tracer, Wave, Swifter, Cabal, and Tornado, all returned from their spaced out locations. Several of them had already been running for several minutes, having heard the earlier howls, since they preferred to not miss group events like that. And the soothing yet warning sound of Bear Heart and Owl Eyes was not do be disobeyed; all came charging homeward at such an announcement.

They all stood there proudly, the pups in the midst of a circle of long legs and fur, and the greetings resumed in their ancient but delightfully predictable manner: tongues lashed out, full of recognition and mutual feeling, muzzles getting dampened all over again. It was accompanied by the most delicate whining, not from sadness but simple appreciation of being part of a united family, whose members lived and loved and fought and still managed to go on together as a largely cohesive whole. The snorting from such excessive "snuzzling" grew louder, as the collection of wet cool noses explored once again the others of their kind. Nuzzling was different, and indicated simple closeness, while snuzzling was bodily exploration of another using one's nose, very canid-like.

There was no additional group howl that night, no need for one other than from joy, for the Chelatna pack remained healthy and whole.

* * *

I've already proffered a warning about not entirely understanding the relationship between my friends Mariska and Jack, and tonight would seem so far to be adding proverbial fuel to the fire. That seems a good analogy, too: if fire is a suitable description of the passion linking two people, then the chemical reactions these two friends of mine share with one another seem to vary in strength from simple accidental spark to massive conflagration, enough to endanger the surrounding woods. Granted, we're in neither Denali State nor National Park, but a nasty fire could easily take hold here, especially with how dry it's been lately. And yes, I occasionally consider analogies along with other thoughts when I'm trying to avoid analyzing the behavior of others, particularly people about whom I genuinely care.

We've now reached a point a couple of hours beyond the moment when Mariska and I spotted those tiny white animals up a steep slope (which I'm still confident were Dall's sheep, even if Iska thinks they're mountain goats), and have located an ideal camp site large enough for several tents, right at the base of the Peters Hills. I'd initially thought the hills might be pleasant to climb for camping and the panoramic vistas likely from atop, but they are, after all, where we'd seen the sheep, and since the damned hills are quite steep, no thank you. Still, now that we've survived our first night together as a group (in three tents, Jack and Iska sharing), we've had a pleasant and relaxing walk through the nearby topography, so far a more relaxing day than yesterday while seeking a good site. Every Sunday afternoon should feel like this.

The site was found by yours truly, I'm proud to say, and lay sufficiently off the trail to not cause difficulties. There are various game trails branching off of here, so we have to avoid them. True, they might be typically run on by nothing more than hares and hoary marmots, but they could just as easily be traversed by larger things, and this is the time of year when black and brown bears are trying to eat as much as possible before taking their super naps. Still, there's a pleasant and relatively quiet creek running nearby, so we've a good water source: Spruce Creek, if I've read the map properly, a skill at which I think I'm improving. Negotiating around a topographic map takes some getting used to, even though it looks self-explanatory at first glance. I once read that you should try imagining the map as sort of a wedding cake, in that it has layers. Each contour line, usually a hundred feet on most American maps (though two hundred on my beloved Gazetteer, which is back in the car) is another layer of the grand cake. So you can try and visualize the cake growing higher and simultaneously narrower. The colors are supposed to help, too: brown for the contours, which suggest mountainous regions anyway, an obvious blue for water regardless of its altitude, and green and white for whatever's left. I guess the thing that frustrates me is two-fold: the green I want to indicate forest, which it may or may not, and the white I want to be relatively clear, which it often is not. And the allegedly simple act of imagining the hills and peaks rising skyward form the Earth is trickier than it might sound; I'm frequently wrong in my assessment of just how a scene on a map should actually look when I'm next to it. And I certainly never see a damned wedding cake, not even an irregularly shaped one.

But I digress; like I said at the outset, this story is really about my friends, especially Dave. So far there's been no fighting, we made it into the "j's" with our demented game of "I Spy" (Mariska gave us Steller's Jays for that one, and we did see a couple of them, though we were of course subjected to another quick history lesson about the German Georg Steller, the naturalist who accompanied the Dane Vitus Bering when he "discovered" Alaska for the Russians in the mid-eighteenth century). So now we've made camp, spent a night, and I'm still pleased with how I managed to convince the others to wallow an entire day away right here. It's just so exquisite a site. We've supplies for several nights, anyway, even if the gummy bears are long gone now.

"Colder than I'd thought," Dave says, who's just returned from a water-gathering trip to the creek. He holds a medium-sized saucepan with a form-fitting lid over it securely, so as not to lose any. It's an entertaining balancing act, fetching water in a kitchen vessel in the wilds. The crystalline liquid appears cool and inviting, though we still want to treat it for cooking. I've already run several bottles' worth through my instantly-cleaning squeeze bottle with its charcoal filter, savoring the lack of carbon taste as much as the delicious water itself. Things do taste differently in the wilderness, I still believe.

"Do you mean the weather or the water?" I say. He stops and thinks; he's my only friend who often literally stops to think, as though he cannot be engaged in other physical activity while cogitating. "Both," he decides, looking back towards the creek.

"Have a seat," I invite him, remembering that Jack and Mariska are still further up the less defined winter trail, which will likely soon see service by the full-time residents of Talkeetna and Peters Creek. Our friends are probably walking hand in hand, pausing at every lovely scenic spot to make out for a couple of minutes like horny teenagers dreading the ill-timed arrival of their parents while slobbering on said parent's couch. And yes, part of my attitude yet remains: I mean, I'm happy for those two, whatever they really have going on together, and I admit I'm still hurting from Charlie's departure from my life even if it's been many months now, and there's part of me that's always wondered about the possibility of Dave and I. It's not a genuine longing, really; sometimes I just wonder if he's ever seen me as a woman as well as a friend.

How is it that these interconnections between and among people develop at all? How do we become part of one another's lives, so wrapped up and intertwined, only to disappear from one another eventually, whether by choice, apparent fate, death? I don't understand this whatsoever. I consider the events which had to occur for me to even meet Dave, or Charlie, or for my parents to meet and then create me. Someone had to be in a certain place at a particular instant, or else things would have gotten missed. It's reassuring that it happens and also terrifying to realize how close you come to missing out on the things and people which become important to you. I know it's often called a divine plan, but that really feels like a copout to me; that doesn't mean I'm insulting the deities or denying their (or His or Her) existence, but it is not really an answer at all. That was an integral part of the first conversation Dave and I ever had: the inability of most people to simply live with mystery, without trying to force another, artificial mystery overtop the already existing one.

I mean, consider Jack and Iska, for example. Maybe I am jealous; not that I imagine some romantic development with Jack, but perhaps it's the simple envy of other people's happiness, when I should be celebrating it. But Mariska's this half-Athabascan, half-German who did her doctoral work in California, compliments of a reciprocal university program which enables Alaska residents to attend schools in several western states at in-state tuition rates. And then while she's doing her student teaching, this goofy younger man signs up for one of her courses, not looking for a date but for a formal aspect to his already worldly education. And then the "chemistry" or whatever seems right, and they become quite intimate as a result, him teaching her of faraway lands he's traveled to, and her teaching him more about the historical details of those lands so they can each appreciate more of each other's pasts. That's the easy nutshell explanation.

But to consider much more beyond, it all gets muddled and befuddled very quickly. What if those university programs didn't exist? What if either Jack or Mariska had attended other schools? What if they'd had their first conversation when one or both had been in a crappy mood for some reason, and then rubbed the other the wrong way? What if one of them hadn't been born, or had died earlier in any one of a million possible ways, what if, what if?

So we want answers. We offer thanks to fate, chance, anthropomorphic deities, animal spirits, a good outcome on a Ouija board, a clever result from a fortune cookie, a useful alignment of the cosmos and its individual stars and planets, a beneficial Tarot card reading... And all this because we decide the proverbial line must be drawn somewhere: there must be some causal explanation that we can rely on, because we demand answers, like when we refused to let Dave off the hook until he answered our questions, even though his answers just prompted more questions. We don't humbly solicit truth; we attempt to grab it by the balls, no matter if it's genuine or useful or simple reassuring bullshit.

And then I tried and have this talk with Dave like I mentioned a moment ago, who proceeded to inform me that the Enlightenment philosopher David Hume once logically shattered causality, and concluded that we have no actual grounds for believing it even exists. Besides, there's a basic principle which insists that for anything to have existence, we must be able to "point" to it somewhere, and thereby acknowledge that it has dimensions, is made of stuff, and responds to the forces of the universe. But without causality, there is no science, no philosophy, no art, no religion. Science must be able to say, "Mix together these amounts of those elemental ingredients, and this will be the approximate result." Philosophy must be able to say, "Take these premises, and then notice how they flowingly if narrowly lead to this conclusion." Religion can do nothing if it cannot claim that, "The gods or spirits created everything, so offer them your gratitude and obedience." And even art goes nowhere if it cannot be stated, "Here is the artist's creation, made by him or her and expressing this view or belief or feeling." I wonder what Hume was like in person: rather well respected in large parts of Europe during his lifetime, which ended just prior to the American and French Revolutions. And while he loved philosophy and science, he had more trouble with art and religion. Maybe he wanted to believe in causality, even if it logically cannot be verified, or at a minimum, remains forever unknown while subject nonetheless to our demands for knowledge.

So I wonder now if the gods grow weary of our superimposed answers. God strolled through Eden and saw it could never succeed, I once read. Parke Godwin's novel about Queen Guenevere after the death of King Arthur, I think it was. And she was frustrated because we choose the apple every time: knowledge, or at least the attempt to find such, over bliss. But that attempt is hazardous, and knowledge is not always sought for its own sake, but for the power it represents. The old adage is true, but for the wrong reasons, I think. Undermining causal explanations is just one example, though apparently one of the more influential and potentially dangerous: people don't want you stirring up their knowledge, or at least what they consider to be knowledge. But everything we know came from a new idea, and with new ideas, someone has had to be first. Some of those first-timers paid for presenting that new knowledge with their lives: Socrates, who showed that simple dialectical discussions, in which the participants went back and forth over the same idea until something which really seemed to be truth emerged; Jesus, who wanted people to believe in themselves and behave less selfishly than was their wont; Hypatia, who argued that no formal dogmatic religion could ever have the last word, and received as her reward a mob who flayed her with oyster shells; Boethius, who translated the ancient Greek thinkers for posterity's sake, only to be bludgeoned to death for wishing to reunify Christianity, which had already split into competing belief structures.

And now I explain to whomever asks that my two friends met at UC Berkeley, and that they have this on-again, off-again relationship which both seem to crave and perhaps need but which seems to lack a fuller explanation, whether emotional or philosophical. That is where I have chosen to draw the line, so to speak, with almost anyone who asks about them. It's too difficult to face the expressions I meet when I want to know more about the details of how they met. And I mean the logical, metaphysical details, not the tawdry minutiae which would better serve the writer of a soap opera.

So why would I want to understand such details? Maybe I'm not even entitled to gain such wisdom. Dave has told me that another thinker, Friederich Nietzsche, believed everything which happens will happen again, just as it has before. I don't know whether to find that comforting or scary, since a second chance often sounds enticing, but if you get the same results as before, then why bother? Dave also let me know how Gottfried Leibniz explained that what we reside in is logically the best world that could have ever been created, and I arrived at the same ambiguous concluding feeling, even if my religious sentiment is, shall we say, untraditional: God could never have made it any better, and it's to therefore be expected that he made it to the best of his abilities. And then the modern physicists tell us that all possible combinations of actions really do occur, just in alternating universes of possibilities. Such is the quandary of quantum dynamics, in which everything really does seem to become possible, even though those same scientists also tell us that none of us, including themselves, can really understand it all. It's as difficult for me to conceive of every possible decision I could have made to correspond to a genuine existence "out there" somewhere as to conceive that there is a singular divine intelligence also "out there" helping to make many of the decisions for us. Maybe I should be reassured: if the philosophers and scientists are both right, then at some indiscernible point I'll be sitting right at this camp site contemplating this all over again, but will I have a memory of having done it before? And will I be relieved by such awareness, or will I just face the thought processes again?

And this means, of course, that Jack and Mariska will meet again, for the first time, whether or not they experience any sense of *déjà vu*. But it also means that there are literally other realities in which they never meet, or they despise each other, or they have an altogether different relationship like parent-child or some such, or one of them does die before meeting the other, and on, and on. Who could ever get a grip on all of this? This really becomes something infinite, the only link to infinity I've ever even begun to consider accepting. If the physicist Hugh Everett was correct with his "multiverse" conclusion about the endless number of actual existences resulting from our decisions, then we'd never have to worry about doing the wrong thing, since we've done the right thing somewhere and at some time. And all your possibilities become realized: all your dreams come true, and all your chances to fail and make poor decisions are likewise manifested. So maybe that offers some reassurance, but I say no; the earlier question yet remains. What becomes of morality, of art, of science, if causality either does not exist or if it becomes pointless since all possibilities eventually will manifest?

Plato said that all learning in this life is actually remembering what you knew in previous lives, which is part of why I mentioned the prospect of eventually returning to this exact campsite, with these exact people, under precisely the same circumstances. Then how does one learn in a prior life, I wonder? Oh, well; I said that the philosophizing could wait, but that was then. We're here now, in the sort of place the great intellectuals of history came to for the purpose of working out their thoughts. Socrates and Jean-Jacques Rousseau and Laozi and Immanuel Kant were marvelous walkers, and had plenty of spacetime alone with themselves for reflection and consideration. The great religious leaders were all walkers, too: Moses, Siddhartha, Jesus, Muhammad, Gandhi. And I grin now, marveling at one of the simpler truths of my own life: I cannot leave well enough alone while in the wilderness. There is never a shutting off of my brain while backpacking. Since I am used to thinking often and regularly, which Dave has told me is why he feels so drawn to me in the first place, I remain unable to simply "switch off," as it were, when I'm beyond the physical trappings of human civilization.

"Dare I ask what's on your mind?" the familiar voice asks, robbing me of my revelry.

It seems Dave has caught me grinning. Can he possibly have remained standing there with that pan full of water watching my revelry for what was likely several minutes, apparently playing catch with a small object? It looks like a stone or perhaps a marble; I really don't know. I'm so often found wholly unaware of the smiles I make, for no externally discernible reason, which often gets the attention of whomever might be noticing me. It actually makes some folks nervous, like I'm plotting something. Apparently one is not supposed to just smile, especially when one is alone with one's own thoughts. "I'm just happy," I say. *And so lost in my own universe I've literally not noticed you next to me these few minutes. And I should have said, "What makes you think that this metaphysical 'I' even exists, much less that she/it has a mind?"*

Dave isn't fooled for a second, his own smile emerging now. I've mentioned that look before: full of pearly whites and wholly natural. It is impossible for this man to force a smile; either he feels like offering one or he doesn't, which strikes me as refreshingly honest. "Is this a general happiness, or something specific?"

"Both, if I'm lucky. But tell me something: why is it that I feel so comfortable discussing things with you that make most other people back away from me several steps, sometimes literally?"

And this man who would rather discuss logic with a stranger than the weather with a friend gives such an easy answer; it's small talk he has trouble with, unless he's speaking to the non-human, like Angus and Cozy. "Because we're friends. There's nothing friends can't discuss, otherwise it's not really friendship but some other relationship."

And that's the magic, the mystery of our own relationship; from any other guy, I'd wonder if those same statements were just a greeting card response subtly masking a desperate urge to fuck me. And that makes me angry all over again; Charlie only ever wanted to discuss anything "deep" when he was horny or drunk or both. "Thanks," is all I can think to offer right now.

"I'm always glad to hear of your general happiness, which hardly needs either qualification or quantification, but simply is. Though I admit the specifics sound intriguing. Is it just being out in the wilds again?"

"That's a great word, you know: 'wilds.' Maybe that's why I can really let my mind wander, when I'm removed from civilizing influences."

"Don't tell me you've again resorted to thinking 'you' have a 'mind.'" Dave grins again, ever the cat licking cream from his whiskers.

"Would you put that water down already, *monsieur philosophe*, and let me just take one thing for granted? Like the possibility that 'I' exist as a genuine entity, and that this funky metaphysical personal pronoun might consist of something non-physical."

He almost looks hurt as I say it. "But you hate the dualists, like Descartes. He was really just a medieval theologian born too late. He wanted to have it both ways: give us bodies and give us minds to occupy them, and that way religious faith need not disappear in the wake of science, which certainly remains unable to locate 'minds' anyway. Science can't even yield a consensus on what constitutes 'consciousness.'"

Leave it to my friend to take a simple statement and subject it to logical dissection. I once saw him spend several minutes having a silent self-debate over whether he was justified in using the word "and." The philosophical paramedic, we sometimes call him. The "Double P." Perhaps that's why he's frustrated with his chosen profession. He needs something to do which intellectually challenges him, and he thought emergency health care would be just the ideal venue. And while he does have to think in very detailed and attentive fashion while doing such critically-timed work, Dave has found it quite problematic that at the end of the day, his co-workers discuss what he considers mundane, perhaps because they've wearied themselves on complex thought processes for that day or shift. It's not bad, Dave admits, far from it, but just a bit trivial for him. It's how his colleagues unwind: talking about families and schools and hobbies and travel plans, so it's a good mechanism for coping with job stress, but Dave is simply more academic, and can find no reason to stop thinking critically when he's off the job. He's not necessarily more intelligent, since he works also with nurses and physicians, people with loads of formal education; he just should probably be in the mind-expanding arena of a university.

The only problem is that he hates schools, believing they stifle thought and creativity, as with his attempts to talk me out of earning my master's, which I think I already mentioned. He's often right in that regard, but to get a job as a professional thinker means playing the political games universities force on people, at least for a while. He has no stomach for that. He can barely handle the politicking which happens in Anchorage hospitals and the fire service, over job security, union issues, pay and benefits, promotions, public safety issues, continual retraining.

How did Dave phrase it once? "Why do people try to stop learning once they finish school? I never finish school, in a sense, since I keep trying to learn." That fact about him so distrusting schools must be killing him.

"You're right, though, you know," he says suddenly, likely noticing that I've managed to wander off again.

"About what?"

"Whatever 'we' might be, whether it's bodies or minds or a collection of funky illusions, 'we' always have to take something for granted, regardless of what we believe or where we live or what language we speak. John Mill noticed that, though he's much more remembered for talking about happiness."

"So does that mean you're still expecting a response to your happiness question?"

"Of course."

And then my own mundane answer for him, though it seems impregnated with meaning, since it feels sincere. "I feel general happiness for simply remaining part of the universe, and more specific happiness for being out here with you three, thank you." He leans over me, kissing the top of my head, and then decides to assemble the camp stove to heat the water. His question, while potentially annoying, also lets me know he's interested in what I'm really thinking, something which seemed distressingly absent from Charlie's ministrations. Charlie, I now realize, is quite a superficial man. Brilliant, yes: he works as a high school principal in the Anchorage School District, but he unfortunately sees the job as something mostly mechanical, rather than as the creative and experimental source of inspiration that all levels of education are supposed to be (and no, I've never uttered that last line to Dave). Handsome, well-to-do family background, pleasant and easy to laugh; I think I was attracted to Charlie mainly as a stabilizing force, a counterweight to all these lofty thoughts and ideas my friends and I have.

Which means that I, like virtually every other person on this planet, is at least occasionally afraid of thinking. Reaching conclusions is a pain in the ass. Why do we only ever want to do it in the wake of our suffering? It's like I wanted to turn that all off, and so I found a very "normal" guy, dated him for two years, and then awoke one morning to a man who found me unrecognizable, an alien being who too often had her head in the clouds dreaming of what might be. Charlie started becoming more distant when I began talking with him more in the manner I'd talk around this campsite, right now. Most couples who fail pin their frustrations on incompatibility or money or some other vague sort of catch-all, or the big one: lack of communication. So how could a man break up with me for wanting to communicate at the most in-depth level I could think of?

"General is the best kind of happiness," Dave says, completing the priming of the stove, adjusting its heat, and then placing the pan atop the blue flame almost reverently.

"There are Buddhist monks who indicate you can find all the happiness you'll ever need in the deceptively simple act of fetching water." He seems to feel obligated to behave for a few moments like one of those monks, briefly contemplating the monumental significance of having fetched our water. That's what people seem to miss: so much of what the great thinkers said is so deceptively simple, like my *sensei* back home would say. There's not a whole lot to lighting a stove and preparing to boil water for cooking, and Dave has nonetheless transformed it into ritual.

"The other deceptively simple act is chopping wood, right?" *The girl has done her homework.*

"Yes," he says, "though the Taoist in me shudders at the destruction of trees."

How many of our conversations have begun like this? "What if the tree is already dead? Plenty around here are. That wood could be rightly said to be going to waste, and Taoists hate waste." Knowing this man and working for a newspaper do wonders for my knowledge of multi-cultural trivia, though I don't mention that: newspapers of course need gobs of paper, even if my new employer is better than many about recycling.

"But what, then, is waste? There's always a utility for something; all must have some purpose, else why would it exist? And why would change even be possible without waste?"

I exaggeratedly throw my arms up in the air, shaking my hands. "Okay, I admit defeat." And I laugh while I say so.

And once again Dave throws me mentally off-balance. "Never, Morgan. Never concede defeat. That's bad karma. And it's not about winning or losing, anyway."

"Why do you do all this, then?" I say, hoping to throw him off instead.

It doesn't work; he's ready. There's a philosopher inside my friend screeching to be let out. "For the same reason we're all supposed to do it." He's still uncomfortable with such an admission, though. He looks down again, frowning now at the saucepan which less than a minute ago was supposedly offering clarity.

"What, ask philosophical questions and hope for the best?"

"No," he says. "But we have these amazing brains, and most of us rarely if ever use them."

"Was it ten percent?" I ask him gently.

"What? Ten percent of what?" He's almost smiling again, but it's the half-assed lip-only pseudo-smile which means he's trying to piece something through and not yet getting it.

"What Albert Einstein said about the amount of our brains we actually use. I think that was roughly his estimate."

"Yeah," he says. "That sounds about so. Although he of course had no experience, to my knowledge, of doing any sort of work in neurology or psychology."

Thrown again; how does he catch me off-guard like that? And I don't mean Einstein. "So what?" I say, trying not to sound peevish.

"Well, that's part of the problem with people thinking right there. Old Al was obviously a genius, and I'm not denying his contributions to science, but the fact that he's clearly an authority in one field, like astrophysics, hardly means that he's automatically an expert in another field, like nervous system anatomy. I love the quote about his assessment of our under-utilizing our mental faculties, but there's no reason to believe, based on his credentials, that ten percent is near accurate. I mean, where did he get the number? Was it based on someone else's research, and the source has been lost? Was it just a number he pulled out of his butt one day while feeling feisty from having argued with Niels Bohr? Why ten? Why not two percent, or sixty?"

I love watching this man get all fired up like that. This is what makes for a good teacher; I'd once told Charlie he should find a classroom in the School District for Dave Thomas to haunt, because talking like this was a wonderful way to get the attention of young minds, particularly those in their teens, who are already open to highly interpretative thoughts, compliments of their efforts to survive the before- and after-effects of parents, puberty, peer pressure, parties, and proms. Charlie had just laughed, not seeing any relevance in inviting a jaded paramedic into one of "his" classrooms.

Fired up or no, this is another of those times when I remain unsure of where Dave might head next. "Why does the percentage matter?"

"It doesn't," he assures me. "And how would anyone ever establish such a percentage anyway? Even if someone eventually does, it still won't matter, because the point is that no one wants to disagree with someone as famously and fashionably bright as Einstein. But genius or no, the man was still human. That means he was still wrong, at least occasionally. He never could come to terms with certain aspects of quantum mechanics, for example, even though much high technology relies on it. He said he hated the idea of God playing dice with the universe, and here was a branch of physics which said things behaved randomly, dice-fashion. Werner Heisenberg said you could either determine the position of a particle of matter or energy, or you could determine its velocity. But never both at once, which introduced the scientific notion of uncertainty. This doesn't mean that science is invalidated or even weakened; it just means that its powers of prediction and of explaining things are necessarily limited."

"But to get back to why the numbers don't matter," I prod, extending the length of the last several syllables.

"Right. Again, the point is, it's okay to be wrong. And I don't know if that is the reason why people are afraid to think, or if it's simply peer pressure, whether such pressure is the covert admonition of your parents asking why you've never been married or yielded grandchildren for them to bounce around, or more overt, such as the ugly unthinking mentality of a group. And you know I hate mobs."

That was another understatement, I knew. Group think, even if it's another obvious oxymoron, seems to be what has motivated so much clandestine book research on Dave's part for the past couple of years now. This is actually my leading hypothesis for his behavior, though I've not shared it with him. Like I said, he once told me there's yet to be a book he won't take to bed, be it philosophy, fiction, biology, theology, musical biography, outdoor survival skills, or economics. Or any damn other thing, for that matter, though those are among his favorites. But the mentality of groups, if it can be called such, scares the shit out of him. The other things that scare emergency personnel: patients who are "unconscious-unknown" (the dreaded "unc-unks," who are unresponsive for mysterious reasons); individuals creating domestic disturbance calls; nasty and gruesome accidents; none of that stuff fazes Dave, really. It's the witnesses (whom he always calls "gawkers") who become unruly and start behaving as a group, even if the individuals who comprise the temporary group could not truly care less about one another, who give my friend the creeps. Dave believes he can handle individuals, at least on a personal and intellectual level, because they can usually be reasoned with, even when they're wasted or angry or both. He even seems okay with the ones who try to justify their behavior by claiming they were "just doing their jobs," or "just following orders," both of which are individual statements which encompass group mentalities. But groups themselves: how do you work with them rationally?

You don't, is his conclusion. "Yes, I know you hate mobs," I say feebly, recalling an incident he shared with me last year, when a popular watering hole in the city had an "incident" in its parking lot. One drunk asshole thought another drunk asshole was hitting on his girlfriend, who was also a bit tipsy. But it was when the hateful comments that emerged: the woman calling one of the men a faggot, one of the men calling the other man a nigger, that things got uglier. Dave's ambulance was the first emergency vehicle of any kind at the scene, and the general mêlée which was already going on by then compelled him to order his partner to drive two blocks away. It took police almost half an hour to get some semblance of social order restored, and by then the injuries sustained by a person who was in no way involved in the initial shouting match had become critical. The fact that this latter man happened to be homosexual and who was simply in the wrong place at the wrong time was ignored by further police investigations, which infuriated Dave after his fear had already been peaked.

For his lovely smile and his strong hugs and his often easy laugh, there are places in Dave's soul where I cannot follow, indeed am not even welcome. He has tried to brush this off before, pointing out that you can actually know very little about another person, truly, to say nothing of how poorly most of us know ourselves. Why else would he mention our alleged inability to even define consciousness? But the expression on his face now, while seemingly mostly nondescript, is nonetheless foreboding and full of darkness. This is not the expression that comes to mind when his favorite thinkers issued the command, "Know thyself!"

He has sometimes scared me when he gets like this, when he won't let anyone inside. Maybe he's incapable of doing so. David so often keeps the whole world at bay, with a joke, often self-deprecating, or with an escort into the realms of the deeper thinkers, or just spending so much time in dark cinemas. But this time he pulls himself right out of it, images of mobs in his head or no. "Morgan, it's like yesterday when Jack and I discussed the notion of opinions. Remember?"

"Certainly. Who would want to forget that? I've honestly thought about that several times since then. But what does the opinion talk have to do with mobs?"

"Well, recall my conclusion, that you have no business holding an opinion without a mix of research and rational argumentation?" I nod for him to continue. "Otherwise, any opinion goes, whether it supports hatred or unpleasant tastes or any other preferences which might disturb many of us. If I just said I was entitled to my opinion, then I could justify anything, really, since I'd be always answering to myself. Saying you have such an entitlement, unqualified, might sound good initially, but it's actually nihilism masking as political freedom."

"Uh huh," I say, still looking for this curious connection.

"The problem, Morgan, is that it's not just individuals who have morally troubling opinions. It's often whole groups. In fact I've come to believe it's usually larger groups. One person gets them rallied up about something, like 'those damned foreigners are taking our jobs,' or 'why should I give anything to the poor, since they're not like me,' or 'why should I worry about the environment, since humans are unique in the animal kingdom and we deserve special breaks,' or any other case where 'you're either with us or against us.' And not only is this hideous and far too easy, but it is in fact hugely dangerous, the simple result of dualistic thinking."

Dualism rings a bell for me, from some of our prior talks. "So, do you mean philosophical dualism? You've already disparaged that a bit tonight."

I'm at once surprised I got it right; I was less expectant this time. "Yes!" he cries. "Any effort to divide up the world somehow might seem convenient, a way of having the world make sense, but it logically begs huge assumptions, and it's also the quickest way to get into this divisive mentality."

"How about some examples then?"

"You remember our talk about Descartes, since, as you say, we already mentioned him tonight?"

I actually shudder to think of it. Old René is one of the famous philosophers, of course, but Dave despises him utterly, along with Aristotle, Augustine, Confucius. This friend of mine has seriously claimed that certain thinkers have been far more destructive of humanity and its potential than the likes of Stalin and Hitler and Mao, simply because people try and shape their lives according to what their philosophical instructors tell them, and these initial examples are of thinkers who specialized in either political or natural philosophy; according to Dave the former wants to control other people, while the latter tries to control the world itself, or some part of it. Maybe he's right. Maybe what organizes us into groups or mobs is just tacit "agreement" with someone whom we've permitted to do our thinking for us. Can thinking for oneself really be that painful? "Yes," I say.

"He's the quintessential dualist," Dave says, "since he more than anyone else insisted on dividing up the entire universe into minds and bodies. Nothing else. Everything is either a body, which occupies space and is physical and composed of material elements, or it is a mind, which exists but occupies no space and is immaterial in a literal sense."

"He also thought that only humans were capable of actually feeling anything, including pain," I add. What intrigues me about Dave's approach to this field is that he reads biographical information about thinkers, and not just their written works, since one of his old college teachers, one of the very few good ones apparently, said that philosophy never occurs in a vacuum; it is always a product of a person living in a particular period of history. It is therefore inextricably linked to every other discipline, since to understand history, it is possible to focus on any other branch of human endeavor that was taking place during the time, such as scientific inquiry, artistic pursuit, literary method, or anything else. And Dave was as horrified as I was to learn that Descartes had no problem in performing vivisection on non-humans, telling his fellow anatomists that the screams of such unwilling subjects were merely the sound effects of machines, automatons. I hated the mathematician turned scientist turned philosopher then as well; anyone willing to nail live cats and dogs to tables and then cut them open to examine them while they twitched and shrieked to death hardly struck me as one interested in enlightenment.

"Correct again. Now I'm not stupid enough to blame every problem on one person; in fact, that's just what I'm accusing so many other people of doing. But this dividing up is automatically antagonistic. It's like all those lame half-jokes when someone says, 'there are two kinds of people in the world,' and then goes on to enumerate that one alleged critical difference which gives the person some false sense of comfort. Take any other division you want: rich versus poor, strong versus weak, Christian versus Jew, Hindu versus Muslim, black versus white, smart versus stupid; all of these things just play upon our fears."

"Sorry, you just lost me. What has this all to do with fear?"

Ask a raging river to stop flowing. I feel guilty for sneaking a peek at the water pan to see how close to boiling its contents might be; the initial steam isn't even visible yet. "Let me explain. You know, as much as I said earlier that I love Taoism, the part about it that I'd rather see left behind is that damned yin-yang nonsense. That whole scheme, which purports to explain all that exists, is divisive, antagonistic, and sexist by definition, and yet the supposed harmony which somehow magically comes from yin interacting with yang makes everything okay. I can't identify with that. But that's the same mentality of our own legal system: two lawyers, trained as good logicians of course, verbally beat the crap out of each other and of every witness called to testify, with the assumption being that in the process of this fighting, the 'truth' will emerge."

"And yet it often works," I say. "There are plenty of worse legal systems than ours at work, or at least there have been historically."

"True. But how many reputations and lives are destroyed in this process? Have you ever watched a trial? This is spooky stuff, since the lawyers can say anything they want, though they're supposed to be doing what I insist upon by making an argument. But what I'm asking for doesn't berate the hell out of whoever is on the stand. I want to learn something, not make someone else feel like complete shit for trying."

"But why focus on being antagonistic?" I say, getting a bit flustered now. Has Dave equated me with one of these pains in his ass? Are he and I being divisive with each other now?

"I know what you're thinking, and the answer is no. You and I are presently behaving socratically, dialectically. This is not a confrontation; it is a pursuit of knowledge, of truth itself. And to answer your question, I'll offer some more examples.

When did you last watch the news, especially something cheesy like political stuff?"

"Um, let's see. You know I try not to do so, though I still gander at CNN and MSNBC a lot of times. If I'm going to keep writing for a paper, I've got to keep informed somehow. I'd rather read it than watch it."

"Granted, though I've learned that when I want to find out something about my own country, the best thing I can do is read another country's paper. Anyway: when a politician has his or her image put on American television, what information is presented along with the person's name?"

I think about it for a moment, briefly savoring the thought of maybe writing for the London *Times*, or some other big international like Dave's mentioning. "The station will list the person's position, obviously. And the state they're from, usually."

"But that's not all," Dave says, really lit up now. The look of darkness has fled once more, replaced by an intensity I can only really describe as fiery eyes. Much hotter and more piercing than my own chocolate browns. I used to think the former description was just a cliché. "What else is there?"

"After the politician's name will always, always be listed a pair of parentheses with a letter inside of them."

And I remember now. "Sure. An R or a D to show political affiliation."

His head moves back and downward, the expression of a teacher whose boneheaded student has corrupted the day's lesson. "And you approve of this?"

"I didn't say either way. I was merely explaining it."

"But don't you see? Once you paste that little letter R or D up there, what happens in the mindset of the viewer goes something like this: 'I can clearly see that because that idiot or asshole there on my TV is a member of the political party which I tend to vote against, I am obviously safe and secure in not listening to whatever he or she has to say.' It's like people describing themselves as 'liberal' or 'conservative,' though most don't know what those terms really even mean. Minimal government is actually liberal, though it's used by 'conservatives.' Conservation is also liberal, but it's basically the same word as 'conservative.' Both types are 'bleeding hearts,' but for different causes: the homeless and disadvantaged and ill for liberals, folks in law enforcement and the military for conservatives. And both want to spend profusely, regardless of what they claim, whether for social programs or for war, universal health care or social security."

"Dave, slow down. With this divisive stuff, do you really think people are *that* cynical?"

"No, Morgan, I think people are really that *stupid*. Laziness of thought leads to laziness of action. And when there's laziness of action, anybody can justify and get away with anything, since there's no interference."

"This sounds like what you used to say about gawkers," I say, not really sure what else to add. Maybe I'm not ready to admit to agreeing with his assessment of television news viewers. That entire medium is superficial by definition; every second costs a broadcaster money, so of course as much will be crammed in as quickly as possible, never mind whether it contains anything substantive. But do people really turn off so quickly once they've immediately identified a potential adversary, or just someone who they think may disagree with them? I have to think about this some more.

Strangely, my comment has yielded silence. Dave is the sort who is scarier quiet than ranting, since you always are left wondering what thoughts are ricocheting through that labyrinthine mind (*sorry, brain*) of his. "Dave?"

"Hmm? Oh. Yeah, you're right. Maybe I'm just a bitter paramedic who's tired of people always staring around like sheep, wondering what's happening. It's easy to see that at an emergency scene, and I still don't know what causes it: morbid curiosity, fascination with illness and injury and death, wanting to be part of something but not knowing how. Some sociologists have even suggested something called 'bystander syndrome,' in that the larger the group, the less initiative taken by any one of its members. I just don't know. What I do know, however, is that I cannot stand the overt violation of another person's privacy that happens in such scenarios. Here's a person lying on a street, bleeding from who knows how many injuries, and people just stare. Here's another person who's screaming she's just been raped or mugged or beaten, and people just stare. Why do they do it, Morgan?"

And it is then, right then, that I start to get a better sense of what this strange story would really be all about. Suddenly maternal, I want to hold and kiss this man and tell him that the world is still a beautiful place, and that it will outlive and outlast humanity's follies. But I also recognize he has to come to terms with what's destroying him on his own. That's the only philosophy lesson which has completely sunk in with me: each of us, whatever and whomever we may be or may become, is partly connected, and partly totally alone. Right now David is alone, in a place where I either cannot or will not follow, I'm not even sure which. All I can truly be is a friend. I shake my head while I finally say, "I don't know. Not all of them do it. I know you think most do, and you're probably right, but I still don't know." He just sits there staring, afraid to even look back at me. Maybe he's deciding how much of an existentialist I am; they always emphasized personal responsibility as the trade-off for actual freedom.

"Here," I say finally, wanting now to shift away from intellectualized philosophy into something more physical, like my beloved *aikido*. "I want to show you something."

"Do tell," he says, in a tone reminiscent of my own frustrated mood of the past two days, but I accept it. And with that, I stand, take him by a resistant hand and pull him up to me, then begin shifting his hands until they hold me in a proper dance position. I've not tried this with him for years, but he recalls.

"Remember the Fire Department Dance?" The same kidlike grin is back now. It can be uncannily easy to elicit a smile from this man. You just have to meet him at his own level; maybe we're all that way, and maybe that's why we so often don't get along.

"Of course. You all looked so dapper in your uniforms. Why was that the only dance you took me to?"

It takes some time to understand the source of his discomfiture. "I like that word: 'dapper;' it's got a nice archaic ring to it. But you know I don't like it when everyone's dressed the same, and you also know people in emergency work: always with the wiseass cracks about whether you and I were really an item. When I said no, the folks at my firehouse decided you must have been a sympathy date for me."

"Never," I console, back-leading for a moment to know that I'm expecting a waltz from him, something I've shown him the basics of a few times. I prefer traveling dances, like this and tango and foxtrot; the ones which stay in place give you more limited views.

Now it's my turn to wax grandiose with the insights. "You know, partner, there are some enlightened souls out there who think that this, what we're doing right now, is the secret language of everything, of life itself."

"Oh, do tell now, Lady Morgan." Dave's holding me securely and closely enough that he cannot see me flush for an instant; he's not called me that for years, either. It used to be a little joke: I was supposed to be Morgan le Fay from the King Arthur legends, and he was whichever one of the Round Table knights she had most recently enchanted, seduced, imprisoned, or all three. Apparently she went through several of them that way, the little heartbroken floozy. Still, she was just looking for a connection with someone, never learning that it cannot be forced, but merely felt. And it took me a while to understand that Dave meant the moniker as a compliment, claiming there was magic in my name because of its mythological origins.

Then again, the last time he called me that was when we'd had dinner at my place, just hanging out together, watching movies and playing with my pets and laughing and drinking some really good wine and someone made a rebuffed pass at someone else... Why can I not remember who tried to kiss whom? What the hell is going on here tonight? Didn't I say I was taking a break from "romantic entanglements?"

Dave's oblivious to such memories, thankfully, or at least appears so. "Morgan? What's this about a 'secret language'?"

"Right. Sorry." It's admittedly awkward trying to move and sway while standing on uneven ground. There are way too many tree roots and small rocks right here for safety, to say nothing of the possibility of knocking over the camp stove, which yet remains relatively quiet with its pressurized heating sound. So I opt to back-lead again, a cardinal sin for women dancing, but since I already described switching dance roles when I act as an *aikidoist*, hopefully I can be forgiven. "Here," I motion to him. "Take me right back over this way," and the swaying stops for some clumsy moments while we navigate to a point roughly equidistant between our two tents: my own tiny one and Dave's infamous "little burrito." Jack and Mariska have been sharing a third between them: a tent, that is, not a burrito.

Then I adjust his hands properly in relation to the rest of me: his right on my back, roughly off-center, a couple of his fingertips resting on the scapula, his left simply grasping my own right, though I have to extend my arm to get him into a decent lead position. A lot of men have really weak dance frames, but this man could be formidable in a ballroom if he put his mind to it. "There. Better?"

"It feels fine," he says. "Though I still await an answer."

"It's coming, Sir Accolon." *Holy crap! Am I flirting with this man?!*

No time to worry about that now, I decide, admiring his smile. *I wonder how he remembers that night. How long ago was that? I think I'd just gotten back from a weekend with Charlie, and we were talking about Mom, and Dave had just returned from Chicago and being with his son who still lives with that dumb bitch who never knew a good thing...*

I suddenly have to stop. My heart rate has actually increased. What on earth is going on here?

It takes me a moment to salvage some semblance of dignity before I can meet Dave's too-perceptive smile. "Let's try a little waltz, and I'll tell you what I mean."

I'm just about to start back-leading yet again when the man surprises me by remembering. Waltz is unique in the ballroom repertoire, since it relies on a three-four count to each measure of music, and Dave correctly begins by driving that left foot of his forward, towards me, with his right following to meet it and then immediately extending to the right side. There's even an appropriate lilting of his whole frame which I mimic as a reflected image, and then his left foot in turn follows his right, so we've taken a step forward (backward for me), then a step to my left, in three counts.

I know it would be easier and more entertaining if you could watch us do this, but describing it helps me try and understand the simple if painful honesty which was hovering around our campsite this night. Anyway, Dave's right foot now leads backward, and he completes the opposite of what he's just begun a moment earlier. With the end of this first motion, we've completed a simple box step, the basic foundational movement of waltz, foxtrot, and rumba, to name a few.

Dave leads me into another of the same, lifting his left arm along with my right after the first half of the motion, so that I'm encouraged to execute a turn beneath his raised leading arm. The second box step finishes, and I can barely believe he remembers even this much.

"Not bad. Now, what I was saying?" I begin, barely perceiving the fact that Dave is now leading me backwards for the full two counted measures of music which does not even exist here, so we have to imagine it. He's taking me into progressive steps, which glide while covering more distance, but since I promised him an answer I don't yet have time to comment or to praise him.

"Dancing is like life?" Dave says.

"Oh, no. Better than that. Dancing is life."

Those soft eyebrows raise quizzically at my phrasing, and I resist the urge to take my gaze from his face, just to see if he's leading me someplace safely. Sometimes you just have to trust and let someone lead you. Maybe I should tell him so; perhaps he's not quite ready to hear it. "How so?" he says, forever the inquiring thinker.

"It's like this," I say, not missing the fact that he has now steered me rather impressively around the second of the two smaller tents, and is about to do what looks like a large figure-eight around the pair of them. "And I'll describe it philosophically for you."

"I can hardly wait," he says, finishing his nifty loop which has intertwined our two tents in that figure-eight, even leading me through a traveling underarm turn, which takes a touch more balance than its easier counterpart executed during a box step. I wonder if he realizes he's completed the ancient symbol for infinity with our motion and line of travel; probably.

Still, it's a delight to just be led by him. Dave now tries a little series of alternating three-eighths turns, switching left to right to left again. These, my teachers drilled into me, represent the basic flowing motion of the waltz, and you need to be able to do them around a dance floor indefinitely. The trick is that when you turn to the left, you can just start the step right away, with no planning or setup, since there's a lead step in that direction. In other words, Dave leads into me for the first one-two-three, starting with his left foot, then guides me with the next two steps until we've traveled a little bit but also have turned 135 degrees or so, thus the three-eighths reference. Then, for the next measure, he comes back right at me with his right leg, and we finish the first half of the motion facing roughly where we started. For the second half of this motion, he steps backwards and we stay almost put, and then the final step is forward for him again, and we're ready to keep encircling our dance "floor." It's really just a big, rotating, elegant way of covering a lot of dance space very quickly, but you have to be confident of where you're either leading or being led as well as fully cognizant of where the other dancers are so there are no collisions. Or, in our case, you have to keep track of where the trees are, and for that matter, I'm taken aback by the fact that we've yet to trip over any big roots: the trees' legs, for purposes of my analogy.

Enjoying the comfort of the moment, I whisper the answer to him that he awaits. "Tat tvam asi," the archaic syllables emerge, the relative lack of wind ensured by the surrounding trees enabling such a soft intonation to reach him.

"So you *were* listening!" he says, almost in disbelief. And he almost loses me in the continuing motion, but recovers, keeps his balance, and even does a couple of swaying steps which simply stay in place, then resumes a largely unpredictable series of alternating basic steps. I'm as startled by his remembering little waltz details as he apparently is now in me.

"Of course, dingbat." There are other times when I don't actually wish to follow where that ever-active brain and/

or mind might want to lead, but that one phrase has always stuck with me.

I refer to a proclamation of the ancient Hindus, a simple Sanskrit saying which pervaded their early religious philosophy, and which dozens of cultures since have tried to regain, though we Westerners tend to overcomplicate things sometimes, perhaps because we're the ones who created formal logic. Mathematics, and its sense of formulaic completion, is more Eastern; asking questions forever is more up our proverbial alley, and we seem more content to obey the rules of our own logic than to wonder about the answers it may or may not offer. Still, I digress: *tat tvam asi* translates most approximately into modern English as "Thou art that," which could just as easily be stated as "that thou art." But to really understand it requires one to go a bit deeper: it refers to mutual self-identity, and the notion that all the divisiveness in the world is actually illusory. In other words, there is no difference between subject and object, yin and yang, male and female, black and white, predator and prey, good and evil... everything that exists is instead interconnected with absolutely everything else. We just artificially and logically divide up it all to try and make sense of some aspect or feature, only to forget that these are *our* projections of meaning, *our* conclusions, *our* truths, and *our* divisions. The whole world is one. Or, as Baruch Spinoza said it, God and Nature (which share respective masculine and feminine traits) are one. But then, Spinoza was an ostracized Jew living in Amsterdam, which, despite its general and historic cultural open-mindedness, nevertheless encouraged both Jews and Christians to shun him. And he was really referring to God's essential nature rather than Mother Nature, but either way, Dave was right; I was indeed listening. And Spinoza was trying to reconcile something which everyone except him thought was divisive. And since we already mentioned Einstein, when asked whether he believed in God, he replied,

"I believe in Spinoza's God." Old Al realized how bigoted and judgmental the question really is.

Of course Dave, the suddenly good dancer, is aware of the ancient Hindu proverb, being after all the one who explained it to me. But since I feel such a connection to him now: physically, emotionally, it seemed wholly appropriate. Though I also know him well enough to recognize he'll continue to rationally torment himself until he figures things out, or at least arrives at an answer which seems to satisfy him on some level.

Linear thought and trying to plan complex bodily motion are simply incompatible goals, which I am reminded of while seeing the puzzled yet curious expression reflecting back at me while simultaneously feeling what quickly becomes the heavy clomping of masculine legs receiving mixed signals from their controlling brain. Dave can't think and dance at the same time; no one can. It's the same with my martial arts experience, something Jack once confirmed for me: he said (and I've since learned) that as soon as you start analyzing, you miss your target, which for his *karate* means getting punched or kicked, and for my *aikido* means doing what Dave just did: stopping cold and looking befuddled, with the danger of simply falling down thrown in for good measure.

I try and help. "Shall we continue to dance or keep talking?"

"Tell me something," he says, as I raise my eyebrows, still feeling, surprisingly, that he has yet to relinquish his solid dance frame, like he's afraid to let go. "Have the modern scientists finally caught up with the ancient Indian and Chinese and Greek thinkers, then?"

"What does that mean?"

"You already said it: tat tvam asi. The lack of divisions. This is the huge metaphysical irony, in that we probably have to imagine the world as a bunch of separate things and beings in order to try and understand them: this is a house, this is the sky, this is a dog; but they're really not separate after all. It means that what those ancient thinkers were trying to tell us is now confirmed by what are described as the most basic tenets of science."

Okay. I'll bite, still enjoying this feeling of proximity, that strong arm holding me in place by the shoulder. "How so?"

He leans back subtly, bringing me with him. Our legs are still touching at the thighs and knees, as any good dance frame should exhibit. "Matter and energy are the same thing, Morgan. That's it! There's no discrepancy anymore; that's what the physicists and chemists are telling us now. We've known for centuries that matter and energy are neither created nor destroyed, but that they merely alter their shapes and appearances, what the philosophers have called 'qualities' and 'properties' for so long. Oh, don't you get it?"

No, I really don't. Where are you going with all this? All I can think to do is shake my head and keep waiting for another dance.

He smiles. "I promise I'll tell you before the end of the trip. My brain's very tired right now. But stay tuned: when I'm done you'll understand how we're both going to live forever."

Foolishly desperate to sound intelligent (*why am I trying to impress him?*), I opt for another tactic, probably just to escape the thoughts of my late mother that his last sentence is already threatening to bring about. "So what's the difference between philosophy and science, then?"

"There's not one anymore, remember? Philosophy and science and religion and art are merely the four avenues to knowledge, and each of us lives primarily according to one of them, while ignoring or trying to allow time for the others."

Smartass. "Well, humor me. After all, doesn't it at least seem like things are separated? How could there be a 'you,' or a 'me,' unless 'we' were somehow distinct from everything else?"

And like almost every other time on our trip so far, he's prepared: "We're not. The sense data 'our' bodies provide are a matter of convenience. But if you like, look at it this way: your own body is made up of trillions of little sub-creatures who are actually each alive, each with their own objectives. But they can't survive on their own. They need the 'you' which is just an aggregate of them all. That's one of the most beautiful things science has ever confirmed for us. Imagine how Anton von Leeuwenhoek must have felt when he became the first person to notice all that cellular activity under his early microscope."

"True," I grant him, recalling that Leeuwenhoek was a contemporary of Spinoza's and also Dutch, and how Mariska has repeatedly insisted that creative ideas are most possible in more open-minded societies like that one, "but are the people and trees and bugs and bears and bats on this tiny planet then analogous to my own body: trillions of other 'aggregates' of life strolling about, each, again, with its own agenda?"

"Yes. That's the whole point. See? The divisions really are just artificial projections. What our bodies tell us is largely for survival value: those individual cells of ours want to go on living, so they tell 'us' what to pay attention to, what to ignore, what to flee from or to pursue. Does that make more sense?"

I think about it, just like I was starting to think about whether I should just plant my mouth directly over his, partly because I suddenly really want to and partly because there are times, much as I care about Dave, that I wish he'd just can it. "I'm trying. Let me go back to your assessment of different types of knowledge, then. You told me once that what you'd really want, more than anything, would be to explore as much as you're able to about what you described as the main venues of human knowledge. At least, I think that was how you described them." He nods.

"So tell me, then, perpetual student, to repeat: what's the difference between all this philosophy stuff and, for instance, the science you needed to study to become a medic?"

Not even a pause from him: "Money."

Interesting. "How about between philosophy and religion, which I know you tend to shun?"

"Hmm. Control, I should think. Or at least the attempt to achieve it."

Yikes. "The only remaining field of human endeavor, according to you, is art. So what separates philosophy from art?"

"Method of expression. I'm not sure art can ever truly be analyzed, which some might take for a criticism, but which I mean as a compliment."

"But couldn't you analyze something which is both artistic and, say, verbal, like poetry or literature?" I say.

He still hasn't let go of me. We must look like two confused and excited teens trying to conclude a first date, just standing there in the woods trying to decide whether to risk something as defining as a kiss. Instead, we're trying to unlock the secrets of the universe, arms clutching each other, though my right arm, still extended with his left, is getting pretty tired. And I briefly wonder what it would be like having chats with "normal" guys, and then I remember: I'd get another Charlie, who, in this same position, would definitely gamble on the kiss and all which might "naturally" follow it, and neither of us would actually be any closer to understanding each other, or anything else. The trillions of cells comprising "Charlie" would simply be encouraging "him" to get laid.

"Well," Dave tries, "with something that's more of a piece of creative writing, the message could be obvious or it could be more subtle. That's a tricky one, since some of the best philosophers are remembered primarily for their fiction: Sartre, Dostoevsky, Rousseau, Rand, Camus, Pirsig. More recently we've got Jostein Gaarder and Carol Gilligan writing novels. Formal philosophy is more direct, though literature is more interesting for most of us to actually read; but those damned novelists seem to feel they can say anything."

"Perhaps they can, if they've earned the right to their opinions, like we concluded recently."

"I love knowing that conversation wasn't a waste of time."

"Fair enough," I say. "But getting back to artistic interpretation: so it seems there are some things even you can't pigeon-hole."

He glares back at me, like I've offered the gravest of insults. "I have little wish to 'pigeon-hole' much of anything, thank you very little. That's where the effort to control comes from, you know."

"You're right; sorry. Now, how about that dance?"

So quickly I'd have missed it if I'd not been staring right at him, Dave actually *clears* his mind (or brain, or whatever's in that noggin). He literally shakes his head, slightly adjusts his hand positions in relation to mine, and then briefly closes his eyes before reopening them to look, well, different. It's like his head's one of those "Etch-a-Sketch" toys from the '70s that he likely had as a kid, as I did, and now he's cleared it up, so it's ready for more input.

"Tango?"

"What?" I must sound foolish answering him like that. I just keep gazing at him; it's probably putting him off, but the curiosity is just about to kill this old red-headed cat, even when I'm not sure if I want him to shut up. But I've never been more intrigued by what anyone was thinking, even myself. How does he do that?

"Tango," he says again, like he has all the time in the universe. And without waiting for a response, he sinks lower just slightly, a feeling I'm well used to from *aikido* practice, and then I find myself being inexorably led backwards again, this time to the unmistakably romantic yet marked cadence of the immortal tango. And like a good martial artist or dancer, Dave's moving me from his own center: just below his navel is his own physical, possibly spiritual, and gravitational center, and that's the source of the power of human motion. It's like what I mentioned back at the *dojo*.

The movements now are smooth, almost polished, though Dave doesn't know any advanced steps. Still, it's far better in ballroom to be really good at the basics than to try and show off with complicated things which take quite a while to try and master anyway. He remembers the *promenade* I showed him years earlier, and he doesn't weaken his frame while leading me into it. Then it's a couple more basic moving steps, followed by a *corte* which has him leaning slightly back while he pulls me directly into him (*did I show him that?*), and then a quicker-paced variation of the simpler foxtrot step. I almost demand to know when he's been practicing these, debating if my need to have an answer is prompted by a sense of wondering how he manages his time or simple jealousy, like he's out every weekend dancing with other women. I know he's not, and why should I care anyway?

He remains in place for two measures, shuffling his hips back and forth twice in a rock and *corte* combination move, looking confident and assured, with me wondering why we've not danced more together and when and where he might practice, and I can faintly hear the words of my dance instructors: *the tango is the sexiest of them all, Morgan; any time you do a tango with someone, you're basically having a three-minute affair with him, because no other dance, even in the ballroom catalog, insists on closer bodily contact than does the legacy of* Buenos Aires.

Is it getting warm out here in these near-winter woods? I wonder sheepishly.

By the time the pan full of stream water on the stove has reached a boil, I'm already making a silent promise that I'll never attempt to analyze who first kissed whom, but we remain standing there like two hormone-infused high-schoolers when Jack and Mariska return to the campsite, Jack at once expressing dismay that he didn't have his beloved camera at reach to capture the moment. We don't even hear their approach at first, only their amused giggles of recognition which they will later claim resulted from what they "knew about you and Dave for a long while." All I remember is an oath made by this man about the evidence that we will go on, that perhaps it's not all in vain like his strange profession keeps suggesting to him.

* * *

Scenario Three:

The likes of Germany and Iraq, two vastly differing sources and influences of human civilizations, now recede behind us in the storytelling. Granted, it remains difficult to locate traces of wolf-kind in either of those modern nations, though lions and elephants once roamed both. Between the ancient recesses of the Black Forest and the contemporary hazards of the Arabian Desert we can confine our considerations of lupine encounters to other historical periods and varying locales.

Take now, for the latest example: East Asia, including China and Japan, Russia and Mongolia, Korea. The nation currently known as the Russian Federation, which generally has healthier environmental policies and openness than its Soviet antecedent, likewise possesses the world's largest wolf population. Impossible to count with tremendous accuracy, of course, but then so is the planet's assortment of humans: the Russians are considered to live with close to one hundred thousand wolves total. Mongolia, bordering to the south, has perhaps a quarter as many. In the other Asian countries here mentioned, the canids struggle to continue living, but can be found nonetheless, if one knows where to search.

Prejudice toward and respect for wolves remains typical and par for the course in most of the Asian lands, but in one of these nations, we can concentrate on one of the most unusual approaches to these animals ever known. As we will see, during part of the feudal Edo *period of Japanese history, a* samurai *named Kiyomori Shinsaku could encounter wolves in a manner yet unconsidered.*

Trained as an expert in the combative arts which will eventually filter their way down to our protagonist Morgan Greene in a revised and more peaceful form, Kiyomori finds himself with a disturbing problem, one he dearly wishes would not have escalated up to him for judgment. Still, as a young samurai *managing a parcel of his lord's lands near the feudal capital city of* Edo, *he recognizes the shame he will face if he cannot come through with a sound decision for his dilemma.*

The peasants working the farm lands he must occasionally help in managing have begun to complain of an invasion.

That is how the superstitious peasants choose to phrase it, *Kiyomori thinks, trying to keep bitterness from his need to plan. At first he feels excitement, even elation; he has been raised and weaned on tales of the Mongol invasion of earlier centuries, turned back by the* kamikaze, *the divine wind which he knows shall forever protect the Japanese homeland from foreign incursion. He is picturing the gleam of his polished swords held high in the light of the rising sun when the peasants clarified what they meant.*

This would be an invasion of four-legged interlopers, they said: mostly deer, with some scattered boars and even monkeys.

Kiyomori is briefly tempted to take the head of one of the meager farmers right then, but his upbringing has also taught him that even if the peasants are worth less than their social betters, they nonetheless have intrinsic value, and the slaying of an unarmed farmer by a highly trained servant of a man who in turn serves the shogun *seems shameful for its disparity. So Kiyomori laughs off the peasant's fears.*

But the farmers remain as anxious as if the Mongols or the Chinese are really about to launch an attack themselves. The young samurai indeed has not seen such an expression of concern etched on another's face since the rumors that the Dutch were plotting to land in parts of Japan other than Nagasaki; the national government, the bakufu, *has been in a brief uproar over such hearsay. But the Chinese and Dutch are only allowed to land in the southern port city, and that has been the case since the year the gai-jin call 1639. Japan is now so thoroughly isolationist that foreign religion, foreign books, foreign medicine, and foreigners, are all banned throughout the empire. So in this year, 1685, the notion of genuine foreigners seems far-fetched at best.*

"Deer? And monkeys?" Kiyomori asks now, his arms crossed over his chest, his brief vision of glory already receding. He takes it as a source of pride that he was born in the mighty city of Edo 28 years earlier, right at the time of the Great Fire which devastated the wooden metropolis. His panicked mother informed him when he was old enough to understand that her own waters had broken right as the shouts of "Fire!" came from the sentries, and now the son, grown into an intelligent and honorable man, takes his curious birth as the inspiration for his own sense of indestructibility which comes from being young and brave. And relatively untested in combat.

The farmer, an old man wrinkled more from years bent over in the sun than from age, nods while continuing to look towards the earth. Kiyomori generally does trust this man, named Hino. Family names are not typically spent on those who do not need to trace their genealogy, but Hino's family has a reputation for forthrightness; it would be unlike him to panic. "Yes, master," he replies as extra emphasis. "There are too many deer. The monkeys our children can frighten away or just shoot with their slings. But the deer are always nearby, and the boars are too dangerous for us."

Deer will remain a curious staple of some large Japanese cities such as Nara even into the twenty-first century, where they entertain the tourists and can be found in parks, among automotive traffic, and exploring the grounds of temples and shrines, rather like the brazen Anchorage moose with which Morgan Greene will become familiar three centuries after Kiyomori's death.

In the meantime, of course, the problem remains. Kiyomori has never seen a boar, though he has hunted deer successfully. Like his knightly counterparts years before in Europe, he is accustomed to feudalism and its social contract, part of which concerns harsh punishments for poaching, which is one reason why the peasants have done nothing about these pesky deer. The other reason is that they feel simply overwhelmed by numbers. "How much damage have they done?" he asks.

Hino releases a pent-up sigh, fearing his safety again. The deer are one thing; an angry samurai something else entirely, though the respect between these two men flows in both directions. "My son and daughters are still estimating, but we think, perhaps, thirty, maybe forty koku worth of crops, mostly vegetables. Deer do not eat rice."

The unscarred samurai cannot keep in an involuntary gasp. Forty koku! The koku is the main unit of accounts in old Japan: it is officially regarded as the amount and corresponding value of rice needed to feed a healthy man for a year. The kind of crop damage Hino is suggesting is almost reminiscent of an invasion after all. And he vaguely recognizes that it took genuine courage for Hino to admit to such a loss, even though it is not his own fault.

"Thank you, Hino-san," Kiyomori replies, adding the respectful epithet, which is normally unwarranted for the lower social classes, but the gesture shows that Hino and his family are still considered trustworthy. Peasants know enough to not alarm their lords unnecessarily, so much so that some of Japan's political problems, whether regarding taxes, foreign influence, or the costs of food, go unreported to the proper authorities, often resulting in successive rounds of finger-pointing while trying to save face. And Kiyomori feels his own *social face may be threatened by news which might be comical under other circumstances; whoever heard of deer eating so much food? How could they have multiplied their own numbers so greatly as to become a threat to the empire's vital agriculture?*

Kiyomori's friend and man-at-arms, a lower-ranking samurai named Chosokabe Yorihisa, still tends both men's horses back at the edge of the farmlands, and has not heard the warning conversation. Kiyomori feels only distress as he walks back and mounts the steed which has carried him around the Edo environs for the past three years. "You look like someone important just died," Chosokabe utters, noting how the higher-ranking samurai has not even glanced at him. Childhood friends, Chosokabe would never dare mouth something so potentially insensitive to any other person.

When they finally make eye contact, Kiyomori looks like he might be contemplating seppuku *without being asked, the ritualized honorable suicide beginning with self-induced disembowelment and ending with decapitation at the hands of a respected equal. "What then will you say to me when someone of importance is actually dead?"*

Kiyomori's gaze looks murderous, and Chosokabe looks humbled in answer. "What is the problem with the farmlands?" he asks, to change the subject. He has little interest in the ways of the farmers; for Chosokabe, indeed to most of their class, such persons are merely a means to an end.

Kiyomori explains it, as the pair slowly rides back in the vague direction of Edo. The city which will later be known as Tokyo has been completely rebuilt and often improved upon since the Great Fire. The former imperial capital was Kyoto, and while the Emperor still lives there most of the time, the real government, the bakufu, *operates out of Edo. This has been a period of relative peace, though the regional* daimyo, *or feudal lords, are often at each other's throats, sometimes literally, in the ongoing effort to get ahead socially and also please the Emperor, who is often seen as indecisive and insecure. But the order of society is what matters.*

Feudal Japan is what we moderns would call a "sustainable society," in that its fanatical isolationism, which forbids international travel, the importation of much beyond exotic foods and weapons, and a relative ignorance of most of the world, has produced a culture of dedicated recyclers. Farming and animal husbandry have evolved into true art forms with strict regulations. Rights of access to different types of goods are rigidly controlled, though there is of course a black market lurking in the cities. There are legal dealers in used paper, used wood, used clothes, used wax, used metals, used construction materials, and perhaps the most interesting: used food. The allegedly best quality is "night soil," the fecal remains of none other than our own species, which has also been put to good use by Hino and the other farm laborers. Prices of night soil vary according to the social station of the person who generates it, since the wastes of the nobility are regarded as leading to superior crops. For a nation which has always been geographically small, topographically and agriculturally challenging, and in Kiyomori's time already populated by millions of humans, the goal is maintenance of a strict balancing act. Kiyomori and Chosokabe might be part of a very restrictive social hierarchy, in which it is quite rare for one's position to change much in a lifetime (at least for it to move upward; going downward socially is a possibility for almost all). Yet this very rigidity has yielded an efficient and environmentally conscious culture. That is precisely why the massive crop damage is so catastrophic; the Japanese people, and in particular the bakufu, will never consent to importing additional basic foodstuffs to cover the losses. If Kiyomori can resolve the situation, he will likely earn another step up the social ladder; failure might just mean an order of seppuku after all.

The sun feels hot overhead during the ride back toward Edo. Kiyomori and Chosokabe live among several other resident samurai at a house, more of a barracks, on their lord's estate near the governmental district. This gives them easy access to all parts of the city, which helps, since they are busy retainers of a lord named Hachisukan. As a lord focused on urban affairs, he has only a small cadre of loyal samurai, *and will never be a war leader on his own. Still, Hachisukan has a reputation for honesty and fairness, and Kiyomori and Chosokabe are both proud to remain in his service. It was difficult for the former, a* jiro *or second son, and the latter, the son of a blacksmith and occasional archery teacher, to have become* samurai *in the first place. It is most often a title of heredity, and as such jealously guarded.*

The young samurai *are both glad to have worn hats on such a bright day, though they have always savored longer rides, no matter the business at hand, since it feels liberating simply to perch atop a warhorse. Kiyomori feels almost ashamed for having told the tale to his underling, since the problem seems so asinine, even funny from a different perspective. If they were to hunt so many deer on their own, it would take time, more resources, and permission of both Lord Hachisukan and the other lords whose interests prevailed in these farmlands; and even if all those things became available, Honorable Lord Hachisukan would likely be unable to let them go for so long. How long might it take to secure so many deer, anyway, to say nothing of the boars and monkeys? Weeks, Kiyomori thinks glumly,* and by then the harvest shall be upon us and the crop damage still affecting us all.

"Do you think we could get the necessary men to hunt?" *Chosokabe says. That is the main part of their relationship that Kiyomori savored; Chosokabe usually knows approximately what his friend and master is thinking.*

"I do not believe so. And it is regrettable that something as elating as a deer hunt would have to feel like face-saving work. It could become a waste of the deer, too: all that meat rotting in this sun before anyone truly has a chance to benefit from it." Chosokabe nods in acknowledgement of these unpleasant realities.

"We could try posting more ashigaru *as guards, perhaps at key access points to the farmed areas," he adds, also recognizing the gravity of their situation; whatever fate awaits Kiyomori will likewise be faced by Chosokabe as his immediate underling. And the use of peasant warriors, the* ashigaru, *would keep the* samurai *free from*

questions dealing with honor, since it is beneath them to perform most forms of physical labor, while the ashigaru have no honor to speak of and are the massed infantry portion of the armies of Japan. Still, the problem remains: ashigaru would have to be taken from somewhere they might otherwise be needed, and even though they are relatively inexpensive, the question of funding such an operation would come up as well, although Kiyomori smirks at the thought that at least there would be plenty of meat with which to feed them.

"I have considered that as well. Hino even suggested it just before I left him. But I do not know where we could find enough. And not many of them are good enough archers for our task."

Chosokabe appreciates the subtle reference to his own father's mastery of the art of kyudo, the way of the bow; had there been sufficient time, his father could teach perhaps two dozen ashigaru to shoot well enough for the job, but time is already working against them. Firearms are available too, though in small numbers, the gunpowder and ammunition usually having to be imported from the gai-jin like the Dutch, and such weapons are likewise considered dishonorable by any true samurai anyway: too easy to use, and able to kill at too long a range. They are for cowards and peasants and anyone else who lacks discipline.

Almost as desperate as his master to think of something practical, Chosokabe proffers the one idea he has not yet tried. They will be back to the city soon, and might have duties in the various districts already awaiting their attention. Kiyomori and Chosokabe act as minor diplomats, law enforcement personnel, bodyguards, property guards, and official messengers in all of Edo's major areas: the Nihonbashi trade district, the Hibiya administrative district, the temple districts (Honjo, Asakusa, Zojo), even the legendary Yoshiwara pleasure district, which must be locked up at night. Few knew the city better than these two, though Chosokabe almost dreads returning now.

"Master?" he begins. "What of the monks up at Nozomi Temple?"

Kiyomori is taken aback, yet almost welcoming of any distraction to his problem. "What about them?" he says, trying to focus on little other than the evenly repetitive clip-clop of their horses' hooves along the well-groomed and traveled road.

Chosokabe explains that Nozomi *Temple is a typical Shinto facility, tracing its origins to the ancient Rin Zai tradition of Zen practice. The monks living and working there will likely be little different from those in almost any other part of Japan, save for one detail.

"They have a deal of excess land. Part of it they utilize for extra crops."

"Chosokabe-san, are you suggesting we have the farmers travel all the way to Nozomi to plant more crops?"* That is the only reference to the extra land he can conjure. Monks are hardly known for massive land holdings; the daimyo would tend toward violent jealousy of that, at any rate.

The younger of the two warriors looks earthward, gathering his resolve, and continues with his strange idea. "Not exactly, Master. But I understand that on part of their extra lands they keep, well, hunters."

"Hunters. Excellent. Perhaps there are enough for us to hire to use against all these deer."

"I believe they would have to be hired, yes, but these are different types of hunters. These are, well, wolves, actually." He says the final two words quietly, almost embarrassed. Kiyomori will not chastise him unduly; still, Chosokabe feels rather unsure of himself for such an odd idea. But then, if it is really so strange but nonetheless true, then the monastery and temple must be earning money for the practice.

Kiyomori reins up short, putting himself in front of his subordinate. "Wolves, you say? True wolves?" I have never even seen one. But they are terrible, and frightening to behold. All they do is eat! *He is not about to reveal such a strong childhood fear in front of another, good friend or no. His mother had told that, *in the wake of the Great Fire, some of the human survivors had been attacked, even eaten, by monsters.*

But not wolves? he wonders now. I cannot remember exactly.

Chosokabe looks downward, avoiding the other's glance. "That is what I have heard, Kiyomori-san. *The monks supposedly keep a few full packs of them, with a couple of extras who do not work well with the others. The individuals, so it is said, are almost beloved pets of the monastery, though the pack members are the true hunters.*"

"Do you know of anyone who has ever actually," Kiyomori struggles for the right word, "rented such savage creatures before? And what might the results have been, eh? Perhaps the wolves got loose and devoured their handlers. Maybe the monks are secretly raising them as new weapons of war for one of the daimyo." *Kiyomori will likewise not admit that he finds himself intrigued by the prospect; he truly fears no wild animal, at least none that he has ever encountered, and he is clever enough to know that the monks must be able to handle them somehow. That is, if the stories of this strange* Nozomi Monastery *are true.*

"I confess I know of no one who has actually used such animals. But think of it, Master: I was always told as a child that wolves were vicious and cunning, capable of killing untold numbers of other animals, including wild deer I should think. If they could be introduced into the farmlands, and we posted ashigaru by the main points of access anyway to help keep them in, then perhaps this could work."

Kiyomori is surprised to find himself smiling, the heat of the late summer sun no longer making him feel excessively warm in his light armor, as a breeze comes up, perhaps a divine signal of the approaching pleasant night. "If wolves are as cunning as it is said, then perhaps they could easily escape from the likes of the farmers and the ashigaru, so I rather think that the monks themselves would need to help us work them."

Chosokabe feels sudden shock at the proposal; he cannot quite picture two samurai leading an assortment of peaceful monks and snarling wolves like a war party aimed at controlling the local deer populace. And for the first time, he wonders if wolves are capable of catching things like monkeys and boar. He supposes so: wolves have just as bad a reputation as boars.

Kiyomori reads the chagrin on his compatriot's countenance. "Chosokabe-san, if the monks do not lead such animals, then perhaps we shall have to do so ourselves."

That is too much for the other man. "Master, surely you do not mean for us to denigrate ourselves like peasants. It would be indecent!" Chosokabe is moved by the realities of social roles as much as anyone; if nothing else, anyone who saw them would at least laugh. Two proud warriors who lived and died by honor alone, walking about with animals big enough they likely have to be kept on iron leashes.

"Think of it this way: it is honorable for samurai to use hunting birds and hunting dogs, even though others take care of them. So why not the use of hunting wolves?"

Chosokabe is still so aghast he has almost forgotten that the very idea has come from his own mouth, as well as the initial surprise that Kiyomori has apparently warmed to the idea; either that, or he recognizes their desperation. He keeps his silence as Kiyomori asks him the way to the monastery, explaining that time is important, and they will simply have to return home to the manor of Hachisukan a bit later than planned.

It requires more than two more hours of riding which would have been quite a pleasant amble through the countryside if not for the concerns of the two samurai. Chosokabe knows how to reach the major monasteries in the region surrounding Edo, since he has tended to pay more attention to the spiritual aspects of his heritage. His family of course is thrilled by moving up in society with their son's acceptance as a loyal servant of one of the lords, though they have raised him to believe in the power of the gods, as well as the influence of one's actions. He is part of a period of Japanese history in which Neo-Confucianism holds sway, with its particular emphasis on interpersonal relationships, always described as both mutually respectful but also hierarchical, as children had to obey parents, wives had to obey husbands, and servants had to follow the dictates of masters. Still, the thought of the gods themselves, who had made these beautiful islands long ago, reassures Chosokabe and reinforces his belief in his society's strengths.

The Shinto religion already has a thousand-year history in Japan by this time, something Chosokabe reminds himself of as the two men ascend their way into the Kanto Mountains, southwest of the city. Fuji-san, the most magnificent mountain in all of Japan, with its instantly recognizable snow-encrusted volcanic flattop, lay to the west of them. It has already been two days since they left Edo, and they know they have to get back shortly or else risk their master's ire. But Kiyomori has clearly decided that the chance of finding a solution to the farming problem outweighs other concerns; he had just better be right.

But in the meantime, Chosokabe keeps considering the influence of the kami, the spirits or gods, on the lives of all the people and a cornerstone of Shintoism. These are not anthropomorphic deities perched on Fuji-san, like the Greek gods residing on Mount Olympus; rather, they are the spirits of all living things, the creative forces, the remaining souls of great individuals who have lived before. And they reside in the heart of the Japanese people along with the influences of Buddhism, with its emphasis on recognition of the inherent suffering of all life and the need and means of lessening suffering or escaping it entirely. Chosokabe has more reservations about Buddhism; how can suffering ever be eliminated? And if the self is to be vanquished, as the religion prescribed, then what need is there for lords and servants such as himself? No, paying respect at the shrines and following the dictates of the Neo-Confucian code of bushido, the warrior's code, is a far more satisfying way to live, and he can always call on the kami for spiritual assistance.

When the two samurai locate the Nozomi Monastery, however, they at once understand the urge to escape from the rest of society. *The view alone from the forested* Kanto Mountains *would be well worth retreating to; neither of the young men has ever been this high before!* Near the red torii *gate entrance to the compound, they have an opportunity to pause and gaze upon the city. From here they can see everything, it seems: the castle and imperial palace, the city districts. Individual smaller buildings cannot be identified from this distance, but the sight humbles both men to the extent that for almost two minutes, they forget their mission.*

The torii *gate behind them represents passage from the physical to the spiritual, and is composed of three pieces of wood, the number being of sacred importance to the* kami. *Recalling their purpose, Kiyomori and Chosokabe offer the requisite trio of bows upon entering the gate, and at once make their way toward the few visible monks, who show no sign of offense or fear at the new presence of warriors. Kiyomori silently thanks his partner for the tenth time for not only knowing of this place, but its location as well. Some religious centers do what they can to remain hidden, and visiting them can be perceived as a potentially untrustworthy act.*

The man in charge of Nozomi Monastery *is an old but very peaceful man named Okahito, whose eyes fill with more light than those of Kiyomori or Chosokabe. He is shorter than they, with a rounder face and more angular nose. Indeed, the pair of* samurai *are sometimes taken for brothers, which amuses them, though they insist that most of their class look similar, with their dark hair kept in a tight and short pony tail in back, and shaved down to the scalp in the front but not the sides. Yet Okahito presents a far more serene expression, the look of one who knows the* kami *personally and who has found contentment in a happy life. The two* samurai *have not been surprised by the almost total silence of the monks, matched by the tranquility of the monastery itself, perched non-threateningly at the base of the mountainous woods. But they have already heard howling, and know that some of the monks have found wry amusement in the jumpiness of the courageous fighters which has accompanied that sound. The* noise seems unearthly, like the plaintive cries of lost souls. Perhaps the wicked and shameful are cursed to return to the world to live as wolves.

The wolves, too, recognize new sense data in the form of smells, though these particular canids have lived long enough around humans to not be bothered or feel endangered by the odors. They live quite well in Nozomi, though they all have their phases of feeling trapped, kept, isolated, wanting the risk mingled with autonomy which both come with freedom. Three of the wolves, to be sure, actually walk around the grounds without regular escorts; these are older former pack members, no longer able to get along harmoniously with their families. This can be quite common among captive predators: in the wilds, a wolf might either be unwanted or else become a lone wolf seeking its own pack, and in both cases, the whole world seems to beckon with the promise of this freedom. But here, where the regular packs live in large pens, emotionally isolated wolves must also be physically isolated or they may be simply killed by the rest of the pack as nuisances.

By now, Okahito has of course extended his hospitality to his curious visitors, who have politely declined, citing their need to return to the rest of civilization. Kiyomori is pleased that he has been able to discreetly broach the topic of wolves, praising the animals for their strength based on their noise. He delicately inquires about the prospects of hiring their services.

Okahito offers the most subtle of smiles at the man's request. "You have troubles on the farmlands to the south, then?"

For a moment Kiyomori feels he should be surprised at such knowledge. But then again, what other purpose would these wolves have, at least in terms of their working for a living? "Yes, Master Okahito. We seek to bring as many of the wolves as possible into several plots of arable land, which are even now overrun by deer."

"Perhaps planting should not occur where the plant-eaters are so plentiful," opines the master, though the samurai refuses to feel chagrined at this time; he has a job to do, and chooses not to answer. "Tell me, young samurai, what is it you truly want? The wolves, to help the farmers, or to ensure you do not risk the wrath of your lord?"

Chosokabe, *following the conversation, knows his own answer, but of course will not interrupt the other man's efforts. Kiyomori considers it, then answers: "All. I wish all of those things."*

"What ambition," notes Okahito, offering another of his miniscule and indiscernible smiles. "Very well, we can supply you with this service, and may we wish you and your lord well." The samurai does not seem to realize he has just been subtly insulted; he is both too young and too worldly to notice.

Samurai *as well as monks were never born to haggle, so a fee for wolf-service is agreed to quickly, Kiyomori wondering if it is too much, Okahito not in the least concerned either way, for he has long since learned what a transitory thing money is. The funds will go to the monastery's maintenance anyway.*

But it is when the warriors receive their first full glance of the beings whose labors they have just purchased that they both silently question the wisdom of their course. The animals are huge, silver and tan and black, with eyes that reflect the sun itself, even though it is now setting to the west, looking as though it will be swallowed whole by the angry opening of mighty Fuji-san. Just what have these men gotten themselves into?

Their concerns are allayed only slightly as they learn that the wolves will indeed be escorted by handlers, humans who have already known the beasts for years. Kiyomori and Chosokabe marvel at the simple torso and arm strength required to keep on one's own feet while attempting to walk something as powerful as a wolf on the prowl. Kiyomori has insisted that they leave at once, and this is acceptable, since wolves travel equally well diurnally or nocturnally. Still, the two nut-brown horses are having none of this. The two men have to run after them when their mounts first catch a whiff of the predators.

No amount of training, discipline, or sheer threats can force even the bravest horse to walk within mere paces of a wolf, and Kiyomori rapidly decides he will not chance losing face to a bunch of already grinning monks by attempting to cajole the horses into his desired behavior. "Chosokabe-san, you must lead the horses back to

Edo. *Once there, inform Lord Hachisukan of what we have done, and
request a detachment of ashigaru armed with naginata and daikyu
to follow you back to the farmlands tomorrow.*" *Both men realize that
this will be a hard ride, with Chosokabe arriving back to their lord's
holding late at night as it is, but that cannot be helped. And they do not
want more* samurai *involved: better to utilize peasants for what they
still view as a peasant task. Armed with the long halberd-like weapons
known as* naginata *and the longbows,* daikyu, *the infantrymen should
be able to assist in directing the monks and the wolves to the greater
concentrations of the other animals they now must hunt.*

*Kiyomori watches his friend leave, riding his own horse and
leading Kiyomori's by the reins. His hand then comes to rest across
his waist, as he feels the comfort of the sharkskin and silk-wrapped
covering of the hilt of his own* katana, *the elegant lightweight and
extremely sharp and subtlely curved sword that is the trademark of
his class. Anyone else handling such a weapon faces death; Kiyomori
often feels his own soul resides partly in his body and partly in his*
katana. *And right now he is just glad to be continuing with his strange
but not altogether unpleasant task. Sending Chosokabe ahead serves
two useful functions: informing Lord Hachisukan of their decisions
while removing the skittish horses. He hopes now that Hino and the
farmers shall prove more amenable to the idea of working with wolves
for a common goal.*

*Truly strange is this little episode, forgotten by most historians
and almost all contemporary Japanese as well. But there actually was a
time, perhaps the only one in known human history, when wolves could
be hired to assist with the hunting and killing which was considered too
troublesome or time-consuming for people to do otherwise on their own.
Kiyomori-san had no idea he had participated in a ritual so ancient as
to be almost beyond comprehension; he knew of no people who looked
like anything other than Japanese, though he had of course heard of the
white demons with their round and blue eyes who were only allowed in
Nagasaki for the purposes of trade. He certainly knew nothing of the
ancient Germanic persons who approached a new litter of wolf pups in*

the Black Forest almost one hundred and twenty centuries earlier, the only other souls we have considered who contemplated the prospect of attempting to utilize wolves for their own purposes: hunting, guarding, pulling, simple companionship.

The Nozomi wolves did prove their mettle and utility over the next few days, delighting in the easy hunting around the Edo farmlands for which Kiyomori and Chosokabe were responsible. Lord Hachisukan praised the young warriors in front of his whole household later, for the foresight of a creative idea. None of the skittish farmers or anxious infantry was hurt, though one of the wolves did escape from its monk handlers, the allure of wild freedom too strong to ignore, even in the presence of relatively easy pickings like deer. Being good jumpers as well as fighters, the wolves also killed a number of monkeys and boars. Hino was ecstatic, even overcoming his initial terror at the sight of the beasts to walk along with one of the monks. He could not contain his smiles or his relief as he ran his hands down through the fur of one of the wolves, letting his fingers explore between the longer guard hairs while feeling the softer and denser undercoat.

Getting so close to a captive wolf might be a rewarding experience, though in the wild they will continue to remain elusive to this day, as we catch up again to Morgan and her companions.

PART THREE: THE GREAT DIVIDE

"If you have men who will exclude any of God's creatures from
the shelter of compassion and pity, you will have men who will
deal likewise with their fellow men."
  - Francis of Assisi

"All beings tremble before violence. All fear death, all love life.
See yourself in others. Then whom can you hurt? What harm
can you do?"
  - Siddhartha Gautama, the Buddha

"You're hallucinating right now, you know," Jack says,
bordering on the annoyed but still smiling in that
childish manner that seems to make Mariska melt.
"You just don't realize it."

Dave is at once intrigued, knowing that such a statement
is likely a prelude to the sort of talk he has craved lately without
fully understanding why, rather than just a smartass comment
about recreational intoxicants. "Do tell," he says.

I can only barely hear this, of course, staring at the
brightly colored interior of my trusty tent. Jack's tent is
occupied by Mariska, who lay still asleep so far as I could tell,
since sounds travel easily through tent siding, and I think I can
pick up the sound of rhythmic breathing. At least I think she's
still out; we had a late night, and there hadn't been much "girl
talk" between her and myself prior to our crashing for the night
from simple fatigue, though she did want to let me know more
of the latest about her daughter, Rebecca.

I confess a mild envy for the close familial tie, and the
obvious emphasis on shared culture, something I occasionally
wonder about. Mom was more into our Irish background than
I ever was, or Dad for that matter; certainly neither of us speaks
Gaelic or anything, and it's of course quite easy to get swept

along with the good-spirited but often inane activities focused around Saint Patrick's Day. I still remember the shock I felt the first time Dave described his time in Chicago while working with the Fire Department, where the residents dyed the river green for the occasion. Maybe we've reached a point where we feel entitled to just pick and choose among varying cultural celebrations, to make ourselves feel like part of a particular group without any lasting commitments. Take Christmas. Despite the name, the holiday has nothing at all to do with Jesus, who was born in another season anyway, and now there are elements of Jewish Chanukah, Roman Saturnalia, Scandinavian Yule, the birthday of the Persian deity Mithras, all rolled up into this funky mélange of brightly colored materialism with spiritual elements trying to get noticed at the same time. In this country, it seems most of all to be about being a kid again, a way to bond with the younger ones. Maybe a cultural ritual is another type of hallucination, and I momentarily wonder about getting into the morning talk with Jack and Dave.

But a real kid, like Rebecca, or Dave's son Dennis? Is it to have someone to share one's experiences with, even though our species, or at least those who are part of American culture, seems notorious at resisting the proverbial wisdom of the elders? Gods, I can barely figure out my relationship with one of these two men out here, and other people think they can figure out children, whom Dave has described as the ultimate philosophy students because they keep asking: why? Why do we insist on learning so much the hard way: is it simple stupidity, or basic need? If the experiences are not our own, after all, then there seems little reason to pay attention to them. Weird. I've never really wanted kids, and there are lots of reasons, going back to that stuff I mentioned as a teenager the other day to Mariska, and I couldn't get some of this out of my head last night, and... well, shit. I mean, Dave never wanted children either, but he adores Dennis, talks about him like he bore the little guy himself, and I know Jack gets along famously with Rebecca, though that still leaves the question of Jack and Rebecca's mother, who isn't exactly known as a morning person.

But right now neither am I. The first nights back in the field are always the hardest, and that I couldn't turn off the old brain until very late did not exactly help. I can still fell Dave's arms holding me in a dance position, and while I admit I really wanted to share a tent with him last night, there was the oddity of Jack and Iska's timing, plus the fact that these one-person tents really are pretty snug. *Keep justifying and rationalizing, silly bitch. Why will you not admit you've probably always had something for Dave?*

At any rate, an early start today should prove a boost, especially since we're trying to cover a lot of ground on this trip. Considering our supply of food, we can afford to go one or maybe two more days uptrail, before we should really turn back, just to be on the safe side. We've not covered as much ground as initially planned, but that's fine; I've really liked how we've spent these first couple of nights so far.

Jack's voice again this time. The campsite is sufficiently secluded, but small enough that the trio of tents remain quite snugly near one another. Witness the myriad tracks left by Dave and yours truly last night from an improvisational round of dance. "Well, as soon as Iska limbers up enough to pull herself out of this mummy bag, I'll give you all the details," I hear from outside.

Grumbling from inside their shared tent, in an unmistakably un-feminine sounding voice: "Boys, go talk your highbrow stuff somewhere else. Some of us do not exactly function well without our daily caffeine fixes." She sounds surprisingly coherent for five hours of snoozing. I could hear them giggling last night, and while Dave managed to get to sleep quickly from the sound of things, I kept laying there thinking, and at one point could have sworn I heard Mariska and Jack having what must have been the quietest sex I've ever wanted to avoid hearing in the first place. Body fluids around a sleeping bag? Yuck! What effect would such have on the down insulation? *But there I go again, possibly just being jealous. How long now since someone besides yourself has brought about your own orgasm, eh, Morgan? And without the odd risk of Cozy mimicking your delighted shrieks or Angus jumping on your head right before or afterwards?*

"I'm waiting," Dave says, whose voice is now coming from greater altitude, so I know he's standing at the perimeter of our campsite. He wouldn't miss a glorious Alaskan morning view. That alone can cheer him up. I wish I could've seen his face right then, even woken up to it. So much for packing my larger tent, which still lay back in the car. Childishly and silently, I wish for him to have felt the same hopes. If I can summon more of that feminine emphasis on honesty, maybe I can ask him later.

"Okay," Jack says, over the sound of a tent zipper being opened and closed while he escapes the nylon sanctuary. I'm still intrigued by how a good tent will feel like a divine little respite when you crawl into it wet or exhausted or both, and like a stifling tomb the next morning when you just want to eat and hike more. The phrase "mummy bag" seems fair, though that's a reference to sleeping bag design. Still, I'd never want to stay in a tent much past daybreak, even in the winter. It gets boring in here, if for no other reason than your inability to see anything, although just listening to these friends keeps me content for the moment.

"I meant it, Dave. You're hallucinating right now. Trapped in the limitations of your own body. And the punchline is that it isn't really even 'your' body in the first place."

I can almost hear Dave's thick eyebrows crawling for the far reaches of his forehead, and can sense that he's looking my way, as though to summon my own input on such a question.

Who the hell can talk this way so early in the morning? "Explain how, then. And tell me also if this is your juvenile revenge for losing the argument two days ago about holding opinions."

Is that how long we've been out here already? "This is a counter-argument, as per your anally-retentive yet logically compelling request from that day. Vengeance has nothing to do with it. And I thought it wasn't about winning."

How long we've come from just last night, when physical activities dominated all, or so I thought. Now we seem headed back into intellectual pursuits. Actually, last night was hauntingly lovely, and I can still savor the laughter and conversation and ideas, although now that it's morning I can reconsider those with which I might actually agree. And I'm still trying to figure out how Dave got back into philosophy proper; I've always known him as a reader, but I typically see works of fiction in his hands. And then I remember his assessment that according to one modern thinker he's studied, there is more truth in fiction than in non-fiction. Weird; that one will take some time. Perhaps novelists truly are far more trouble than they're worth, since they seem to feel entitled to say anything at all. Maybe that's why I'm trying to work in journalism.

But still, working on the MFA at UAA *(is that enough letters for you?)*, most of what I had to compose for coursework was fiction, with occasional poetry. My actual journalism courses were fewer and further between, but at least reporting has a particular structure recognized the world over: writing in third person, with no emotion, and attempting to remain nonjudgmental, which of course these oddballs out in the woods with me think is impossible, though it might still be worth trying in the name of fairness.

The morning debate intrudes on my recollections and musings again. Having assured Dave of egalitarian intentions, and with Dave having assured Jack that arguing is indeed not a contest as such, Jack begins. "See this?" he says initially.

I of course cannot see "it," but Dave helps. "A spoon?"

"Yes. Describe it for me."

Dave pauses, wondering where this might lead, but he cannot resist leading questions, even if he ends up ambushed. "It's of a certain length, width, depth. It's made of titanium and is notched so the handle can act as a repair tool for your stove, since it was manufactured by the same company. It always accompanies you on your trips, so much so that you've never been the sort to accumulate those goofy collector spoons from tourist shops all over the world."

"Come on, Dave," Jack quips, acting more like Dave than like his usual accepting self. "That's the simplistic textbook answer. Next you'll tell me what it's for, and Mariska can probably let us know how long people have been creating and using spoons in the first place. But what else is it?"

Another pause. Then, "I genuinely don't know what you're after, Jack. It's just a spoon."

"No!" beams Jack. "You wanted to know the secrets which escape our notice, so here's one: this spoon is almost entirely empty space."

"Well, you're right. I mean, basic chemistry tells us that a single atom is mostly empty space, while basic physics tells us that the space might not actually be empty either, but might be occupied by other subatomic particles which are so unbelievably tiny that we'll likely develop headaches just contemplating them. But what are you getting at?"

"Your notion of a spoon is a hallucination," Jack says proudly.

Great, I think. *Who needs drugs when you have friends like these?*

But I'm also curious by how Dave, the inquisitive one, doesn't seem to be getting this. "Look at it this way," Jack explains. "If it's mostly empty space, why do you perceive it as 'solid' metal?"

"I admit I was still thinking of the empty space itself," Dave says. "I once heard an analogy to baseball and subatomic parts: if an entire Major League stadium was the atom itself, then the nucleus, consisting of all the protons and neutrons and accounting for almost the entire atomic mass, would be like a single baseball left lying on the pitcher's mound. And the electrons would be like fly and foul balls zipping around the stands, moving at the speed of light so the fans wouldn't even see them."

I wonder if young Dennis got that same analogy when Dave was still in Chicago; apparently they'd gone to ballgames at Wrigley Field a few times. I'll bet so, and further wager that Dennis thought the analogy was both cool and spooky.

"I like that one," Jack says. "That's good, but you haven't answered me."

"About the hallucination?" I'm sure Jack's nodding now.

"I guess it's just an accident of my limited nervous system. Since I can't perceive the atoms and all the vacant space they contain, my brain fills in the gaps, so to speak, and I am led to conclude that this 'spoon' is really totally solid. And it's not just my eyes that are in on the deception: it feels solid, sounds solid."

"Yeah. See? So this adds to the ambiguity, and to the relativism. Of course we can't trust our bodies, since they bullshit us constantly, so much so we don't realize it. So what's left? Reason?"

"What on earth got you interested in such a topic so early in the day, anyway?" David asks, mirroring my thoughts, to my infantile glee. Though I'm sure he's pleased to have found another backpacking philosopher. Jack only acts flaky sometimes, mostly since he switches jobs so much, but he's often quite insightful.

Jack's voice now sounds topographically higher as well; he's standing outside the larger tent, walking about the site and probably trying to warm up while doing so. It was pretty chilly last night. Inside my own tent is the evidence: the moisture from my breath condensing onto the linings. It's even a bit frosty along some of the zipper seams. "It's what you said last night after Morgan and Mariska went off to chat."

That perks up both ears. Probably Iska's, too, I should think, though there's no more sound coming from their tent. "Morgan, I apologize, but we weren't eavesdropping or anything last night. But we did hear that part about the unity of all things."

Should I reveal that I wasn't eavesdropping either, but that there's something about listening to other people's love which gives me just a bit of the creeps, especially if it's people I know? "No worries, Jack," I say from the bowels of the nylon burrito. "So what's on your mind this lovely if chilly morning?"

"Well, I don't want to sound nihilistic or anything," Jack says, with a confessional, conspiratorial near-whisper. I can at once hear Mariska rustling about in their tent, like she can't wait to hear what's going on. "But if we're all connected, and yet we have these limited bodies which give us limited and often flawed versions of the world, then how can we ever claim to know anything at all?"

"Ah, from metaphysics right into epistemology," Dave says. "That's a brilliant segue, actually."

"You just don't want to admit you're hallucinating," Jack insists.

"I haven't disagreed with you yet. I'm just waiting for your counter-argument."

"Well, the world as we know it exists at different, what shall we call them: levels. Right? I mean, there's the perception of our own selves and bodies, and the tents and trees and whatever else might be crammed into another of our 'I spy' lists. But there are other things we can't see, can't even detect at all, even though we seem to know a lot about them."

Emerging from my tent now, which seems fully real since I can see and touch and hear it, and after enough nights outside, I can smell it as well. And, hoping that nothing will be weird between Dave and I, and still refusing to care a great deal about how I might look after sleeping, I at once encounter both Dave's morning smile and Jack's apparent insecurity. That seems to be the emotional weakness of being asked to think.

"Such as?" David says, still meeting my own smile. *Good! At least he's not looking away or any other goofy shit like so many people do after a night of, well, of... what happened between us last night, anyway?*

"Such as the workings of the subatomic world. We could discuss quantum mechanics or individual atoms or the fact that no one's ever seen an electron, or a quark, or the big bang, or evolution actually occurring."

"Jack, do you want to talk about science, or about philosophy?"

Jack is more prepared this time. "According to you last night, there's little difference between the two. What was it you said, exactly? Money?"

"Sure," Dave adds casually, getting the joke, as am I, that he is currently poised over the same damn little stove which seemed to operate for us metaphorically just a few hours ago. He's already been savoring a classic early morning camp treat: hot cocoa from an instant powdered mix. Like I said, it all tastes great when you're removed from the trappings and temptations of civilization.

"Well, then, what does that mean? I'm getting tired of feeling like a dumbass here."

That, strangely, elicits a frown from Dave: one of *those* looks, when he's either angry or scared but doesn't want to show anyone which cards he might be holding. "Have I made you feel like a dumbass?" he says, the smile dissolved.

"No, you haven't, but our talks have."

"Jack, I talk about weird stuff like this because I'm trying to understand the meaning of life, if you'll pardon the asinine cliché."

"Why is it asinine?" comes Mariska's voice, herself crawling rear-first out of their vestibule, her boots sliding back onto her feet with the laces stored within them; they feel more relaxed that way. Once you feel your hiking boots securely tied, it feels like you need to get going right away, instead of savoring the morning.

Dave looks from Jack to Mariska to Jack again, though not to me. "Because it makes a bunch of assumptions: one, that life has meaning; two, that this meaning is singular and not plural, which rules out anything relative; and three, that I or anyone else is ever entitled to learn such meaning in the first place. But I never want anyone to feel stupid."

Mariska is still mid-stretch, her arms reaching for the heavens themselves. "On the first day of many of my classes," she says, "I inform my students that they should never feel intimidated by the people who wrote their assigned readings. I tell them instead that they should ready themselves to greet history on its own terms, try and make it a friendship, a meeting of minds."

Dave seems to like the sound of that. "Yeah, that's it. One of my old profs told me to," and he clears his throat and deepens his voice into a suitably academic growl, "never take any guff from these old thinkers! You should figure out what you believe and feel first, and then see which of these folks agrees with you."

"Did you really have a professor like that?" Jack wants to know.

"Yes, luckily. He was one of the few who kept me from dropping out of college and probably going through paramedic school that much sooner."

"Are you glad you finished the degree first, then?" I say, mentally taking notes of all Dave's gestures and mannerisms this morning. It's probably unfair to catalog them, but he does have this way of encouraging you to pay attention to him, on all levels.

"Yeah, I am, even though I haven't wanted to go back. Maybe I'm just taking that old prof's words to heart, and doing what may be no more than an ongoing independent study. I'll never get credit for my solo research, but what matters to me is the asking." Another turn to Jack. "And don't feel dumb, my friend. Certainly not on account of anything I have to say."

"Then tell me why money is the difference."

"Hmm? Oh, right: between science and philosophy. Well, the old test for science used to be testability itself." Mariska nods along with this; she's organized seminars on the history of science for her students. "And that was fine, so long as you were always dealing with the empirical, or the stuff we take for granted based on what our bodies tell us. Like Jack mentioned, there are tents and trees and ourselves right here, and we could hypothesize and experiment with them however we might want."

"Fine," Jack says, already sounding more relaxed. "And like the lovely Professor Kline here might tell us," a significant nod to Mariska, "that was how science really emerged as its own discipline, apart from pure philosophy and religion. We had to empirically test things to see if we could really understand how they worked or perhaps even what caused them."

"That's a good summary, Jack. Now, two things happen with science, roughly at about the time we enter the twentieth century, when a lot of people, including many scientists, felt that all the major discoveries and truths and facts had been learned."

I can't help sighing, personally. I'm still watching Dave and the others, but have opted for a seat on a nearby log adjacent to the stove, preparing my own steaming mug of chocolate mix. The smell is helping me become more attentive to my surroundings, and I can only sit back and wonder what kind of intellectual distance today's conversation might reach.

And I notice Dave casually but discreetly playing catch with some small object again, like a stone. But it looks blue or maybe green. I'll have to ask him about it later. The others don't seem to notice it.

"Maybe it was the notion that we had scientific 'laws' now," Jack opines. "That's the sequence: you notice something, you wonder about it and create a hypothesis, then you test the hypothesis." He seems like a prepared schoolboy; Dave elicits such responses from people, whether friends, coworkers, or strangers. Even his patients. I wonder how many others have heard about the cardiac patient he was once working on in the back of his ambulance who was close to death who wound up almost jumping out of the emergency bed two hours later to hug Dave for being so insightful about the meaning of death. Not the meaning of life, mind, but the meaning of death. That heart patient described Dave like part priest, part counselor, and left the hospital very much alive with a glow on his face.

Mariska, not about to be left behind (and not one to ever feel like a "dumbass," I'll wager), says, "And the hypotheses which seem to work most clearly and rationally become theories, and then the theories which no one seems able to falsify might get called laws. Although there are very few such laws: gravity, thermodynamics, the behaviors of chemical reactions which get named for their discoverers. And it is fascinating how every scientific law I know of deals with the physical sciences:

chemistry, physics, geology. But I do not know of any for the life sciences."

I finally pipe up. "Life is unpredictable. Who would've guessed we'd be debating the meaning of the universe after several days of no showers?" *And what, then, of evolution? You can't do biology without it, but it's still not a "law," even though it necessarily and truly occurs.*

Dave looks unabashed, finishes his drink, and tears open a pair of envelopes of instant oatmeal with which to complete his breakfast. "You're both right, though Mariska's getting ahead of me just a bit. The two things that happen to science are these. First, the emphasis gets to be placed on something later called falsifiability, rather than testability, which Iska just hinted at. After all, like Jack told us, we can't actually run tests to confirm the positions or activities of individual electrons, at least not directly. We can only infer and deduce their existence and actions from larger-scale effects, the kind we can actually see and touch and manipulate. That works brilliantly; it's perhaps the best example of truthful deduction I know of, since such proofs deal with what we can't see, and there's no longer any way to really deny that things like electrons exist.

"And then secondly, there's the start of a move away from the notion of science being a source of truth, but more as a source of what is the best estimate we can make at the time. Science is always supposed to be written in pencil, but a lot of people take this to mean that anything goes, that everything is relative, and that we really need something like religion to avoid the abyss of nihilism. It's like people will accept those same deductions, but they still want the comfort of relying on what their senses tell them, even though those same senses are very limited, and sometimes just wrong with the information they impart to our brains, like with Jack's spoon."

"But people want to know, don't we?" I say. "Why study science or read philosophy or practice religion unless we wanted to know things?"

"I agree," Dave says, "but then there's Jack's question from earlier: how the hell do we really know anything at all?"

That's the sort of devastating show-stopper of a question which silences us all, which is usually only asked by smart-assed teenagers who've just discovered the logical merits of skepticism while not yet realizing that the line separating skepticism and nihilism is genuinely quite subtle and easily missed. So instead, we take turns gathering our thoughts and proceed through the comforts of simple breakfasting and greeting a morning which appears promising. The brightening sky is clear, even if our minds aren't.

Although at a distance, to the northwest it seems, I could swear the snow line within and about the mountains is a little lower to ground level than when we left. We call it "termination dust" around here, an odd nickname for the inevitable arrival of another winter; you can just watch the grand white line sink lower and lower while the fall foliage completes its color changes, until the line catches you and you start planning to spend your days wearing more clothing and wondering when to possibly change tires to avoid sliding.

"But I'm not a nihilist," Dave's voice announces, from nowhere it seems, stirring his steaming oatmeal. "That's the last thing I'd ever want to be. That was the whole purpose in my argument about holding opinions: if we all really can just have any damn opinion we want, then again, anything goes, all is relative, truth vanishes along with responsibility, and nihilism reigns. And everything I believe and love and hope for is bullshit."

"I can only imagine what the members of the AFD must think of you," Jack says, whose expression seems to reveal a mix of awe and pity.

"I don't know, Jack. Maybe I no longer care. I think I need to get out of that business anyway: too much dealing with angry and frightened people, and the breaks that finally come after transporting a patient are filled with the truly intellectually stimulating activities of filing paperwork, and cleaning and restocking an ambulance." Dave quickly glances my way as if to offer silent thanks for our talk last night. "I like the people I work with, but I don't know what the hell to do anymore. You three are the only ones I can talk to like this."

I'm about ready to toss my arms around him and plant another comfort smooch on his saddened face, but there'll be time later, or so I promise myself. And besides, when a small group of persons you actually care about have made the kind of conversational progress like we have so far on this trip, are you ready to just give it up? I can think of several of the scenes of one of movie-junkie Dave's favorite films, *The Breakfast Club*, which all four of us probably had memorized over twenty years ago while making that agonizingly awkward move from middle to high school. There was a group of five stressed out teens in that movie, apparently having nothing to do with each other, who took advantage of time away from their regular lives during an enforced weekend detention to face their fears, remaining skeptical but never nihilistic. That's all that film was about, really, and it was magical. And since the four of us are already friends, shouldn't we be able to make even more conversational progress?

So here we all are now, in wilderness detention, each having that sense of a new fear: what if I'm not good enough? What if my loved ones don't love me enough? Am I doing the right fucking thing with my life? Is this really what life's about? Why is my dear friend Mariska the one who seems the most sure of who and what and where she is? Is it her cultural background, her temperament, or just good life decisions? And on, and on. It's like I told Dave: we want answers, never mind if they're actually true or not.

"Strangely, I know what you mean," Mariska says now. "You should hear the talks in my department sometimes. I like working with them also, but most of our meetings are just about procedural nonsense, and dealing with research, or problem students, or budget concerns. When is there time to talk about history making us into who we are, which is the reason I chose my field?"

No one says anything. There is just nodding. I can hear a woodpecker, and only Mariska turns toward the sound, forever on the lookout for avians. She told me once it must be the greatest gift of all to be able to fly, but she refuses to take piloting lessons, even though that would be an easy thing to do in a state where two percent of everybody has a license; she said she didn't want the magic of flying to go away. She could always alter her perspective by imagining life as a bird instead. Instead, it appears she's had a nerve struck. "The problem is that my field is also the one most susceptible to personal and political influences. A single history course only offers so much time to cover some period and place, and the decision about what gets left out seems a more sensitive and emotional consideration than what gets put in."

"How do you mean?" Jack says.

Turning back toward us, Mariska says, "I mean that if you do not know your own history, you can never know yourself. That probably sounds like another cliché, coming from an indigenous American, but it applies to us all. We all have our heritage and culture, which are as inescapable as these flawed bodies you two gentlemen have been discussing here today. But the problem is that there is little agreement about which parts of our histories need to be taught; recall what I mentioned recently regarding the elimination of a language."

"What do we do, Iska?" wonders Jack now.

"We accept the horrible along with the heroic, and try and learn from both so that future histories have less of the former and more of the latter. If you wish to be human you have to accept all of yourself, not just the glorified bits."

I once heard a silence described as "pregnant." That's what we have here, now. Some moments just have no words.

"So, as a counter to nihilism," Dave says anew, with just the trace whisper of a smile, "why not focus on what we really value?"

"That's it," concludes Jack. "I'm packing up so we can hike our way out of here." His tone is unmistakably friendly, paradoxically. He's likely as intrigued and/or perplexed by the recent changes in his friend. It makes me wonder why people seem anxious about asking questions in the first place, and when all is said and done, that's really all Dave's been doing all along. The part that scares people is that questions lead not only to potential answers but also to more questions.

And he's just been frustrated with his answers, despite the near smile reemerging. And in the meantime, I know how to peak Jack's interest again. "Dave, didn't you suggest last night, in no uncertain terms, that you'd impart the secret of living forever, some time before our trip ends?"

The playful Dave, the one who greeted me at my apartment recently to amuse my pets, beams through the uncertain countenance. "But I've yet to answer Jack's question."

The named friend shakes his head. "I don't even remember it anymore."

"We know what we know because we say we know it, Jack. Yes, that's begging the question, and makes me guilty of taking something for granted. But every belief is a value judgment, an assessment, an interpretation about the world. We have such tremendous leeway in terms of what to believe, but we have no say at all in whether we will believe."

Jack and Mariska steal a glance at each other, as if to say, "what the hell," and they start going through the motions of breaking down a camp to continue moving, an activity which really needs to be done earlier in the morning anyway, otherwise the will and the impetus both tend to diminish. Dave doesn't mind; he seems to recognize that we'll all hear, and hopefully actively listen, to whatever comes next.

And I think, right then, that there's something else, something mundane, that David Thomas has not shared with me recently. There has to be: no one just talks this much about such deep and heady stuff without some major event lurking in the background. Not during one's free time, anyway. Another one of Dave's favorite movies, I ♥ Huckabees, features a firefighter (okay, not exactly a paramedic, but still someone to whom Dave can relate for working with people having really shitty days before calling for help), who has a major crisis of, well, what exactly? Faith? Career or family issues? And this fireman has these curious "existential detectives" literally spying on the intimate details of his life to try and figure out what makes him tick, but in a more profound, philosophical sense. So this character poses the question: why is it only during a crisis or a time of major doubt that we ask the questions that otherwise only crop up in Philosophy 101?

"All I wanted to know is why money separates philosophy from science," Jack retorts. "You said they ask the same fundamental questions." He's inspecting their tent while he says this, acting as though he will actually pay monumental attention to a small spider working its way across one of the seams. He no longer kills them; it's like Dave's talks about karma got his attention. Or maybe it's just how Mariska once told him that the world would be overrun with insects, including Alaska's feisty mosquitoes, without the web-spinning arachnids. I still remember how entranced I was to learn that spiders fed certain intoxicants, particularly LSD, would spin flawlessly symmetrical webs, and that some American Indian tribes considered the effects of peyote, which was basically identical to the synthesized acid, as what might be called a *de*hallucinogen. Not a reality-blocker but an illusion-remover. So the purpose of a vision quest, in any culture, is to try and perceive the world as it truly is, at least in as open a sensory fashion as our bodies will ever be able to handle. Do the drugs allow more perceptions, enhanced perceptions, false ones? I don't know, but there's no denying that we do inhabit rather restrictive fleshy vessels. Try spotting what an eagle sees, or listening to a dog whistle, if you have trouble believing me. And those examples are pretty minor.

"And so they do," Dave says. "If you want to test one of those scientific hypotheses, because you think it might offer some insight into the workings of the world, then how do you test it?"

I can feel the wood of my perch securely beneath my posterior, and wonder if any of my companions have noticed that I've not taken my eyes off Dave for several minutes. Then I wonder why it took me so long to notice this fact myself.

"Simple," Jack says. "You design an experiment, designate your test subjects, and decide which is the crucial control variable, and then start observing what happens. That's why the experiments in school are always so boring: you always know ahead of time roughly what to expect, so they're not really experiments at all."

Mariska chimes back in again, apparently not ready to rummage through the same tent and start pulling out the stuff that needs to be organized back into her pack after all. "That is true. It is really only an 'experiment' if you do not know what will happen in advance. Otherwise, those science texts are just cookbooks for laboratories."

"Agreed," says Dave. "But what does it take to keep one of those laboratories up and running?"

"University funding, of course." This again from Iska, a veteran of more than one fund-raising event. I've heard her argue convincingly that a percentage of all corporate profits should be spent on public education, just like with the precedent for public spending on art.

Dave's grin is relocated. "Precisely. So, how do you get that funding? Who decides, in other words, which experiments will get tested, and which won't?"

Oh, shit, I think, scared of the knowledge that I recognize right where he's going with all this. It's my second serendipitous moment on this trip, so far, after that recognition during my seemingly random hiking break to notice the simple and yet painfully elusive truth that I am not separate from my surroundings after all. No, wait: is this my third such moment? Does realization that you might be in love with someone count as serendipitous? *Shit!* Now I can't even add.

Jack looks to Mariska as he guesses. "Aren't there college committees to decide this stuff, like which departments get which funding?"

And she's not skipping a beat. "Of course, but we in the humanities fields usually get considered last. Dave is correct: those labs are quite pricey. I surely do not work in one: there is no laboratory by which to study 'empirical history,' though I suppose funding for something like an anthropological study or an archaeological dig might come closer."

"But doesn't this mean that there has to be an agenda?" Dave suggests. "I just said that each of our beliefs is an interpretation: maybe it's literal, absolute, unshakable truth, but even then, how would we know other than to make a leap of faith? Or maybe the belief is just the best we can come up with, which does explain why our beliefs and our knowledge continually change, and why we differ so strongly, even violently, over them. The trade-off is that we get to keep learning, at the expense of having to face perhaps not being able to etch certain truths into marble blocks for the ages. So how do you decide which hypotheses to test in the lab, and which to ignore?"

"You submit a proposal to the relevant parties and ask for money, and the proposal has to be logically argued," I say, keeping my voice in a monotone, like I don't want to go letting cats out of bags.

Dave just nods this time. "Yet there's potentially an infinity of hypotheses, so when you choose one, you betray automatically your own beliefs and values, and try and make those mesh with whomever you're requesting the money from. But a thought experiment, which is where philosophy is left, has much more freedom. Naturally, there's a trade to be made here, too."

"How so?" demands Jack, frowning as would anyone, I suppose, who has just been told that the world is relative and not relative at the same time.

"With the scientific experiment, you get results that others can read about and replicate. You get agreement on a certain level, since anyone with just a little background education and training can follow your work, so long as they too have access to the lab. Plus there's the appeal of learning something about the 'real world,' so to speak. But with the thought experiment, you can test any damn hypothesis you want. You just plug in a little logic and then rationally try and assess the results."

"An example, if you please." Jack has finished paying attention to the spider.

"Wouldn't it be great if our gear just packed itself up?" Dave says. "Or my now empty mug of oatmeal cleaned itself in this beautiful clear running water? Instead of rolling up the bags, and unfolding the tent poles, and cleaning our breakfast dishes, wouldn't we rather just keep talking and listening to the birds and not worry about these artificial toys we lugged in here on our backs? There was a great commercial for something like that once: a woman gets out of her car, pushes a button on her electronic keychain, and the whole car folds itself up into a lightweight miniature and even jumps into her purse for her. I think it was the Sci-Fi Channel: no more looking for parking spaces or paying for tickets."

"What does this have to do with philosophy and science?" Jack wants to know.

"Everything. Wouldn't it be cool if we didn't have to fuss this way with our gear the morning after?"

"Sure, I guess. But what are you getting at?"

"I'm just conducting a thought experiment. I made some observations, considered what I might desire to come about, and then thought about the possibilities. If there really is a way to make our equipment and tents do all that, then I can test the hypothesis, invent something new, and make a damned fortune. In the meantime, all I can do is bemoan the fact that I have to do some age-old physical labor to help break down the campsite today."

Jack nods. "Okay, I think I'm getting it. I'll bet the scientists will be pissed off for your division, though."

"Why? I love science. All I've done is point out that it has a price tag, while philosophy, at least initially, is free. But true science, like true philosophy, is not supposed to ask ahead of time which questions are worth asking or testing. And since science needs technology and therefore needs money, we ask questions ahead of time anyway."

"When does philosophy accrue costs, then?" I think to add.

The same specter from last night crosses Dave's face, like it does when he describes the ugly scenes he's had to sometimes work as a medic. "Sometimes it can cost you your life."

I really don't believe Dave is trying to score points by introducing a dramatic flourish to his conversation; he's already been dramatic enough unintentionally, throwing some of his thoughts our way recently. As we all gaze at him, there is no sense of him wanting to be an actor offering some Shakespearean soliloquy to the chorus, like some Greek stage work. He doesn't even look at us. He's alone again. "Dave?"

He finally recalls us. "Consider those who asked others to think. Socrates. Laozi. Hypatia. Boethius. Wat Tyler. Joan of Arc. Albert Einstein. Helen Keller. John Kennedy. Martin Luther King. John Lennon. A thousand other philosophers. People who challenged others to use their heads. Or maybe those are extreme examples, since their celebrity factor is too big or because some of them were executed; thinking can still get you ostracized, your reputation ruined. We could consider Copernicus. Galileo. Rousseau. Hume. Spinoza."

My first time to feel like a dumbass today. I hate name-dropping; it's like a variation of using jargon to confuse, though I doubt Dave means it that way. "Dave, enough. We haven't read all these people, okay? Come back to us." I hope it doesn't sound pleading or angry.

"You're right. 'Sorry."

Leave it to Jack to lighten a mood. "Hey, buddy, since you're done with your breakfast, how about some help with this tent, which I'm fairly confident will not, after all, fold itself neatly up and hop into my backpack."

Mariska pauses at their tent, looking back at Jack. "Do you think that control exists?" she asks him.

"What control?"

"You mentioned control when talking about experimentation. You are supposed to control a test variable, which is allegedly the only difference between the two groups of test subjects. But do you think such control actually exists, or is it another assumption?"

Jack looks befuddled, but Dave laughs aloud: "There's no such thing as control! It's another belief structure." Jack winces.

"Then tell me, master, what good is experimentation?"

"It's actually very useful. I didn't say it was wrong." He pauses himself now, mixing some of the cocoa in his mug over the scant remains of his oatmeal, possibly as a stall tactic, leaving me wondering how much hot water is left. "I only said it requires belief. But every argument, every belief, every judgment we make, requires taking something for granted. We have to assume at least one thing as given, or else we could get nowhere. We couldn't even have a conversation otherwise."

"Like what?" Mariska says. "What, in other words, are you assuming right now?" She's actually started to pull the tent poles out of their securing eyes to fold them back up.

"That's easy," Dave says. "At the moment, I am assuming that I am truly in the Alaskan bush, that I am in the company of very good friends," another playful glimpse my way, "and that you are each able to comprehend what I'm uttering. Those are actually some major assumptions, if you really think about them."

Jack nods, seeming to like that better. "So then what about control?"

"With control, I'm just not sure there's any such thing as an independent variable. In fact, I'm convinced there's not."

Mariska, casually dropping the poles, then sneaks up behind Dave and starts tickling him, aggressively. I'm halfway between jealous and amused; Dave's as ticklish as Jack. "What are you doing to us?" she demands mid-laughter. "What has gotten into our old friend?"

Jack goes back to releasing the last of their tent poles from its eyelets, so that the structure starts to gently collapse. "Yeah!" he shouts. "You were easier when you just wanted to keep traveling as much as I try to. Now there's this huge crisis of faith. And maybe now you're Mariska's control test subject, and I'm the experimental one. God knows she tickled my butt enough last night."

"Literally?" I say, then decide maybe I don't really need to know.

"Well, not exactly. Modesty forbids..."

In between laughs and retaliatory gestures aimed at Mariska's nether regions, Dave tries to reply. "It's not a crisis when you're trying to figure out what you believe. My whole life, I've just believed the regular stuff: go to school, get a job, have a mid-life crisis, gripe about getting old and about how things used to be better as a way of reassuring yourself that you made some right decisions and held some right beliefs. But I'm tired, ouch, Iska, of the conventional crap."

"So now who has control of whom, Dave?" Mariska says. The two of them have squared off, separated, doing that goofy instinctive and wary circling of one another that members of other species might do when sizing each other up for potential combat.

Dave loves the attention; who wouldn't? And he's good at retaliating, too, eliciting some playful yelps from Mariska. It's good to see her lower her guard more on this trip; she so often has to display her own social "control" too, like with her job. Perhaps that's why people "escape" into the wilderness at all, to forego some of that social control. Maybe that's why we so often envy Jack, since he's the most carefree spirit among us: the world traveler, the job-dabbler, the one who seems aimless from a conventional perspective but who's likely the most "grounded" of us all, even if he's been befuddled lately by the results of Dave's off-duty reading list.

He's also completely refusing to help his erstwhile lover now, too, despite her appeals to him for aid. He just adds to the talk, instead. "Iska, it's like Dave said: there's no control. Just look at you now. Dave's got you."

"It's like with animals," I say, unsure where the comment comes from.

Mariska and Dave are on the ground now, completely filthy and mindless of the scratches they've likely accumulated by what my mother would have called "rough-housing," or my father would label, as my own favorite, "grab-ass." They pause long enough to look my way and await a response. They've not been this captive an audience for me since I howled the other day.

"Do tell," implores Jack, starting to roll up the tent, the dream of some nifty tent-rolling technology forgotten. "These two certainly look like animals now." Indeed, Mariska and David help each other up, still breathing heavily, and dust the major soil off themselves. Apparently they've had enough for now, and seem to await me.

"Well, I remember this talk I had with a couple of the staff writers at the *Daily News*. One of them was chatting about hunting and trying to predict the behavior of what he was after. I think he was trying to obtain a bear permit that year. Anyway, he thought that we could more or less control animal behavior, in the sense that all species are predictable. But the other writer disagreed. She said that bears and many other species, including us, have at least some free will and at least some consciousness. She insisted that most living things are too complex as individual systems to merely be automatons." *Despite what Descartes kept saying, the prick. And if "I" am really a conglomerate of trillions of cells like Dave reminded me, then how could someone ever hope to reliably predict the behavior of the composite "me?"*

"So what did you all decide, then? Or was there no resolution?" Mariska says.

"Oh, I added something I got from my high school biology teacher. There are only two things I remember from old Mister Browning's class. One is the archaic taxonomy, which has been highly modified since then anyway: kingdom, phylum, class," and the others all chime in mechanically, having received the same basic education. "Order, family, genus, species," we all chant together, giggling, probably each recalling images of dissected frogs and diagrams of the "branches" of organism classifications.

"See?" Dave says, his regular breathing restored. "Another attempt at control. It's an attempt to establish order. It works somewhat, but it's just a tool, a human filing cabinet. Not everything fits into it cleanly and neatly."

"God, Dave, let the woman talk," Jack orders. "And the second thing?"

I can still picture short Mister Browning, dressed always in that stereotypical tweed jacket, like he was disappointed for not teaching in a college instead of a public school, though he was a fine teacher. He loved playing in the lab, watching things grow in petri dishes, and tending to our assorted "lab pets:" a snake, a pair of frogs, several freshwater fish in a tiny aquarium. I wonder what he'd think of our talk of science and values. "The second thing was another way to describe a species. Like Dave here, this teacher of mine loved logic, and he thought it was cool that there were four basic categories in this case. He used to illustrate this point using a square divided into four equal sections, like you do in biology with Punnett squares to predict the genetic ratios of offspring." *But you can only do that with very simple traits; most of them are far too complex to be predicted with much accuracy, and since genes don't seem to possess free will or consciousness, it seems this is another vote in favor of the inherent unpredictability of bears and other creatures.*

Nods from around the campsite now. They remember. "Man, I hated studying Mendel. He always seemed so boring," Jack complains. "Still, it's impressive what he accomplished, though it must have been mind-numbing to watch all those pea plants grow. That's life in a monastery for you."

"What were the four options?" Mariska says. Dave is actually leaning forward, hanging onto whatever words follow.

"A species, and any of its members, whether it's a plant or an animal, can be either tame, or it can be domestic. Additionally, it can be both, or it can be neither. We wrote those four possibilities in the squares, with the headings 'tame,' 'untamed,' 'wild,' and 'domestic.' And then we just considered a bunch of examples."

"Like what?"

"Well, how about dogs?" I ask them.

"Domestic," Mariska says. "And hopefully tame, too, though perhaps not."

"No doubt," Jack says. "We've probably all been chased by mean dogs before."

They seem to be getting it already. "Okay, then, what about horses?"

"Wouldn't that depend on whether these are domesticated horses, or wild running ones that no one's ever 'broken' before?" Dave asks.

"Exactly," I answer. "Genetically, they're the same. They could interbreed and have fertile foals, but their behavior's totally different. The tame ones are those you can ride or hitch to a wagon or sled. But the wild ones have to be tamed. And they're still considered wild or domestic, depending on their behavior."

"So are horses ever truly domestic then?"

"According to what I've said, I don't see how they could be, at least not to meet the definition. After all, if you turn one loose, it might do okay on its own, depending on the environment, unlike most domestic animals, which tend to lack the survival skills of their wild counterparts. Horses would die here in the wilds, since it's too cold and they need shelter just like us, though a released horse in Wyoming might be fine. But the whole point of that class period all those years ago was to consider genetic changes: a 'domestic' animal is one that has undergone genetic alteration, typically at the hands of humans."

I let that sink in, then ask, "What do you see when you look in a mirror?" I can still hear my old teacher's voice asking the identical question.

Some heads shaking now. "The answer is," I tease them, "a domesticated primate. That's basically what we are, what we became. And the genetic changes became more pronounced, though it took a while. We can't interbreed with other primates, not even the other great apes. But wild horses can interbreed with farm horses or with race horses. And dogs can interbreed with wolves and coyotes and dingoes. The problem is in labeling, like Dave was saying. Ability to interbreed is supposed to mean that you and whomever or whatever is sharing your bed is a member of the same species. But we saw the problem with horses. And this now begs the question about the differences between dogs and, say, dingoes or foxes."

"I think I see part of it now," Jack says. "The tameness of something is its ability to handle being around the likes of us, but whether it's domesticated depends on what we did to its ancestors."

"A bit crude, maybe, but that's basically it. It's like shopping for groceries. All the fruits, vegetables, and meats came from domesticated species. You can't buy venison in a supermarket anymore than you can buy crowberries. The items wrapped up in the food shops are different now: we raised the plants to grow faster, or taste 'better,' or grow in environments they wouldn't have been able to survive in before, like those pumpkins nearing four hundred kilos people raise for the Alaska State Fair. And the flesh comes from domestic livestock, the animals we raise. In Alaskan markets, the only truly wild foods I've seen have been in the seafood aisle: fish and crab caught in local waters."

"But there are a couple of weird things about all this," Dave says now.

"True," I continue. "Like you were saying, there's always a price, and not just with the logic and the imperfections of what you called a filing cabinet. In the case of domestic animals, they're just not very bright compared to their wild ancestors. Domestic cattle and sheep are especially stupid. I mean, it's not like wild cattle and sheep are geniuses, but they have more going on upstairs than farm animals do. And in the case of domestic plants, typically they're just bigger, sweeter-tasting, and maybe more resistant to certain insects and diseases, or sometimes less so, like when a bunch all fall prey to some infecting organism. That sort of thing has happened to both Central American bananas and French wine grapes, just in the past century, and both crops almost vanished forever. And when you see something like all those types of wild berries growing around Alaska, they'll always seem tiny compared to what you can find in the shops."

I knew that would get Mariska's mouth watering, a woman who grew up running about in the summer and fall with her relatives to harvest those fruits and who knows which other plants. I can picture her with several shades of dark berry stains on her hands and clothes, rushing about with the excitement of one who wishes to pick every last berry in the world. She knows ancient medicinal uses for so many leaves and roots I can barely take it all in, and she's long since memorized recipes for not just the berries, but for other parts of our wild plants, too. And yet there's never been much agriculture up here. That's what I was talking about with subsistence during our drive, and "living off the land," but the indigenous Alaskans have managed that for millennia without farming, without forcibly domesticating other species in an effort to control them (with the possible exception of wolves), without noticeably changing the landscape.

And that was the Great Divide, I recall her saying once before. Historically, the very advent of agriculture was what gave some humans the notion that they were separate from the rest of the world, from nature itself. But only some: people in Africa and Asia and America typically held onto the more ancient view, though they came to be seen as primitive by the Europeans, who really got it into their heads that they were different.

And when you're "different," you're either an outcast, which no one wants to be. Or you're special. And what better proof of being "special" than to be able to say, "Look at all these creatures I've domesticated, plants and animals alike, so that I now have a food surplus and can designate more creative tasks for my clan and tribe members, and try and dominate them as well as nature. Look at the civilization which grows from this."

Agriculture enabled the coming of religion to replace mysticism, thoughtful art to replace simple imagery, and philosophy and science to show up at all. And it also gave us the illusion of being separated from the other creatures upon whom we depend for simple survival. And it turned old allies into new enemies.

Mariska once told me about wolves in particular, or maybe I'm just remembering it now that we were just talking about canines: how contemporary research was beginning to verify that these social pack-based creatures taught us how to work as a team for hunting, and how to work together to raise our young (things the other great apes do very differently, so we couldn't have learned such from them). But when we had domestic livestock, the wolves began to be perceived as a threat, so we had to try and tame them, too: turn them into "man's best friend."

These images race through my mind, and I'm then whisked back to the conversation, recalling something about domesticated foods. "And if the logic holds, Jack, then we should actually be less intelligent than wild primates, shouldn't we?" Dave says, grinning like the Cheshire Cat who teased Alice. That gets Jack laughing anew, so he has to pause while gathering his gear.

"Dave, remember when I used to tease you for having a big head?" Jack says. And I recall that it wasn't the typical commentary about having an inflated ego; David literally has a larger than average melon sitting atop his shoulders. He nods in response.

"Don't you see now that Morgan's given us an answer? Size doesn't matter after all. Hooray! Insecure men the world over can rejoice. Insecure women, too, one supposes."

"What the hell are you on about?" Dave says. "And you think *I* talk strangely!" Mariska and I are already giggling. I can hardly take time to wonder about the most fundamental chapter of human history when Iska, in a gesture out of the vision of the men, grabs both of her breasts and simultaneously lifts and squeezes them, in a universally accepted gesture that size shouldn't matter after all. I actually hunch over from laughter at that; if her students could see her talk about the Great Divide now!

"I mean, you're right. And since we also know Morgan's right, but we don't want to admit that we might likewise be less brilliant than our wild genetic counterparts, well, it just reminded me of something. What the hell are you two laughing at, anyway?"

That, of course, just makes us laugh even harder, to the point that Mariska and I have tears beginning to shine in our eyes. Why are things even funnier when shared with just one or two others?

Jack just shakes his head, another confused male unused to the fact that we women will be just as rude and raunchy as men, but we keep that little agenda usually hidden. Dave just raises an eyebrow and listens to Jack. "I used to actually wonder if you were so bright because you just had more actual brain tissue in that scary head of yours. But then I remembered: by that logic, whales are far and away the most intelligent things on the planet. Elephants should be able to do calculus from birth onward. And even the local moose around here would outperform you on any standardized test. That just struck me as funny."

"Size doesn't matter," Dave repeats, shaking his head. Mariska and I can still hardly keep from laughing; between the two of us, we've probably tried the false comfort of that line on several different men, knowing how asinine it sounds in its usual sexual context. I mean, to be a good lover, attitude is what matters, far more than the size of the "naughty bits." Well, that, and a simple capacity for joy. *How much joy is left in Dave's heart?* I wonder. I want him suddenly to still be able to feel, and to be more hopeful. I'm no longer sure he's cut out for this emergency work; he cares, sure, but maybe he's too close to the job now for it to be healthy. *At least he's in a good mood today. Like last night.*

Wanting to change the subject a bit, Mariska veers off, with Jack yet none the wiser about her copping a self-feel: "There remains something I wonder about now, though. Morgan, you mentioned that discussion with the other newspaper writers. How did you resolve that?" She wants to get back on track with the guys, our private girl joke having run its course.

"How do you mean?" I say back, flicking a tear from each eye and deciding that it might truly be time now to finish collecting our gear and pressing onward. We've already been at this site long enough, delightful though it's been.

"I mean," she says, "what did you all decide about this ability to predict behavior, of bears or of yourselves? With what we have discussed here about control, is it just a way to reinforce the belief that we really are free? Do we truly decide our own destinies?"

Leave it to Dave to answer before I have a chance. There are times when that gets annoying. "We want to believe in free will. But desiring something hardly makes it automatic; think of my tent-packing toy. The existentialists emphasized freedom along with responsibility for your actions. But a lot of psychologists, meanwhile, and some other philosophers, said there's no such thing. Skinner insisted freedom is an illusion, another of Jack's hallucinations."

But I insist on my own answer; my sympathy for Dave does not include being outshone by him when I can hold my own. "It's difficult, Dave, partly to explain and partly since I need the chance," I begin, "since Skinner has to be right in order for conditioning, or any type of training, I suppose, to take effect. And anyone taking a basic psychology course gets introduced to Skinner, though I don't imagine many of those college freshmen get into this underlying consideration of what's really at stake. And I want freedom to exist as much as anyone. I can't stand the thought that I had little or even no choice but to accompany you all out here."

"What do you mean about training?" Jack wonders.

"Think of our earlier examples, like dogs and horses. We like them so much partly because those are both eminently trainable species. It's why some people dislike cats, but cats are no less trainable; it just takes more patience and more repetition, since cats are smarter than dogs and horses, and would thus prefer to follow their own agendas. The cat-haters just reveal themselves to have less patience. But you can pretty easily get a dog or a horse to do some basic behaviors with a simple system of rewarding. It soon becomes habit, for them as well as for the trainers."

"The same applies to us," Dave says. "That's what I was alluding to before by mentioning my avoidance of the 'typical' life so many of us lead."

"Then, the gods themselves help us," Jack says, "but we're becoming a bunch of wilderness loving existentialists!"

That amuses Dave and Mariska, but now I opt to return to Dave again. "So now you've answered Jack's queries, but again, what of the immortality you promised last night?" Maybe I'm demanding just to get back at him for verbally cutting me off.

"Yeah," says Jack. "Don't tell us you've found religion."

"I tend to believe that religion finds you, Jack," suggests Mariska. That's one of the loveliest sentiments I've heard from her, though I suspect Dave might tear it apart rationally. Then again, religion's so easy to abuse, which is why he'd want to tear it apart at all. Instead, he teases us. "This bit about free will is part of the immortality. But let's save it yet. Like Jack, I'm looking forward to hiking some more."

* * *

John Graydon was trying to decide if his younger brother had gone utterly crazy, or if he was starting to make sense. Benjamin insisted they could get in one more excursion to the area south of the Denali Park lands, both National and State, before winter really decided to set in. He was not about to admit to his elder brother that he was still a little shaken up over being temporarily left alone with the wolf carcasses, when he all but swore he could hear other creatures out to get him. He spoke instead of how the most beautiful hunting was to be done in the fall: gorgeous colors, prey which were easier to spot and track, a decline in mosquitoes and temperature.

In the meantime, the pelts had brought some decent money, and were still being processed even now, after their initial sale, to provide the eventual wares which would line the shop windows in downtown Anchorage. Either locals or tourists might take interest in them at that point, though many of the latter, depending on where they hailed from, still felt guilty about buying furs, even if Anchorage was not a city in which a human wearing a fur coat was likely to be splashed with red paint from protesters. The Graydons always had trouble understanding that: such coat owners often had individual possession insurance policies, so the insurance firms would replace the coats anyway, which in turn perpetuated such business, which automatically entailed the slaughter of more fur-bearing animals. And additionally, the protesters seemed to ignore the leather which often comprised their shoes, belts, wallets, jackets. Even the plant fibers making their jeans were parts of things once alive, but no one protested the cotton or flax or hemp industries on charges of cruelty. John and Benjamin had killed the wolves quickly; they made a point of doing so. That was what had so irritated John about the poachers: trapping was based on fear and painful, stressful death, typically by strangulation. And baiting completely eliminated any thrill of discovery or chase: any moron could lay out food and then shoot whatever creature came along to inspect it. He'd tried explaining this to his younger brother several times, and he thought now Ben understood how John felt like their attitude was in between the extremes: the counterproductive and senseless cruelty of trapping on one side and the often irrational and even hypocritical protests of those who opposed all forms of hunting and farming. In the case of the one, there was no moral justification to be any less sympathetic than the world already was, and with regard to the latter, where on Earth did the protesters think their food came from?

John Graydon had been having such thoughts while walking with his brother, admiring the admittedly brilliant fall blaze of color emanating from the surrounding vista, already indicated by Benjamin: the taiga in this region was exquisite, and he sometimes wondered why most tourists didn't stick around long enough to enjoy it. With the peskier insects quickly dying for the year, and the fiery gold and crimson in the countryside, what was there not to love? Even those who suffered from "bearanoia" could take heart in knowing that Alaska's residents of the ursine persuasion would soon be retiring to their dens for the winter, so why not savor more of the landscape now, before it was completely covered for another long winter?

Talkeetna was quite a small town, though connected enough to the larger world for those who began to miss it. Wintering here was far easier than, say, McCarthy, which lay at the western edge of the gigantic Wrangell-St. Elias National Park; that town was considered crowded if it had more than a few dozen souls in the summer, and in winter its human populace fell to perhaps twenty or so, and they were truly isolated. So were countless other settlements in Alaska, but the Graydons enjoyed access to the trappings of civilization, at least once in a while. They both loved jazz, for instance. On more than one occasion they'd stolen down to Anchorage for a night over in a cheaper bed and breakfast just to partake of a night at the local blues club, and rarely went to hear someone more famous at the Performing Arts Center downtown.

And even Talkeetna had a place where furs could sell, though it offered little by way of live music (the occasional bluegrass or local jam session notwithstanding). It only had a few hundred intrepid people willing to live there year-round, plus a miniscule station for the Alaska Railroad, and the airstrip where the brothers had landed coming home recently, before hurriedly driving out with a pickup truck and a flatbed trailer to fetch their well-loved ATVs from the boat. And now, in this place which could feel its own isolation, Ben Graydon was apparently itching to return to the wilds already.

"Where exactly were you thinking of having us go?" John said, as they finished their walk and found themselves back home. On the one hand, John loved having no family commitments beyond his brother: a wife had left long ago, no longer wanting to be so removed from an urban area, and she'd headed back to Denver, which she said was sufficiently mountainous for her. The running joke about Alaskan ratios of men to women ("the odds are good, but the goods are odd") had finally gotten to her, and John had begun to seem too much like some weird mountain man for her. And neither brother had kids, and while they knew many of the other residents of Talkeetna, they preferred to keep to themselves in back country: too many persons on the same fishing or hunting expedition were clearly a case of too many proverbial cooks spoiling the soup.

"What about that area where we had good luck with that moose last year?" Benjamin said.

"What, you mean just west of home, here?"

"Yeah. We're still in GMU 13, but you're not suggesting we go after moose again, are you?" John peeked above and behind his brother's head; as they sat now in their small but workable kitchen at the dinette table, preparing to brew some fresh coffee. He thought he knew the answer, but seeing the calendar, his brother's choice with bikini-clad women of Alaska photographed enticingly for each month, confirmed it. "It's past moose season now, anyway."

"Well, sure it is, bro. And I don't want to be dragging some big-ass moose back home this time of year, anyhow. I'm talking about smaller stuff, or at least, maybe just a little fishing."

"Ben, if we try fishing west of here, we're only likely to have much luck near Chelatna Lake, and the ATVs won't get over the Kahiltna River." The river was fed directly from the glacier of the same name just to the north, so it was silty to the point where you couldn't really see the bottom even in the parts near the banks where depths could be measured in mere inches, though the rapids could be many feet deep.

There weren't exactly many species of fish lurking in such an inhospitable environment.

"Right," Ben said. "But over towards Little Peters Hills, or even a bit further north where the mines are, would be good. It's gonna be a long winter." Benjamin, in truth, was a poor climatic prognosticator, and often said it would be a long winter, just because there wasn't as much hunting and fishing to be done. And living in this small town throughout the seasons wasn't just potentially lonely, despite the friendliness of many of the locals; work was quirky here. Summers were easier: plenty of folks worked as guides, for hunting, fishing, photographing. Many others sought regular, if seasonal, employment with the Railroad, or acted as flightseeing pilots. Then there were the numerous contributions to the hospitality industry, though business at the local B&Bs, inns, and restaurants of course dropped quite notably during the off-season, and there weren't many jobs here in educational or governmental fields.

On the other hand, the Graydons, taking pride in their mutual spirit of wilderness-loving, had done most of these jobs at some point. Benjamin had an aptitude for small engine repair, had done some schooling all the way down in Seward at the local vocational college for that, and was considered about the best in town. Older John had done everything from high school security and teaching to guiding fishermen to entertaining tourists riding the rails with his tales of life in the Bush. He knew he had to get in line again for work this fall, and it was too late to get involved with school, unless he wanted to just work off and on as a substitute, which was not his favorite vocation.

But he was good with money, or more specifically, not wasting it. That was the other thing about his soon-to-be ex-wife; Denver was also a far more impressive place to go shopping, and while she hadn't exactly spent to the point of breaking them, she nonetheless hated the way Alaskans often dressed, and was likewise not altogether fond of John's very well broken in pickup truck, or the house he now shared with his younger brother which, while sturdy, dry, inexpensive, and easy to maintain, just wasn't very showy. The brothers had stopped lamenting the fact that some women were just more focused on being showy, especially those from outside the state; they knew that those concert-goers down in Anchorage would wear everything from t-shirts and jeans to tuxedoes and gowns.

So the thought of heading out one more time was a possibility, at least from a financial perspective. It was far cheaper to hunt in Alaska when you lived in the thick of it, without having to buy airline tickets and hire out guides and equipment.

"Remember that old black bear who got away from us up in the mines?" John said. The empty ghosts of several placer mines were still in the main Peters Hills, the more dedicated locals and tourists alike taking pride in periodically venturing out with their pans past the end of the Petersville Road to try looking for specks of gold the old-fashioned way. John didn't think he'd ever pulled out more than a couple hundred dollars that way, but it was fun as hell, made them both feel like old mountain men from another century.

Benjamin laughed, pouring coffee for both of them, one of the few products for which both men were willing to spend a bit more money on the good stuff. "Of course! That pesky old critter just stared you down, like it was ready to quit. I think it must have laughed itself silly when you noticed your safety still on."

John indeed had felt embarrassed that day, but appreciated that maybe that bear wasn't quite ready to cash in after all, despite the lightening of his hair and his slight limp; he'd still managed to escape into the woods, and the brothers had lost him within a couple of hours. "All right," he agreed.

"Let's get outta here again. But next week, it's back to work for both of us!"

* * *

The brown bear was huge, even for the standards of its own kind. Foxtrot, Puddles, and Sterling could hardly believe the enormity of such a creature, and they were already trying not to whimper while silently wishing that Bear Heart and Owl Eyes were close by. They would know what to do!

The pups were feeling mischievous, especially Foxtrot, whose muzzle was well on the mend in its absence of quills, and, like adolescents everywhere of every kind, the trio felt the need to prove themselves. Maybe it was just the excitement of seeing what they could get away with. So they'd spent most of the morning, while David Thomas and Jack Godwin debated the inadequate sensory experiences of spoons, dashing further and further from the rendezvous site and leading poor Tornado along to keep up as best he could. The large wolf pups had already covered over three kilometers, and the other adults were once again largely on independent prowls. Summertime and even early fall were periods of solo exploration, a time to get away from the pack for hours or days or weeks, until winter encouraged the regrouping of all members; smaller prey animals were more difficult to find and catch in winter, which left the larger species, which in turn were more challenging to bring down and required multiple wolves.

The younger wolves meanwhile did not quite comprehend that the reason for this bear's size was her recent gorging of a delectable mix of fish from Chelatna Lake. There existed a luxurious fly-in lodge on the lake for the humans, and the bear wisely avoided this facility, even if the people who frequented the place were more likely to merely hope for a glimpse of bears, rather than to bring home a future pelt and a great deal of gamey meat. But humans or no, the lake was too good a resource to pass up: all five types of salmon returned the huge distance from the ocean in order to spawn within, and the long narrow body of water was also inhabited by two kinds of trout, plus grayling and pike. The brown bear sow, who was also pregnant and thus prone to eating even more than the already huge amounts one might expect from a bear soon to be in search of winter quarters, had trouble with the indigenous lake fish: smaller, harder to spot, though she did once plunge her head into the chilly water and snag a surprised pike in her maw. Fattened up now on hundreds of kilos of easier to catch salmon, especially their fattier skin, she was merely heading southeast, and unwittingly into the pack's territory.

That was the curious thing about marking territories, whether via the urine marks and scat piles left by wolves, or the walls and political borders created by humans: only members of one's own species really cared about (or could even typically recognize) those boundaries. Accordingly, the sow had no clue she was venturing into wolf terrain. She was used to scent marks, of course, but typically only paid attention to those left behind by other bears.

Foraging on the now ripened berries and seasonally omnipresent sedges and other greens, she might have barely noticed the inquisitive wolf pups had they not been feeling feistier as of late, particularly after their run-in with the porcupine. Granted, there seemed little reason to flee at the sight of a bear, even an invasive one like this; maybe she could be persuaded to play. Young wolves never tired of games.

So they watched, at least for now. The bear was still young and strong, only in her fourth year, though the wolves noted that her movements were a bit ungainly, usually a sign of inherent weakness that could be exploited while hunting. Tornado hoped that the pups would not foolishly try and take advantage that way, but he need not have worried: the bear was simply too big, as well as too strange and unexpected, for the pups to take much closer notice.

Or so he hoped. Tornado's gaze alternated between the pups and the bear.

Filling up on as much of a high fat and protein diet as possible for weeks at a time did have a way of making one a bit clumsier and slower than usual; the bear would be thin again come spring, the extra calories needed to get through winter in a den, especially with the extra fuel needed to bring live young into the world. Despite what many believed, pregnant bears did not hibernate through their deliveries (any pregnant mammalian female should be glad to confirm otherwise, since birth pangs do have a way of waking one even from the deepest of slumbers). But slightly off-balance or no, a pregnant she-bear simply trying to cover some ground was not a creature that one typically blocked or otherwise interfered with. Still, the pups just had trouble resisting.

Tornado, still realizing his responsibility, wondered why these three pups in particular were the pack trouble-makers; *he* certainly never acted in such worrying ways when he'd been this age. So he continued to try and keep all three of the youngsters simply in view. Sterling was easy: the female's coat almost reflected the sunlight on a day as bright and clear as this one, and she could be spotted from a greater distance because of it. Puddles, a mix of tan and black and very little of the lighter shades which typically colored *canis lupus*, had an easier time camouflaging himself, though he was so adept at making noise by bounding about that his shading sometimes hardly mattered. And Foxtrot, with a lighter belly shifting seamlessly to beige flanks and black and silver back striping, was the only one among them who could stay both quiet and close enough to the ground to often escape detection by other creatures. Like his namesake, he was quite adept at skulking and sneaking, sometimes taking delight in getting as close to the adults as possible, especially Rendezvous the *omega*, without being noticed. He'd likely prove the most capable hunter as an adult.

All the pups had to do in the meantime was survive that long. Tornado remained unconvinced that toying with a bear was among the better ways to do so.

Draw a huge 's' and rotate it ninety degrees in either direction, then widen and superimpose it with one end encompassing the East Fork River to just south of where it gets continually fed by the glaciers of the mighty Alaska Range, and rest the opposite end right on the far side of Mount Yenlo, eighty kilometers west of Talkeetna, and you have a rough assessment of the Chelatna pack's homelands, contained within the border of this area. Tornado and the pups currently found themselves north of this mountain and south of Chelatna Lake, right at the border of their territory in part of the straighter portion of their grand 's.' And they kept observing the sow from the safety and reduced visibility of a blend of marsh and low woods. It was like alpine tundra, with its lower amount of tree cover, and the marshlands were often a good spot to locate moose, though the caribou cared less for it. It was also easy and fast to travel upon when frozen, though millions of mosquitoes also took advantage of these wetlands during the summer. Fortunately they were already dying out rapidly for the year, not to be missed by mammals.

The sow, content just to amble for now, remained yet wholly oblivious of the presence of the predators. Her concern was primarily with checking on her old denning site, which lay on a small hill overlooking Sunflower Creek. The waterways in this area (dozens, feeding into active wetlands) did flood a bit with the spring thaw, right when the bear would emerge from the den with her one-to-three newly born cubs, but the site was well protected and the waters would not be so dangerous for those cubs, who would be as curious and playful as Sterling,

Puddles, and Foxtrot very shortly after their crawling out of wintry darkness.

The fact that Tornado had never previously encountered this bear was what caused him the most concern of all. She was heading right for the center of their territory; indeed, her old den site lay just a short distance beyond their farthest border, and he, like the other adult wolves, had scent- and scat-marked the area many times. So how had they missed the sow? Carefully positioning himself downwind, and making sure the goofy pups had done likewise, he already knew by scent alone that he'd never laid eyes (or nose) on this bear.

The reverse of that applied, too. The sienna-colored sow was content with a much smaller territory, and while she was hardly predisposed to permit other bears to often travel through her home (the now absent father of her future cubs notwithstanding, who himself was now north of Chelatna Lake, working on his own feeding and other winter preparations), she was willing to tolerate minor incursions. She stopped suddenly, for no reason discernible to the wolves, and sniffed.

All types of bears could stand well-balanced on their hindquarters, sometimes for minutes if properly motivated, just to take in the additional sense data offered by occupying more vertical space. Ursine nasal passages seemed to be as sensitive as those of wolves, and their vision was just as good, approximating that of humans, and the view truly was more impressive when one could, even if just temporarily, take it in from an altitude of two to three meters instead of just one. The female bear, however, portly from her piscine predations, had enough trouble waddling on four feet; trying to balance upon just two, even for a few short moments, just seemed too much to demand of her sleepy form at this stage. So she let the scents wash over her: the subtle earthy aroma of tiny tundra leaves as they lay on the ground, gloriously turning into their bloody and amber hues; the crispness of the tangy wind, far gentler down here among the hills from where it began minutes earlier, high in the snow-enclosed peaks; a pair of foraging arctic ground squirrels, desperately trying to remain both silent and hidden, as they had likewise noticed the bear from her heavy and ungainly steps. They need not have worried; if the bear could have laughed, she would have, knowing that she'd never be able to catch squirrels in her current state. They were good bear snacks in summer when she had the requisite agility, but now she'd just tired herself out to no avail.

The wind pulled slightly on and through her cinnamon fur, its rippling and changing pattern indirectly visible in the flowing of individual protective and insulating hairs. The sow liked the wind, always had. She could still remember the breezes catching the fur of her mother those years ago, as the tough old female tried to teach her cubs the ways of their kind so quickly, in just the span of a few short seasons. Then it was off into the wilds on their own, even being chased away by their mother if necessary. The sow's brother, the only other cub born to that mother, only survived until this time of year. He was perhaps too playful, always looking for trouble, and he was just convinced that everyone wanted a cute friend.

The sow's mother had valiantly fought off the adult male near one of these creeks when her twin brother had gotten too close. But it wasn't enough to save him. The older bear had jealously guarded his own fishing site, and was not about to tolerate an interloper. Fortunately the cub's injuries had been sufficiently great to kill him quickly, since mother and sister would have been unable, at least emotionally, to finish him.

Presently, this equally tough she-bear could process the fleeting imagery, but was unable to keep it within consciousness for very long at a time. That was good, though; it was best not to dwell on the past. And her recent mate was the first male bear she's allowed herself anywhere near since her brother had died on the bank of a creek.

Then the sow's ears pricked up, automatically. For just a moment she actually thought she heard another of her own kind, and was almost ready to panic, realizing that her preferred den might not be safe this season after all. What if some foxes took it over instead? That would be all right; she could chase them out. But another bear?

And cowering down as best as possible in the nearby tundra, young Sterling tried frantically not to repeat her sneeze. The winds were blowing up tiny bits of plant material, some of which had swept quickly up her nostrils before she could turn her head. The sneeze was dainty, but she wondered if this big lumbering creature had heard her.

Tornado, at the same time, was about to panic himself. The pups were between him and the bear, and while many an Alaskan standoff featured a single bear surrounded but standing up to the members of a wolf pack, he was the only adult here. The bear could probably slaughter all four of them if it really wanted to. He had taken the time, though, and managed to keep track of the rather precise positions of his charges. And he wondered if Bear Heart and Owl Eyes, had they been present, would have simply announced their presence to avoid surprising the bear, or attempted stealth, which now seemed to be failing the pack members.

But the bear decided just to keep moving again, apparently unconcerned now. Tornado could partially see Sterling's sheepish glance back his way, a meek attempt at an apology. And right at that moment, with his eyes focused on her and not on the other pups, he missed catching the movement of Foxtrot and Puddles.

This was not a gesture of boyhood bravado, as might be displayed by other male mammals, including many humans. After all, Sterling herself was slowly inching herself closer, just to see how much fun, if any, a bear might be. Rather, her two brothers had just opted to cover for her, as it were, and jump right out of their hiding places, as though to offer their finest canid greeting to someone who was, technically, not yet in their territory and therefore on potentially amiable terms.

But the sow's eyes revealed an equally surprised response, as she was wholly unprepared to find herself staring down a pair of wolves, who just bounded out of the undergrowth without a care. Indeed, she was about to stand her ground, when she noticed the size of these two characters. She could hardly run her usual fast speed in a pregnant and overfed state at any rate, which was otherwise at least as quick as the wolves.

But weren't wolves larger than this? And didn't coyotes live mostly alone, if that's what these creatures were instead?

The two young males were equally dumbfounded. What was the point of jumping out and surprising something if all it did was stand there staring at you, like you were the one with the problem? They looked at each other, as though wanting to ask what to do next, but then the she-bear was again taken aback at the abrupt manifestation of two more of these odoriferous animals, one clearly female by her scent, the other much larger than the others. A leader, maybe.

Had Tornado been able to gauge the bear's thoughts, he might have found some small and wry amusement at the notion of him qualifying for *alpha* status, something he'd never really aspired to nor held out much hope for achieving. He was just the biggest wolf here now, and that was the wilderness stereotype: usually size truly did matter after all, despite what David Thomas and Jack Godwin had recently discovered.

None of the animals moved for a handful of heartbeats. There was not much tension, truly, though humans looking on might have felt edgy at the prospect of a confrontation about to turn violent. But no violence was present here; the bear was too tired, the wolves too few to cause any real damage, so why bother? Instead, the five animals simply stared, the bear taking the measure of each of the interlopers.

She offered a low rumbling vocalization, which sounded rather like a moan, deep and throaty and something like a loud exhalative snore. The wolves didn't flinch, although Puddles instinctively backed up a step; it was like nothing he had heard before, but he remained curious. Why kill something just because it's looking at you?

Tornado, in fact, was the only one of the five animals who felt any sincere trepidation about the encounter, partly since he still recollected his responsibility, and partly because he knew bears were almost indestructible, at least from the perspective of wolves. He barked once, then let the sound linger and soothe its way into a howl. He knew his own voice would carry further than those of the pups. But the youngsters did not comprehend why Tornado would howl at all; they had no understanding of his wanting to call for help, since they felt no fear of this larger creature.

Again the bear considered standing vertically: in addition to the enhanced perception, the posture looked far more intimidating. And again she opted against it, feeling too bloated and weary. So she did what anyone else might do in such a scenario: she resumed walking.

Puddles was most directly in her way, but the sow did not challenge him, nor even look him in the face. She was merely attempting to remain on the most direct line towards her den, hoping that these strange wolves or coyotes had not invaded her winter home. She had a bit of trouble smelling them, as the wind kept shifting subtlely, so she was unsure if they had been marking the terrain.

Sterling and Foxtrot slowly followed the bear, staying out of sight right behind her, while Tornado ambled over to Puddles to make sure no challenges took place. The bear gave another rumbling vocalization. Tornado wondered if the sound might carry itself even further than his own howl, and also pondered how far away their packmates might yet be. Their territory was geographically smaller than it might otherwise have been for a dozen wolves, since prey was so abundant within, but it might still take a couple of hours if the others were at the furthest reaches.

Yet the encounter remained almost comical for its lack of aggression. A bear was just walking home, and some wolves were just out for mostly leisure, and they happened upon one another. Foxtrot and Sterling, feeling feisty, lightly barked near the bear's hindquarters, trying simultaneously to get close enough for a good sniff of her. They could hardly believe how large the bear's feet were, as her muscled legs plodded over the tundra. She knew they were there, but seemed not to care.

But then she stopped, just adjacent to Tornado and Puddles. This time she gazed at them, not threateningly, but more as if she was soliciting information. Some body language was essentially universal, but she did not "speak wolf" any more than they could "speak bear." Yet she was vaguely aware of not wishing to be followed all the way to her den, which still lay just a couple of kilometers further. True violence between wolves and bears was rare, but it usually focused around denning sites: bears pulling out pups or wolves pulling out cubs, all in the name of territorial possession. Disputes over food sources were likewise extraordinary, though the two species might locate one another's caches and dig them up. Still, the location of her one genuinely safe locale was not something the bear wished to become revealed to anyone else.

And Tornado finally began to relax as he returned the questioning expression on the bear's face. Rather like a wolf's, really: equally alert ears, a similarly largely proportioned nose, which he could hear inhaling and exhaling. Teeth arranged like his own. And the unmistakable penetrating eyes, so clear he could see himself and Puddles and the topography reflected within them. Before becoming conscious of what he was doing, he actually offered the large bear a play bow, lowering his front legs while keeping his back ones upright, with his chin almost touching the ground. This was an expression of curiosity and friendliness, which Puddles immediately copied.

The bear had witnessed this gesture previously, but that was in another part of the land; those wolves had smelled differently. And she knew these were wolves now: coyotes simply did not act this way. Deciding she was in no great peril after all, she resumed her slow pace.

Tornado did not take offense to the bear's refusal of his offer to play, suspecting that she was pregnant, and he knew that they never saw bears during the winter months anyway, although he wondered where they disappeared to during those times. So he vocally commanded the pups to rejoin him, and the four wolves sat together. As the bear lumbered by, Sterling and Puddles yapped each a time or two, still hoping for some play from the strange but not unfriendly thing. They could not comprehend that the bear was on a schedule, and would be slumbering away in just mere weeks.

Several minutes later, the sow stopped and turned back towards the wolf's position. She could now only see the one adult, the younger ones either hiding or just too small to pick out in the tundra, which could hide many larger creatures. Content for the moment, she started walking again, guessing correctly the wolves would not follow her, perhaps even if she strolled into their own lands, which she did not.

* * *

Dog-chaser awoke to the familiar feel and scent of his muzzle being licked. Wolves knew this sensation from their days as pups, when they would continually lick the adult muzzles, triggering the regurgitation of carried food, which was what pups survived on between the stages of milk and being able to eat directly at a kill site. And Dog-chaser had been dreaming, at first peaceably and longingly, of the Time of the Herd.

There were gigantic herds of caribou occupying Alaska and northern Canada. Some thirty-two alone occupied the lands of the former, and went by colorful monikers granted to them by field researchers: Porcupine Herd, Forty-mile Herd, Central Arctic Herd, Mulchatna Herd. And while these numbered in the tens of thousands, even hundreds of thousands, the caribou herds which went traipsing through the wilderness west of the Denali Park lands tended to be far smaller. But when several hundred of the animals venture into your territory unannounced and unexpectedly, you might get as excited as these wolves did that day. It was over a year ago now.

Midnight and Shadow, both black in coloring and female, and respectively the *alpha* and a *beta*, had located the slowly migrating herd first. Midnight had accepted the task of returning to the rendezvous site as the best location from which to gather up the rest of the pack. She yipped and yapped and howled, but only for stolen instants here and there, since one could not really make such noises while running, especially at a full lope. She was excited, even though she knew the caribou would not get far, and even if they did, she similarly realized that her packmates would track an animal for days, even weeks, if that was what was required to bring back enough food for the pack and its pups.

And Dog-chaser recalled seeing Midnight run that day, so sleek and elegant and beautiful, darker than anything else he'd ever seen. He twitched now in his dormancy, paws clawing uselessly through the morning air, his canid brain trying to reconcile the image of his lively packmate with the last image he'd had of her, the day the humans brought their man-thunder and went about killing.

And that was as far as Dog-chaser's dream had gotten when he felt the damp warmth enveloping his muzzle. He automatically returned the greeting, opening his eyes to find Trap-dasher staring at him, though he of course had already known who it was by the scent. He rolled over, stood, and looked about inquisitively for the reassuring presence of Oak and Paddler. He dimly wondered if the caribou from his dream might materialize nearby; a single one of them could feed the four wolves quite well.

But caribou hunts would remain a future question mark for now, at least for wolves who were still on the run. They felt less fear now of the humans, but since they still had yet to establish a new territory, their situation remained quite precarious.

And it snowed last night. The four of them had been so utterly focused on their immediate survival they had barely considered the inevitable. Dog-chaser had savored his dream so thoroughly that Trap-dasher had actually licked bare traces of snow from his whiskers, gone unnoticed during the night. The flakes each felt like little chilly piercings on the *beta's* tongue.

Granted, the insulating combination of a dense undercoat with the longer colored protective guard hairs meant that wolves could survive rather extreme temperatures, in ranges which would scare moose south and make even caribou sleep more closely together for shared group heat. But to face winter in the mountains, while possibly still being pursued, without even having a home or much feeling of safety: that would prove a new experience for all four of them.

Rising off the dappled tundra, now featuring white in addition to its other shades, Dog-chaser stretched fully, arcing his back for the forelegs, then thrusting himself forward for the hind legs. His muscles felt chilly from the overnight cold, but he knew movement would feel normal soon. He followed the cold calisthenics with a return greeting to Trap-dasher, tasting the familiarity of his packmate while readying himself for what was an *omega* wolf's most important and most difficult task.

To be the pack morale leader. No matter how trying matters became.

Alphas might lead, and *betas* might struggle to maintain pack order and cohesion, while pups just tried to keep up while aping their family members and learning wolf ways, but the *omega*, in addition to serving as the receiver of group frustrations, also faced the sometimes herculean task of making sure no one was affected so negatively by challenging situations that they lashed out at any of the others, nor at the *omega* him-or herself, more than usual. At its most extreme, individuals might even leave the pack to try life on their own, but they had to reach a feeling of complete hopelessness for that to occur, to take such risks. The pack needed its whole strength, especially during winter.

So Dog-chaser was used to being on his own for long periods, to eating last, to being picked on; the need for solitude was in fact what had enabled him to find the courage to wander so far out of Fire Creek territory and brave the human settlements. He might not know it by the human's names, but Dog-chaser had actually disappeared for most of a previous summer, venturing due south to Nikolai and then east all the way to Kantishna.

That was scores of kilometers from their old home. It was dangerous. It was irresponsible, and it likely had sealed his fate as a permanent *omega* wolf. But it had also come in direct response to Tumbler's abuse.

Tumbler was dead now, of course, one of the other pack members brought down by men, though Dog-chaser had strangely not given his late brother nor his fate much thought since the day of the slaughter. He didn't even recall seeing Tumbler's body among or near those of the others, but the survivors had tried calling, even after they'd fled. No doubt their short but mournful baying howls had been heard by the men, but they would have also been identified by any other surviving packmates, and there simply were none. Maybe Dog-chaser was just glad, in his own often put-upon way, to be freer now.

The other pack members never knew where he had gone those months past. He couldn't verbally explain to them that Tumbler had drawn blood in a misplaced show of dominance, though they of course would have smelled and seen it. Nor could he explain that he just wanted some time away, which did happen more often in summer than winter. He had just wandered, following the sun or his nose. He had crossed the border of some other pack's territory, though he very carefully stayed near the edges, where the scents were fainter and where he thought he would be less likely to be attacked if located. His frustration with one of his own packmates had grown sufficient to make him take a huge gamble. Dog-chaser had not expected to remain gone for so many weeks.

So off he wandered, just a touch south of the Kuskokwim Mountains initially, and then the topography opened up into flat, often wet, often heavily wooded lands heading east. He couldn't get over the size of the gigantic mountain that he'd seen several times to the south; not many wolves got to actually see Denali up close.

While human residents would generally consider Nikolai a sleepy little hamlet, the sights and sounds from the perspective of a wild wolf were as overwhelming as a human making a first visit to the likes of New York or Tokyo: too many strange forms of strong sensory input. And without a guide, Dog-chaser fled rather quickly. He thought some of the locals were initially wolves, but the dogs proved far too anxious when they detected his presence, indeed made such a racket that the lone wolf fled after a quite short visit.

Still, even that had offered him his first experiences of the odd bipeds, with their artificial homes and technological noises.

So by the time Dog-chaser located Kantishna, just by wandering eastward for a while, he felt more determined to remain for longer by not becoming so fearful. His travels had seemed to take him to the ends of the earth, and he had never realized how the land just kept going on, and on, for so long. The world just never ended!

It had required an additional full day of scouting and probing among the strange new scents after the wolf had first located the settlement at Kantishna for him to summon the nerve required to invade human space. Trepidatiously, he had managed to isolate other smells which were similar to those of wolves, yet somehow just slightly alien; Dog-chaser had no idea that domesticated dogs lacked the tail scent gland which wolves possessed. It had been bred right out of them, though that did not presuppose a lack of marking behaviors from the more slobbery relatives of wolfkind; they were just limited to the potent urinary and fecal scents, and sometimes rolling to leave their own fainter odors behind.

The other nearby scents at this strange place Dog-chaser could of course place immediately: several ptarmigan, the recent passage of a young bull moose, even a handful of caribou. There were animal odors he couldn't quite make out, though they were a bit like the caribou; there were multiple animals involved in leaving these, and they could easily be traced to something dark and protective like a den, but one which rose above the ground, rather than having been dug into it. But these other new and queer scents: they almost literally knocked the inexperienced wolf over!

He'd never smelled trees so potently before, with their insides exposed and sliced into manageable pieces, like those comprising the horse barn. Several dozen planks, freshly cut earlier in the year, lay stacked in an orderly fashion off to one side of the settlement. Close to these, Dog-chaser found something shiny, reflecting the sun like water did, but it smelled nothing at all like the almost fragrance-free water he'd known all his life. This stuff reeked of foulness, and it was weirdly opaque. Curious all the same, he'd followed it, just wondering vaguely about its source, and then automatically dashed into some nearby trees when he had suddenly been overwhelmed by the loudest noise he could have ever imagined.

It was like a bird, but so huge, and so loud! He couldn't yet have made the connection between the winged machine and the traces of oil it had inadvertently left on the gravel landing strip at the western end of Kantishna. The young but very curious wolf hunkered down beneath the protective shade of the evergreens, hoping that he would not be seen, and that the scents he'd just located would be strong enough to mask his own presence. He had certainly not been foolish enough to try marking the extraordinary territory himself, so he should have been fine.

The wolf almost bolted as the single-engine fixed-wing airplane touched down, its experienced bush pilot requiring a very short distance to safely land, but Dog-chaser realized he would have likely been easily spotted had he emerged right then. He could feel his hot heart banging away in his narrow chest, and hoped it couldn't be heard, since the reverberations he could make out in his head. He was terrified!

The aircraft quickly taxied to a halt, and some of Dog-chaser's anxiety was briefly overcome as he watched the propeller spin to a stop; his own eyes traced the three blades as they wound their way down. Together they looked like a fun toy, but the wolf was hardly about to approach the machine, especially since now there were emerging out of its belly: humans!

This was, of course, prior to Dog-chaser's emotionally excruciating introduction to the horrid man-thunder, though this was the first of the smelly shells he'd ever encountered, and this one flew! Why would the humans allow the huge stinky bird to eat them, only to climb out of it again later? And how had they survived in the first place? Was this thing really a bird?

Dog-chaser knew ptarmigan, ravens, eagles, of course. They all ate different things, but none of them, he thought, would ever feast on something as large as a human. And this loud thing, now thankfully much quieter, surely smelled nothing like any bird. So he kept watching, hoping the bipeds would not venture too close and ruin his hiding place, maybe even killing him outright for crossing their border. The wolf was glad that the humans were the only animals he could see at the moment, since their sense of smell did not seem that strong; how could they not sniff around the machine, or near its tracks, like Dog-chaser himself had done just minutes earlier? Did they not realize how much the terrain could impart to them? At one point, it looked like they would get down on all four extremities like any proper canid would, and likewise smell the ground appropriately, but they ended up just stretching and looking around.

Then again, the eyes and noses of these strange tall beings seemed awfully far from the ground, rather like a bear when it reared up. Dog-chaser tried that maneuver sometimes, but could never keep any semblance of postural equilibrium that way, and certainly couldn't walk like that. It seemed stupid to him. But the human's eyes were quite expressive; he could see that himself from beneath the lower branches where he remained as motionless as could be. He had calmed down, and fortunately he had not been out of breath when first finding the hiding place, so he could keep his mouth closed to breathe. Silence was now to be prized.

Some base part of Dog-chaser, perhaps part of the simple fright-flight-fight response, informed him he had been truly lucky thus far, in his efforts to keep clandestine. He indeed wished to explore more of this area, wondering if he could ever persuade any of the other pack members to inspect this place with him. He doubted he could, and even if he was mistaken, why bother, anyway? Part of this adventure of his was recognition that he had come here completely on his own, faced his fears, and remained safe. So far.

And thankfully, the humans seemed to be finishing their quick survey of where they'd just landed and emerged from the huge flying machine, and walked past Dog-chaser's safety tree, laughing and making other guttural noises that the wolf could not begin to comprehend, save that they sounded pleased. He heard the distinctive noises of wooden doors opening on slightly squeaky brass hinges, not understanding what could be happening, but he did at once figure out two new bits of data: the humans were now inside one of these straightened piles of assembled trees, and that a new batch of scents emanated from within. Some kind of food, though unrecognizable, and traveling more quickly and potently for having been cooked, and another scent, much like Dog-chaser's own.

Could there be a wolf in there? Dog-chaser could not conceive of it; no wolf would be caught in such a place, although he failed to make the connection between his using a live tree for safety and shelter in much the equal way as the humans reconstructed dead ones for essentially the same purpose. He wanted so badly to get closer: both types of smells were hugely enticing. How he yearned now to return to his packmates with the scent of a strange wolf and strange foods worked into his fur! That alone would serve as an olfactory report of his doings and bravery. He slowly began inching his way forward, keeping himself as flattened as possible against the low bushes next to the tree, which offered a trace of cover, though it was still better than the all-gravel landing strip.

As he drew closer, trying to remain silent (though he could still hear voices, now coming from inside the building), Dog-chaser noticed a whole assortment of these strange collections of dead trees, assembled into roughly uniform and neat stacks. He didn't comprehend this at all. Since they hardly seemed dangerous, and since he could tell the food scents were potent enough to mask his own, he crept right up to the side of one of the buildings. He could hear nothing within it, though it also smelled of the recent passage of these strange creatures; there was an overpowering fruity sort of smell, too, which Dog-chaser didn't like at all, but again, it would help cover up his own.

Not being familiar with nor caring about perfumes and colognes, the young wolf peered longingly around the corner of the small building, one of several two-room rental cabins which provided the primary income for the seasonal human residents of Kantishna, which had once been, if not a boomtown, then at least a boom-village, a century before when gold had been found this far inland. Most people associated the gold rush of the late nineteenth century as a coastal or river phenomenon, but the odorless soft yellow metal could be found almost anywhere in the Great Land (which Dog-chaser had also found in streams before, and regarded as worthless except for the playful way it could reflect light in the moving water). In fact, the wolf could also look further to his side, back towards the landing strip and his prior hiding place, and notice the much darker wood of the old assayer's office. It even smelled older, and the roof was so old now that it was overgrown with what appeared to be its own lawn. Still, it remained in good condition, a popular photographic target for some, but Dog-chaser thought it looked dark. He crept a bit closer to investigate.

Underneath this old mining assayer's building came a hissing noise.

It captured Dog-chaser's attention, naturally, and as he was already curious, he poked his nose under the building.

Something small and furry was under there. It had vicious-looking eyes reflecting the sunlight, and it backed up from the wolf and hissed again, emitting a deep throaty growl afterwards. Its attitude clear, Dog-chaser decided to ignore the cat, who had escaped from the lodge earlier in the day and taken to exploring the area.

And then, in between these two extremes of his sneaky vision, the wolf noticed a tremendous one of these wooden stacks; what could the humans be thinking, to have created such a huge building? What purpose could it serve? If it was for shelter, it was too much, unless dozens of humans slept there. Wolves themselves rarely used any type of true shelter, and even a winter den was only for the pregnant female and her coming pups, and even then was usually not much larger than the minimum needed to provide insulated cover for mother and babies. Dog-chaser could see some motion inside, and was confused by how the light played tricks on the doors; it was the first time he had taken a good look at glass, which comprised much of the area of the main doors leading into the lodge.

Dog-chaser could then no longer tell if what kept him in that spot was curiosity or fear of discovery. Probably both, it seemed to him, since he could experience both emotions by that point. He could hardly imagine such buildings, would never have been able to reconcile something as grandiose and immense as a city with his own very limited experiences with humankind; as it was, he simply felt glad that these vertical beings seemed to want to stay here, and not venture out without their noisy fake bird.

That was until he noticed the all-terrain vehicle, which, while scary in its own right, was less so (and less noisy) than its flying counterpart. But oh, how it stank! Dog-chaser could hardly keep from coughing and retching as the thing passed, with thankfully just one person on it. It did not slow at all as it passed him by, but kept heading towards the first building the wolf had been near: the barn, whose inhabitants Dog-chaser had forgotten about, which he thought had smelled a bit like moose. The small but noxious cloud which belched its way aggressively out of the machine's rear remained in the air for several minutes, and Dog-chaser lowered his head again, keeping his front paws over his face in a vain effort to stifle or escape the smell.

And now there were dogs in tow: a pair of them, running alongside the ATV and its driver, occasionally yapping and making a nuisance of themselves, at least to Dog-chaser's way of thinking. They didn't seem to mind the engine exhaust; maybe their senses of smell had deadened. The wolf was about to call it a day, not wanting to tangle with things which looked more or less like wolves themselves, and had just about risen from his latest location when the dogs stopped. They were a few yards behind the vehicle now, for the moment forgotten by the driver whose dogs they were. And they began sniffing the ground, right between the cabin and the tree where Dog-chaser had crouched down just minutes before.

Were these truly wolves? Since running right now would give himself away, Dog-chaser took to studying them. The gait was a bit off; they were sloppier walkers compared to him and his packmates, but otherwise they moved as wolves, walking and sensing alertly. The ears were all wrong, partly folded over the sides of the heads, like they'd been bilaterally injured. The muzzles were shorter, and the chests seemed rounder and thicker. Most telling of all, the two tails, though eagerly wagging, remained at a roughly horizontal level: neither the low curled posture of an *omega* nor the vertical pride of an *alpha*. Being almost completely color-blind, Dog-chaser still could discern that one of these creatures was very dark, indeed all black. The other was colored more like a wolf: white underside, with white also prevalent on all four legs, and darker flanks. The face seemed especially wolf-like, at least from what little the true wolf could see of it as it ran past.

Dog-chaser now realized that his previous luck with timing was at an end, though he didn't know just how practical it would be for him to leave now. More humans were on their way back, several of them in a large wagon drawn by the horses who resided in the barn, and a smaller group returning from an afternoon hike, and all of whom would be giddy with delight over what a productive day it had been for spotting wildlife. Some would rave about seeing brown bears, others speak boastfully about witnessing a moose and tiny herds of caribou, and all would likewise be ready for dinner in the lodge; thus the powerful food smells the wolf had already detected. So he had to go. He could only imagine what it would be like to find himself suddenly surrounded by humans, including the temporary residents of the very cabin he was hiding near.

So it was right then, while facing the decision, that Dog-chaser inadvertently though simultaneously confronted the countenances of the strange wolves. The humans might have found it comical, but already the three canids were on full alert and ready for whatever danger the stranger represented.

The ATV's driver had by then just shut off the engine, and the other sounds could be heard more accurately: birds, human chatter, open-mouthed breathing of anxious canids, heavy human footsteps. And the dogs had noticed the wolf. Dog-chaser did not realize exactly what had given him away, but figured they must have already noticed his scent, and he was an interloper after all.

These other wolf-creatures would surely kill him. And he would never see home again.

But strangely, Dog-chaser did not comprehend that the two dogs, the large Labrador and the Husky mix, were actually as trepidatious over his presence as he was nervous over theirs, even if it was their turf. The wolf smelled mostly canine-like, and in appearance seemed visually much like them, but something was off, and the dogs were consequently on guard, automatically remaining close to each other.

And even more strangely, things might have had the chance to become ugly if not the serendipitous interference of one of the humans. The ATV driver had already headed into the lodge, apparently wholly unconcerned with his dogs, as if forgetting that dogs liked to explore and they were in the middle of a tremendous wilderness. It was a child instead.

The young girl was one of the horse-drawn wagon passengers, still thrilling over what she'd seen that day, and no longer missing her friends back home in Indiana quite so much during her holiday "to the middle of nowhere," and still allowing herself to fantasize over having a horse of her own after getting to know the huge working equines who'd trudged her and her family and some other people along for several hours. So she was taking her time. And she noticed the two dogs. And she of course noticed how they seemed totally focused on something. And then she saw the wolf.

She might not have noticed at all, but being a dedicated animal lover, the girl had already fetched and was now carrying a new friend: a tabby cat who'd begun hissing furiously upon noting the wolf's presence. Dog-chaser didn't recognize the animal that had just minutes before been hiding beneath the old assayer's building, nor had he noticed the cat skulking its way back to the lodge, apparently deciding it didn't need to be around all these dogs and wildlife after all.

It really is a wolf, the girl kept telling herself, and then, with her twelve years of life experience in a large Midwestern city, tried to decide whether she was supposed to be scared now. She reckoned she should be; after all, this was a *wolf!* Were people in any danger around wolves? The girl quickly glanced around, noting that the doors to the lodge with their spotless glass panes were just a few yards away. And she surprised herself by not screaming. She indeed had no recollection afterwards of consciously deciding to remain quiet and curious; she just did so. She'd already released the terrified cat, who'd largely forced its way out of her arms and gone scampering back into the lodge to hide.

But Dog-chaser by now had had quite enough himself. He was also scared to death. One of the humans was actually staring at him, and who knew what such creatures might be capable of doing to him? Never mind the risks from the dogs; he had to get out of here.

Flee, was the simple non-linguistic command his brain gave him. *Get back to the pack.* He charged the dogs, hoping surprise would be good enough.

It seemed like it wouldn't be, at first. The pair of dogs split themselves apart, and the wolf sprinted through, baring his teeth but not slowing in the slightest to actually risk a fight. He just wanted to scare them. And then he headed for the landing strip, past the airplane, past the footprints and the smells of humans and dogs and horses. And he just ran, as fast as he could.

And the dogs pursued. Bear, dog, wolf, cat: they all tended to chase anything crazy enough to run from them, either for sake of curiosity and play or for a potential meal. Never mind their initial fear; the dogs simply knew they had to chase this invader. Only the concerned calls of the girl made them eventually pause.

That, and the speed of the wolf. The Lab and Husky pair were both in good physical shape themselves, but were a little older, and a little slowed by richer, less energy-efficient diets, and so the wolf simply outdistanced them. He never looked back, never stopped to howl, never acted otherwise aggressively; he just ran from fear.

As for the girl, she felt a thrill at what she had just witnessed, and called the dogs over. They obeyed, having already become comfortable with the young person, who by then had already spent two days in Kantishna with her family, without once being bored, like she thought she'd be prior to coming.

And thus did Dog-chaser acquire his name, quite a strange one for his kind. He did indeed return home quickly, still smelling just vaguely like domestic dog when he arrived. And that drive to chase through, to face fear, to overcome obstacles, was what the wolf knew he had to get his packmates to keep doing back in the present. Else they likely wouldn't last out the winter. He vaguely wished, however wolves go about wishing, to be able to share the story of his venturing to Kantishna with his packmates; they would have loved it, had they been able to comprehend it, but they would have had to witness it themselves.

Such linear thought did not systematically transpire through Dog-chaser's head, and he didn't think in linguistic terms as humans so often did, but he did fully recognize what lay before him now: when the others showed any signs of wanting to truly quit, it would fall upon him to keep that individual going. Maybe that was part of the reason for Trap-dasher seeing to him first this morning, as a gentle reminder.

His muscles felt newly invigorated now. Dog-chaser was done stretching, and done with his reminiscences. He padded lightly over, with Trap-dasher in tow, to the *alphas*, Oak and Paddler. After an exchange of morning greetings, Dog-chaser recognized the futility reflected in the expressions of his packmates. In a species which relied as heavily upon body language as on the subtleties of the nose, the *omega* wolf felt unusually pleased to have this task to face: to encourage the others. This would likely entail group howling, which helped with group focus, and very active nuzzling and muzzle-licking, even with the risk of being snapped at or even bitten by a frustrated wolf of higher status. It might even include behaviors such as simple play-bows mingled with genuine play, with the same accompanying risks; *omegas* were sometimes treated rather

brutally by other pack members, but if Dog-chaser could brave
a human settlement, then he felt he could certainly risk being
bitten a few times by packmates who might vent their own
frustrations and fears at his bodily expense.

* * *

Scenario Four:

> *For all our considerations of wolves and humans and their
> interactions, or lack thereof, there remains another historical issue to
> ponder, though giving it its proper intellectual due also necessitates
> venturing into the macabre and horrific.*

> *Consider for a moment the shape-changer, a character found
> among cultures around the globe. The Japanese believed in those
> individuals who could become foxes. The Irish had a similar belief
> in the ability of humans to transmogrify into seals. Were-tiger tales
> appeared in India, and the Trickster, usually a coyote or wolf or raven
> and typically with form-altering ability, was found in many American
> cultures. But there is a difference separating these legends from
> those of the original lycanthropes, the werewolves: these other weird
> combinations of humans and other species might act for general good
> or evil, sometimes being benevolent or even creative forces, or possibly
> sometimes devouring the unwary. Yet werewolves, universally, are
> loathsome, creatures worthy of complete extinction and nothing less.
> Lycanthropy might be a gift in some cultures; to the Europeans and
> their cultural descendents, it is unequivocally a curse.*

> *It might all be a joke, of course. After all, no one really
> believes in such monsters, right, even if anyone ever did? But some
> superstitions, which of course are nothing other than beliefs receiving
> a biased name, die hard, even in the face of contrary evidence. There
> exist those cultural beliefs which simply do not dislodge easily, so
> much so that their literal truth or likely falsehood becomes a moot
> consideration. Even if members of such a believing group have no wish
> to make admissions in public, the prejudice of time and place might*

remain inviolable. Such is the case with the evil shape-shifters, the ones known the world over as lycanthropes.

"Lycanthropy" itself is a term which today will only receive attention in three types of publications: reference works appearing in the inappropriately-named "New Age" shelves of bookshops; psychologic and psychiatric journals, most likely under the heading of "Rare Clinical Neuroses and Psychoses," or some such; and horror fiction. In this modern sense, there is the appeal to the dramatic and monstrous in the first type of book, and to the socially scientific and medical in the second. Werewolves within novels, meanwhile, seem to be in little danger of vanishing, likewise with their filmed counterparts; there remains something horrifically appealing in the idea of being able to transform into a monster, perhaps for reasons of vengeance, maybe to simply run wild, or even to savor an abrupt change, especially of one's own perspective. Whatever other explanations may abound, the curious diagnosis officially known as lycanthropy is exceedingly rare, in which the individual afflicted with the mental illness believes, actually believes, that he or she is either a wolf or a werewolf. This individual typically presents with symptoms such as preferring to eat raw flesh, walking about on all four extremities, and howling when the moon is most visible, never mind that true wolves do not participate in the latter activity, as we have witnessed.

Regarding the curious mental illness, it seems that those few who have been isolated and contained with this condition have almost universally made claims of being werewolves. Perhaps being a wolf isn't dramatic enough, or sufficiently terrifying, or maybe full wolves are somehow superior to their monstrous fantastic counterparts. Maybe there is some ill-tempered desire to get even with some element of human society, and becoming a monster seems a way to do so. Or perhaps there is the dim recognition that, since wolves are truly no threat to humans, but people are often scared of them anyway, then what better method to exploit an archaic fear than to become half-person, half-beast? And it has been observed that the idea of the werewolf elevates the man, while insulting the wolf, though some might disagree.

The most sensational cases require us to travel back through the mists of spacetime for another visit to our collective past, though on this excursion we need only go back a handful of centuries. One of these places we have walked before: Germany, though at this time it is still the Holy Roman Empire. Its immediate neighbor, France, will also offer a stage for this danse macabre: *actual alleged werewolves, their hunts, their captures, and even their trials.*

This is now the 16th century, just prior chronologically to our previous adventures with a certain pair of samurai in feudal Japan. Returning to Europe, we enter the wake of the world's other major practitioners of feudalism, in a time now called the Renaissance. Propaganda being what it is, the mass superstitions, institutionalized racist policies, tortures, and executions which we moderns often associate with the medieval period did not really get into full swing until this latter "Renaissance" timeframe, though as with wolves, old biases are difficult to dislodge: most of us use the term "medieval" roughly synonymously with cruel or barbaric or just plan backward. The focus of European religious war has shifted by this time, from Christian versus Muslim during the Crusades, to Christian versus Christian, in the immediate aftermath of the Protestant Reformation and Catholic Counter-Reformation. Paranoia and suspicion might always come more or less easily to those of our species, but this is a time when it becomes both more politicized and continues to increase, in terms of the number of potential evils people are told to fear: Jews and Muslims were insufficient adversaries, perhaps; now we had to walk in trepidation of our neighbors and fellow Christians.

Granted, the Renaissance, or rebirth, as the term actually means, does serve as a tremendous inspiration for progressive movements within painting, sculpture, music, political and moral and religious philosophy, the growth of science as its own discipline; and it also witnesses huge growth in simple literacy, as Johannes Gutenberg's printing presses begin not only to make more books and other publications available, but start also to print in non-ecclesiastical languages. Greek and Latin thus begin to get displaced, and far more people outside the nobility and clergy aspire to become persons of letters, even if they never acquire any of the costly books of their own. The Church is often displeased by such notions nonetheless; people who can read seem almost automatically more likely to think about and discuss what they have read, whether a text contains love sonnets or a logical justification for armed revolution. And we get back to the issue of werewolves by considering one book in particular.

The Malleus Maleficarum first goes to press in the year 1486, just prior to when most Europeans will first learn of the vast "New World" which lies beyond their older maps, in the regions which were formerly labeled "Here be Dragons." Though Europeans (and Asians) have "discovered" the Americas centuries before, this is the year Christopher Columbus receives financial backing from a foreign crown to take his ships past the map borders. However, his expedition underwriters, in the persons of Ferdinand II and Isabella of Aragon and Castile have, just a few years prior to this, reinvigorated the Inquisition, originally created as far back as 1231 with the express purpose of "combating heresy." This tool of the Catholic Church will have exterminated numbers of human lives impossible to calculate now: from as low as two thousand according to modern Catholic apologists, to some ten to fifteen million by the time it is officially dissolved six centuries beyond its beginning, almost always on charges which can only be labeled as superstitious. Admittedly, the official Church-sanctioned executions represent a tiny proportion of the overall number of Inquisitorial casualties, but this is also the period of mass persecutions: of Muslims, Jews, and most particularly women, the latter on charges of witchcraft, midwifery, practicing any level of health care, earning too much money or working for pay at all, or whatever else might have offended the neighbors that year. Like the Holocaust, the Burning is a term which tries to simply sum up one of the more tragic periods of our collective history.

Still, perhaps one must take the beneficial with the horrid sometimes. Concurrent with Columbus' voyage is Vasco da Gama's sailing around the Cape of Good Hope, Leonardo da Vinci's painting of the Mona Lisa, even the invention of the toothbrush in that land of fabulous creations, China. Yet by 1492, as the Italian sailor reaches the Caribbean, and as the aforementioned Spanish monarchs expel the remaining Jews and Muslims from their kingdom, the Malleus Maleficarum has already begun to make its influence felt. This is the period of the worst of the Inquisitions, the one with its uniquely Spanish flavor.

The idea behind something like the Inquisition and this interesting book which helps support it is logically simple and concise: it is to remove the "undesirables" from one's midst, with the goal of being able to rest more easily among one's true fellows. This is a regular occurrence among countless animal species: "keep the others out" is the basic strategy, though this naturally necessitates a method of identifying those annoying "others," and making sure they have no way to get their greedy paws or mouths or hands on your possessions, be these food, land, or females.

The troubles begin in recognizing that this is also part of an ancient philosophical as well as political problem, at least where our own animal species is concerned. Wolves practice this basic separation, too: woe to those canids who venture into territory belonging to another pack, as death from members of their own kind has a good chance of being the end result. "Intraspecific strife" this is called: being slain by members of one's own species. There are examples with other mammals, with avians, with fish, with insects, with reptiles, and of course, we ourselves often specialize in such behavior, something to which Marine pilot Daniel Collins could relate. But with the wolves and these other non-humans, there is always something easy by which to distinguish "member of my group" from "non-member." For the wolves it is primarily scent; a canid that smells differently from the ones they know is not to be trusted or welcomed, unless it perhaps can convince the others that it means no harm and might even be an asset to the group. *Eventual adoptions can and do occur this way, which are also a practical method of keeping genetic options open; a group which takes its own isolation too seriously will of course eventually end up inbred and severely disadvantaged.*

But what options does this leave for our own kind? And since there are so many of us, and our family lines intersect and overlap in such complicated ways, as Morgan Greene has attested, how do we keep track of who is an ally and whom an enemy, who a friend or family member and whom a threat to our way of life? The combination of our more limited sensory apparatus and our extremely detailed social and cultural patterns compels us to create labels in the search for this comfort we mentioned.

The Inquisition was quite talented at this creation of labels: "You! You stand accused of heresy or blasphemy. You are a Jew or a Muslim or a Protestant or a natural philosopher or, worst of all, a woman. You are therefore clearly up to no good. Confess now, and may God have mercy on your corrupted and tainted soul." This does not leave very many other choices, unfortunately. And this new book, as close to a bestseller as books get in those days, proves an insightful way of separating the heretics from the faithful or fearful.

Literally, the title translates as "Hammer of the Malefactors," and while it only mentions werewolves as such in a handful of instances, it devotes page after tedious page to the identification of witches. A huge part of this tome is the culmination of the European and Christian notion that women are simply involved in evil activities: they're inherently flawed by both biblical and ancient philosophical accounts. Indeed, the Old Testament (so central to ancient Jewish, Christian, and Muslim beliefs), as well as thinkers as varied as Aristotle and Confucius, all mistrusted the females of our kind: the first set of "others," and always easy to identify because of simple bodily differences. Eve was of course allegedly fashioned from Adam's spare parts, and the notion that a woman could be educated, or know more than a man, or have more money or strength or power than a man, was just too fearful a notion to face. And women certainly could not be *trusted with any sense of reproductive freedom. Witches, beware, the book says: your days of evil influence are numbered.*

And allied to these alleged feminine troublemakers were, among others, the nasty animals and their ilk. Some inquisitors and hunters who became familiar with the tome took it for what it was: an early how-to manual on ridding the world of particular types of vermin, but these were vermin in deceptively human forms.

Gilles Garnier thus clearly deserves mention here, and he already had a strike against him: not a woman, at least, he was nonetheless a hermit, and like the lone wolf, who better to be suspicious of than someone who lived alone and tended to shun the company of others? What might those hermits be up to, anyway? Garnier might have been a 16th-century Ted Kaczynski, plotting some unholy and unspeakable vengeance upon others. And small towns in particular, such as Dole in France, tend to be more susceptible towards distrusting anyone seen as an outsider.

Garnier exacerbated his problem by "confessing" to a certain predilection: on holy feast days, he had a disturbing tendency to acquire grotesque hungers, and villagers appear to have observed him attempting to eat a young girl in November, 1573. They said he looked like a monster, though: furry, moving on hands and feet simultaneously, showing off teeth and fingernails long enough to be regarded as claws. The girl escaped, a few of the villagers chasing off the hairy beast with shouts and pelted rocks.

An assortment of other children of both genders during the next few weeks fared more poorly, however, and they were found with various parts of them missing, with plenty of bite marks in evidence around the wound sites. Still, it took a while for the villagers to put it all together and begin suspecting Garnier; it seems he wanted help, as though he was vaguely cognizant of his ill-doings and wished to stop.

Bushy eyebrows and heavy facial hair did little to assist in his legal defense. In truth, modern pleas of "temporary insanity" have their roots in Garnier's squalid trial, and we would likely find aspects of the proceedings troubling: what prompted the actual confession was Garnier being treated to an encounter with one of the Inquisition's prouder tools, the rack. Torture-augmented confessionals notwithstanding, the court remained unmoved by Garnier's pleas, and he was burned at the stake, another popular method of dispatching the annoying at the time.

Across the border in modern Germany, we can proceed to meet another loner, though one reputed to be a sorcerer. Peter Stumpf (spellings of his family name varied) was a prosperous farmer and widower, with some influence in the local community, the town of Bedburg. There are few persons from this period with more detailed legal records than Stumpf, and we can begin by noting another series of rack-inspired confessions, among them that he had practiced magic since the age of twelve, and that a pact with none other than the Devil himself had yielded a furry belt or girdle, the donning of which would transform him into a ravenous and huge wolf. The change was supposedly possible during any time of year; no full moon was necessary.

Fourteen children and two adults, along with numerous goats and sheep, allegedly fell prey to Stumpf's exclusively carnivorous proclivities, and one of the younger victims named was his own son. Unfortunately for the family, Stumpf's other child, a daughter, was accused of being in league with him, as was his apparent lover; both women were strangled to death, their bodies eventually burned with Stumpf's. His own execution was one of the grisliest on record for the period: put to the wheel after the rack, flesh was then torn from him with red-hot pincers. The longer bones in his extremities were then hammered, a treatment with the purpose of keeping him from returning from the grave. He was finally beheaded, and all three bodies fully immolated, in October, 1589.

The Holy Roman Empire was then amidst the throes of the violence between Catholics and Protestants, the castle at Bedburg eventually becoming a Catholic stronghold. Accordingly, it has been suggested that this werewolf trial was in truth a thinly-disguised political show trial aimed at persuading the dissident Protestants to rethink their *ways and beliefs. At any rate, werewolf trials were sensational media theatre, generating plenty of talk and publicity, the religious undertones aside; after all, it was felt, Stumpf did sell his soul for greater power in the form of the magic wolf girdle, an act only capable by those on the wrong side of Christian doctrine.*

So much for French and German efforts to resolve the lycanthropy problem. Across the Channel, there might have been fewer werewolf trials, but there were more werewolves. Indeed, the British had a history of believing the curse could be passed along familial lines, so that multiple generations might harbor dark secrets. This is a theme even picked up today in role-playing games and action films, as entire clans of werewolves and, for that matter, vampires, vie for supremacy. And there were precedent-setting chronicles set down in British documents: Cnut the Dane wrote of werewolves when he was King of England in the eleventh century. Likewise, James I of England (previously VI of Scotland) attempted to account for the persistent beliefs of commoners in the monsters, writing as late as the sixteenth century; one can only speculate what he might have thought of Garnier and Stumpf, whose trials took place just before James ascended the throne. How werewolves could be explained as possessing "a natural superabundance of melancholy," as he described, might seem a bit reaching, but it raises the question: how does one account for something which is not supposed to exist, when religious, scientific, and philosophical explanations fail? Is it just acting out, or a mere mental illness, however frightening?

While the British have a strong tradition for lupine shape-changers, it is currently unusual to locate anyone who still professes belief in their literal corporeal existence. The notable exception is the Russian Federation, particularly in the east, getting into Siberia. The ancient arctic passage of Beringia is of course what connected this land to North America, so one might hypothesize if very old stories of werewolves might have been brought from Asia to America via this route, since the American Indian peoples do exhibit a sampling of shape-changing traditional beliefs. Making a charge of superstition or primitiveness is easy, but from a modern and, hopefully, more enlightened perspective, the question remains: how does one explain the history of werewolves?

Perhaps etymology can help again. "Lycanthropy" is named for Lycaon, an ancient king of the Greeks, whose dinner guests one evening included none other than Zeus himself, the father of the Olympian deities, who had a penchant for sometimes traveling disguised as a mortal. Eventually the father-god revealed his identity, which nonetheless went questioned by the host Lycaon, who opted to attempt a cruel test. Killing one of Zeus' innumerable human children and serving him as part of the feast somehow seemed like a way to verify the truth: would Zeus recognize his own upon sampling his flesh? Arcas, the victim, had been the son of Zeus and his human lover Callisto, and was now unwittingly part of the entrée, the ruse of which Zeus saw through immediately. Enraged, the god hurled a lightning bolt at Lycaon which immediately transformed him into, of all things, a wolf. Apparently living as one was already considered a curse so many centuries ago, although strangely, there are those more contemporary werewolf tales which suggest lycanthropy does offer a type of bodily immortality, as supposedly does its undead counterpart of vampirism: the feeding on mortal humans is the one curious and unwholesome prerequisite of both conditions. But maybe mortality, even if of a bodily rather than a spiritual version, has its perks.

Then again, according to some accounts of Lycaon's fate, Callisto was his own daughter, so maybe there was an element of human vengeance in the tale. Zeus had, after all, deceived Callisto by appearing to her as her favorite deity Artemis, only to then rape her (sexual assault and deities otherwise behaving as poorly as humans were of course grist for the mythological mill for the Greeks). Still, the ancient Greek fascination with wolf transformations hardly ended there, as a later shrine built to Zeus on Mount Lycaeus allegedly witnessed more rituals entailing human sacrifices, and whomever feasted upon the slain bodes would likewise become wolves. And even during periodic tributes to Zeus held each nine years, sacrificed animals went into a ritual soup (and, typically, a human boy to spice things up), and whomever happened to dine upon the boy's viscera would become a wolf until the next such ritual. In this last case, the person undergoing the change would return to human form provided he or she ate no more human flesh during the nine years spent as a wolf. One could still avoid the curse if one were careful. This speaks of temptation, however; recall that true wolves remain quite frightened of humans, so humans transformed into wolves would, apparently, overcome this trepidation and potentially hunt humans.

Like countless other religious and mythological tales, there is clearly an element of sacrifice here. The sixteenth-century executioners of Garnier and Stumpf believed their sentences were passed justly onto men who were either naturally demonic or who traded a soul for a form of power. Becoming a wild animal again, removing oneself from the mainstream society, has a price: wildness and greater potency might seem their own reward, as with immortality, yet people remain suspicious. Perhaps that is the true lesson of the historical werewolves.

Still, for the most terrifying example, we must consider France once more, this time during the latter part of the eighteenth century. By now, religious wars in Europe have largely ceased, and this has become the Age of Reason, Europe's grand Enlightenment. Our story transpires a quarter-century before Enlightenment ideals will receive very bloody political and social tests in the French Revolution, at a time when the British colonists of North America have just won a state of relative freedom from their French and indigenous American Indian foes, though another decade will pass before the Yankee colonists rebel again against their British forebears. The Industrial Revolution has been creating factories in Europe for some years as well, as machinery and technology utterly transform production and livelihood, and raise moral, economic, and environmental questions. The notion of people being essentially equal to one another, at least in a political sense, is gaining ground, and science comes into its own more than ever, almost wholly divorced now from religion, though these scientists still refer to themselves as "natural philosophers." So the Age of Reason was *accordingly rather ill-equipped for the troubling occurrences of the Beast of Gévaudan.*

To begin with, eyewitness accounts differed, as they always seem to do, a fact which troubled the authorities in the Garnier and Stumpf cases also, but which tended to get glossed over for the sake of ridding two communities of their local monsters. Torturous confessionals were largely out of vogue by then, and there were no particular suspects in any case. In the early summer of 1764, a girl became the Beast's first human witness, and while her farm dogs were terrified and fled, the bulls of her family farm she was tending at the time scared it away. Yet accounts of the creature from this girl and from others in the vicinity of Gévaudan yielded a description of something which was not especially wolf-like after all.

The Beast was the size of a cow with a correspondingly wide chest. It had a lion-like tail, long, flexible, and with a noticeable tuft at the tip. The head was described as roughly greyhound-like in appearance, though such an otherwise peaceful countenance ended with the requisite huge fangs easily visible in its gaping maw. The paws were either like hooves, or had six-inch long claws. The creature was capable of carrying off a sheep by itself, and could wade upright across streams like a biped. Such varying elements gave it the sense of being a chimera, a mélange of other species with fearsome traits (the chimera itself being another legendary creature from ancient Greece).

The Beast demonstrated early a preference for the meat of children and women, so it may have feared men. King Louis XV himself offered a very motivational cash reward for whomever could dispatch the Beast. And so by September of 1765, one of the more successful hunters did manage to bag a huge wolf: close to three feet at the shoulder and weighing some hundred-thirty pounds. Those who study wolves in our own time will at once know that this is a tremendous size for a wolf: rare, but still possible. And the French villagers breathed easier, believing this had to be the monster terrorizing the countryside.

But two months later, the killings resumed. Dozens of them. And the modus operandi of the killer remained the same: women and children, dying not of broken necks or loss of blood as might be expected from predation, but of decapitation or massive head trauma. The Beast was either severing heads or crushing them in its jaws, so its skull must have been rather larger than the suggested greyhound form.

Again, an explanation is necessary, though we currently might not feel quite the pressing need for one as did our French forebears many decades ago. Belief that the creature was a true wolf faded, and more people, even in the Age of Reason, began suspecting a werewolf. Some women told of how a kindly gentleman had offered to escort them through the local woods, and as they refused, they noticed the excessive hair or fur on the backs of his hands. Human serial killers were and continue to be proposed as answers to the Beast, though no human evidence was apparently found near the bodies of the slain and partially-devoured.

Some modern researchers suggest the Beast was a relocated hyena taught to do ill, though hyenas, while very intelligent and certainly trainable, cannot apparently be made to simply attack humans on command from a distance, especially in daylight. They also usually lack the requisite head size to kill in either manner, and no one else was observed by surviving eyewitnesses anyway. Other theorists, including modern crypto-zoologists, speculate that the Beast was a mesonychid, a far more ancient carnivorous ungulate, a scavenger and hunter of fish. If this were so, the Beast would become something akin to the fabulous monster in Loch Ness: an old relic unable to escape its environmental niche, surviving precariously into modern times long after all others of its kind have vanished into history and paleontology. But even so, there would have to be a line of such creatures for them to continue to produce offspring, so where are the others? No such relatives of the Beast have ever been found again, or were before.

What if the beast was a hybrid? Of course, wolf-dog hybrids retain some popularity into the present, and their keepers often proudly describe their pets as containing a certain percentage of direct wolf ancestry, never mind that such numbers are wholly impossible to verify. The hybrid hypothesis seems most plausible, however: hybrids typically retain much of the intelligence of wolves, but with the additional lack of fear towards humans mentioned before. Perhaps it was even trained a certain way; domestic dogs, just like humans, can be taught to become exceedingly violent with minimal efforts. But how does even a dog gone wrong manage to slay from five dozen to over one hundred persons?

Whatever the Beast truly was, it has ensured its continued notoriety. One of the most successful French films of all time, translated into English as "The Brotherhood of the Wolf," seeks to explain the Beast once and for all. It offers an intriguing account of the monster, complete with quite graphic accounts of the hunting of wolves which had been blamed for the Beast's attacks. Like werewolves of fiction and probable fantasy, normal wolves too so often receive persecution and blame for actions they have not committed, or for simply being themselves, and thereby perceived as threats. On this note, the region of Gévaudan itself, once known for a healthy wolf population, likely has none today, partly in response to concerns over the monster of the eighteenth-century.

The Gévaudan Beast was finally slain, as late as 1767, by a local farmer named Jean Chastel, who succeeded where Louis' finest hunters and soldiers had failed. Despite the Beast allegedly being immune to musket fire, Chastel managed to put two lead balls into it at extremely close range. Some believed that these were silver musket balls, blessed by a priest, so it should be easy to see how some elements of the werewolf legend were added at this time. And, unfortunately, the Beast's body has long since disappeared, making any additional studies of it impossible.

The curious allure of the werewolf remains, despite all these strange and terrible stories of old. Why do we curl up in darkness, intentionally scaring ourselves by watching Lon Chaney Jr., Michael Landon, David Naughton, Tom Everett Scott, and Benicio del Toro morph into monsters? What is it to truly run with the wolves? Why has this become such a potent and tempting archetype, handed through millennia of human civilization, with influence drawn from cultures across the globe?

What, in other words, might we have lost by becoming domestic creatures?

PART FOUR: THE ACCOLADE

"The question is not, can they reason, nor, can they talk, but, can they suffer?"
  - Jeremy Bentham, *An Introduction to the Principles of Morals and Legislation*

"The love for all living creatures is the most noble attribute of man."
  - Charles Darwin, *The Expression of Emotions in Man and Animals*

I remain delighted by the good fortune we've had on this trip with the weather. I mean, I'm not the sort to really let climatic effects get to me emotionally, so that rain and "bad" weather don't bother me much, although it can be frustrating to hike or work on other outdoor activities when you're soaked. Still, in the northern lands, many folks are really messed up by this sort of thing; we even have a name and its correspondingly amusing (to me) acronym for the basic influence of annual alterations in amounts of available daylight: seasonal-affective-disorder, or "SAD," which I think used to just be cabin fever. Some people really hate the almost 24-hour sunshine in the south-central part of Alaska, including Anchorage, which we get around the midsummer period, and they likewise cannot seem to tolerate well the scant six hours of light we're left with at midwinter. But I love it all; it just takes some acclimating. At any rate, since we began this trip, the weather's been deliciously cool, like autumn should be. Maybe that's the reason it's my favorite season. I don't see it in terms of everything dying, but everything celebrating life and preparing for regeneration. If it was such a downer, then why would all the living creatures up here make the elaborate plans for getting through the upcoming winter that I mentioned all the way back when I first left my *dojo?*

So now the sound of *crunch, scuff, slide* has returned, though thankfully without the accompaniment of "I Spy" this time. We seem more content with not talking for the moment, probably having done more than enough of that while packing up earlier today. This gives me time to not just savor the landscape, but also to face the simple truth that Dave is completely occupying my thoughts, and I'm wondering, like an infatuated young teen, how much he's considering me. As a group, the four of us have again alternated with lead positions: men in front, women in front, one couple in front. And Dave took my hand in his while Jack and Mariska were in the lead for a while, also like young teens not wanting to get caught before the parents of one of them arrive home. I missed the comfort of that strong paw when he took it away, although it is awkward to hike with a full pack and try and hold hands; the packs themselves, especially those with external frames, just brush your hands away.

But I wonder now what's been accomplished by this little trip of ours, other than providing the escapism we'd all hoped to attain. Indeed, it seems like none of us want to start talking again, not for fear, I don't think it's that, but maybe more from a sense of wanting to resolve something.

Why do we think that way? It's like the feedback Mariska offered me once when I asked her about both the best and the worst things about her job a few months ago.

The best: good breaks during holidays, with most of the summers free, although, being Iska, it's not like she spends much time away from the university on her posterior, and devotes those summers instead to doing work she wants to do: volunteering at the Alaska Native Heritage Center, running about with young Rebecca, traveling, sometimes with Jack.

And the worst: encountering students who seem to believe they headed off to college for the purpose of obtaining answers. Simple, clear, unambiguous, universally recognized and acknowledged answers. And I know this really frustrates her, especially if she also happens to be thinking about her daughter at the time: all three of these friends of mine, who haven't bathed now for days and who have revealed quite personal parts of themselves through simple conversation, agree that we've each been lucky to not have been made utter morons by our educational system.

So maybe that's a question for today, taking various forms. In other words, why does Dave feel misunderstood by his coworkers, even though they really do seem to respect him and enjoy his company and his emergency care expertise? Why does Mariska fret about her little girl being fed a bunch of ready-made responses to ancient timeless questions which we still have to consider and debate, perhaps because they might be only answerable through very subjective and cultural means? Why is Jack perceived as a smart-aleck, when he has such a sensitive ability to lead others through wilderness and city alike, and possesses such a delicate touch with a camera lens?

Should I bring this up? I wonder. Glancing around, I notice how the terrain has grown patchy, in a loose sense: smaller clumps of woods here, softer taiga there, so there's less uniformity. Our maps have this whole area shaded in green or just left blank as white patches, like I mentioned before during our drive north, so when you're up close and in it, you never quite know just what to expect next. Maps are just guides, after all: they can hardly reveal everything. One thing does stand out, however: that termination dust is lower than yesterday. And even with my overall positive assessment of the recent weather, it can grow overcast and foggy and even snowy around these parts quite quickly.

For the first time, I wonder briefly if we should head back, though we are making a loop of sorts. The Kahiltna River beckons before us, though we've not quite sighted it just yet. We still each carry extra food, plus emergency reserves like snacks and energy bars, and after mulling it over this morning have decided to try and spend a night as close to the river as safely possible, then work our way out of here tomorrow, which would make it three nights. None of us knows of any safe crossing, and we don't have sufficient time to seek one. And the snow will probably avoid us until after we get home.

It's still lovely, at any rate. Looking about, I recall that despite my considering Jack's skill, I've hardly seen him take any photos on this trip. His camera is with him, a weathered thirty-five millimeter beast owned by him for probably twenty years which he swears is all but waterproof and which has allegedly survived dunkings and droppings in six continents. He also has these cute little binoculars that he takes along on trips like this sometimes, though maybe he's already used them without my knowledge; like many tricky photographers, sometimes you just don't notice when he's up to something. The binoculars, too, are some nearly indestructible item much prone to travel abuse, a souvenir from one of his earlier intercontinental excursions. I think he said he's had them as long as the camera.

Considering how old the camera is also, it's of course not digital; Jack has sworn he will never stray to the dark side of the Force like that, pointing out that even though the newer technology has come a long way, it's both still too slow to really capture motion as he prefers to try, and you can still tell a digital at once if you try and blow up the image for a print later.

But I remember: he has probably two dozen shoeboxes full of photos at home. Mostly filled with rejects, too: Jack's the sort to not really make scrapbooks nor even collect organized albums, but he'll simply put together some of his better pieces into little flip-albums, and let the images speak for themselves.

He receives high praise for them this way, and feels his creativity is fully contained in the images, without any additional need for decorating them into albums. He has sold a bunch as well; even my latest employer has considered hiring him as a staff photographer, but he insists he wants to shoot whatever he wants to shoot, and not just fires or cutesy holiday events or sports or whatever readers of the paper consider news. Spoken like a true *artiste*, damn him. Maybe I'm just jealous. Of Jack doing whatever he seems to want to do, of Mariska for having such a great kid and being able to spend time away from academia playing and learning. I should be happy for them, whatever their future together or apart holds.

And yet I'm not jealous of Dave. I don't pity him, either, but I'm still feeling protective, like last night. Inquisitive, too, since now I've belted up like everybody does so much of the time, scared to broach a sensitive topic.

Why can't we just say what's on our minds? *Assuming, of course, that we really do have minds in the first place.*

Dave notices me grinning at that thought. "What are you thinking?" he says softly. Jack and Mariska are in the lead again, and don't hear him.

"Dangerous words, those, Mister Thomas."

That gets his attention. I knew it would, but I don't want to toy with him. "Why dangerous?"

"Because, as with our conversations on this expedition so far, who knows just where a seemingly innocent question or subject might lead?" Gods, I'm good sometimes; the words are so simple, and yet I can already think of several ways he could interpret what I said. Maybe I should be more precise, like he's always on about lately. But somehow, right now I just can't stop flirting. *Silly bitch.*

"That's the beauty of talking with genuine friends," he says. "There's no need to try and arrive at any particular destination, just like with this long hike of ours."

That feels quite reassuring, actually. Simplicity, again, and yet something so difficult and unpredictable in a "relationship." I have to dare this. Who said that, anyway? *Dare to know.* Plato? Kant?

You're stalling. Just ask him! "Dave, have you thought anymore about last night?" *Christ, you sound like an eighth-grade sappy dipshit wondering if she'll survive her first period.*

"Of course. I loved being with you. I especially enjoyed the dance lesson, though I'm sorry for tripping over all those roots."

I can tell he's also nervous. Why do people never get any better with this stuff as they age? Is it just the emotional vulnerability, or concern that we'll never find that eternal bliss that those damned childhood fantasy tales promised? I'm so tired of being afraid of feeling close, of risking emotional proximity and depth.

We used to call each other Morgan le Fey and Sir Accolon. But Accolon, at Morgan's urging, stole Excalibur from Arthur, and was killed for his trouble, which is the fate of all those who want knowledge or anything else to which they're entitled.

Enough, already. Enough. This isn't Charlie, and he's not any other schmuck you've dated, slept with, not called, dumped, fallen in lust with, or fantasized about. It's just Dave. Sweet, brilliant, frustrated Dave. "Yeah, well, most dance floors don't have so many gnarly roots. We should perhaps confirm that little fact sometime."

"I'd love to, Morgan. Maybe there's something coming up next weekend back in Anchorage. Club Soraya, or the Fred Astaire studio, or maybe even the Golden Lion."

I can take comfort in two things: one, he's not wimping out or masking feelings, and two, a fond reminiscence. And I strangely wonder briefly how much time he's logged at the other dance venues he just listed. "Do you remember that night at the Senior Center?" I say.

"Ha!" he laughs, prompting Mariska and Jack to turn around, wondering what we're on about. Seeing smiles, they resume hiking, lost in a universe of their own conversation probably. "I thought you were taking me to a retirement home, or just any place where you wouldn't have to confess to knowing me."

"Never that, sweetie." *Did I just call him that? Never mind.* And the Anchorage Senior Center is a recreational facility adjacent to a genuine "old folks home," a really clean and modern one, actually. And every few weeks, there's a live band, usually quite a talented one at that, playing jazz and swing and other tunes appropriate to the sort of ballroom dancing we were trying to finagle our way through last night amidst the trees. Maybe that's why some of the older folks in the city practice such: partly for the memories music brings, and partly since dancing is life, like I said, and who wants to focus on life for life's sake more than the elderly? "I just wanted somewhere that you'd feel more relaxed, before we hit the town for the Ball."

"You were a fine teacher then, and again last night. And you haven't answered."

No more backing out. Take a chance. "About what I was thinking?" He nods. "I was trying to picture the two of us together. Again at the Senior Center. Walking playfully and deliberately bumping into each other just for the contact, like those two goofballs up in front of us."

"I don't know, Morgan. I'm not sure how kindly Cozy and Angus would take to that. Didn't they both really adore Charlie?"

Still riddled with that stupid emotional anxiety, it takes a moment to realize he's kidding again. And I wonder about my cockatoo and ferret, and also about the very human son

Dave has in Chicago. Would Dennis handle a new woman in Dave's life? Would he be pleased, or threatened?

"They both really adore you. And Charlie always hated Angus; the little guy used to scamper all over him and his stuff at inopportune moments. He even crapped in his shoes once."

Dave laughs softly but open-mouthed at that, knowing well the feeling of the tiny paws on sensitive skin, if not the rapturous joy awaiting those who find their footwear victimized by vindictive small mammals. But Dave enjoys the sensations of those same little feet, doesn't find them threatening at all. "You know, you really should meet Dennis sometime."

For all the stories I've heard about this ten-year old boy, and all the photos I've seen of an eager kid who has his father's penetrating eyes and fellow love of loud sirens (he's made noises about wanting to join the Chicago Police someday), I've never before really considered the fact that I don't actually know Dennis personally. We've only been told of each other. "Why? What have you told him? About me, I mean." *Come on, woman; keep showing some backbone.*

"That you're one of my closest friends, among the best I've ever had, and that I could never risk losing you." My hopes feel dashed for an instant, an emotionally charged sigh escaping me as I imagine the "friendship speech" coming on at any moment; how else does one help ensure that one doesn't lose an already valuable friendship? But I'm premature: "He once said the two of us should 'hook up,' I believe was how he put it, since I seemed to care about you so much."

Wow. Maybe I should meet the young guy. "Did you and Dennis' mom part on very good terms? You never talk much about her."

"Mostly. She really is a city gal, and can't picture herself up here. She's got a well-paying job with an advertising company, which I always thought was too superficial and trite, and I know that contributed to at least some mutual resentment.

But I suppose she's just mostly afraid, like the others. Another contestant in the rat race; I reckon you have to be to be able to afford to live directly there in the city."

I doubt if this man shares the typical jealousy of a wife (well, ex-wife) who pulls down more money than he does; he's never struck me that way, and why else bother with a comment about "superficiality?" Still. "What do you mean, 'mostly afraid'?"

"Well, I mean she's afraid of, um..."

I don't want to pry, but the curiosity is making me want to. Badly. So I try to help coax it out. "It's like we've talked about before. Remember when we were hanging out at Title Wave, partly for me to reminisce and partly for you to drool over the options of used books?"

"Do you mean that time last year when we were so loaded up on caffeine from the coffee shop next door that we were sitting in the book shop giggling like a pair of stoners, waiting to come down off our high?"

I smile hugely at the memory. It had been pouring rain all day, and the two of us were just running errands. I had a few old books to unload, after Dave had gone through them himself of course. He had expressed semi-outrage at my wanting to trade in a Michael Crichton title: "State of Fear." That was what had actually gotten us talking, but at the time, he was still excited by work (how had it gone so far downhill so fast, and did paramedics really get so fed up so quickly?), and I was still trying to work things out with Charlie (and Dave was my proverbial and literal crying shoulder throughout all that crap), and, *wait, where am I going with this?*

Dave looks like he's still awaiting an answer, but one of the most glorious things about hiking is the lack of necessity to keep talking, and maybe that you can only maintain direct eye contact for so long, else lose your footing. Americans fret terribly over not knowing what to say at any given moment, like there's another clock ticking somewhere and punishment awaiting those who can't think of anything appropriate for speech right then. Other cultures prize silence, recognizing its power.

And I remember now. "Yeah. We kept laughing at the table where the visiting writers give their little talks, like two kids making too much noise in a library. Some people even looked at us like we were in a library."

"Until you said something typically golden, like, 'Hey, bite me, this is a goddamned store, not a temple.'"

What a delightfully wicked recollection that proves. Maybe I was just testing the patience of the patrons of my former employer. Or maybe I was just giddy from a temporarily caffeine-increased blood pressure.

When I stop laughing now, in the present, I remind him of Crichton's warning tale. It's about people living in fear of, well, *everything*, it seems. If it's not terrorists, it's the ozone, or now global warming, or fossil fuels (or alternative fuels), or diseases, or politicians, or the shit level of education I mentioned, or unexplained metaphysical things (whether God or the structure of spoons or the nature of true reality), or any damn thing at all which catches on and makes us all run and hide or at least consult our televisions until we decide we can feel safe again. I share this with Dave.

He nods. "That's more what I mean with my ex. She accused me of not knowing what the hell I wanted in life. I accused her, like I said, of being superficial, of wanting a job in which she tells people to part with money they may not have for stuff they certainly don't need."

"Ouch."

"Yeah. Anyway, it's hell to keep any relationship afloat when you don't support, in fact can't even believe in, what the other person does. How she defines herself. But I think she is a good mom, weirdly enough. She's great with Dennis. I've got to get the guy up here more often."

"I'm glad the two of you had such a great time over the summer."

"Definitely! And thanks, too. I'd rather have that, something continual like that for a period of weeks, rather than just the every other weekend thing that so many divorced parents have to contend with."

"So what is she really afraid of herself? Other than the usual maternal things like her job and her son's health and education?"

He really stops talking to think that one over, and we both simply spend a few moments noticing our boots gaining more miniscule amounts of wear. "You mentioned terrorism. Let me put it this way. I know I've already argued to you about how the word just means fear, and that the whole thing just becomes another irresolvable relativism."

I nod. Being told to fear anything at all, especially when little or no reason is given, makes the deliverer of the message, literally, a terrorist. A body count is unnecessary. What matters is that fear precludes thought, better than any drug could. And there's no better way to instill fear than to become dualistic and divisive: us versus them, this political party versus that political party, civilized versus wild, this religion versus that religion, allies versus enemies. It's usually given as an either/or scenario, and I don't know of any such case where there's not at least a third option, and often many more. But when you're afraid of something, anything, the ability to reason vanishes, along with the ability to make genuine distinctions and measured choices.

Sometimes that ability to reason never seems to come back. That's what worries Dave. That's what makes him want to leave his job. He can keep his own cool in an emergency. So can the other paramedics. And firefighters and police and hospital staff and soldiers. Usually. Hopefully. But even the best can get shell shock.

"So what's not relative, then? Anything?" That's why I don't do much reading of formal philosophy myself. I may be guilty of falling too much or too often into the "it's just a bunch of creative bullshit" camp. But then there's this guy next to me, pointing out that philosophy just asks "why?" Why act a certain way? Why believe a certain thing? Why fear anything? And if you can't arrive at answers, especially plausible answers, then it really becomes creative bullshitting. Maybe that's why teachers and theologians and lawyers and scientists and politicians are so good at the bullshit portion: giving the illusion of providing answers when they just spew their own beliefs in an effort to mask their own fears themselves, and those of their hapless listeners.

Dave half-answers my own question. "I think that the need to consider the questions is universal. We're all trapped with these higher brains, like it or not. We have tremendous leeway in terms of how to use them and how to act on the thoughts they produce. In other words, we have plenty of room to decide what to believe. But we have no choice at all as to whether we will pick something to believe."

"Yeah, you said that earlier, but it almost sounds religious. Should I be nervous?"

"I'm not talking about religion at all. Belief encompasses so much more than that. I'm talking about *any* beliefs. Like that I'm actually here, savoring this luscious fall day, with people who actually care for me."

From any other man, even Jack or my father, that would sound like sappy romantic greeting card crap. Only Dave could get away with a word like "luscious," because he means it. "So you feel 'trapped' by these 'higher' brains? Most people might consider them a gift."

He stops. I mean, he literally stops again now, his boots scraping over the vaguely defined trail through what have become thicker woods making grinding noises like punctuation marks. "You are kidding, right?"

He's staring at me rather intensely now. What the hell do I say to that? "Um, well, no. I mean, isn't this advanced processing power inside our skulls a good thing?"

"I think so, certainly. Even with the disagreements and the uncertainty, I absolutely believe that. But most people don't want this 'gift' at all. It's the ultimate accolade, and in my experience almost no one gives a shit."

"What?!" I've stopped hiking now, too, of course, briefly looking ahead to Mariska and Jack, who have disappeared behind some of the nearby trees. "Dave, much as I love you, aren't you the one who's kidding now?" *Gods, what a way to sneak in the "L" phrase.*

"Morgan, have you ever considered how many people actually use their brains? And I mean truly *use* them, to think independently, to grapple with issues other than what to have for breakfast or how to get the job promotion or why their kids can't stand them? What would most people do if they had original thoughts? Actually, no, that's not fair." He throws up his hands, catching himself. He doesn't want to sound preachy; I've seen him this way before.

I sigh, almost relaxed, but this is the calm before the storm.

"Really," he says now, "people do have real thoughts, about genuine questions and not just the superficial transient shit, but they shut those thoughts away. They're dangerous, or scary, or just weird. I barely know anyone who doesn't second-guess themselves. Christ, why do you think people have such a shitty attitude towards philosophy? You should see the looks I get, and the questions." He's calming down a bit now, though he's pacing back and forth like a trapped animal, and

I'm surprised our friends haven't seemed to notice the sudden change in vocal volume.

Dave pauses and looks about us then, like he's taking in the simple beauty of this very wild land, but I doubt he notices it at all. His voice briefly changes. "'What'cha readin', Dave?' 'Philosophy? Do you meditate too, Dave?' That's what I get these days, from anyone. If someone starts a new activity, like an exercise regimen, or a hobby, or a different job, or an address change, or a new relationship with a new partner, nobody bats an eye. But those things all resulted from philosophically weighed decisions, didn't they? People don't have to read Aristotle to pull this off, and they do it naturally as kids, but *their parents actually squelch this in them*. And when as adults they spend this one little snippet of time *thinking*, then they just pull out the brakes and it goes away, and they're right back into the mundane."

I'm feeling less protective from last night. And, I really want to know. "Do you think it was accidental?"

"What's that?"

"These 'higher' brains," and I point to the side of my head and tap at it. "The cerebral cortices, resting on top of mammalian centers, with reptilian raw instinct below. Is there a 'why' in the question as to how we turned out this way? Is this evolution of very complex brains, which occurred pretty quickly (which is why those brains are crammed so tightly into our heads), simple pure accident, or purposive?"

"It has to be purposive. It has to be good for something. Otherwise it would be another failed experiment: the Earth could phase out its test run of the cerebral cortex, and we could just go through the motions. Maybe we're already starting, if you think about it. We're making ourselves more and more stupid all the time, and the ability to critically consider seems to be becoming a progressively rarer skill, even a liability. Thinkers are still respected in some cultures, but Americans hate them."

I'm nodding now, intent enough on our talk to not even notice Jack and Mariska heading back our way. Their concerned shouts to get our attention are barely entering our perception. Like Dave said, we only pay attention to what seems necessary at the moment. All living beings are like that. And maybe that's why we spend so little time thinking; these brains are so evolutionarily new, maybe we don't even know what to do with them. It's like the analogy to high technology: it's advancing so quickly, and so many folks wonder if we possess the requisite intelligence to handle it all, but we go right on with the inventions anyway (some vaguely useful, some completely idiotic), because we can't imagine not doing so. And it's a cycle, too, since the new toys are just distractions, more escape mechanisms from thinking. The simple acquisition of them is another way to avoid thinking, and then we can't figure out why they were so supposedly necessary, and we get bored with them, too.

Like we grow bored with each other. Because we don't think.

"So what are we to do, then?" I say to Dave.

"Eliminate so much of this meaningless 'structure.' Set aside at least a couple of hours a day to just daydream and fantasize, no matter how old you are. Insist that kids interact with their teachers and their parents, instead of just trying to futilely memorize raw data to frantically recall on test days. Realize that we are all accountable for our actions, even if it seems like plenty of folks are getting away with all kinds of nastiness. I guess, above all, don't be passive unless you're specifically resting."

"Don't we have to be passive sometimes?" By now I am noticing the others, who've returned to our peripheral vision, but are standing quietly and observantly. After what Jack and Mariska have noticed lately, they're perhaps thinking that Dave and I are "talking through the relationship," or some such.

"Yes, Morgan," Dave says, "but again, I mean when resting. We otherwise have to work to stay alert, and I don't mean jumpy, like by using caffeine as we were joking about a minute ago, or any other drug to try and make us more attentive. Don't worry: I won't resume talking about hallucinating again. But I'm referring to avoiding passivity when it's just empty exposure to something which requires no thought: sitting on the couch watching television, sitting on a pew listening to a religious sermon. There's a way to sit and be involved, to 'actively do nothing,' if you will."

"Zen again?"

"That's one version, with actually loads of structure, but it doesn't have to be so serious or so dedicated. I just want people to pay attention."

"You know, that was how the natural philosophers began studying the whole world. The entire body of human knowledge is very largely based on simple observation, a form of passive acceptance."

He likes that, as I knew he would. "And it wasn't until much more recently that people realized," he says, "that no matter where we are or what we're doing, we're interacting with our surroundings anyway. A lot of folks were pretty distressed over what that logically implies for scientific observation, which is supposed to be completely objective, but I think subjectivity is inevitable. You can't subtract yourself from the world, not even when you're dead. You always affect things, willingly or no. Just existing therefore has a moral component to it."

"So do you think we're different, then?"

"What, you mean from other creatures, because of these nifty brains?" I nod my response.

"You know," he says, "I've thought about that a lot. So much of the stuff I've read just presumes that we're somehow different, and then we make the mistake of taking that and adding the even more egocentric assumption that we're therefore special. It makes me want to retch."

"Why? What if we are special? Don't you think Dennis and our friends, and I, are somehow special?"

"Nice try. And to me, of course you all are. But to the rest of the world, not really. And that's not negative, just true. I mean, if I drop dead today, I like to selfishly think that a handful of people will miss me, but will the world stop turning? Will the sun not rise tomorrow as a result?"

"Of course not, but why are you being so morbid?"

"I'm not trying to be, really. What I'm trying to say is, we matter to one another, and that's beautiful, and we do matter to the world, for the reason we just mentioned: everything we do has repercussions, even if they're tiny, or subtle, or if we never have a chance to learn what they are in the first place." I notice Dave's looking at me very tenderly right now, like I was attempting to do with him last night. He had trouble making eye contact while we danced, but maybe that was just embarrassment or uncertainty over the proper steps; whichever, it appears to have vanished now.

"That's the basic conclusion of Taoism, you know, Morgan: each of us is both hugely vital and of utterly no consequence, simultaneously, which is why that doctrine advocates not trying to selfishly interfere with what's going on, because you affect things anyway. The apparent contradiction of that, and the fact that one half of it seems like such a bummer, is why Westerners have trouble with it. But while we're talking about Asian thought, the basic conclusion of Hinduism, like we mentioned earlier, is that we are all interconnected, like it or not, so that what we do automatically affects everyone and everything else. This is the same conclusion you just brought up again, with the impossibility of scientific objectivity."

"And meanwhile," he keeps going, spellbindingly, "back a bit westward, one of the ancient conclusions of Judaism is to maximize your own potential to be a better person, and Christianity holds out hope that each of us might have that intrinsic value which we already have but forget, and Islam reminds us to keep trying. All these wisdom traditions just tell part of the story, but there's a common thread to all of them: try to be less of a selfish asshole, they warn us." I can't help giggling now, despite Dave's apparent seriousness. "Because there's a way in which you really do count, and another way in which you're just another speck of cosmic dust. There are no such things as VIPs. There are just composite wholes thinking they're each comprised of billions of individual little bits of consciousness."

Why does one of his phrases ring a bell? "Didn't you once say we shouldn't take religious teachings in particular at face value? Like how some followers believe that only they really matter because their faith is the only thing that matters."

"Yes, that sounds right. Siddhartha seems to have said it best. He told his followers to specifically *not* create a religion around his memory and teachings, and that no one should accept anything at face value unless he or she had considered it themselves, and weighed it according to their own reason. He was opposed to blind following. To my knowledge, Jesus said roughly the same, but both men were ignored. Entire religions were built around their memories: Siddhartha became the Buddha, and Jesus became the Christ. I'm glad I found that little truth out later in life. As a kid, my own religious teaching was so spotty and scattered that I thought 'Buddha' and 'Christ' were surnames. Like you could hop over to visit Joseph and Mary and see a doormat by their house which read, 'Welcome to the Christ residence.'"

I laugh again, and note that Dave's at least smiling, though so much of this clearly pains him. And I immediately remember, right then, at that magical moment of insight, my own little serendipitous observation from the first day of our trip, when I felt *connected* to all of our surroundings. I was lost in the vastness of the wilderness and yet knew I was an undeniable part of it at the same time. I felt pathetically small and also grandiose all in one indescribable instant. And I also confessed to myself that it took work to reach these feelings of, what? Enlightenment? "So are we getting into a debate on religion or ethics next?" I don't really want to; I just want to devour the intensity of all these feelings and insights, so I'm smiling while I say it. And I remember now too the note about "cosmic dust:" Richard back at the *dojo* said something similar once, about how even Einstein took notice of the insignificance of the individual. And ethics would seem to be next, since Dave can't seem to shut up about how to behave.

And I love him for it. I won't embarrass or distract him with a kiss, but listening to him, it feels like being in love for the first time. I feel connected. My *aikido* instructor Miss Rogers would be proud; she's forever on us about making these connections with one another while we train. Simple, but never easy. Usually that phrase annoys me.

"Ethics. Well, let's consider it. Hi, guys; welcome back." Dave turns toward Mariska and Jack, who have hiked back the short distance to rejoin us. "There are several versions and forms of ethics, and we have a huge stake in all of this, since everyone wants to know what's right, and how we should behave, or at least how all the other assholes should behave." Amazingly, Dave can keep going like this, just casually switching from one tremendous topic to the next, like awaiting the next course at a feast. And it *is* a feast, make no mistake: we're feeding ourselves with each other's ideas, a very different but just as vital form of nutrition. Those cerebral cortices make sizable demands, in more forms than one.

Grins all around. Mariska this time: "More light conversation, we hear. Let me see, now: virtue, command, obligation, utility, rights..."

"Sure. Those are the traditional, probably the only major forms of ethical influence. Which applies to the Athabascans, Mariska? Do you mind my asking?" Like Jack and I, Dave, too, feels that stupid political correctness shit just enough to wonder if he's offending, since Mariska's part of a culture which is largely alien to the rest of us, though there's no reason it should be.

Mariska's not put off, though. I've never seen her, at least that I recall, as animated as on this trip. "Virtue ethics, surely. Indigenous Americans tend to base their ethics on respect, usually for the Earth itself."

"Like what we spoke of a couple of days ago, right?" I say to her. "In other words, don't take more than you can use."

She nods. "That is simplistic, but true. I rather suspect other species tend to see us as a race of users, without being appreciative of what we have. I still offer my own thanksgiving even when I simply head into the bush to harvest plants and berries, and of course also when fishing."

"What about you, Dave?" Jack says. "I mean, you already know I think ethics should be built upon rights, and that means it's primarily about not infringing upon the rights of others."

Dave absorbs that, hardly surprised; Jack has indeed been affected by his international excursions, horrified by what he considers violations of basic human rights above all. "I think Mariska's on the right track, with virtue ethics. It's the only type that starts with the individual and then extends outward. Other ethical approaches begin with consideration of everyone else, with you playing catch-up."

My turn: "I think Jack is closer, really. All that social utility stuff makes the most sense, and it's also democratic, even egalitarian."

"Something's to be said for them all, clearly."

But Jack's having none of Dave's obvious plea: "You have yet to answer me. If there's one theme of this whole trip, it's that you have to come up with answers to the old questions, and you're no exception, my friend."

Dave can't quite hide a new smile, even though the challenge is back to him now. Turnabout's fair play, though, as my father would remind us all. "Let's see, now. None of us cited divine command, although Mariska mentioned it for the list. So none of us seems to feel we should behave in any particular way because some potentially hostile deities tell us to do so."

We make bodily gestures to concur. Now why is it that three highly educated persons, one with a master degree and another with a doctorate, keep appealing to the quite newfound wisdom of this friend who almost dropped out of college, picked up a degree in forestry mainly because he had most of the credits and couldn't decide on any other specialty, and whose qualification for this impromptu discussion group is filling most of his spare time reading as a mainly emotional response to career frustration? This is how cults begin, isn't it?

He's your friend, and you may be in love with him already and not ready to face it, so stop bitching. And you've never known anyone more loathe to have others quote him verbatim or look to him for personal guidance, though he might make an exception for his kid. Remember the sour expression on his handsome but unwashed face as he described the humble Siddhartha and Jesus becoming deities; David believes it a hideous transformation of lived wisdom.

And besides, almost all cults die out; only a very small number survive and evolve into religions. And even then, that initial cult-status only applies to those who opt to give up their ability to think; each of us would regard that as intellectual anathema, especially Dave.

And he now continues. "Okay, so no gods: whatever any supernatural entities may desire, their wishes and even their existence seem to remain unempirical, which means we're left questioning what they want in the first place, though plenty of philosophy started by asking such questions. What else? Oh, moral relativism as an ethical system fails logically, since you can't universalize it, which leaves the proverbial door open to all kinds of abuses, since it claims that nobody's standards are any better or worse than any others."

"I'd agree to both of those," Jack says. "But you're stalling with your own answers. Don't tell me you're afraid of disagreeing with us. And I thought like crazy that you were a relativist. What else was the discussion about reality dealing with?"

"No, it's not that exactly, but I do respect what you're each saying. Which one's next? Right: your own notion of rights-based ethics has its promise, Jack, but like we talked about with opinions a two days ago, when we talk of rights we too often forget the accompanying responsibilities."

Jack nods his very tentative assent. "Shit, how could I forget? Let's not get back into that again; I'll conditionally agree that the two have to exist together, or else people will likely tend to get spoiled and bitchy for their entitlements."

Mariska, I notice, is following every syllable, but with the unmistakable glint of her own challenge to Dave's latest conclusion. "What of virtue, then?" she says.

"I'm getting there. First, the utility Morgan mentioned is, despite its admitted democratic appeal, still quite susceptible to abuses of the majority: if what is right is what we decide via majority vote, then what becomes of those who hold the dissenting view? What do we do with them? And Mariska's background in history can certainly inform you of the kinds of extreme injustices which have emerged out of that: usually we isolate or punish or simply kill them outright."

This is covering huge amounts of ground quickly, and Mariska is indeed nodding. She once told me the main reason she went into history was to challenge the injustices of the past.

And she, too, believes we've gotten dumber as a species, and loves pointing out that no modern person actually truly knows how the Pyramids or Stonehenge or the Hanging Gardens were actually built, even though we think we're smarter than those ancients. Yet she's as idealistic as Dave, thinking we really can learn from the past after all. If we're willing to listen and think. "Are there any even left?"

"Yes, other than virtue." Dave's on a roll. It's strangely fun to watch him in action, so to speak. "Duty ethics, or deontology, likewise falls apart when you think it through. It's a good starting point, especially for kids as a learning tool, since it might help to instill some sense of respect like Mariska emphasized, but you're eventually going to ask, I would hope, why exactly you have a duty to do something in the first place. And then the answer becomes: because doing it or avoiding it has certain consequences. And when you consider consequences, you're right back to utilitarianism and majority rule, with its attendant bad side effects. It's *Star Trek* ethics: 'the needs of the many outweigh the needs of the few or the one,' but you're still left with what Mill called the tyranny of the majority."

I've just decided I need to write an article for the *Daily News* about my insightful friend. "Backcountry Paramedic Reveals Mysteries of Universe," I can call it. Maybe. I could get it into the Life section, perhaps for the big Sunday edition as a human interest story.

And then I'd be guilty of exploiting him. I doubt Dave would ever go for it. He'd complain that there are too many egos out there allegedly spouting wisdom as it is. Like Siddhartha said and Dave paraphrased, we each have to work it out on our own. And like I realized twice on this trip, it takes work. And the fact that it takes tremendous, often lifelong effort, is precisely why we turn the messengers into gods: Siddhartha, Confucius, Socrates, Jesus. They each warned us we had to think things through on our own and not act like sheep. The sheep might get messily devoured by the wolf, speciesist imagery notwithstanding. And sheep are almost always found in flocks: strength in numbers, or at least the false feeling of strength, that "tyranny of the majority."

Dave would insist on individuality, come what may. He's aware of the costs.

Maybe I'll just write an article for the Friday edition about what it's like to backpack during autumn and how to survive the deep conversations which may likely result among you and your fellow hikers. I think I was already thinking along some such lines when I left the *dojo* last week and hurried home to pack.

I share my conclusion. "Dave, you want virtue ethics, not so much because it starts with the individual as such, but because you insist that *everything* has to start with the individual: before group identities which lead to thinking like the group instead of thinking like a person."

He looks ready to kiss me again. "Morgan, that's beautiful. If only I had some paper and a pen, or a mini recorder or something!" From any other man, I might've taken this as offensive, but I'm glad that he appreciates my mirroring his insight.

Mariska then offers a potential obstacle. "Which virtues are we discussing then?"

"What do you mean?" I say.

"Well, I have already professed that tradition as my own, but it becomes difficult to qualify further. In a sense, you almost have to make a list of virtues to discuss virtue ethics. So, which should we admire and follow? Or is this another relativistic thing?"

Dave and I both take that in, and I can see Jack making a mental listing of the great virtues; at least, that's what he seems to be doing, if I had to guess. That's the catch with the virtue model: you have to eventually identify the ideals you wish to live up to, and then expect, perhaps selfishly, everyone else to live up to them as well. "I suppose the risk is of people using their own alleged virtue to become self-righteous, and we all know what the likely outcome of that is," I say, receiving nods. The greatest killers in history never seemed to suffer from self-doubt, after all.

"Yeah," Dave says. "It can't just be posing. Politeness might be a virtue, but without understanding the reason for it, it just becomes stuffy and empty."

"Did Confucius not say that one had to understand the meaning behind all the social rituals?" Mariska asks. "Like with generosity and justice. You have to understand why those things are worth pursuing."

"Yes, and Aristotle said that the whole key was to have neither too much nor too little of any particular virtue. With courage, for example, which was one of the Greek's favorites, too much made you a vainglorious idiot and adrenaline junkie, while too little made you indecisive and cowardly, suffering from Hamlet Syndrome."

"Is that an actual affliction?" Jack wonders aloud.

"I think so," I explain. "It's about fatal indecision and the need to act. For all the philosophizing, you eventually have to make a decision and follow it through."

And we shortly find ourselves making a laundry list of sorts. The four of us arrive at our own compilation of the ideal virtues, including those we've already mentioned (justice, courage, generosity), and others we just keep adding impulsively, like faithfulness, thankfulness, gentleness, simplicity, tolerance, compassion, even humor, the last of which is offered by Dave, curiously, who for all his seriousness about his life recently still remains convinced that life itself is a comedy.

Then Jack pipes up again, aware that we've made a nifty list, but haven't really accomplished much concretely. "But Dave, what about specific cases?"

"Like what?" I, too, wonder how we can start applying this to specifics, though maybe we can never get past Aristotle's model of the golden mean, of acting between the two extremes with each trait. Still, the gift from those Greeks, I think, is the notion that virtue, all virtues, are inherently teachable, that all children can learn them. The Chinese and Indian traditions would agree, and those three cultures are the birthplaces of philosophy.

"Such as," and he steals a furtive glance at his erstwhile partner Mariska. "Such as, for example, having kids? Those to whom we have to teach about these virtues?"

"Having them, or raising them?" Dave says, and I wonder if I'm the only one who detects the subtle challenge in his tone. And what made Jack choose that as an applied ethics issue? The big three, I recall, are abortion, euthanasia, and capital punishment; nothing charges an ethics discussion like consideration of the possibility of death.

Socrates said the entire purpose of studying philosophy and thinking rationally was to come to terms with your own mortality. And his fellow citizens murdered him for it. Where did that cheery memory come from?

"Either. Why is there any difference?"

"Because this whole time since you two got ahead of us on the trail, Morgan and I have been discussing one thing, albeit along varying perspectives, and that's human selfishness, which led right into ethics. And there is a difference."

Jack appears to recognize the answer, but he's weighing his words, perhaps not wanting to risk offending Mariska. But I suspect she can again take it, although I'm also wondering if all our talks have really been so simplistic, in the end. "Raising kids may be the most selfless act of which any of us is capable. It has to have huge effects on ethics."

Dave nods, as does Mariska, the only parents among our foursome. Jack looks to me as though for support, since, while I may have extensive babysitting experience and a smattering of youngish relatives, I'm still not directly a mom as such, unless you consider those two little critters back in my apartment. Most parents don't consider pets to be "kids," though the animal-lovers often disagree. And I've been known to point out to some parents that during the first year or so of a child's life, "pet" is precisely what the child is: adults talk to the kid like it's a pet, and expect it to do tricks for their amusement. They're just different kinds of tricks. Talk about objectifying: no wonder kids start thinking rationally. They're busily trying to figure out how to escape such social bullshit.

Jack risks continuing. "Fine, I'll say it. Having them is hugely selfish. The only way to offset such an act is to go through the trouble of raising them, and doing a good job at it. You've got to try and instill those virtues in them as you go, but the initial act is selfish. Maybe that's the Aristotelian golden mean."

But Dave wants this clarified, or at least voiced. "Why is it selfish, Jack?"

Jack's getting flustered now, realizing he's at the midst of one of any society's biggest taboos: we've talked about education, sure, but now we're raising the accompanying issues of children themselves, the future generation, those who will initially judge us for posterity. "Look, gang, I love Dave and I love Mariska and I think you're both exceptional parents. But when you have a kid, you're essentially asking everyone else to behave differently, and that's why ethics exists at all. And with having kids, the reason's just so you can pass on your questionable genetic material, and keep an alleged 'line' going, and give someone else your name. And before you all lynch me, let me say that a lot of parents, probably most parents, stop at that point, even though most people mention love first, which strikes me as quite untrue considering what I've seen. What they see is the cute little gurgling creature they've just created as though by magic, and don't consider the responsibilities, or the costs, which we all have to pick up, or the fact that this child will not always appreciate these older beings which have brought it into existence." I suspect we all notice how Jack emphasized the "r" word there, no doubt to get Dave's attention. Having children is considered a right, for some ill-defined reason; responsibilities do tend to get mentioned far less often.

"So why don't you have kids, Jack?" I say, which, surprisingly, gets some laughter from the group.

But his response is wholly serious. He again goes out of his way to address all of us while answering. "Because that selfishness has horribly overpopulated this poor planet, which is why we have such problems agreeing on ethics. Because there are hundreds of millions of kids who need homes that their parents either wouldn't or couldn't provide after all, but most people don't want to adopt, since like I said, they want to pass on their own DNA as though that actually matters where love is concerned, and I think love's the best virtue of them all. Because I'm too immature and I can't imagine giving up traveling, even though traveling and seeing how shitty so many kids have it is what got me thinking this way. Because I already love Rebecca and Dennis and don't need to be around other children. Because my own ego does not insist on my creating little Godwins to trot about, much as my folks would love grandkids. And because modern parents demand that no one interfere with teaching or raising *their* kids, no matter how bad a job they may be doing teaching or raising them on their own." Jack is almost breathing heavily after this all comes out.

"You are not immature," Mariska proffers. "We all need a mix of playfulness and maturity, and you balance them well."

"Thanks, Iska. There are just so many costs with this, which people never consider: education and health care and food and housing all cost, and not just money, either."

Mariska nods, then turns to us. "So, how much further does anyone suppose we still have to go today?" A bit more good-natured laughter at that. We've already been hiking for a few hours, and have more to finish if we're going to reach an appropriate campsite somewhere closer to the river. Not receiving a verbal answer, Mariska suggests, "Why do we not take a break, then? We already are, really."

Packs get slid off slightly sore hips and backs, the sudden loss of weight eliciting contented sighs from sore and tired bodies. I pull out an energy bar. The others have their own snacks, though Jack has again reverted to his delightfully youthful ways and begun comparing his own snacks to those of Mariska, claiming of course that hers are better and she should share.

Relaxing, I'm ready to try a more radical question now, with all of us sitting, like we're the only ones left in the world. "Dave, has Dennis ever heard you talk like this?"

"Sure. But you should hear his mother when I try and speak this way, even though I don't use any jargon and I just encourage the young guy to use his brain. She can't stand it, gets on my ass about filling his head with all that intellectual crap. And all I'm asking him is to be human. That's what we are, you know: the great philosophers through history have tended to classify us as rational animals, or reasonable beings, or some version of the same phrase. Supposedly this is what makes us different from the other creatures on this planet, even though it gives a false sense of superiority."

"Yeah, you mentioned that earlier, too. I wasn't sure how you would answer that: do we deserve special treatment after all? I think I'd just accused you of being morbid."

"I remember. And I think the only thing that makes us different is facing the fire."

"What does that mean?" I force out between bites. The cool weather has made the bar extra stiff and tough to chew, so

I have to wash it down with some water from the Camelbak, which is likewise quite cool.

"Remember what we said about fear. You said it, actually, I think."

"What's that?"

"If there's anything that makes us different from the other species with whom we're fortunate enough to share this world, then I think it's facing the fire. I had a friend once who took this to mean: 'what, you mean cooking?'"

I love that image. And it's true, actually; we could come up with a new philosophy based entirely on cooking as what makes us stand out from other animals. Those folks on the Travel Channel would love it. I chuckle while Dave continues, between bites, wondering who the better cook out of the two of us might be; considering how little I do myself, it could go either way.

"But anyway, what I mean by facing the fire is that everything alive on the planet is instinctively terrified of it, including us, although individual animals can get used to it, as long as it's relatively contained and not torching a whole forest. I wonder how many eons had to pass from the time we first started walking upright to the time when we took the chance of getting closer to fire to watch it in action. It was probably on a small scale; I can't imagine our forebears sticking around to watch an entire forest conflagration, especially since every other creature nearby would have been frantically trying to escape it. And then I wonder how many more millennia elapsed until we were able to actually start to work with it. Think of it, Morgan: everything we consider part of civilization emerged after we'd first domesticated fire. That was the first living thing we tamed, to work with metals, and to create the longer-lasting pottery which archaeologists love finding so much, and, of course, to cook. All the really good tools are products of fire. And of all the primordial elements, it was introduced as the possible key element of the universe because it represents change; everything fire touches gets altered by it."

"I'll bet the firefighters at your station are amused by this particular thought of yours, considering their job descriptions."

Dave laughs himself at that, nodding as well. "Yeah, they do. They just don't like it when we lose control over it. But you know I don't think there's any such thing as control, anyway."

"So what else does 'facing the fire' mean?"

Dave takes another minute to both gather his thoughts and chew his way through his own energy bar which is still the consistency of hard taffy from the cool weather. I have to keep foods like these in my pants pockets to help them warm up a bit. "Look at it this way: getting over that trepidation about fire was the smartest thing we ever did as a species, at least from the perspective of it leading to our more advanced tools and the cultures and civilizations built with them. Now we get scared mostly of ideas, which don't bother the other animals: most of them are still scared shitless of fire. Even just the presence of smoke is enough to drive off the most determined animals. The problem is, we got both cocky and complacent."

"You're losing me." Even though we're all sitting down, Jack and Mariska are reclining a few yards from us, just laying back and enjoying the view. I glance in their direction, and notice what they must see: the clouds to the east have gotten lower, puffier, and greyer (at least, I think it's the east; the going has been thicker through this portion). Some snow or rain soon, to dampen our mood along with our gear perhaps? I'd sooner get to our next site before the weather turns for the worse, preferring to listen to rainfall on my tent than to hike through it.

"Sorry," Dave says, sounding slightly further than he is. "When I was referring to my ex, I said she was afraid. But not of the typical things one might suppose: she's fearless walking around her huge city, and she's unafraid of business meetings and proposals and deadlines, which are more the sorts of things to make me a bid edgy. And yet she'd never even think of joining one of these talks of ours, and not just because it's with me, or because we're currently in the middle of nowhere."

"I thought we were in the middle of everywhere."

"You know, I really love when you talk like that. You're a poet."

"And don't know it?" I say.

"Ahh, you just ruined it. It's not when you're being all cliché. It's when you're just expressing yourself. Small wonder you're a writer."

But I'm not really writing what I want. The paper's a good job so far, and decent pay, but doesn't every journalist aspire to write that great novel or dissertation or collection of poetry?

"Plato said we have to leave the cave, you know."

I'm still thinking wistfully over the what-ifs in my life. "What was that?"

"We have to leave the cave, and face the fire."

"I must have missed that one, Dave." *Damned Greeks. Why do we keep going back to them?*

"The job of the philosopher, according to that cantankerous old fart, was to lead people out of the cave of ignorance. See, the analogy appears in the *Republic*, Plato's best known work. The main part of it is his outline for an ideal society, which was rather undemocratic and tending towards totalitarianism. I should tell Jack to read it, since people don't get to raise their own children in it, and they're raised by the state instead. And there're three social classes corresponding to the three parts of the human psyche, to use a modern term, and the book does give women the benefit of the doubt, at least sometimes. But the cave is the strongest imagery."

"So what happens in there?" says Jack this time, having pricked up his ears at the mention of his name.

"People are living in there. But they're chained in place, so tightly they can't even turn around to see the cave entrance. All they see is the wall in front of them. I'm unsure if they can even see one another, so how much would that suck? Anyway, on the wall is a never-ending series of dancing shadows, created by a fire behind them, so these shadows are partially the images of the people themselves, and partially whatever and whomever else moves in front of the fire to cast darkened pictures on the cave wall."

"This is charming," Jack says. "What cheery message was old Plato trying to give us with this one? And who chained the people up in the first place?"

"That's just it, Jack; it's not literal, and I don't know who locked them there. It's an allegory. It was supposed to be gloomy as hell, but even scarier from our perspective since these prisoners have no idea that they're prisoners in the first place. Plato was trying to scare us into the realization that he believed that was actually how almost everyone lives. In daily life, no matter where we come from, what we believe, or whom we love, we're content with the images on the wall. I think Plato would've had conniptions over something like television."

Wouldn't he just? And what, then, of Marx's allegory of religion and opium? He'd probably crap frogs over television as well. "So how does the philosopher come into this?" Mariska wants to know now. Apparently snack time is over, though Iska and Jack still face away from us, watching much more grandiose things than mental stone walls.

"Plato felt very heroic in that sense. He thought the philosopher was on a rescue mission, very dramatically so. The liberator comes dashing into the cave, chopping away at the chains, and slowly, very slowly, leading the people out of their lifelong imprisonment. It's kind of like the surgeon who worked on Val Kilmer in that movie he did with Mira Sorvino: 'At First Sight.'"

Jack acknowledges what he regarded as a lackluster film in which a man blind from birth receives radical new surgery and can suddenly see, though his senses are utterly overwhelmed by all the new intake of information. Jack decides then to stick on this point. "Why slowly, though? Why not just pull them right out?"

"Look at it historically instead of analogically." Dave pauses, trying to mentally scrounge up an example. He snaps his fingers, really into it. "Mariska, when the prisoners in the concentration camps at the end of the Second World War were liberated by Allied troops, a lot of them still died shortly afterwards. Some of them were just too far gone to be saved: starved and worked and infected with disease to death. But some of them also died surprisingly quickly when their emaciated bodies were provided with sudden stores of food from those same Allied soldiers."

Mariska nods. "Their systems could not handle much food at once. When you are starving, you must eat in very small amounts and build your body back up slowly. The system shock will kill you otherwise. And I see how this fits Plato's cave."

Jack gets it, too. "Too much daylight at the cave opening, too much light all at once. The poor buggers would be blinded!" he says, mimicking a Scots accent, something he sometimes does when making exclamatory remarks.

"But not just blinded," Dave explains dramatically. "Dead. Like those other liberated prisoners, the historical ones. Their systems couldn't handle the shock, either."

"Truth hurts, right, Dave?" I say to him. "Ignorance is bliss?"

"The only way to know if ignorance is bliss is to lose your ignorance and think it through, but by then it's too late, of course, so it's a genuine dilemma. It's the same problem with the realization that youth is wasted on the young."

Jack's still playing with the allegory, though. "Why would it kill them?"

"The lesson is just that no one can handle too much of an upset all at once. It's too much input, perhaps even fatally so."

"But why would knowledge be lethal?" Jack demands.

"Jack, it's a story. It's about having to undertake a lifelong quest, to continually seek knowledge, to continually seek to improve yourself by staying out of the cave and never venturing back inside, no matter how appealing the shadows might have been."

"That cave may be a gilded cage, but it's still a cage, is that it?" I say. Who wrote that, I wonder? I probably had to know it for a literature class.

Dave just nods. Jack seems to want to stay literal for some reason. "Face the fire," he says, then adds, "How the hell did you end up working with firefighters?!"

That strikes us all as hilarious, and Dave laughs like it's the funniest thing he's heard in years, bending over at one point from the isometric workout his abdominal muscles are now getting. It's amazing how laughter does that. Maybe laughing is a version of stepping out of the cave, too.

"We just have to think," Mariska says.

"And then there's you," I say, pointing at Dave, "living up to your potential, and you're also not a speciesist, with all this talk about us feeling all high and mighty compared to other animals, and since I know you think the likes of Angus and Cozy can think, too, even if it may not be on the same level as us."

"Morgan, look, I wouldn't trade this weekend out here with you three for anything, but if you're going to insult me, then maybe we should just continue on, and..."

"Hey! I did *not* just insult you. That was a compliment. You're helping to keep me on my toes, too. Why do you think I just took a job as a writer? It's a job that requires thought, even if it's not always deep or of such a character that it'll just change the world."

He mulls that over for a moment. I swear I can almost again hear the gear wheels in his cranium whirling about. "Good point," he says back.

I look then at Jack and Mariska, sitting next to each other, hands held and resting in the grassy rocky terrain. Am I out of the cave now? For a while, at least, savoring all of this, knowing it's too much to take in at once, like Plato's prisoners encountering the light?

And what happens when we head home? Are our homes and jobs and daily routines just other caves? They offer safety, but they're also artificial, devoid of meaning except what we can force into them. Like those kids in *The Breakfast Club* again, wondering if they're doomed to become their superficial and dull parents.

And then we count down the days and weeks until we can venture out like this again. To regain this feeling of complete, true freedom. It's not a vacation; that's a type of escapism. I'm (we're) trying to immerse my- (our)- selves in all of this vastness, to feel like we're truly a part of something: of ourselves, of each other, of this whole great land. And in between such excursions, we opt for the mini-escapes, the smaller versions of sneaking past the cave opening for a glimpse of reality: the sudden laughter, the sense of accomplishing, the getting lost in a good read, the experiencing of an orgasm. All little items and events to shake us out of that cage, however gilded it might or might not be, to face the fire of reality.

My friends look so peaceful, even though one of us has to shortly take the initiative and get us all moving again. Dave hasn't noticed that my staring has shifted to him. I cannot take my vision in any other direction right now; I just devour him with my eyes, feeling love for these three souls. And also, strangely, for myself.

And as I force my gaze from him, with Dave remaining wholly oblivious of it in the first place, I now cannot get this idea of love out of my head, what Jack said is the greatest of all the virtues. Is that what motivates us all; is it just that alone? Is it enough, or does passion require the admixing of reason, the impetus behind all our wilderness talks on this trip? And what about this nonsensical phrase "making love," anyway? Talk about some politically correct bullshit, an ancient phrase from the time prior to when "political correctness" came to be known by that name; it's just more dishonesty, a collection of euphemisms and dysphemisms to conceal questionable behaviors. What a term, though: I've never understood it literally. Can love, devotion, loyalty, truth, be *made*, actually created? Planted and reaped? Is "love" just a beggar for affection, or worse, a dictator, a chemical addiction? I've "made love" with men for love, for pleasure, for fun, for trust, for loyalty, for mourning, for healing, out of boredom, excitement, and insecurity and the idiotic need for approval, and even for no definable reason at all. But what *is* it? What is actually created?

* * *

Of course, it was difficult enough for a lone wolf to escape detection by a foreign pack. But four wolves traveling together were bound to elicit attention from the members of the Chelatna pack. And now, right at the time that the Fire Creek survivors were at last feeling like they might be safe, protected between the immense mountains while winter was about to set in, they nonetheless realized that they were now invaders.

The Fire Creek pack members by now understood that they had to move quickly through this other pack's territory if they were to have any genuine chance of continued survival. The good news was that the men and their thunder and dogs were far enough behind them, in both days and distance, to have been largely relegated to memory. So with the likes of men, dogs, and ornery moose and wolverines behind them, at least for the time being, the wolves now found themselves ironically at their greatest peril, from members of their own kind. If they could avoid confrontations, naturally.

Their journey had covered over a hundred and fifty kilometers in a matter of days. By human reckoning, these wolves had found their slain packmates less than a week before. And none of these intrepid survivors could imagine more difficult terrain than what they had just traversed, only to find that the very end of it was the clearly and unmistakably marked borders of another territory. The scent marks and physical remains found by Oak, Paddler, Trap-dasher, and Dog-chaser in this vicinity suggested that a minimum of a half dozen other wolves lived not far away, and there could be others as well. Considering how recently the markings and droppings had been left, it meant either a smaller pack with a smaller territory and enough time to regularly patrol their borders, or a larger pack with a larger territory, and possibly patrolling the same way, but in larger numbers. Either way, the odds of detection were against them.

But now, the elements were as well. The four wolves understood that true winter was about to set in with undeniable force, and that the route of the last quarter of their quest would soon be closed. Possibly with them still caught in the middle of the forthcoming snow, if they deigned to retreat at this point. Whoever comprised the territory they'd unwittingly set foot in had chosen the terrain well: the Fire Creek members found themselves facing southeast into the Chelatna homeland, among the multiple rapidly rushing braids of the West Fork of the Tonzona River; their introduction to this river had been the presence of a feisty and possessive wolverine.

The river followed a rough Z pattern, southeast then southwest then again southeast, and while it had been usually comparatively easy to keep the river in sight these past few days, what sobered the wolves was the dramatic change in terrain. The former home of the Fire Creek wolves in the shadows of the Sunshine Mountains scores of kilometers away had its share of hills and challenging map features, but nothing like what awaited them while they ensured their distance and accompanying safety from hunters and other creatures. Granted, they'd totally escaped another wolf territory during their quest, but they knew they could hardly establish themselves anew in the western portion of the mighty Alaska Range. Between the extreme cold, the tremendous peaks, and the general lack of food that these characteristics ensured, there was no home for wolves or any other endothermic creatures there.

Mystic Pass was the name the humans used for this rocky channel: a severe narrowing leading south through the mountains, with the river the only feature by which to even begin to navigate; even when out of sight, the wolves could almost always follow it by sound. And even its temperature grew colder as they had ascended. The total elevation change was just a few hundred meters, but the exposed rock and scree and sharp edges had yielded bloody paws and a dearth of prey. The trees thinned, the rocks grew, while dozens of glaciers surrounded the wolves.

Yet the wind was the worst part. Accelerating through the narrow mountain channels and broadcasting the more severe weather which would follow in its wake, the icy gales came screeching down from the peaks and left the tired and hungry wolves sufficiently on edge that they'd hesitated even allowing their feet to get wet since their drying would be uncomfortable, even painful. Still, the cuts and scrapes emerging on their protective footpads relished the occasional quick dunk into the rushing water, and the wolves took turns grooming and licking each other's feet; Dog-chaser went out of his way to make sure Oak and Paddler still had full use of all paws. Such care had taken place each morning, after the four had slept huddled together to share warmth.

And now those same two *alphas* turned around from their current position, stomachs grumbling for lack of ingestion for two days, and even their last meals had been a random mix of ground squirrels and a couple of careless snowshoe hares. A lynx had startled one of the hares right into the path of the trotting wolves, then wisely let the canids have it. One to one, a lynx and a wolf might prove almost a match, considering the cat's proportionately huge feet and mean claws, but the felines tended to stay as far from wolves as possible. They seemed to know wolves usually had friends.

Oak and Paddler, thus reversing their view, simply panted at the partial sight of what they'd all just ventured through and dared. Grey clouds hung over this portion of the Alaska Range, probably signaling more snow; they'd already felt flakes on their noses and eyes while working their way through the treacherous Mystic Pass. They couldn't last the winter in there, certainly had no wish to go back through it to the flatter regions, and were now hemmed in by their tracks in that direction on one side, immense mountains liberally sprinkled with glaciers on their flanks.

And another pack's homeland on the fourth side, in front of them, beckoning and threatening simultaneously.

The *alphas* knew they had no good choices now. But they wouldn't go back. Part of leadership meant making decisions and following them through, even if they turned out to be wrong via hindsight.

But they didn't think this was a wrong decision. Just an unfortunate one, since they would now have to be as alert as they ever had been, knowing that their next meals would have to be taken from an area which would no doubt be jealousy guarded by others of their kind.

And Dog-chaser, still quite cognizant of his responsibilities, noticed the defeated looking Trap-dasher and the emotionally exhausted Oak and Paddler. Dog-chaser had already started to venture straight southward, along a line which looked like it would skirt some smaller and lower mountains which thus far remained free of whitened summits. It also appeared to follow the border of the newly discovered if alien territory, so hopefully it would be less likely to be traversed as regularly as the rest. He had also detected both scents and physical, partly digested remains of good prey in the demarcating scat left by the Chelatna wolves: moose and caribou definitely lived around these parts, and not just smaller food sources like rodents. It was eerie to get that close to markers left by wolves he didn't know, but he felt strangely reassured by the clear presence of good food sources. If there was truly enough to go around, then maybe the Fire Creek wolves could avoid trouble with the already established residents.

This was at the western end of the S-shaped territory belonging to the Chelatna pack, whose members were right then scattered more to the east; the signs of their dominance had been left days before, fresh enough to easily gain the attention of the Fire Creek pack, and which would last for another couple of weeks before really needing replacement. The Chelatna members were diligent enough to keep their borders well defined this way, making regular patrols which served the additional function of locating the likeliest whereabouts of larger prey species. This territory was roughly five hundred kilometers squared in area with its curious shape largely defined by mountain and river features: a bit smaller than might seem necessary to support a dozen wolves ranging in age from less than a year to almost seven. But the prey was indeed plentiful here, consisting of a variety of species requiring specialized skills to bring down. Any wolf traveling on its own could of course catch hares, rodents, slow-witted and slow-moving birds, and even the occasional fish. Larger prey was far riskier, unless it was too young, too young, or ill or injured. The ravens sometimes helped with spotting prey; indeed, Chelatna wolves were known, along with many others of their kind, to follow the glossy black airborne opportunists to realize that the avians could be useful allies in the hunt, later benefiting from the remains of kills after the wolves had taken their fill.

And once again, Dog-chaser crawled over to Oak and Paddler, nuzzling each of them gently and thus helping to encourage them to continue, tired or no. They needed shelter as well as food, since this was a highly exposed area, and even the comfort beneath larger trees, which could be rare in these parts, would be most welcome now. Dog-chaser knew the *alphas* would resume their courageous leading soon, so he moved over to Trap-dasher, who sat apart from the others, eyes half-closed.

Dog-chaser was feeling wiped out, too, but he edged his way ever closer, and rather than stand in what might be taken as an effort to intimidate, laid down instead, nudging his head in next to his brother's. Trap-dasher resisted at first, then gave in to his fatigue and let Dog-chaser nuzzle him. The latter then rolled over onto his back, exposing his belly to the elements, and playfully wriggled back and forth, the motion largely preventing Trap-dasher from completely resting. He would have to move now in order to fully stretch out and relax.

Both of them, in fact all four of them, could have easily fallen asleep right there, but all realized how vulnerable they were. It was indeed getting later on in the afternoon, but they would have to plod onward, knowing that Dog-chaser's proposed route did appear to truly be the safest bet among their disappointing options.

* * *

The Chelatna wolves, meanwhile, had both regrouped and remained wholly unaware that their territory had just been invaded. And interestingly enough, there was surprisingly little that wolves did to prepare for winter. Bears, like the pregnant sow the pups had recently encountered, were of course finishing their preparations for hibernation. Caribou still clustered in their herds, content that their snouts would still find foods in plant form beneath the snows. Moose merely altered their diets, focusing more on exposed branches now that fruits were mostly gone for the year and lower plants would soon be covered. To the wolves, winter would just be another part of the cyclicity of their lives.

But confronting other wolves, and the dangers that represented, was not typically on the seasonal menu of activities, something Rendezvous and Cabal were well aware of when they actually sighted the bedraggled looking interlopers from a distance of several kilometers. This was far more serious.

The snows to the west had yet to venture this way, and the two wolves, Cabal an older *beta* male and Rendezvous, the Chelatna counterpart to Dog-chaser, had ventured up a hill on the far side of the Yentna River. The foliage was less dense in this area, and while the hill was shorter and more gradual in its ascent, it afforded enticing views westward. The pair had just been relaxing in the late fall day when they noticed the strangers.

Rendezvous, as another *omega*, tended to keep rough track of where the others of her pack were, and thus realized that their packmates were scattered mostly to the east. This recollection may have been all that kept her and Cabal from trotting down to greet the others, who might have been easily mistaken from such a distance as packmates.

But in the case of unknown wolves, such a greeting coming from Cabal and Rendezvous might be met with intimidation or even attack; wolves might commandeer another pack's territory, or part of it, as they might take over a denning site from other wolves or other species. Such behavior was quite rare, typically an act of desperation. That was the reason why buffer zones usually existed around wolf territories, which none of their kind claimed.

That was the Chelatna pair's first clue. The second was the fact that two of these four wolves were all black, a coloring which simply had not occurred among the Chelatna wolves for some years. Scents were unnecessary: these wolves were visually and obviously strangers, and heading in their direction.

The Fire Creek wolves remained unaware of their detection, simply skirting the southwestern edges of the Chelatna territory. Oak was the first to be spotted by Cabal and Rendezvous, and, like Trap-dasher, was indeed almost completely black in the shading of his fur. Paddler had tan and white mixed in her flanks to set her apart, and Dog-chaser was the lightest colored of the four, with grey and silver and white blended in a roughly uniform fashion, lighter tones mixing into his underside. Keeping their muzzles earthward, they kept up the fastest trot they could manage, and hoped this territory they'd trespassed would either end soon or at least offer sufficient hiding places. As it was, they could still detect enough traces of the Chelatna wolves to follow their territory's contour as it approximated the base of some far gentler mountains than the Fire Creek members had seen for some days. Soon they would find themselves heading due eastward, through the woods and marshy terrain leading to the Yentna River.

Rendezvous, for her part, remained motionless now, observing the other wolves every few minutes or so when they would briefly reemerge into her field of vision. Cabal had already ventured off to begin summoning the other pack members, and both wolves knew that someone should stay put to try and keep the positions of the invaders known. Cabal would remember clearly where the female *omega* lay in wait. It might take hours to summon all the others, with the decision to be made about who would remain behind with the pups, eager as they'd be to join the party, and for the adults to head this way and offer whatever discouragement might be necessary to keep their territory free of unwanted guests.

What Rendezvous did not realize was the sheer hunger and fatigue of those same unwanted guests, who in turn were less likely to notice any other wolves precisely because they were tired and getting close to ravenous. Taking down something big would require too much energy and probably a few more wolves at this stage, so the Fire Creek members would have to continue seeking out smaller prey. It took a while to locate something suitable; they did actually observe a small herd of caribou, maybe twenty or so, who looked alert but not threatened, and they were at any rate further into the Chelatna territory, which automatically meant that pursuing the caribou would prove much riskier. So the Fire Creek wolves plodded on, eventually locating a fat white ptarmigan and another careless snowshoe hare, though several other members of both species managed to escape. Those quickly downed nibbles would have to get them a few more kilometers, and nary a trace of either animal remained afterwards. Dog-chaser was lucky to get one of the hind legs of the hare as his share, the others were so hungry.

The small dead bodies vanished into the wolves in mere moments. They ate so fast there was barely any noticeable blood around their muzzles, a sign of a more contentment-inducing feast. Rather, Dog-chaser and his packmates displayed the behavior which had centuries before led to the adoption of the human phrase, "wolfing one's food." Only vaguely satisfied, they kept trotting as best they could, refusing to sleep either so close to the rushing and heat-sapping Yentna River or to the Chelatna homeland.

Rendezvous, for her part, remained quite curious about these new wolves. Like many of her kind, she simply did not know wolves from beyond her own pack, and she had never aspired to either try and rise in the ranks or to venture off on her own as a lone wolf and attempt to locate either another male or a whole pack which might be looking for a humbled new member. She felt content enough with her lot, even if she remained at the bottom of the social order.

Yet that same low status was what enabled her to feel this vague interest about the strangers. Not having to make the decision about when or how to confront these other four wolves, she could simply wonder about them instead. It would be up to Bear Heart and Owl Eyes to determine the appropriate course of action, and Rendezvous did not feel particularly threatened by the Fire Creek survivors. She whimpered briefly and softly, looking about her as though expecting Cabal and the others to trot right back at that moment, but of course they would take much longer. It was the inability to keep the four other wolves regularly in her sight that made her anxious. Were they drawing closer to her position? Did they already know of her presence, as she of theirs?

The wind was also softer now, mingling in no discernible pattern, and thus making scent detection more challenging. And the vista before Rendezvous, while vast and expansive, nonetheless contained plenty of limitations to her excellent vision. Sometimes many minutes would pass in between her sightings of the Fire Creek members. And sometimes when they did become visible, it would only last a moment, and then they would slip behind another cluster of fir and birch or a tiny hill which would not even reveal itself on the limited two-dimensional maps of the humans, the likes of whom Rendezvous had certainly never seen. And this sudden sense of isolation helped make the female wolf realize she might not have what was required to become a loner; she crouched down, flattening herself to the earth and tried to be patient and observant at the same time, rather than afraid.

She did not happen to witness another of the occasional breaks made by the Fire Creek wolves. Paddler it was who made eye contact with the others, bidding them pause while she pointed her snout eastward and tested the slowly moving air. She offered a subtle growl, more of ambiguity than hostility, and wondered if she'd been wrong.

She thought she'd smelled a wolf. Just for a moment. But her packmates had the same weary expressions on their faces, apparently having missed the olfactory cue. Perhaps it was nothing after all. Paddler took another few quick sniffs, still looking in the same direction, then decided it was of no concern. Granted, they were still in the new territory, but it was either very large or its keepers were highly dispersed throughout it.

They continued onward, soon reaching the drainage of the Yentna. The good news was that it appeared easier to cross if they followed it just briefly downstream, which in turn would appear to take them a bit out of the territory. The not so good news came in the form of seeing that the river appeared to lead into boggy terrain; the wolves did not yet know that even further south, it opened up into a collection of hundreds of little lakes and ponds, which, still unfrozen, would slow them down and probably offer little by way of suitable prey. And everywhere they looked behind them now, back to the west, was mountain after mountain, so they were still hemmed in.

So that meant they would likely have to reenter the other pack's homeland. As Oak and Paddler led their two lower ranking packmates down towards the river, they could see a steeper incline leading up to a smaller, relatively isolated mountain. Yenlo, the humans had named it. The most appropriate route seemed to be around this mountain to the north, which they guessed, correctly, would take them right towards where even now Cabal was beginning to locate his own packmates.

* * *

The Graydon brothers were pleased that they'd found no evidence of poachers this time out, like Brent Muskey and Trey Stone, who appeared to have gone home, and while John remained confident that they would not really find much in the way of prey, especially this late in the season, he was amused to notice the passing of another group of human travelers. Morgan, David, Mariska, and Jack, similar to the Fire Creek wolves, were as yet oblivious about their discovery; it rarely occurred to them that they might be observed by others. By other humans, anyway; such was their sense of isolation.

This other group was clearly just a bunch of late-season campers. They didn't appear to be armed, and in the interest of minimizing noise, John and Benjamin had just kept quiet rather than announce themselves. They looked young, too, this group, but if they were out here at this time of year they were either experienced or stupid. The brothers were content to leave well enough alone; if these four other people were hunters, then let them find their own quarry, and if they were anti-hunting, which they might be considering how they were all dressed, then why bother talking with them anyway? The Graydons recognized the sort of pastel hues common in clothing selected by those who shopped at the mass market outdoor shops, which were harder to come by in Talkeetna. The brothers themselves were once again encased in more appropriate camouflage.

The Graydons were hardly disinclined toward small talk with strangers, in fact loved it in a small town sort of way, but that wasn't their current purpose. They'd been heading toward Petersville, north of Peters Creek, still intending to make for the old mines like they'd discussed, but then decided almost at the last minute to make an alteration, using, curiously, the same dotted red line that Morgan Greene had noted in her large map book which still sat back in her friend's car. It was a winter trail, which, at this time of year, would be more subtlely marked, and likely a useful game trail as well. Deciding they'd have potentially better luck closer to the river, the brothers had left their old pickup truck quite close to the Subaru which had transported Greene's party and then hiked in the same direction.

It was mostly a feeling of a sense of odds that motivated the Graydons now. Like casual gamblers, they would be thrilled by the big payoff, but would also remain content if they just found something worth bagging and bringing home. Their ATVs were back home in Talkeetna this time around, so if they actually did manage to locate something the size of a moose, they'd have to work quickly to prepare it and field dress it and arrange to have it properly transported. The cooler weather would help some, but decomposition would still begin quickly, making such flesh unfit for human consumption, and only of interest to the likes of wild scavengers.

But the men's spirits remained buoyant. As with their earlier expedition in pursuit of wolf pelts, their activities were based more on a sense of adventure than on a dire need for profit, even if both men still had long-term questions to address regarding employment options. The point was to be out in the fall, before the hard winter really set in, with its limited hunting. Not being much for most winter sports, Benjamin and John would content themselves with the occasional day of ice fishing, but neither of them was a skier or hockey enthusiast or any such. And they shared a single snowmachine between them, using it more for work than leisure. Assuming the pesky old thing would even start up again this time around; John thought it had revealed its age more than once last winter, and was likely now to offer its final death throes when they pulled it back out of storage.

In the meantime, the brothers easily flanked the traveling direction of the four other people they'd spotted, and opted to head almost due west. The Kahiltna was at its widest in that direction, arrived at by a rolling hill near the end of the winter trail, so that area might prove an enticing spot for moose to take advantage of the last of the fall foliage. They would not be searching river beds for food once winter arrived.

"What do you reckon those people are after, this time of year?" Benjamin said, his words emerging evenly despite the slightly quickened pace the men maintained. The brothers were in fine shape physically from a lifetime of regular exercise in the bush.

"Who knows, Ben?" the elder said. "They looked like Anchorage folk, the way they were dressed, and since the tourists are gone now. And they didn't look to be armed."

Benjamin nodded his assent to that. It could be awkward carrying their rifles, since they didn't need to remain constantly in hand like soldiers might carry on patrol. But they didn't sling very well, either, so both men had rigged their own backpack holsters, of sorts: flexible casings customized for the guns, attached to the sides of their packs now with a creative use of bungee cords and duct tape. There was a running gag in Alaska that if you couldn't fix something with either duct tape or a hammer, either it wasn't broken or wasn't worth fixing; the state led the way in nationwide per capita usage of the silvery strip adhesive. Both brothers had eliminated plantar warts on their feet with it before.

"No," he murmured now. "No, they definitely aren't hunters. Maybe they're just photographers, or something."

"Maybe. To get some good shots of the colors, though, would need more gear than they must be carrying." Benjamin often marveled at his brother's perception, but John typically brushed it off, always saying that a good hunter is simply observant and pays attention to surroundings. That was the real pleasure of hunting, even on the trips when they returned with nothing but sore joints and wet gear: the simple automatic enhancement of their bodily senses, which people in big cities so often had trouble understanding. You just got used to all the noise: traffic, thousands of simultaneous conversations, alarms, phone rings. Most modern people had no idea how intrusive their technology was, when it supposedly existed to make life easier.

John might have come closer to bragging about having already learned such simple but overlooked wisdom. The toys and gadgets were fun sometimes, but they didn't save time like their makers professed. People spent just as much time on housework, and more time at their jobs, than they did just a few decades earlier. And now they typically had longer commutes to and from those jobs to boot, so where was the benefit, other than the possibility of a larger paycheck and maybe some fickle fame from the others in the rat race? No, the elder brother didn't think he was better than the city residents, nor smarter, for that matter; he just knew when to keep things simple.

Still, both brothers had vague uncertainty of the simple pleasures now sought by the other travelers they'd witnessed today. Why would anyone hike into remote areas like this without a specific purpose? In Alaska, if you weren't hunting or fishing or taking photographs and you were still out in the sticks for several days at once, then some folks might not understand. The Graydons were so similar to these other people, and yet so different as well: love of the wild land propelled them, but for different reasons. Still, all six were out here now partly just to be at one with the rest of the world.

Benjamin nodded again. "Yeah. I think you're right about carrying all that camera gear. Anybody can take good pictures out here, but the really good ones need more equipment than I know I can afford."

"Too competitive, anyway," John said.

"Yeah. Hey, look over that way." Benjamin stopped.

"What?"

Benjamin pointed southwest. He could see the river now. They'd only been able to hear it for the past few minutes, so to able to see it emerge into view so soon meant they had a good vantage point.

"Oh, yeah," John said. In front of them, the Kahiltna displayed four main braids, which were never quite the same from year to year, in size, layout, or even number. The men were still the better part of a mile from the closest of them, so the fact that they could already hear the water gushing past meant that a safe crossing was unlikely to be found. They knew the winter trail picked up again further south, but also believed the other hikers would be down in that area, and the brothers didn't want a crowd right now.

"Let's head a little closer and take a look. I think there'll be a lot of good campsites around."

Benjamin assented. They were just starting to work their way downhill a bit more when they heard the unmistakable droning sound of a wolf howling.

And a few seconds later, it was answered. By what sounded like a bunch of other wolves. Probably just on the other side of the river.

Most people never saw wolves in the wild in their entire lifetimes. The Graydon brothers now wondered if they'd have another opportunity just as lucky as that from their last trip.

* * *

I can barely recall being more bushed at the end of a day's hiking than I am presently. After what evolved into a lengthy break of lying in quite a comfortable spot, Jack had finally been the one to rouse us all back into action, so we could find a new camp site before darkness really set in. We had plenty of light, surely, but it was now late enough in the year that genuine darkness did occur once more, even if late.

But it's proved to be worth the wait: we have indeed managed to locate another gorgeous location, just slightly uphill from what appears to be the winter trail I'd noted earlier in my Gazetteer. It affords a lookout over much of the Kahiltna River basin, and at the moment we're trying to savor the remnants of a spectacular sunset which is making the river itself glow magnificently. It's good to have a useful sensory distraction while we go through the now tiring motions of getting camp set up again. It's been a busy Monday.

The four of us have actually remained rather quiet since that break. Once again, why bother mucking about with a golden silence amongst friends? Besides, I'm not sure any of us, even Dave, could handle much more linear thought this day. This is what hiking's all about for me: when we're hungry, we eat; when tired, we sleep. Dave would be proud: quite the little piece of simple yet elusive enlightenment in there, with no schedules or clocks reminding us of when things are supposedly to get done.

And Dave. What am I going to do with this man now? He's sitting overlooking the vista, having already finished his own little spot with a tent that never looks like it'll be big enough to contain him. His burrito. Jack and Mariska are likewise finishing theirs, as confirmed by the omnipresent sound of modern campsites: tent zippers going up and down and around as people check to make sure everything is in the right place. Our stoves are cooling off from dinner; soon the leftover river water we've boiled will be cool enough to pour into our Camelbaks and extra plastic bottles. Food and food wrappers are all isolated in the Ursacks (Jack and Mariska are sharing one of their own, from a recommendation I'd made to them last year after mine had proven its worth); the yellow invincible bags will then be placed close to the river. The wind closer to the water should help disperse any residual scents so keep away any opportunistic eaters, and the sacks have to be hidden since trees sufficiently high for more traditional "bear-bagging" are few around here.

And I've been watching Dave throughout this little reverie and mental checklist. After all the emotions working their way through me since last night, I'm probably just too tired now to think very clearly. All I know is that I have no wish to let this man stay out of my sight for very long. I smile gently as I recall my earlier thoughts about love, asking the one question I'd not pondered this afternoon when we were lying about soaking up the sun and feeling our skin tighten as the sweat evaporated. What changes with love? Why is it so unpredictable? And why do we even welcome it?

I remember a friend in one of my writer's courses when I was doing the MFA work at the university back in Anchorage. She'd turned in a piece which had something to say of love, with the catch being that she had to read it aloud for the rest of us (as did we all, for our own work). It was partly to hear our own thoughts receive voice, and partly to get over that weird trepidation so many seem to have about speaking in front of a group, something none of these tired hiking friends of mine would likely have much trouble facing.

"How does love change?" she said to the class that day. "Do any of us ever choose our feelings, or do they just come to us?" I still don't have an answer; I simply recall part of what my classmate argued. This other young woman had, in fact, come up with the most gentle and yet determined and rational defense of what is so often mistakenly referred to as simple "lifestyle." I'd known for weeks that she was a lesbian, could hardly have cared myself, but Anchorage can be a homophobic town, and here was this woman telling us, almost soothingly, that our emotions and passions are not matters of choice. They simply are. "Have any of you ever actually chosen who you've fallen in love with? And if it's just a choice, then couldn't you try and persuade the person of your affections to return your sentiment with equal ardor, by pointing out how perfectly matched you'd be? Maybe you could offer this other person a list of the obvious logical advantages of being in love with you in return." We'd laughed at that. Dave would've liked her. And now here I am wondering what makes love transform itself: I've always loved this man, but never, perhaps until now, felt that in love madness toward him.

That student had really drilled her point home. "And if you think gender identity or sexual orientation is mere choice, then it must be possible for everyone in here to 'choose' to 'play for the other team,' to borrow a phrase. But the homophobes never seem to acknowledge that as a possibility. So much for the choice." Fewer members of the class had found that funny, but I'd loved it.

Love is mad; it must be. My classmate was right: how could such a thing possibly be chosen? We're just attracted to different people for our own reasons, most of which likely make almost no sense at all. And again, I seem to be overcomplicating things. One of my specialties, I fear. All I know in the meantime is that I've become conscious of my breathing, like *Sensei* Rogers regularly reminds me of, but in this case, I can probably count the number of times I've sighed deeply while watching the back of an old friend, wanting just to know what he's thinking.

Jack gets our attention this time, catching me watching Dave but courteously not pointing out how I'm just staring, likely drooling almost, but like I said, I'm focusing on respirations, not salivary output. "Hey, I know everyone's tired and all, but don't you want to go and check out those howls yet?"

He's been talking about that on and off for the past hour. We did indeed hear some howling earlier, and it sounded like a wolf pack, considering how it harmonized, came from multiple locations (so far as we could determine), and thus meant that multiple animals must have been involved. But we were just so utterly wiped by then that we couldn't picture ourselves traipsing off to look for signs of wolf activity. I'd love to see them in the wild someday, too, but right now I just want to sleep. Preferably with Dave's arms wrapped about me.

Dave turns away from the last traces of the sunset. "Jack, you know I'd love nothing more, but it'll be totally dark soon. And we're hardly equipped to go looking for wildlife at night."

The perpetual curious kid in the candy shop: "Well, what about tomorrow?"

And that was how it started. The easy question of one who will not be dissuaded. Had we just packed up the next morning and hiked out of there as per our plan, then the following events would have turned out quite differently. But I won't play "what-if" this time, like I promised when I drove home to pack days ago. I'll try to learn something instead.

So, sleep came to all of us quite easily that night, sore bodies packed snugly into three tents. I usually take a while to fall completely asleep, and admit I'm a bit envious of these friends who can seem to knock themselves out just by thinking it, or not thinking about it, which appears to be the real trick. Still, I do recall the evening quickly passing by, and don't remember any more howls. Just occasional other wild sounds: an owl, at one point, or so I thought. And some random rustling through the brushy landscape, plus the dulled but regular roar of the river. I dreamt of running wolves and a handsome but frustrated Marine and somebody who turned into a werewolf, but I couldn't tell whom, and it wasn't scary. Weird. Maybe it was the Marine. I must have been even more exhausted than I'd been prepared to admit. And I thought Dave would have appeared in my dreams, since he wouldn't escape my head much during the day, but I guess my subconscious or whatever opted for a break from passions.

And now morning. With frost. *Holy crap; how tired were we all to have not been woken by this?* I can see my breath easily within my tent now, and note that my cheeks feel colder than I think they should. Inspecting the tent's interior, I notice the extra moisture, a sure sign that it's much cooler outside than in. *How cold did it get, anyway?*

"You guys won't even believe this." Jack's voice again. He sounds torn between glad and anxious, but surprised either way.

I'm not sure I want to hear the punchline to that just yet, as I automatically inspect both the interior and exterior of my sleeping bag, which is zipped up closer to my head than I remember pulling it last night. I must have been too tired to remember waking just enough to complete that little motor skill, though the cold that would have propelled such action should have woken me a bit further.

The sleeping bag appears fine. You may recall I prefer down, the delightfully insulating goose down which also packs more compactly than the synthetics. The drawback is that you absolutely must keep it dry, or you might as well just try sleeping outside of it. Fortunately, the moisture around the edges of the mummy bag is minor, so my breath and the proximity of the bag to the tent walls didn't seem to make that potential moisture an issue.

"Let me guess," Mariska says, groggy again as usual. How do couples consisting of one early riser and one late sleeper ever have a chance? "Snow? Should we be worried?"

"Well, I won't say worried, exactly. The sky's actually cleared up quite a bit, but it's colder, as I'm sure you can all tell, and the snow on the mountains looks, I think, lower from the last few days."

When did I last consider that? I wonder. Was that just yesterday? No wonder most outdoors people bring watches with them; you can really lose track out here. I have to think before figuring out that it's Tuesday.

I hear a zipper now, having missed the sound of Jack's. Dave is apparently trying to drag himself out of his tent. He loves sunrises, too, something I learned about him years ago. *Don't say any of this crap aloud, Morgan; you'll make your friends barf from the sentimentalism.*

"What do you see, Jack?" he says. I decide we might as well get ready. We'd estimated last night during dinner that we could hightail it out of here in just a few hours, and then make it back to the city sometime at night. Probably a bit late. But even now, none of us should be missing work. At least AFD gives Dave a pretty flexible schedule, and Iska's classes only meet on certain days, per her preference.

Unknown to me at the moment, Jack does have his little binoculars with him, like I suspected earlier. For the first time I feel vaguely guilty that we may not have given him enough time to pursue his major interest, but I've already mentioned the shelves of shoeboxes of photos in his disorganized home. Still, I thought I'd have noticed him taking out these cute "field glasses." Like his beloved 35mm, he takes pride in the beating his petite binoculars can withstand, though I didn't know he was using them right then until I heard the shout of pure glee.

"Hey, you guys! Come look." He says the second phrase softer, and we're all wondering what he's spotted, clearly excited. We should've guessed.

By the time I've emerged, Mariska shortly following, Dave is holding the lenses up to his own eyes, a huge grin plastered on his scraggly face. He also speaks softly for some reason. "Jack, you're right. Ladies, you've got to see this."

All I see is woods, hills, and part of the river, but I dutifully take the proffered glasses, raise them, and try to squint out of the side of one eye to follow the men's eager pointing.

They're messing with me. There's nothing out here but us, I think as I keep scanning. *Probably a damn snipe-hunt, like the old joke. They're just trying to distract us from the suddenly colder* weather, which emphasizes the fact that we are now on a deadline to work our way out of here, and not just because we have to return to work.

Dave's attuned to me, though. "Morgan, just a bit lower, to the left. They're on the far side of the river."

"Fine." I can feel the four of us bunching up, as though we'll somehow get a better view if we stand closer together, some weird version of "group think" again.

And then I see them, all at once filling the circular and clear image in the slightly dusty lenses. *Coyotes? No. Too big. The legs are too long, I think, and the heads are big. And aren't coyotes solitary?*

And the realization hits me, just like I'd imagined it minutes ago. I'm looking at wolves. Young wolves: they must be this year's litter, from what little I know about the species, which isn't much. I see three. And the coloring of each is surprisingly distinctive; I'd thought this species was more uniform that way. One looks like I imagined, another has less grey but still with the tan and black effect I'd expect. And one is almost all white. Beautiful! I swear the silvery one looks right at me for a moment, like it knows we're staring.

And if these are the pups, then where are the adults?

"There has to be a way to get across the river," Jack says. "How far do you suppose we are from that crossing we saw on the map?"

* * *

Scenario Five:

And now we have the opportunity to come full-circle, so to speak. We have visited wolves in several differing locales, and have considered them from such a myriad of interpretations and descriptions, some accurate and insightful, others bigoted and narrow. But now we can at last join the wolves in that region of the globe where their very existence has become the most politicized, where they

are the most widely studied, where they are loved and reviled, respected
and feared. We can now venture into the New World, or at least its
northern portions: Canada, America, and Mexico, the places where
contemporary adventurers often shell out intriguing sums specifically
for the chance to see, study, photograph, and perhaps hunt and kill
wolves.

It is at once curious to note the relative lack of observational
study of wolves prior to the twentieth century. Countless conjectures
and fanciful fables have of course been offered through the ages, though
the first genuinely systematic and scientific approach to canis lupus
originates as recently as the mid-eighteenth. Charles Leroy, in 1764,
finishes what may be regarded as the first scientific study of wolves.
This is the very same year as the beginning of the rampages of the
Bête de Gévaudan, whom we saw previously, so any work even
vaguely sympathetic to wolves might not have received the warmest of
receptions right at that time. Leroy's work is not necessarily a defense
of wolves as such, though it does emphasize the high intelligence of the
canids, which he argues must have resulted from simple environmental
pressures. This is therefore a slight preview of the eventual work within
the field of evolution, making its way onto the world scientific stage
a century later. Alfred Wallace and Charles Darwin are not wolf-
lovers as such either, though they use a variety of species examples to
show how those same environmental pressures lead to adaptation or
extinction, including the cephalization which we have also hitherto
considered, just after our visit to the modern Iraqi desert.

Yet it is the likes of Aldo Leopold, Adolph Murie, Barry
Lopez, and David Mech that really bring the field of wolf research
into sharper focus, and all of their work is done throughout various
parts of the North American continent. Leopold gains sympathy for
wolves as he watches one die, though he still maintains a belief in
the need for trying predator controls, believing that a "balance" might
still be possible, without eliminating predators and trying to maximize
available prey species for hunting by humans as well. Murie is hired
by the United States National Park Service to study, paradoxically,

the reasons for the declines in Dall's sheep populations in Mount McKinley (now Denali) National Park, and the general public along with his employers are displeased to hear his conclusions after living among many large species, including wolves: that wolves are an integral part of the Alaskan ecosystem, that predators are in fact necessary for the biological health of all such systems, and that wolves are not even responsible for the occasional drops in prey species, including Dall's sheep.

Lopez publishes a very readable history of wolf-human interaction with his description of the "dance of death" at the time when the "Green" movement is just getting underway, and political tools like the Clean Air Act and Endangered Species Act are about to be signed in the United States, making it the early 1970s. Mech publishes his early research data concurrently, then remains an integral part of wolf research for decades to come and into the present, spending months at a time in environments most of us would regard as hellish to continue his field work. All four of these men, regardless of their sympathies or intentions, reveal huge amounts of new facts regarding predator-prey relationships, with emphases on wolf behavior.

This modern trend marks a complete reversal from the time that the Malleus Maleficarum was published, during the time of New England's own witch trials and bounties placed on wolf heads, along with the influence of werewolves, even though the latter are even now believed by some to plague the lands just across the Bering Sea from our human and canid protagonists in Alaska; Siberian werewolves are documented fact, insist some of the locals. It is still important though to understand that these more recent men were (or are) all dedicated scientists and scholars; no tree-huggers or poets here. These are men who got their hands quite dirty in an ongoing effort to discover truth and to understand some of the most essential details and features of ecology, carrying capacity, and predator-prey dynamics. There is no magical balancing act to be had, they come to realize: the variables never stop applying survival pressures on every living creature, so that what is one year an ideal fishing ground, for example, proves boring and unproductive to the fishermen who visit it the next year, though it might yet again become exciting in the third year. The Earth has its own agenda: even what we call natural disasters are events which simply occur for their own reasons and follow their own rules, and often which may need to happen for a greater good. It is admittedly difficult to appreciate this notion when it is your house that has been flooded, burned, buried, or shaken apart, but the cycle continues with or without your approval or metaphysical moralizing.

That is part of the scientific explanation. Let us come home now, though, to North America, as promised, to consider our final collection of thoughts about the wolves, who likewise have their own agendas, so often reflections of our own. This is a different North America, to be sure, and the lands herein described have been altered by the American notion of "progress," which might be socially and economically useful, but like all things has its own costs, in this case the displacement of humans and other living things.

The eighteenth century has witnessed a number of curiosities in the lives of all human residents of North America, and perhaps even more in those of the tribespeople of Riitahkaac, a young hunter, close in age to his earlier Japanese counterpart Kiyomori and just as eager to please others while proving his manhood. Contacts with the Spanish are still recalled by Riitahkaac's people, which had started promisingly around the time of his birth but ended in bloodshed when Pedro de Villasur led several dozen troops to Riitahkaac's ancestral homelands to try and prove something which no one recalls any longer, though the tribal villagers still speak of the ensuing battle: the Spanish leader was slain along with most of his warband. Since then, connections with the French have led to more encouraging trade, though this Indian village remains wholly unaware of the social conflagration which will erupt soon between the French and another group of similar looking folk whom Riitahkaac has never seen: the British. This is the year 1741 by the white man's reckoning, and the tribes, even those far removed from the European settlements and burgeoning cities in New England, *will shortly face ever more dramatic changes as industry and social expansion engulf the Americas.*

Here, then, is a tribe occupying the lands called Kansa, which the pale settlers will divide into Kansas and Nebraska, though the tribe has been here since the sixteenth century. Iroquois expansion in the Ohio Valley compelled these people here, after an initial migration from Texas and Arkansas. The tribe of Riitahkaac is a branch of the Caddoan peoples, who share similar linguistic roots and bloodlines. His people number as many as ten thousand these days. History will call them the Pawnee, *more specifically the* Skidi *tribe. But they will also be forever known by another moniker, the only indigenous cultural group throughout the Americas so called...*

The Wolf People.

Even their method of identifying themselves uses a canid symbol of their own creation: you can mimic it by making a fist with your right hand, with the palm side facing forward. Then extend the first two fingers so that they are straight and form a "v," rather reminiscent of long pointy ears, like the ones you have likely used behind some unwitting friend's head during the taking of a candid photograph. Now bend this modified fist forward a time or two, and you've got it: you have just identified yourself as a member of a particular tribe. And this is how Riitahkaac's people often reveal themselves, both to each other and to members of other tribes.

For now the young hunter's focus is on a more intimate identification with the wild canids. Riitahkaac and his cousin Ku'sox are experienced paariisu, *or hunters, and they have taken advantage of one of the natural features of their homeland to allow themselves a bit more stealth while they follow, as subtlely as possible, their quarry. They do not use natural cover or hiding places; rather, they have taken to wearing wolf pelts, since their eventual targets, the bison, are curiously less distracted by the presence of wolves than they would be by the intrusion of taller, scarier looking humans.*

This practice does not entail a belief in lycanthropy, as we mentioned earlier; Riitahkaac and Ku'sox do not believe they have actually become wolves, and nor did they kill the two individuals whose pelts now cover their torsos, the front leg portions tied securely around the men's necks and shoulders to prevent loss. These wolves died of natural causes, the pelts lovingly kept by these biped hunters. And the pelts had their own value, often tradable for other goods, from both Indian and European groups.

Still, Indian tribespeople might yet slay wolves, but always for specific purposes. Cheyenne shamans are known to rub their warrior's arrowheads in wolf fur to yield better hunting accuracy. Hidatsa women rub wolf skin on their own bellies to alleviate difficult births. Curiously, the Cherokee tribe refuses to kill wolves; they believe the slain wolf's companions will return seeking revenge. They also suspect that the loss of wolves will lead to the decline of their mutual prey species. One can only wonder if other human groups ever derive their fear of wolves for similar karmic reasons.

But wearing a wolf pelt, meanwhile, does seem fearful to many observers. Ancient Romans, some of the Germanic peoples, and perhaps the ancient Britons, all experimented with such accoutrements, partly, one assumes, for warmth, and partly because such pelts do look impressive. Recall the objective of the modern Graydon brothers: their acquired pelts will likely be sold as intact as possible, with the face, tail, and leg portions still in evidence. Yet for many peoples, the appearance of a wolf (or even of its parts) proves intimidating, so much so that the Comanche and Cheyenne believe the Skidi can adopt wolf traits: effective tracking and the stamina to travel all day. This is the result of identification with the wolf: the paariísu try to become as close to wolves as possible, emulating their desired attributes in a more physical fashion than anyone else.

Both young men of course also wear the pariki, or "horn," from which the name Pawnee derives: this is their distinctive hairstyle, a crude horn shape extending downward from what could be described as a very tightly woven ponytail. It is a scalp lock stiffened with bison tallow to look like a horn. And, as the men operate as scouts in addition to hunters, they have toughened up their hands and knees so much that their skin in both those regions is virtually leather. What else could result from a human, lacking canine or feline feet pads, walking about on all fours, occasionally for quite long distances at a time? And Riítahkaac and Ku'sox have been on the trail for several days.

Their mission is quite simple, though the requisite stamina is daunting for most, something in which the two cousins take pride. This is the prelude to the first of two annual bison hunts. The Skidi have only had access to horses for a generation, and while some of their relatives at home have become superb equestrians, even developing the ability to shoot arrows while mounted and charging, there are simply not enough steeds to go around. And the Skidi do not opt for mass killings of their prey regardless: just a few individuals here and there, their flesh to be rapidly butchered and dried. And another hunt will come in the fall as well: the first hunt after the planting, the second after the harvesting.

The Skidi are farmers as well as hunters, unusual for peoples in this region at the time. Both of the brave scouts are pleased to not have to tend crops, though they have assisted with the rudiments of farming. And the planted corn, beans, pumpkins, and sunflowers do prove a welcome addition to the berries, nuts, plums, and grapes which grow on their own accord nearby. Indeed, Ku'sox presently carries most of their food, largely in the form of nuts and preserved meat, in this case some savory elk flesh from a sizable buck which he caught on his own earlier in the spring. And this reveals another trait which neighboring tribes regard as both strange and awe-inspiring: the aforementioned wolf-like stamina includes the ability to continue tracking potential prey while subsisting on very little food, something wolves do of necessity regularly. By the time they do make a kill, it is easy to comprehend the source of that phrase "wolfing one's food;" you'd be quite hungry too if you spent all day jogging and unsure just when you might eat again. For now Riítahkaac and Ku'sox are getting by on mere hundreds of calories a day. They feel privileged to say, "Ckirhki kuruuriki:" "we look like wolves."

This comes in some contrast to their actual names, which mean golden eagle and left-hand, respectively; Riitahkaac is named for his coloring and Ku'sox for his dexterity. Ku'sox also has a wife, Kskiikarnaku, translated as green leaf for her subtle but strong beauty and health. She thought to give him a sacred or medicine bundle prior to his leaving, which seems like a simple luck charm but which is believed to contain vast potencies aimed at assisting her husband with his appointed task. This bundle contains smoking apparatus and body paints, ritualistic devices to be used only upon a successful mission, in which case they will be shared with Ku'sox's companion.

Those who reside in Kansas today will of course recall that, while beautiful in its own right, it is nonetheless rather flat country, and has never been largely forested. These two characteristics offer few hiding places for the often crawling men, who have trailed one of the smaller bison herds for over a week, only moving about on two legs at night in an effort to get closer. Like all the hunts we have viewed so far, this one too seems a bit drab at first: how exciting is it, really, for two grown men to alternate between short periods of jogging and much longer periods of crawling, just to get close to some dumb animals?

But the dance of death will be played out yet again, as it has countless trillions of times since life began first evolving. And the bison are not as dumb as their lazy gestures might suggest; they are always alert to potential hazards, and they can quickly encircle both young and old alike, facing whatever confronts them with a ring of angry thick shaggy skulls which have devastating horns, like their musk ox relatives in Alaska.

"Do you think they can smell us more or less easily in the rain?" Riitahkaac asks his partner.

Ku'sox considers the question, realizing that the recent weather has churned up fresh mud in some spaces, and while he is thankful for the pelt tied about him, he is also aware of the definitive "wet dog" odor emanating from them. The skin oil in animal pelts never seems to fully disappear. "I do not think so, cousin. Look. See the two young ones playing."

Riitahkaac follows the other man's pointing arm. "Yes. Do you think we should return and tell the others of this herd, or try and secure one of those juveniles ourselves?"

Ku'sox recognizes both offers as tempting, though it would be a feat for the pair of them to drag a whole carcass several days back to the village. And there is also no strict hierarchy at play here, either; from a wolf's perspective, for instance, both men would rank as betas, neither of them enjoying special privileges in what is a largely egalitarian society. "One of us should return and inform the other hunting parties." *The words hang emptily in the air, seeking purchase; neither man wants to leave.*

"That is true," *Riitahkaac says at last. He barely feels the rain, light now but still steady, as it seeks the folds and channels within his clothing. The lodges at home would be drier, of course, but his leggings and robe and moccasins have been well treated to keep wetness at bay.* "And I believe it is your turn."

Ku'sox continues gazing at the herd, measuring his partner's phrase, knowing its truth. "Very well," *he admits,* "but see now the boundaries of this herd. Up ahead, in the direction of whiteness, you can see the branch of the river, and how it traces its way towards us." *Directions for this people consist of shades and colors: the four directions each have a sacred color, which likewise correspond to four basic commandments. These are all based on respect, something a later white man named David Thomas would at once identify as similar to the philosopher Kant's imperatives: respect for the Earth, respect for Tirawa the mother sun, respect for one's fellows and fellow creatures, and respect for freedom. The last is felt most acutely by the hunters: whatever they might gain from hunting was a creature who had to freely choose to give itself to them, which is what prompts the acts of thanksgiving afterwards. That is what the dance of death, a phrase used repeatedly by the modern writer Lopez, really means.*

Ku'sox speaks. "Then, notice how we came from the opposite direction. The herd can be guarded here, trapped, so long as you do nothing foolish enough to scare them away." *Riitahkaac nods. Ku'sox* is *already reaching for the food bundle, readying to divvy up their meager rations, giving twice as much to his cousin since he shall be exposed to the elements longer.*

Riitahkaac has done this before, though he does not care for being alone, and also certainly does not wish to lose the herd. He has only to watch them while Ku'sox, the better tracker of the two, returns with a larger hunting party, perhaps with a horse and litter or two for transport of the bison, which will be fully utilized for food, clothing, insulation, and tools. So Riitahkaac turns to humor to mask his dawning apprehension of what will be a lonely vigil, just him and several dozen huge woolly animals.

"I shall not make the bison so nervous as to try and leave. If they think that wolves are nearby they might wish to flee, but even a single wolf should be able to keep them in this area until you return." Riitahkaac himself sounds both proud and anxious; it is a large responsibility, and his only fear is of making more work for his fellows, so he has to keep this herd largely where it already is.

"You shall act as a fine wolf, cousin," Ku'sox says. "I shall proceed as fast as the wind to fetch help."

Riitahkaac smiles at that. "But I am the one named for a bird; how could you possibly go so fast as the wind?"

Ku'sox claps him on the shoulder, laughing, his hand not getting any wetter from the beads of rain which have accumulated on the other man's pelt. "You shall be fine. It is perhaps too bad that the sacrifice is to ensure the harvest, not the hunt."

The annual sacrifice has indeed already been made to Tirawa. A captive Cheyenne girl had to be given during the Morning Star ceremony during the summer solstice to ensure crop success, and while that had taken place just before the hunting and scouting parties had left home, such a practice bore little effect on hunting. The hunters had to offer their own humilities. Riitahkaac is already going over the prayers in his mind while Ku'sox finishes preparing the meager rations to be left with him. The former will not be able to gather much, and clearly remain unable to hunt, while he performs his landscape-scale guard duty.

"Now go, my cousin," Riitahkaac admonishes gently. "Give my affection to your beautiful wife, and perhaps next year we can celebrate a strong daughter or son from you both."

Ku'sox beams. *Marriages are so often arranged, but he truly cares for Kskiikarnaku. Like all newly married men, he frets constantly about her love for him, and being able to provide for her as a good hunter and warrior should.* "Thank you, cousin. Try and stay warm." *It is indeed warm out, despite the rain.* "And figure out which of the bison should become our prey for when we return."

Riitahkaac nods and watches the other man crawl like a wolf for some minutes before he is sufficiently out of view of the herd, whose members thankfully do not have the best vision anyway. Then he turns back to his quarry, simply watching and observing individual as well as group behaviors with the patience all hunters know. Despite his charge, he loves this activity that later biologists will simply refer to as field study; he never bores of watching the animals, whether insect or avian or mammal.

Still prone, he quietly but determinedly recites the ancient incantations, told amongst his tribe for countless generations. It feels especially uplifting to Riitahkaac, who has after all been named for one of the greater spirits whom he now quietly invokes.

"Oh, Eagle, come with wings spread aloft in the sunny skies. Great Eagle, come and bring new life to we who pray." *This first part of the prayer is for a spirit to work on the minds of the prey, so that the latter might be more moved to offer themselves as prey for the survival of the tribe.*

Riitahkaac now kneels, adding simple hand and arm gestures to the rest of his divine request. "Remember the circle of the sky, and of the stars, and of the eagle. Remember the great giving life of Tirawa, and of the young within the nest. Remember the sacredness of things. This is my prayer.

"Make me like the Great Wolf. Grant me stealth and wisdom and love of family for my purpose. This is my prayer."

Content for the moment, Riitahkaac returns to his prone position, thankful that the ground is less sodden here. The only sounds in the world right now are his own breathing, the occasional surprisingly graceful gallop of the bison as they play or disagree with one another, a few small birds twittering to each other. It will take six full days for the others to return from the village, during which time the young hunter will often wonder about the wolves he has impersonated and where they might be hunting.

Riitahkaac and Ku'sox and Kskiíkarnaku will not survive to experience the elations and tragedies which shall befall their people, though the grandchildren of Ku'sox and Kskiíkarnaku shall: a visit from the Lewis and Clark expedition in 1803, and the Treaty of Table Rock of 1805 which will move them about until they get resettled in a reservation based around Genoa in Nebraska. Their great-grandchildren will weather an outbreak of smallpox in the tribe in 1837, while yet another two generations further away shall savor their last tribal bison hunt in 1873, and the tribe will continue their struggle to maintain cultural independence as they gain land in Oklahoma and forge their way clear into the twenty-first century. A wolf will appear on the flag of their descendents by then, a perpetual reminder of a fundamental part of their identity. In this way, their ancient association with the wild packs will not be forgotten, as it has been in so many other parts of the world.

PART FIVE: BLUE MARBLE

"It appears, in fact, that if I am bound to do no injury to my fellow-creatures, this is less because they are rational than because they are sentient beings."
- Jean-Jacques Rousseau, *Discours sur l'origine et les fondements de l'inégalité parmi les hommes*

"No truth appears to me more evident, than that beasts are endowed with thought and reason as well as men."
- David Hume, *A Treatise of Human Nature*

We had no idea that it would turn into a race; we didn't even know anyone else was out here with us. Anyone human, anyway. Don't get me wrong, here: I'm not opposed to hunting as such, but as with any other activity, it's always permissible to question motivations, as Dave would have it. I totally agree with him on that point. Still, I'd no idea his own emotions were really at quite that much of a boiling point until later that morning, after we'd re-secured the campsite and hidden the Ursacks again.

No, that's not true. You've been waiting this whole trip to see if Dave would come any closer to a resolution in his own life. Jack and Mariska are partially in on it, since the three of us just wanted to get Dave away for a few days since he's been having such a disillusioning time at work lately, and we've been worried about him.

But what gives us the right to interfere so heavily into his life, much as we love him? What does that say about the existential freedom he's talked to us about on this trip? Jack might maintain that love is the greatest virtue; Dave would claim personal freedom as the key. And while I knew Dave had been stressed, I sure as hell was unready for the rest of what happened.

Simple curiosity again this was, the kind that allegedly slays nosey cats and makes us reach for the forbidden fruit. The road to hell is paved with good intentions. Everybody means well, but they mess it all up when they feel motivated by righteousness, which is the feeling that precludes further thought and the possibility that their own views might be mistaken. These were the clichés which strangely began buzzing about my head even when we'd hidden our food stores (what scant amounts were left thereof, anyway), and trotted down to the river, as though a bunch of wolves might actually welcome us. I think it was Jack's curiosity that really got us going, partly since he'd been the one to spot the pups, but Dave and Mariska hardly needed persuading. I seemed to be the only one even vaguely hesitant.

But make no mistake: it wasn't for fear, especially not after the talk I'd had with Dave so shortly before. I do not fear wolves. I've been play-charged by bears on my backpacking trips, have been buzzed by hostile seagulls in Homer, and once had a moose decide that chasing a biped might be a useful way of attracting a mate (though I didn't stick around to see what kind of luck that bull moose had), and I'm aware that I'm always going to be in far more danger from the other residents of my apartment building, and from any other people I encounter, than I'll ever be from the likes of wolves. Also like Dave, I recognize that old habits die very hard, and it feels so much more dramatic to display fear in the presence of something wild. I've never bragged about any of these wildlife encounters I just mentioned; even Jack and Mariska don't know of them, though Dave does. But many people would brag. Most folks would, I truly believe, make a dramatic case out of a little nondescript incident like that.

What I felt while we hiked briskly downward was the drop in temperature, mingled with a slight breeze, and a recognition that, while we were hardly snowed in, there were nonetheless some patches of early snow here and there. Just enough to tease, really; it was more like what would have been morning dew a few weeks ago had just frozen, and frozen slightly thicker in some parts, giving the impression that universal whiteness would arrive forthwith. Even the river just looked colder somehow, and while the summer flows had slowed, we could tell that there would be no safe way across the Kahiltna unless we found that ford site Jack mentioned. And I do remember seeing it; I just didn't want to mention it. Like I was trying to explain a moment ago, chasing the wolves, even though we certainly meant no harm to them, just felt invasive and therefore wrong. I really believe the others felt it, too; at one point Mariska strongly suggested we turn around, and the guys knew it also, but that damned curiosity just arrived overwhelmingly. When else would we get such a chance again? It might be the only time I'd ever see such a species in the wilds like this. What I do know is that we located the ford site less than a kilometer from our campsite, and that the crossing indeed proved easy. I also know the pups had already fled from the initial sight of us, which was to be expected. How many people understand that wild animals are far more afraid of us than we are of them, perhaps because they have excellent reason to be? And then we tried tracking them, which is part of why I feel guilty now. And then the hunters appeared. And then there were more wolves. It's difficult to keep all this in perspective, as well as maintain some sort of chronological narrative. So much for the MFA in creative writing.

* * *

It had proved to be a quite narrow escape for the Fire Creek pack survivors. Still suffering the effects of little sleep and mostly empty bellies, they'd kept up the previous day, ignoring the frost developing overnight, and completed their half loop around Mount Yenlo, approaching the Kahiltna River. But in order to avoid the trickier lands south, they'd had to turn north. Right back into Chelatna territory.

And this time, the property owners had been waiting for them.

Hopelessly outnumbered and underfed, Oak and Paddler knew their best and probably only chance was to run for it, which certainly elicited no complaints from Trap-dasher and Dog-chaser.

The mutual sighting took place on the far side of the inappropriately named Willow Mountain, just a hill among the true peaks, though it did exhibit its share of willow trees so loved by moose. The Fire Creek members had successfully skirted Mount Yenlo only to find, as with their emergence from the Alaska Range, more telltale signs of the presence of other canids like them. Paddler and Oak understood that this territory was likely larger than their old one; it was longer, at any rate, as they'd hoped to be clear of it by now. But they never had learned that they'd been tracked and watched for much of the day. Rendezvous had actually picked up their trail behind them as they passed, since she recognized that these four strangers were heading away from her observation post.

And in the meantime, dutiful Cabal had quickly gathered the other Chelatna wolves. Returning to the territorial center, he'd found most of the adults. Swifter, the young female, had been left with pup-sitting duty earlier, so she was with the trio of even younger wolves further east, close to the river where the pups had indeed been spotted by an assortment of weird biped creatures, who walked and ducked their heads like huge birds, but they seemed to lack wings to fly. Such was Swifter's hasty assessment, and she hadn't stuck around long enough to learn more, growling at the pups to move themselves quickly. Still, the pups had remained curious, and no one within the Chelatna pack had any experience with humans, anyway.

Cabal remained ignorant of all this, of course, still being a ways westward as he'd begun to locate the others. But Tornado and Tracer, two of the younger males, he'd found playing near the marshlands. Wave, one of Cabal's own littermates, and Fisher, who at over six was tied with Bear Heart for the title of pack elder, had been lounging with the two *alphas* on a brushy hillside. Cabal had gathered Tornado and Tracer, and the three had quite startled the other four as they galloped up to them, receiving the usual greetings but with Cabal panting extra heavily and whining, continually pacing towards a southern direction to indicate his fervent need of having them all follow them. He paused only long enough to lap up some cool water from a nearby trickling stream.

And follow they did. Wolf packs did not squander themselves on the equivalent of committee meetings. Instead any wolf, regardless of rank, could summon the others if he or she reported trouble, and Cabal's behavior was such that the others all clearly expected something big, and not a member of any regular prey species. Lower ranking wolves would get in trouble later for "crying wolf," as the strange human phrase went, but still, any individual could sound the proverbial alarm.

Hurrying almost due south, they'd dashed through the narrowest portion of their territory to find Rendezvous, who in turn easily revealed to them the unmistakable tracks of unknown wolves. The eight adults thus understood the problem immediately, and could tell that the strangers were heading eastward. This was a threat for two reasons: the invasion of a territory coupled with the fact that the four interlopers could easily locate the pups, who would not receive much extra protection from an inexperienced young wolf like Swifter.

Death to the invaders would have to be the likeliest outcome, but the *alphas*, Bear Heart and Owl Eyes, did consider it rather odd that there was evidence to indicate the presence of four wolves. The Chelatna wolves couldn't count, and didn't need to; there were fresh traces of four distinct new scents. A whole pack was traveling, which was strange; taking such a huge risk was an activity usually reserved for lone wolves, trying to make it on their own until they could find their own mates or perhaps even a sufficiently open-minded pack to adopt them. But four? No: this was an invasion, and would have to be squelched at once.

So, in total, there were four young wolves to the east, the three youngest of which had already revealed themselves to the humans, plus another four running for their lives just south of them which the young ones didn't know of, and then another eight in pursuit of this other group of four to the southwest of the pups' and humans' locations. And of these five groupings, two human and three wolf, there were curious overlaps in terms of which knew of the other's existence and motives. One set of humans knew of the other, but the reverse was not true, though both sets knew of the wolf pups. And the pups knew of both sets of humans, but had no idea that their territory was in the process of being invaded by humans and wolves alike. And the rest of the wolves as yet had no idea about any humans at all; only one of them had even seen the stinky bipeds before.

And Dog-chaser was far too terrified now to think about it. The howling which came from behind them did little to help. It was the only time that the sounds of his own kind had ever frightened him.

* * *

"Wow!" Jack exclaims. "I assume you all heard that?"

The rest of us offer our breathy affirmations, since we are moving quite quickly now, the fastest speed we'd maintained on this whole trip. The guys had both had a slight dunking in whichever river this was, the Kahiltna perhaps. I can't remember, and I'll try to verify later. The ford site worked out well, but in our excitement, it was easy to step a bit carelessly and let some of the now very cool water over the tops of boots and down into socks. Fortunately those fabrics still insulate when cold. Mostly.

And I am unsure when I've last seen Jack so worked up, or Dave, for that matter. For all the formers' photography background, he'd already told us that wolves were one species he'd never really glimpsed in the wilds, and certainly had none of his own pictures of them. This was the only remaining large furbearer Jack hadn't catalogued on film, and he didn't want to miss the chance. His camera could be seen now, draped in its case around his shoulder but still bobbing clumsily up and down. I wonder all the while when we might cross the line into wildlife harassment, which is illegal and bothers me morally regardless, though Mariska has informed us that the pups we'd seen were old enough to no longer need their original den. So at least we weren't chasing them out of their most basic home and shelter, which I would have found reprehensible.

Now across the river and heading more or less westward, I pause and turn back behind us. Jack notices at once. "Morgan, the howling came from the other direction."

"I know. But I thought I heard something behind us, too. Did you guys pick up anything back toward the campsite, something big?" Heads shaking this time, but I could've sworn my ears had detected larger creatures. Deciding it must've been nothing, we resume our pace.

We could still see traces of the winter trail as it appeared on the Gazetteer, and it is simple enough to follow. But we don't really know how to verify the presence of wolves, so we move, probably too rapidly, and look for any signs we can find. Jack and Dave are so giddy I half expect them to get down on all fours and start sniffing the ground like dogs looking for spoor. And then Mariska notices, near the ford where we've just crossed, the unmistakable signature of wolf tracks. Some of them are huge, the size of my palms. Mariska tells us that only the Great Dane can match them for size among domestic dogs, and that the way to tell they aren't lynx tracks instead is by the presence of claw marks, which these have.

Even the tracks are cool to see, and some are noticeably smaller than others, but there exists an intriguing order and symmetry to them. "They're so linear," I say, not knowing how else to describe them.

"Yes," Mariska confirms. "Dogs walk more sloppily. Wolves walk more gracefully and more in a straight line, almost like they are on tightropes."

So we've found them; the tracks look very fresh, even if I'm not Ranger Rick. More slowly now, we fan out somewhat and begin edging our way southward, following the tracks. I wonder what has become of whomever howled recently.

* * *

Dog-chaser would spend the rest of his life occasionally remembering what happened next. While formal reason might have been unknown to him, he nonetheless could appreciate that these four other beings, so much like the men and the girl he'd once stumbled upon in Kantishna, probably saved the life of himself and his three remaining packmates. The Fire Creek pack simply had run out of metaphorical steam, and although they'd again found the edge of the new territory, they could actually hear the other pack behind them now. And they were closing. And it sounded like there were many of them.

Had he been on his own, Dog-chaser would have completely humbled himself (even more so than an *omega* was typically expected to), and begged not to be killed by these other wolves. He would have rolled over, exposed his tender vulnerable belly, and hoped like mad that the others didn't disembowel him on the spot. Any of his packmates would be able to also, though in the case of Oak and Paddler, a clash with other existing *alphas* might prove fatal anyway.

But Dog-chaser was one of several now. His fate was tied to that of his packmates: they would survive or perish as a group. If nothing else, at least this nerve-wracking, anxiety-producing trek of the past days would end soon, but it also felt so futile to have come so far only to end up killed. They'd braved man-thunder, men, dogs, poor weather, the loss of their own home, the deaths of their companions, and an assortment of ornery other animals, only to face death at the maws of others of their own kind.

Yet such was their desperation that the Fire Creek wolves failed to notice two things: they were even now passing the furthest boundaries of the Chelatna pack, and they were perilously near members of another predatory species which also might slay them on sight.

* * *

It was comical, really. That was John Graydon's initial assessment of what transpired. He and his brother of course knew of the backpackers, and could also hardly have failed to notice the howling, as it traveled for miles. And both men had wondered what the hikers could be trying to prove by intentionally trying to dash madly after a bunch of wolves. True, neither Graydon brother could recall any actual wolf attacks upon humans, but the beasts could be a bit nasty up close, they felt sure. But they also noticed one of the hikers carrying a camera. So even though these four dipshits were making way too much noise with their talking and splashing, they apparently thought they might get close enough for a canid photo op.

Still, the men followed. These crazy hikers would probably scare away everything in a mile radius, but you could never quite tell when you might get lucky when hunting. John and Benjamin had their rifles prepared, and likewise took off in pursuit, curious as to whether they'd have the opportunity to make their presence known to anyone else.

* * *

"Did you hear that?" Jack says, forcing himself to be quieter. He's breathing a bit heavier now, as are we all. I can feel sweat dripping from some unmentionable parts of myself, but our heart rates all recover quickly.

"What, more howling? No," Dave says.

"No, not that. Right in front of us: it sounded like something running through the woods up ahead."

"I heard it also," Mariska confirms, then points. And it's all the time we have to consider, while visually following her outstretched arm and single digit, before we see it. *Holy shit*, we actually see it: the unmistakable form of a wolf, all black in appearance, maybe half a kilometer away in what I think is southwest of us. It just broke right through the overgrowth, and is now near the river. Even from here I can tell it's been exerting itself like us. I can see its sides moving from the respirations.

And then, *I'm tempted to think "holy shit" again since mere adjectives have suddenly failed me*, there emerges a second, and a third. They're beautiful! And they all look tired. And I can hear Jack fumbling with his camera. From this range, he'd never get the portraits I know he'd love to have, but with a lens which magnifies six times, you'd at least be able to verify what these creatures are.

Wolves! I've now seen wolves in the wild. Cross off one more species!

Mariska and Dave release a gasp, and can barely contain their whispers. And that's when I notice we must be upwind, since the wolves turn towards us. We've been spotted. "Not much time," Jack gripes. "We'll likely not see them again once they bolt for cover."

"How do you know?" Dave says. He cannot tear his eyes away from this privileged glimpse.

"They are far more scared of us than humans are of them," answers Mariska. "They have good reason to be."

"Well, not from us specifically," insists Jack, already clicking away with his first few shots of the camera. I glance back just enough to notice his ear-to-ear grin.

I vaguely realize that later I shall never know quite how long we might have been standing there. Seconds, minutes. Old Einstein again: time's relative to observers, and all we wanted to do right then was continue to observe. But then: "Why are they just standing there?" Dave says.

None of us know. But then there's another howl from behind the wolves, and a fourth emerges. Even I know now that wolves can harmonize, but there's no way this new individual could have offered that strong multi-vocal song on its own. Plus, the sound came from the wrong direction.

What the hell is going on here? The first three wolves have glanced at us, but have apparently decided we're not much danger, though they're certainly not making any efforts to draw closer, much as we'd like them to do, especially shutter-happy Jack.

But this fourth wolf, the grey and white one, doesn't merely look towards us. He stares. He gets up near his packmates, sits down submissively near them, and stares. I swear he's (she's?) looking right at me, into my eyes, at all of us. Like he knows us somehow, or perhaps is hoping for something from us. But that doesn't make any sense.

My staring right back at this fourth wolf is interrupted by the unmistakable heart-stopping explosion of the sound of gunfire.

* * *

"Shit!" Jack cries out in a tone partly fearful and partly furious. "Who else is out here?"

Mariska, usually the one to admonish Jack (and sometimes Dave) for their colorful selections of ejaculatory expressions, ignores it this time. Still loving to point things out to the rest of us, she wheels around instantly and gestures angrily to two men just across the river. "What are they shooting at?" she says to us, as though we know.

For the first second or two, I wonder if these noisy assholes are targeting *us*, but as I glance from the wolves to the men and back again, I realize: *They're hunting the wolves. How long have they been out here, and why have we not noticed them until now?*

Some dim autopilot version of consciousness is trying to reconcile whether or not this is wolf season, and if we're in a legal area for such, and whether these armed men have permits, and all that crap about which I know almost nothing, as I see and hear Dave. He's running to go back across the river.

"Dave! What the hell are you doing?!" demands Jack, who is still holding up his camera, though he's not shooting anything at the moment. Mariska is mostly watching him, still probably wondering how best to handle the situation. I've never heard of hunters going off the proverbial deep end up here and targeting other humans, but I'm not used to having rifles discharged this close to me, either. I mean, the men and us and the wolves form a narrow triangle with our positions, so if this damned hunter or poacher or whoever he is had shot just a bit wide, well...

Don't think about it. Just act. I look back towards where the wolves are. It takes another moment to realize that I don't hear any more howling, and that three of the adult wolves we just saw have disappeared, *and where are the pups? We haven't seen them at all for a while now.*

But this I don't understand at all: the fourth adult wolf, the curious one, is still sitting there, calm as can be, like this is all a show. I can only imagine what it must be thinking. And didn't Mariska say that wolves are scared of us? Why hasn't it run away?

And then I'm completely bowled over to notice that behind me, Dave has reached the river fording site again, and appears to be yelling at these other men. *David, what on Earth are you thinking?*

* * *

Dog-chaser was through running. He felt too tired now, anyway. And he was sick of being afraid of the man-thunder, however horrible the noise was. Oak and Paddler and Trap-dasher had quickly hidden behind his current position, but went no further: they wished to announce their location to neither the men nor to the other wolves.

Dog-chaser sniffed and looked about from where he sat. He did not hear the other wolves, those strangers whose territory they'd run through twice. He could not smell or see them, either. Perhaps they were scared of the man-thunder also. That made sense; why would they not be so, after all? It was loud enough to hurt.

The four humans that the *omega* had seen closest to the river had clearly taken an interest in him and his packmates, but had not deigned to come any closer, which seemed odd, and they made much less noise than any of the other various humans Dog-chaser had seen before. The other two humans could now be seen heading into the river to come across. The wolf did not know how the noise-makers worked, did not even fully appreciate the connection between rifles and dead wolves; he just knew that men and louder noises were clearly conjoined with the deaths of his family members.

That made him scared, but he just needed rest. He'd not only kept up with his three remaining packmates, but had exerted more energy from both motivating them and from eating last, and therefore less, than they had. And since the wolves who'd been chasing him just moments before appeared to have stopped, he was just going to sit and observe whatever happened next.

The humans appeared to be establishing their own pack hierarchies, via usage of gestures and shouting, rather like wolves and their body posturing and growling.

* * *

It begins with shouted warnings, and not direct physical assaults. "What the hell is wrong with you two idiots?!" Dave demands of these two men, one of whom has just finished levering the bolt action of his rifle and thereby placing the next round into the firing chamber. The three of them have made a hostile rendezvous on one of the more solid bars of land in the midst of the river, which still offers a line of sight to where we'd just seen the wolves.

I can't hear what the men reply to Dave. They look surprisingly calm; I suppose they would have to, since they're the ones with the guns. By this point, I've already more or less womanhandled Jack and Mariska into following me back over to where the three of them are bickering, but it hardly takes much persuasion. Strength in numbers, and all; I think Jack has already obtained another clandestine photo or three of this little incident, and am hoping like mad that such images won't ever be needed as any kind of legal evidence.

We're almost to the river ourselves now, the voices coming clearer. For just a second I remember the impetus of all this nervous human energy, and turn around again just long enough to notice that that same crazy wolf is *still* sitting there, watching us. Looking back towards Dave, I can tell that these men, dressed every inch the way I picture Alaskan hunters to look, right down to the camo jackets, are likewise aware of the wolf's continued presence. They seem a bit taken aback by it as well. They also seem intent on getting another shot.

But someone else appears to have forgotten the wolf entirely. He's too busy shouting to notice much else. "Let me guess: Insecure trophy hunters? Bush and Palin voters? Immigrant haters? Who else would be this goddamned stupid! Do you two inbrednecks even have permits, or do you just feel like killing anything that moves?"

The professional writer in me is, for just an instant, impressed at Dave's new term, since he's always joked about how rednecks and inbreeding seem to go hand in hand, and I can, perversely, barely stifle a giggle at this, but I have to keep running to reach them all.

"Look, sir, we have every right to be out here as anyone else," says the one who appears the elder of the two, and I notice that there's a clear resemblance between the two men, even though the younger one has more facial hair and looks a bit skittish. "And if I may say so, it's rather 'goddamned stupid' to be out here unarmed." The voice sounds controlled, tempered, though the other man with him seems edgy.

"Why?" Dave says, shrugging his shoulders overdramatically. "In case I chance upon other armed people? Are you threatening me as well?" I must admit, Dave's tone frightens me a bit.

"Mister, we're not threatening you, but we are indeed hunting, and you four have probably scared off all the game in this area by now."

Dave shakes his head. Always one for terminology, he focuses on that. "Sure. To you it's a childish game. To those you're targeting, it's something else. And besides, you're the ones making all the noise!"

The younger of the two pipes up this time. "Hey, asshole, we're not causing any trouble for you and yours, so why don't you just leave us alone? People have a right to hunt."

The object of my newfound affections strangely smiles at this, which I can barely see on the far side of the river from him, like he knows he's got something useful now. "To hunt, yes, to obtain something which helps them survive. So are you two asking me to believe you're going to go home and make some wolf jerky?"

"What we do with a kill is none of your business. I wouldn't expect a tourist to understand." This again from the older brother. John Graydon did feel himself getting angrier at this demented shorthaired hippy. What kind of retard charged armed men in the open when he wasn't even armed himself?

"Tourist?! Do I look like a tourist? Why don't both of you turn around and hike your butts back home? Somehow I doubt it's even legal for you to be out here, and the idea of blowing away a wolf smacks of cowardice."

That last word triggers something. No god-fearing red-blooded American hunter is about to let go of a charge like that, even if it's only implied. "It is legal," the older man says now, finally looking directly at Dave and taking his eyes off the wolf, or at least where the wolf was. I haven't dared to look back that way again, and even now, Jack and Mariska and I are sizing these men up, wondering what will happen next.

We've finally reached where the three are standing. I'm barely aware of the water which has again seeped over the tops of my boots from where the three of us just carelessly splashed back across the water. Jack tries to defuse things before they go any further. "Look, guys: my friend doesn't mean any insult, so why don't we all just part ways?" I know this tries Jack cruelly, since he completely agrees with Dave's assessment. He knows no one eats wolves, so these guys must be trophy hunters, which all four of us have vehemently opposed for at least as long as we've known one another.

Yet the strange men are having none of it. "You know what cowardice is?" the older man says menacingly. "It's people like you who don't realize where your food comes from, or where your freedom comes from, or just how easy you have it. And then when you suddenly want safety or luxury or the daily necessities, you whine for it. Who do you think provides that?"

"It's obviously not you," Dave says, "and I'm hardly a whiner. And just so we're clear, it takes no courage at all to squeeze a trigger, ever. None! Go kill a bear with a knife or your bare hands and I'll be willing to reconsider your 'bravery.' And standing up for what you believe in, regardless of what it costs, takes far more courage than either of you two pussies will ever even comprehend."

The Graydons had pretty much decided that this character, whoever the hell he was, did at least have some balls, even if he was hopelessly misinformed. Or maybe he was just nuts, which might make him dangerous. "Back down, mister," John admonishes. "Just back down and walk away, all of you," and he makes brief eye contact with me for the first time, along with Jack and Mariska.

And then he makes the careless mistake of raising the rifle again.

Neither Dave nor I look towards where the gun must be aimed; we haven't the time, and to my astonishment, Dave throws himself at the big man, roughly his own size, and grabs onto the rifle as it fires, at once ruining whatever aim the shot might have had, and as we notice an instant later, clearly panicking the other, younger man.

Up until now, I'd only really been annoyed by the fact that two dipshits were destroying what should have been a happy future memory for me and one of my most exciting wildlife experiences. But the fact that I now have a gun pointed

at me and my friends is utterly infuriating. Dave trips, unable
to get much of a grip on the one rifle, and falls to find the gun
pointed at him. And then the other man keeps pointing his
own at Jack, Mariska, and I, repeatedly and in turn.

Maybe I'm so angry now because I'm the closest to the
younger fellow, unwittingly having put myself adjacent to him
as I walked up here with my friends. "What the hell are you
trying to do?" the older man says, but then he looks anxious for
some reason, and as though he's not even sure to whom he's
posing the question.

I've no time to wonder why. As the younger man again
directs the rifle my way, I realize that I'm the leftmost member
of our little group, which allows me to step quickly to the right
of the offending weapon while simultaneously moving directly
into the man's personal space, placing my left hand on the rifle
barrel and my right in between his hands, on part of the stock.
I dimly hear Jack take my lead, accompanied by Mariska's gasp,
instantly followed by the sounds of groans as a pair of well
placed kicks connect with the older man.

And it feels strangely fluid, this dance of death, as I
pivot just slightly on my right foot, the one closest to this young
scared armed moron, and throw my hips into the motion, so
that my shoulders and arms and hands all follow this full bodily
circular movement. The arcing path of the rifle is undeniable
now; this young man has no idea at all what he's in for, as my
hands circle in front of him, still clutching the gun, and as I
finish the circle the gun is still in my grasp, out of his, and he
collapses involuntarily onto his left knee, having had to release
his grip of the rifle; my rotation, what we call *kokyu* in the *dojo*,
has torn the weapon from his hands and left it in mine.

Was it just three days ago I'd been naively wondering
what it would be like to disarm someone of a genuine weapon?

From there all I have to do is step back and, now engaged
in a skill about which I know next to nothing, raise the rifle and

point it at him. "How does it feel?" I say to him, forcing myself to remain calm, to let the fight, flight, or fright chemicals work their way through me. Dave has explained to me that everyone gets the shakes at some point after a truly dangerous encounter; the body simply tries to get rid of the noxious cocktail it just produced for survival functions. It's what makes some folks puke after a really stressful incident; Dave has confided in me that he's sought out the occasional alley or nearby dumpster right after getting a patient loaded. "Is this really loaded and ready to fire?"

It takes Benjamin Graydon moments to find his voice, so startled is he by both being disarmed, and having the action done to him by a woman. He is incapable of believing what has just happened. He just nods instead. "Jack?" I say.

Later on, Jack will describe his own action, which was based not on my blending motions of *aikido* but on the more aggressive nature of *karate*. Jack noticed Dave's erstwhile assailant turn his back to him, and he capitalized on it, performing a side snapping kick to the back of the man's knee, and when the man was then collapsed on the ground and already in pain, following this up with a roundhouse kick from the other leg, connecting with the face. Neither kick did much damage, but both hurt, and the man would have a sore knee and noticeable "shiner" for a while. "I'm fine, Morgan," is all Jack says. "Iska?"

Still startled but realizing the danger is now past, Mariska responds affirmatively. "Dave?" she asks gently, still taking in the scene, with me holding a rifle on one man, and Jack gripping the other rifle, with three other men on their knees.

The third of those men is of course David. And like the hunters, he's also breathing more heavily than he probably should be.

"David?" I say now as well. Like the older hunter, Dave is down on all fours. Well, three, anyway, since he's probing his right armpit with his left hand. And his breathing, while it sounds labored a bit, also sounds like he's forcing it to retain its rhythm. *Oh, shit.*

I swear, if this son of a bitch has hurt Dave... But then, weirdly, I notice that Dave seems to be laughing. Not a full guffaw, to be sure, but he really does seem amused by something. But it only lasts a moment or two, and then he says, "Does anyone have a cell phone?"

I don't remember any of us bringing one, and doubt we'd get any reception out here, even if we were less than forty kilometers from Talkeetna as the eagles fly. And if my map-reading ability is halfway competent. "Well, gentlemen?" Jack says to the hunters, slurring the term of respect into a sneer, to receive shaking heads in return. They both seem dumbfounded by what has happened.

Dave's wincing now; his searching hand must have found something. *Surely he wasn't... no, don't even think that.* "Jack," I say, "put down that other rifle and take this one." And I gesture to the hunters. "Both of you, on your feet." They comply, albeit a bit slowly for my enraged preference. "Back your asses up," and they step away from us, while still facing me, and then I feel Jack's reassuring hands take control of the offending piece of wood and steel I just commandeered. Part of me just wants to collapse and twitch for a while, but I don't think any of us are going into shock just yet, thankfully. Still, I'm now quite cognizant of the fact that, being a former EMT, I'm the one with the most health care expertise of anyone out here except for David himself.

And he's forcing himself to speak. Coldly, detached, analytically. He's already slid off the lighter jacket he'd been wearing. It's probably good he's such a warm hiker, so he's wearing one layer less than Iska or I. "No penetration trauma, which suggests no apparent fragmentation. I'd also suggest possible cavitation, but if that was so, I'd not be talking."

This crazy hunter of hunters is assessing himself like any of the other hundreds of patients he's dealt with over the years.

I kneel next to him. He briefly makes eye contact with me. "How's the wolf, Morgan?" is all he says.

The what? Oh, right. Our position by the wolves is behind where Dave now kneels, sitting in *seiza* as I do so often on the training mat. Glancing back, I can already hear Mariska's surprise. "That one wolf still is back there. I cannot believe it."

Nor can I, but my focus is now on Dave. Jack speaks now. "If he's able to walk, Morgan, then we'll have to get out of here. There's no phone, and I don't think this place offers the smoothest of landing sites for a plane or even a chopper. Mariska, I want you to grab that other rifle. Just strap it over your shoulder. There's no bullet loaded right now, so it's safe, but we'll latch the safety on it, too."

At least someone else among my friends is relatively calm. "The wolf's fine, Dave. You just saved it." *You crazy, dear man.* And that's when it hits me. He just risked his life, and is now injured, we don't know how badly, and all to decrease the risk to a wolf. Is this dedication or madness, or something else?

"It hurts like hell, Morgan, but there's some good news."

"What?" I say, blinking away tears while I gently grasp him, and a vague attempt to offer some kind of comfort. I've never felt so helpless before, not even when Mom died.

"Fortunately, I'm not very thirsty, and I haven't found very much blood. The end of the gun barrel must have been right under my armpit, but I don't remember the gun going off. So the bullet didn't actually enter me, else I'd be in pretty bad shape. Still, it feels like there's some burn damage, and a little blood loss. It may just be a nasty proximity burn. If I can just keep the site fairly clean..."

His eyes lock onto my own then. I can see what he doesn't want the others to know, and I can already note that his face is a bit sweaty, though hopefully it's just from the sudden exertion of sprinting across a rocky dangerous river and confronting armed men.

But it's shock he's mostly worried about, which is why he mentioned the thirst. You don't give anything to drink to shock patients, even though they may be hugely thirsty and get really bitchy about wanting fluids. They can be combative, even if they don't realize the kind of physiological trouble they're in.

And the fluid issue is because of the risk of hypovolemia, and also from the risk of creating an airway hazard in case the person suddenly becomes unconscious. Unresponsive, basically comatose. And I don't know, really, how much damage there is.

I decide to help him stay detached and analytical. After all, he's just another medical case. *Stop it, bitch!* That thought elicits a few more tears, which I furiously brush away with my lightly gloved hand. "You said there was no cavitation, right?"

It works. He's already hostile again. "That's what I hate so much about fucking guns, Morgan. The high-powered ones especially. The bullets travel so fast that the energy of the wind they generate en route forces its way into the wound site, opening up a far larger hole that you'd expect from just the puncturing bullet itself. That's what makes them so goddamned difficult to treat. Rifle bullets are even worse, since they tumble on impact, and bounce around inside the victim, but the bullet doesn't appear to have done anything to me."

"Let me see," I gently but firmly command.

I'm met with either masculine denial or that annoying tendency of health care people to become the worst patients when they're the ones who need help. And they all do, eventually; they just hate admitting so. "It's fine, Morgan."

I can already see some blood on the right side of his shirt, with a little around the vest. I think of my own first aid kit back at the camp, which is of course roughly seven kilometers or so from here. The bleeding's not bad, or so it seems to this EMT whose certification has lapsed. Still, you use the best stuff you have first. *What do we have out here which is more or less clean, since I doubt there's anything truly sterile?* The best I can think of is, well, it's back at the campsite; I'll get it later. I'm sure Dave will find it amusing, which may go further toward helping him avoid shock.

"Can you stand at all?" I gently say. "And tell me, what else about guns?" This is the same person who, after all, informed me that in an emergency, a useful antidote to the fear, which can exacerbate shock, is simple anger.

Normally, the antidote to fear is love, not anger. Its opposite may be courage, though its cure is love. But right now there isn't time. I'm going to try and keep this man energized enough to survive until we can get him to a hospital, which means I have to delay telling him how much I love him and that he has to hang on.

Very slowly, and with some help from Mariska and I, Dave gets up onto one foot, with the knee of the other leg still on the ground. Jack is still covering the men, though I can't even see that at the moment. But Dave can see them, and he's chosen this curious time to offer them a lecture. Fine, if it keeps him talking and further from hypoperfusion.

"You know what's wrong with what you're doing?" he demands of our dumbfounded captives, who look utterly nonplussed; none of this seems to equate with any of their own experiences in the backcountry. Dave's moving precariously.

"It's an attempt to gain control, but there's really no such thing. You think you can control this land and its creatures, but you can't even control yourselves. And the guns are just ways to cheat." Dave grunts a time or two, then slides some of his weight onto the other foot, and, to my surprise as well as perpetual gratitude, he is actually standing, though I can feel him leaning demonstrably on the combined strength of Mariska and I.

"It's cheating," he repeats, "and that's what makes it cowardly. It's like someone who claims 'they say' when wanting to make a point, but that makes it meaningless. 'They say that wolves are bad,' or 'they say that we need to drill for oil,' or 'they say that we need to go to war against someone who's never harmed us.' You want to hunt, fine: go hunt. But do it because you need to eat to live, and don't you dare gloat over it. My friend here could tell you that you have to respect Nature's bounty," and Dave squeezes Mariska, "but you two just come out here like you own the place, and try and kill a species which is no threat to you and which you will never need in order to survive. And then you rant about the city folk, having forgotten that the creation of the cities was prompted by that same stupid notion of control that you're trying to maintain out here, so you conveniently sidestep the responsibility."

He's sweating again. We have to get him moving. "Come on, Sir Accolon, let's see if those legs still work."

Jack's voice again, from my flank. "Change of plans. Here, Morgan, take the other rifle from Mariska, and Iska, you take this one." He knows neither of we women present have any experience with firearms, so I suppose he suspects I'm more on edge than Mariska, and perhaps still of a mind to blow these hunters away for hurting someone I care about, but as Dave just reminded me, that too would be cowardly and wouldn't resolve or answer anything. But who would even know, out here?

We would. Always. "What do you have in mind, Jack?" I say.

He's already worked his way around me, handing off the guns and getting most of his own weight beneath Dave's left shoulder. Mariska and I almost drop the damned rifles, and

I'm glad we made the hunters back up before we started all of this.

"Look," says one of them, the older one I think. "It was an accident, and I'm sorry. Now what can we do to help?"

I wheel on him. "You can go on ahead and make sure help is ready by the time we get back to where we left our car."

"Fine, we'll go. The last thing we need is a classroom." And they turn and head off. I'm amazed; I didn't think they'd really move. And I'm strangely glad that the elder of the pair seems able to move quite well despite just having gotten kicked a couple of times by Jack. I've seen Jack use stronger versions of those same kicks to shatter solid pieces of old wood, so I can only imagine what they might do to bone.

Dave takes his first uneasy step while leaning on Jack. Mariska and I have relinquished our holds, both begrudgingly. "You know why I hate guns?" he says, much more softly.

"No, why?" I ask, surprised suddenly by the appearance of Jack's camera around my neck. I hadn't even noticed him give it to me or that I'd taken it along with a rifle.

"Guns allow liars and cowards and weaklings to become killers. That was the epiphany I reached when I worked on my first gunshot victim in Chicago. It was a kid, an unwilling participant in a robbery gone bad. The kid never had a chance. And I know what the robbers and the gang-bangers and the cops and the soldiers want us all to think: that without the guns, they get no respect. But all I'm respecting is the power of the gun itself. For the person hiding behind the trigger, I have nothing but contempt for the coward who refuses to talk, refuses to try, and refuses to accept responsibility."

"Come on, Dave, save your strength," Jack admonishes. The pair of them have taken about ten steps now.

"Jack, I'm managing. Besides, we teach that keeping potential shock patients involved is the best way to minimize shock's effects, or even to keep it at bay for as long as possible. Where was I?" *So much for not mentioning shock*, I note.

"Responsibility," Mariska says to remind him, glancing trepidatiously at me. I smile feebly in return.

"Oh, yes. Time was, to kill someone, you had to get your hands dirty. But with a distance weapon, you can avoid getting messy. That makes it easier. All these goddamned guns are just penis substitutes, a way of saying, 'Look how big mine is.' God, it makes me want to puke. We kill animals and each other not so much to eat, but out of dick-fear, out of the fear that we're not good enough on our own, so let's beat up on someone else. It's the ultimate form of bullying, and just as psychotic."

I'm still going over a mental checklist of sorts. There's no cyanosis, or bluishness of the skin, in evidence with Dave. He's weakened, but apparently not critically. If he does have a burn from the muzzle discharge, then we can treat it superficially at the campsite with my Second Skin. We might also need the Betadine, and the Advil if the pain gets worse. If we can keep him from actually going into shock, then I'd guess offhand that he'll likely be fine.

But he's hesitant to allow the rest of us to see whatever wound is actually present. That's worrisome. He probably just wants to avoid alarming us, but maybe he doesn't want to acknowledge something potentially bad when we're still this far from help.

And there's very little you can do for shock "in the field." Keep the fluids away, elevate the legs to encourage gravity to keep blood in the torso and head, but we can't do the latter since that same gravity might make any bleeding near his right shoulder worse, and of course he needs to be moved. On a whim, I reach for his left wrist, draped as it is over Jack and easily within reach. His hand feels cool, but I notice a strong and mostly even radial pulse in the wrist. And I haven't noticed any more bleeding near that arm. So far, so good.

"Didn't I promise to tell you guys about immortality?" Dave says suddenly.

Christ, no. "Why don't you save it, Dave?" I intone desperately, trying not to sound hysterical over what might, in my brief moment of dark fantasy, become a backcountry deathbed confessional of some sort. "You've had us wait this long."

"No, it's time I mentioned it. But tell me something first."

"Anything, Dave," Mariska says.

"Is that wolf still anywhere in sight?"

I'd all but forgotten. That's the second time he's asked about it now. Glancing back once more, I genuinely cannot believe my own eyes. That one wolf, the curious one, sits there yet, gazing towards all of us. I cannot help but wonder what it must be thinking about these noisy bipeds who just happened upon its day. I laugh at my own anthromorphizing as I wave to the wolf, and savor the knowledge that it and its packmates are at least safe for one more day. Dave absolutely loves hearing about it. It helps keeps his spirits up for quite a while, despite his griping about the hunters.

Seeking distractions myself, I allow my thoughts to wander where they will; somehow the sighting of these wolves has provided an impetus and an opportunity for such. And witnessing Dave yelling at people likewise permits me to consider part of what just motivated him. He's been needing a release, and these hunters represent, for him, the worst of what he finds at his job. Their implied identity as those who permit Dave and the rest of us to go on living now prompts my own thoughts, even if I'm not screaming them at others.

I can actually almost feel the primitive intense hormones coursing through me, making me reflective. It's quite a heady mix.

I know David in particular would relate to this immediately, though he'd still find it as horrifying as ever. For him, the hunters embody the group-think mentality, which Dave's confessed to me on a couple of occasions over the past few months is *the* reason why he's burned out on the job. He hates gawkers. I mean, *hates* them. When he's at an emergency scene, he has apparently shouted at the gawkers present, telling them to stop staring, that what they're doing when gawking at the victims of the scene is a severe violation of privacy, and even a form of rape (I've never been able to verify this, though he's been written up for it). But the people keep right on staring, either obsessed with death or glad it's not them who've been hurt in some way or maybe just taking pictures with their damned cell phones or plotting to sell their video footage of the event to the television stations. They're so caught up in the dramatic that the consideration of either trying to help the victims or looking the other way and leaving another's dignity at least partly intact never occurs to them. And then they'll preface the next family dinner with, "Guess what I saw today!"

What drives that? Are people's lives so monstrously drab and boring that they need to embellish the mundane and everyday into the grandiose and epic? Perhaps: why else would photos and tales of celebrities be worth so much? But for the moment I'm not focusing on Dave's work. I'm concentrating instead on wildlife. I still remember the Alaskana sections of the Anchorage bookshops, with a whole sub-category about bear attacks. Imagine that: other writers like me capitalizing on fear and the fine art of blowing things completely out of proportion. Yeah, sometimes wild creatures harm humans, though the rate at which humans harm and kill wild creatures is so much greater it can probably be expressed with astronomically sized numbers, but this is a talk I've actually already had with Jack, not Dave.

Jack is equally sick of this. He seems convinced that the psychologists must have some name for whatever condition compels people to overly dramatize things. People get freaked out up here whenever a bear or wolf glances their way, but the animals are just curious. These creatures don't strut about, altering their plans, while sizing you up as a potential entrée. They just go about their own activities. But people think the wild animals are scary, and they don't realize that it takes a gigantic human ego to believe that another animal is going to modify its activities for the sole purpose of ruining your day.

With fear, once again, size doesn't matter, since people are phobic about things as small as bacteria and ants and spiders, and also as big as Alaska's bears, but this time I'm no longer grinning at the notion of size not mattering. I'm just tired of wild animals being persecuted for being themselves.

It's like this, and hopefully this'll help summarize part of what we were all getting at with parts of our talks, about ethics and ideas and the rights to opinions. You can't justify killing another creature unless you either need it to survive and eat or unless it's an act of self-defense, both of which are generally sanctioned by every major philosophical and religious tradition known, no matter how pacifistic. But our species thrives on the dramatic. And I'm guilty of hypocrisy of a sort here, too, as I narrate my way through this mental obstacle course. All novelists are guilty of this, since fiction is a form of manipulation (but so is truth, otherwise we'd never have discussed the reality behind the composition of something like a spoon). Read a story, hear a storyteller, see a movie or play or musical, and let your emotions get carried away with you. And people act on their emotions, especially fear, which is the real bitch of it. To paraphrase Dave, those old Greeks were well aware of this power, partly because they gave theatre arts to us as part of their legacy. Aristotle said that the theatre had a cathartic effect: go reread Euripides and Sophocles and Aristophanes and keep in mind the influence they have on your feelings. You enter the theatre, participate in a group activity (which used to be in a lit setting but now takes place in darkness, so you can't participate in the experience with other people anymore), and feel some degree of empathy with the characters, who will have to be undergoing major life changes if the story's going to be any good and not put the audience to sleep.

And thus the drama. Tragedy and comedy alike have the same effect: experience some raw emotions, and you'll be ready to deal with your own life a bit better, since at least you're not as badly off as the tragic characters or you've just laughed at the comic ones.

So what happens when this tremendous storytelling power gets misused? Storytellers traditionally have been the central personages of their cultures, whether they appear as bards, troubadours, minstrels, actors, playwrights, humorists, poets, theologians, shamans, or teachers. They all tell stories. And every story has its own wisdom, whether the participant decides to share in it actively or not.

So when you tell a story involving wildlife, what happens? Well, to make it dramatic, you offer an old parable. But to really get the audience into it, you scare the shit out of them. Snarling bears, rampaging wolves, greedy lions, stampeding herds of wildebeests, anxious rhinos, disturbed hippos, growling cougars, clouds of locusts or mosquitoes or bees: what better metaphors to suggest that humans are different, that we need to escape from these terrifying things?

And then we miss the ego trap I mentioned a moment ago: we actually dupe ourselves into believing that we're somehow *better* than these other animals, even though we're the ones slaughtering them, and not the reverse.

Let me explain the effects of the storyteller another way. Leo Tolstoy became a philosopher himself once, after he'd decided late in life that his writings which are now so worshipped were complete crap, and he rejected the trappings of wealth. He focused on the topic of what constitutes art, with a deceptively simple title: *What is Art?* And he said that any art, all art, is a moral activity. With moral justification and moral consequences. I had to read that book for my own master's program, and I don't think Dave's gotten to it yet, but I know he'd love it. Because this is where the storyteller is held accountable, and Dave's conversations with us on this trip, starting with the notion of the entitlement to our opinions, finally get fleshed out.

Because the storyteller is responsible (or any artist; old Tolstoy tried accounting for painting, sculpture, music, and basically anything else which might be said to have any level of artistic merit). That's why opinions have to be earned. I'm absolutely not advocating any form of censorship; indeed, in order to make rational and measured judgments about anything, anything at all, you have to be able to consider the things themselves, and that in turn requires exposure which can only come from freedom of access. What this does mean is that yes, you can say and portray anything. But you're also responsible for the effects your portrayal might have.

Back to the wildlife stories: picture those goofy Three Little Pigs. A moral fable, of course, or at least a primer in the merits of basic construction materials. And like all good dramas, there's a villain. And not just a wolf, of course, but the big, bad one. The evil one, the one which must be conquered and eradicated. And make sure you don't let your kids or pets out at night, because the wolf might be out there.

Or take that caring yet inattentive youngster, Red Riding Hood. Another moral story, to be sure, and here the antagonist even receives the same name: Big and Bad. Perhaps he survived the ordeal in the pigs' brick-enclosed kitchen. Perhaps he had a twin. Either way, the imagery remains the same, and storytellers have traditionally escaped with clean hands, just like those who complain about "terrorism:" these are evil monsters, and you must have nothing to do with them.

So just how the big bad wolf acquires tremendous breath power in the one tale and a taste for geriatric cross-dressing in the other might remain a mystery. But what is less difficult to ascertain is the legacy of fear inspired. Hiking back now with a wounded and now quiet Dave, I never felt the slightest fear of those wolves we sought; I did however feel fear for them, especially once the other humans nearby materialized, and I witnessed directly the effect on Dave. That was how I learned that he was not just engaged in some quirky intellectual exercise about opinions and the need to get past behavior motivated by fear: he really believes these things, has proven them rationally and logically.

He once put it like this: he's noticed that using reason makes us more likely to do anything *for* each other. And he's likewise noticed that a lack of reason makes us more likely to do anything *to* each other instead.

Sorry. I know I got a bit carried away back there. I'm still attempting to reconcile all of what just happened. And I've become more hectic and immersed in the ancient adrenaline rush myself, essentially because I'm now terrified about David.

* * *

Paddler, Oak, and Trap-dasher had rejoined Dog-chaser where he sat by the river, his tired tongue still drooping from his panting mouth. The others were in much the same shape themselves: fatigued and hungered to the point of just collapsing right there by the water, come what else may. Paddler had tried to growl her conviction into the minds of her packmates that the river might be swum, but they were having none of it.

They had all taken turns lapping up some of the cool but silty water as it rushed by them, always in even more of a hurry than the wolves themselves. Once again, they'd had to take turns with such an action, perpetually on the alert for other animals, including others of their own kind.

But where were the Chelatna wolves now?

Dog-chaser would never understand whether the pack that had just been chasing them had been frightened off by the man-thunder, or whether they had just charged in a threatening manner like the bull moose the Fire Creek members had encountered recently, merely to scare them away. He was also vaguely aware that he and his surviving family were now past the borders of the other pack, so maybe those wolves had just given up on the chase, their point having been made. He doubted Oak and Paddler and Trap-dasher would dare to reenter the territory which came almost up to this river.

They wouldn't follow the humans, either, of course. That eliminated two directions. Only the river was left, and it looked as if it ran southward, away from the new pack's territory. If the four wolves could just obtain another meal or three, they could be on their way, hopefully without having to worry so about their own survival.

For their part, Bear Heart and Owl Eyes and their packmates remained keenly aware of the presence of the other wolves. Chasing anyone beyond the borders of one's own homeland was always risky, something these wolves had never had to do. And the incredible sound had indeed scared them off, at least initially. But as the humans realized, there was truly strength in numbers, and the two Chelatna *alphas*, along with the older adults, including Fisher, Wave, Cabal, and Rendezvous, now approached the river again. They'd only ever seen it from a greater distance, and they also wanted to know if the invaders, human and wolf, were still around to make a nuisance of themselves. Trying to establish a territorial claim at or around water was rather meaningless: the effects of the water itself would too quickly wash away markings.

Tornado, Swifter, and Tracer, as the younger adults, had been made to stay in hiding with the pups, Puddles, Sterling, and Foxtrot. They were all more easily excited, and were less tested in the hunt anyway. They would likely only create difficulties if presented with strangers, regardless of species, and the risk was considered too great regardless.

The more mature members of the Chelatna pack thus slowly but boldly made their way closer to the river, realizing at once that they were beyond the scent markings which delineated their home, as clear to many other species as signposts and warning labels. But they had to know; simple curiosity drove them.

Strangely enough, it was the two *omegas* who did the most to defuse a potentially violent confrontation. Oak and Paddler were immediately on guard again when the strange wolves began to emerge from the woods, upwind to mask their scents and able to make undetected noise which was covered by the sounds of the river. So the wolves were noticed the same way they would have been by the humans: by visual cues first.

Trap-dasher was still drinking his fill, and Dog-chaser continued to watch where the humans had been, almost as if he perversely wished them to return; his curiosity about the odd creatures was such that he almost felt prepared to chase after them, but he also knew he had to stay with his family.

Two pairs of *alpha* wolves simply stood now in a small clearing, their subordinates arranging themselves behind them, ready for whatever would happen next. Full wolf wars were extremely rare; usually problems only arose when a lone wolf or perhaps two ventured where they weren't supposed to be. And all of those present now realized that this could only end badly: the Fire Creek members would be destroyed, and the Chelatna pack would suffer grievous casualties, even with the younger adults and the pups safely tucked away elsewhere.

Dog-chaser, for his part, was barely interested. He just wanted a new home, and was too tired to really care much about canid politics at the moment. And he was surprised, as were they all, by the appearance of a strange female wolf, colored like himself but with more tan at her flanks, and slightly smaller. She oddly, yet boldly, strolled up to where Bear Heart and Owl Eyes stood erect, greeted each of them, and then moved in front of them, lay down, and rested her head on her forepaws.

All the wolves recognized the peacekeeping behaviors of *omegas*, but this was strange indeed; a lower-ranking individual would hardly put herself automatically in harm's way, not without good reason. Dog-chaser was intrigued by Rendezvous and her gesture: submissive, but submissive to all present, as though she was indicating that she was prepared to weather whatever abuse was necessary to ensure peace.

Dog-chaser tentatively approached her. He was so exhausted he would have preferred to just roll over and sleep until the first snow arrived. But at this stage weakness of any kind would be exploited by either side, something he couldn't afford. He offered a similar greeting to his own *alpha* pair, Oak and Paddler, and then lay in the same position in front of them. Fewer than twenty meters now separated the two *omegas*, while the *alphas* and *betas* continued watching each other, warily.

It would have seemed comical to any watching humans, had any been present, and maybe it was also to the wolves. But the two *omegas*, one male and one female, slowly inched their way toward one another, crawling on their bellies, even their legs flattened to the ground. It was uncomfortable, to be sure: this close to the river, the landscape was strewn about with dead branches and plenty of rocks, in varying degrees of smoothness.

None of the animals growled, or barked, or raised their hackles from fear. None of them postured defensively or aggressively any more. Only the subtle presentations of lethal teeth betrayed the tension. And all eyes alternated between watching the enemy and watching the *omegas*.

Still flat, still avoiding body posturing which would indicate hostility or dominance, Dog-chaser and Rendezvous finally arrived to a single body length of each other. They had kept eye contact all the while, and now that they were close enough to detect more complete scents of each other, just sat there for long moments experiencing each other.

The *alphas* and *betas* of both packs did not quite comprehend all of this; who could ever really follow the thought processes of mere *omegas*, anyway? Yet they had nothing to prove, and because of this simple fact, enabled the rest to avoid bloodshed. Dog-chaser and Rendezvous gently eased their way ever forward, until able to actually share very tentative greetings: sniffing followed by muzzle licking.

That was enough. The *betas* sat down first, shortly followed by the *alphas*. The tension had eased, though there was little other compromising. After all, the Chelatna pack could not afford to allow so many new members into its territory; the homeland would have to be expanded, which in turn might yield canid casualties after all. Borders were quite precarious, but still, no one wanted a fight. Oak and Paddler were the first to behave from the obvious conclusion: they would move away, and continue on until they found a new home. Fortunately, some good land for that purpose lay to the southwest, which they would find with just a bit more travel. The *alpha* pair grunted to gain the attention of Trap-dasher, who was thrilled at the prospect of escape, and Dog-chaser, who lingered for a few moments with his new tentative friend, then rolled over to show he meant no aggression, and stood, eyes downcast, and slowly walked away. The Chelatna wolves watched them until well after they had followed the river's course southward.

Rendezvous kept staring in that direction for another hour even after that.

* * *

I warned back at the start of this little tale that I might wind up having reservations about telling it, but it was the discovery of something personal of Dave's which has strangely helped me get through all of this now. You will likely wonder about his notion of the value of personal sacrifice, but since my entire purpose has been to discuss things and beings of value, perhaps you might find yourself reconsidering. You may wonder in addition if my entire story has been about running the greatest possible risk for the sake of saving a single wild animal. On one level, that is true; but I remain far more interested in the background of this man I find so irresistible which drove him to take that risk in the first place. That's what I think this is really about.

That one particular wolf whose life was likely saved by my dear friend David Thomas had us all utterly mesmerized, I admit, mostly from its own obvious curiosity towards us, as were we curious about him. That does in fairness seem almost foolish now, but when you encounter something truly wild, there's almost a magic to it, which is a reversal of our more traditional feelings toward the wild: fear, mixed with a desire to try and control, since that seems the only way past the fear. I know that sounds trite, like my earlier claim that martial arts practice and reading enough books would somehow serve to improve me as a person, but the feeling is the same. And as for the foolishness, well, one of my favorite novelists once said that anyone who has not made of fool of him- or herself for some cause has lived only a shadow of a life.

And the counter of fear, recall, is love, or at least acceptance. Courage, the opposite of fear, is just a cover: I tend to think that the only genuine difference between courage and stupidity is the outcome. A good outcome merits praise, while a bad one reminds us anew of those potential Darwin Award recipients; the same action might get vastly different interpretations.

Let me put it this way, instead: for so many centuries, members of our species have remained thoroughly terrified at merely the prospect of seeing wild creatures up close. Especially the larger ones, and particularly if they have big teeth and claws. And now, whether you're a hiker, photographer, hunter, or just otherwise going about your day, and something like a moose or a bear just happens to cross your path, you might be more inclined to appreciate the fact that the animal in question permitted you to have a glimpse of it, rather than running and screaming about the nasty and ornery monster that you and your fellow townsfolk will clearly have to kill to make everyone "safe."

I understand not everyone agrees with this, and I'm trying to kind of sum up part of what Dave was talking about, or writing about, as it turns out, and, well, I fear I may be getting ahead of myself again. At any rate, suffice it to say how delightfully surprised we all were to find the waiting ambulance back at the tiny parking area where we'd left the car days earlier. For all Dave's ranting about those "damned 'inbrednecks'," you had to be impressed by how quickly they'd hiked back, eventually receiving piecemeal cell phone service on the way, and making sure that a unit from Talkeetna was there with a crew ready to drive fast. It took us all hours to get back; thank goodness we'd gotten started early that morning when we'd found frost in and around the tents. I think about fifteen kilometers passed from the river to the cars. I'd always think afterwards that the simple determination to keep going was the biggest part of what enabled Dave to keep shock at bay. We managed to finish the hike, exhausted, in four hours, probably as ready as our wounded friend to pass out.

The real issue with any kind of shock, which can actually result from nothing other than fear, is a mix of timing and fluid consideration, since all the various kinds of shock involve insufficient fluids, especially blood, getting to where it's needed. The body can compensate for shock for a little while, though for how long depends on both the person and the circumstances. Dave was able to focus his slowly decreasing energy into a heady mix of righteous anger and analytical detail, as all medical technicians and paramedics are taught to keep their shock or potential shock patients involved as much as possible. Laughter can sometimes help this, too. Being amused was for a while scoffed at by the medical authorities, until they noticed how it helped healing. In Dave's case, he almost collapsed, not from weakness or injury but from laughter, when I suggested at the campsite that we use my remaining pair of clean panties as an improvised bandage.

Of course, he'd roared at the previous suggestion, compliments of Mariska: a tampon or panty shield. I'd never heard that, but Dave admitted he liked the explanation of the fact that such items were lightweight, flexible, clean if not quite officially sterile, and naturally highly absorbent. Jack had almost blushed at that, but also found it funny. And it amuses me, some of these gender details: why do men sometimes feel they can't laugh at something feminine, if the women are already laughing themselves silly about it?

Dave hadn't bled as much as we might have feared, but we still exhausted our supply of gauze from the various first aid kits (mine was better equipped than the one shared by Jack and Mariska, who admitted they'd not really checked theirs very thoroughly for some time), but considering that we were trying to deal with Dave's armpit, the underwear was just the thing to lay atop the gauze, and then wrap the whole mess into place with another undergarment: in this case, my long underwear pants. Needless to say, the shirt would be disposed of soon, too, considering its new hole, though we left it on him then, partly for warmth. Poor Dave had had to remain awkwardly on his back while we worked on him this way, and he was the one who kept on acting as a cheerleader to keep us going, and encourage us all to get moving. He knew the value of what he was doing. Maybe there's a little *omega* wolf in each of us.

In other words, "keep 'em talking," as I've heard Dave say in reference to conscious patients. And I hardly need to point out that on this trip, not talking was not a problem from which David seemed to suffer. The hard part was recognition that someone had to move forward with him, and someone had to break down the camp. But then, we realized, if the hunters had really gone on as we'd demanded, then they too would have had to leave behind their equipment, even temporarily. And with time mattering, we mutually decided we'd cross that proverbial bridge when we reached it: the gear would stay put for now.

It's funny, now, almost. I'd insisted on riding in the ambulance, but considering how cramped the space in back was for treatment, I had to ride up front; even that little gift was only awarded when the medics found out Dave was one of them. And I had to listen to the harangue, and in some ways continue to encourage it, for the drive back as far as Palmer, site of the newest hospital in Southcentral Alaska. Jack and Mariska had very graciously offered to head back for our gear, and then bring the car back later. There was little else they truly could do at that point, but I know how the decision pained them; they wanted to be at Dave's side as much as I did. They also told me later how exhausting it was to carry double-loads; I'd promised to take them out to dinner for it, at a place of their choosing.

"Did those idiots relinquish their surrogate penises yet?" the still conscious and feisty potential love of my life yelled from the back of the ambulance.

"Do you mean their rifles, Dave? Actually, Jack and Mariska are probably still talking to those guys. I'm not sure what's being discussed as such, but I suspect it has something to do with promises on the one hand to not trophy hunt mixed with counter promises of not going to the authorities with news of anything other than a hunting accident."

He wasn't about to be mollified by this, of course. "Accident?! Shit, Morgan, we both know it wasn't accidental. And gunshot wounds have to be reported as such."

But it was my turn now to become the analytical one, if only to help me survive emotionally during such a rapid drive southward. "The actual firing, no, that was no accident, as we all realize. But the injury you sustained while trying to minimize the firing's effects was, in fairness, accidental. At least from a legal perspective." *I think.*

Dave seemed to mull that over for a time, even closing his eyes while I wondered if he was drifting out of consciousness. The medic working on him helped keep him talking, too, while rechecking the awkward yet comical bandage and dressing, and steadfastly keeping Dave breathing oxygen directly from an onboard cylinder. The gas, in a more pure state than that found in air, did wonders to increase tissue perfusion and thereby help minimize shock. "I guess we can inform the ER staff that it was just accidental. I don't know what the police might want to do about an inquiry, or about finding the actual gun. I doubt they'll do anything, since the State Troopers would have to look up that asshole, and since the bullet has vanished. And it doesn't look much like a gun wound, considering."

I thought about it all, too. This thing could become some big entangled mess if anyone wanted to press and file charges, but the most that could really be done would probably entail fines, and that was if those guys were hunting illegally, which I still didn't know either way. And I supposed Dave could start a lawsuit for "wrongful injury," or whatever this would have to be called, but that might be awkward to prove.

And he'd be required to then explain what inspired him to cavalierly charge an armed man. Maybe we'd all get into some variation of the "temporary insanity" stuff.

So I'd sat there in the cab, wanting just to hold Dave's hand and feel his heart beat through his wrist, looking back inquisitively at the medic sitting adjacent, wondering how soon we'd be at the hospital. I basically spent that drive trying not to freak out, and felt vaguely reassured by the fact that the other medic, the one driving, never did turn on the siren. They're not supposed to be used up here unless the person in the back is having an extremely bad day and was potentially unsalvageable, so hopefully the lack of a siren's wail was good news.

At one point I looked up quickly, startling this poor driving medic. I was brought back to the present, finally taking a moment to look outside the ambulance. I laughed slightly to myself, shaking my head. The paramedic asked me what was wrong.

"Oh," I told her, "it's just that when we came out for this trip, my main concern had been about the possibility of snow, and there's still almost none to speak of. I never thought I'd have to worry about an injury like this instead." Damn it. I felt my eyes getting wetter at that.

But the medic took my hand and squeezed it, looking at me. "He's very strong," she said. "And he knows how much you care about him."

Several hours later, I'd been encouraged by the Valley medical staff to go on home and visit Dave again in the morning. He'd been stabilized. And of course he'd been vocal throughout his ER treatment, describing in detail the injury, its circumstances, how it had been dealt with "in the field," and how "minor" it was. They'd conditionally agreed, but wanted him kept overnight for observation. Dave had expected as much, though he'd offered a smattering of protest. He just wanted to be home.

I called Mariska when I got in, then Dad. Angus and Cozy were thrilled to have me back, though I broke down and sobbed for a while, selfishly wishing I had something bigger, like a large dog, who'd be easier to hug and better able to absorb tears. Angus nonetheless diligently stayed around my face and shoulders throughout, allowing his coat to get wet. And Cozy flittered about, actually asking where Dave was, which of course made me cry that much harder. And it made me think all over again of the emotional and intellectual range of species to which we falsely feel superior.

That thought was what got me off the couch, along with the phone ringing. It was quite late at night by then. I'd left messages on both machines. Dad appeared to still be out somewhere; this was Iska. "We got everything back okay, but it took hours. I guess the hunters did also, though we didn't see them again."

"What do they intend to do about all of this?" I said.

"Well, Jack and I discussed that some on the way back south. We spoke with those two fools, who seem genuinely scared of Dave's response. They still cannot quite appreciate how he ran at them, nor for that matter how you and Jack disarmed them. I felt a bit useless at that point, I must admit."

I'd not considered that before. "Never, Iska. You were right with Jack and I when we chased after Dave. We all faced down armed men, not just him."

That seemed to mollify her, and she asked how our crazy paramedic was doing.

"Oh, argumentative, naturally. He was protesting hospital food when I left."

Mariska laughed. Such a melodious laugh, from this other friend of mine, never harsh or judgmental sounding. "I shall make sure Jack and I stop in tomorrow to visit him."

"Thanks. He'd like that, though you might want to call first. I'm not sure when he's due to get out, and it'll hopefully be early. Give Jack a squeeze for me, and tell him thanks, too."

Mock effrontery: "What makes you think Jack might be here?"

"Come on, Iska," I prodded. More giggling from the other end: it sounds like Jack playfully wrestling with young Rebecca, who must be back from her stay with Mariska's colleague in the history department. I hung up the receiver, pleased for all three of them. Wondering at the stories I'd have to tell co-workers at the newspaper and training partners at the *dojo*, I was unaware of drifting off.

* * *

I woke up the next morning still on the couch, a cockatoo watching over me and a ferret resting on my belly, and still wearing the same stinky hiking clothes.

It was after the mechanical feeling of showering, changing, unpacking, and feeding and cleaning up after my pets that I noticed my kitchen table. Where did *that* come from?

And I remembered: Dave had sneaked a peek towards the kitchen on our way out of here Saturday morning. I hadn't thought much of it then, since I was eyeballing that stupid still empty pewter frame I love so much and which I suddenly wanted to contain a photo of Dave and I, but now it was obvious: he was looking at what he'd left for me.

A stack of papers, typed and double-spaced, like you'd find with anything being submitted for consideration for publication. There was a yellow sticky note attached to it: "'Had to type it...you've seen my handwriting! 'Hope you enjoy, and we'll talk more about it on the trip. - D - .'"

He must have sneakily left it here when I was grabbing the last of my gear and making sure Angus and Cozy were all set for a few days on their own together. He wasn't sure when he might be back over here, and he clearly wanted me to read this. It's the only time I've been privy to his writing.

There were multiple items, really. As I read, it became clear that David was trying to figure out how to make them mesh into a single more coherent whole, so the work remained still in the early stages, making me feel even more privileged; it's vulnerable to have your words read, even when you think they're "finished," though my editor at the paper feels otherwise. But I felt surprised by what I found. Most people, if they can write well at all, tend to be either good at prose or good at journalism or neither. Dave has a flair for both, making me want to be right at his side that much more.

The first piece was about Jack, though he didn't use any names. It was a report about "wildlife management," which Dave was quick to point out was another misnomer, just a silly misguided oxymoron, since "wild" was unmanageable by definition. I knew it was Jack because I could remember Jack telling us about this.

Jack made a sojourn some years back to eastern Africa, and improvised a safari trip around some parts of Kenya. I say improvised because organized safaris like that are rather pricey, even if they take place in poorer countries. Jack was intrigued by how much cost could actually be involved, so he'd done his usual asking around, while making his way to some of the major wildlife reserves, like Maasai Mara and Samburu.

The costs had to do with the value of wildlife, he learned. And now it was really starting to click for me. The Kenyans figured out that they could hunt the elephants and lions and other big exciting creatures. Or they could leave them largely alone, and charge foreigners to come and see them instead. And they learned that these animals were worth more, far more, in terms of simple money, alive than dead. And the government was prepared to back this basic truth up with force.

There would be no more illicit hunting, no more poaching; the government even made sure that the international news media had a chance to film the burning of tons of ivory, which could have been illegally sold for a large sum to help a developing nation.

I remembered doubting Jack as he'd told us this: the Kenyan Wildlife Service, which helps manage the reserves like our Park Rangers, has the legal sanction to shoot poachers on sight. They don't even have to warn them, and they shoot not to scare or harass but to kill.

It remains the only case I know of, anywhere in the world outside a declared war, by which humans are given authority to hunt other humans. I was astonished. Jack used to joke that we should do something similar in Alaska.

"Why?" I'd asked him that day.

"Think of it, Morgan. Try and imagine what would happen to poaching with a local law like that." He'd worn that usual smarmy Jack-smile as he'd said it.

I had imagined it, and was somewhere between intrigued and horrified. But the underlying premise did start to take hold: Alaska might instead be part of the world's wealthiest nation, rather than one of the poorest, but we're nonetheless hugely dependent on outside income. Revenues from tourism are number one here now; there's less to be had from minerals and fossil fuels, and we have no major manufacturing sectors. And I mentioned before that poaching does take place in Alaska, in addition to many kinds of legal hunting, which ranges from quick mercy killing to tortuous trapping.

The way Dave wrote about Jack's story left the sense that maybe they were both hoping I'd revise it to make it presentable to the *Daily News*. I didn't know for sure if that was the intent, but it did feel that way. Dave even left some margin notes, which indeed required careful reading, that probed gently for additional questions and tips about making such a piece more widely distributable. The thesis was two-fold: all ecosystems need predators, and wildlife is worth more alive than dead. The perceived values have shifted, or so Dave and Jack were hoping.

The second piece Dave left behind was a short story, and it read almost like a kid's tale, or maybe teen or young adult, if you pay attention to such categories. It seemed in fact like it had been written for Dennis, and it felt like he wanted my approval or something first, like he was embarrassed to send it onto the kid. Apparently it was based on one of the talks they'd had when Dennis had visited Alaska. Maybe he'd wondered if this was coming on too strong or something, since his ex-wife had chastised him for encouraging Dennis to ask lots of questions.

"Packs," the story was called. And it was about wolves. And about humans. And about the need to become an individual and the need to also belong to a group, and the pain that such often mutually incompatible goals and needs created.

I felt another tear leak out and cascade its way down my skin as I realized now why Dave feels so frustrated. He's a loner who desperately wants companionship but doesn't know if he can handle it. He's lived in a bunch of different places, I don't even remember them all, but the outcome has always been the same: a few close friends spread out and left behind, while the new folks encountered typically remained acquaintances, although they were still pleasant to be around: I've met some of them, and have hardly been unimpressed. But Dave just knew something fundamental was missing. He moved up here to find a smaller community, in the belief that the bigger the city, the worse (ironically) the sense of loneliness. And he became part of a very tightly knit group: firefighters and paramedics are almost legendary for their sense of comradeship.

But even then he didn't feel like he belonged. He doesn't understand the balance between the need to be part of groups and the need to pursue solitary interests. And the groups are inescapable: we're all born into families, as citizens of particular countries, and we develop our own beliefs in addition to keeping or dumping the ones those initial groups pile on us. All these things mark us as members of this or that group, and the overlaps can cause their own conflicts from divided and often misplaced loyalties.

And David was still walking the line between the two, unsure where he fits in: the lone wolf. And the only person I've ever met who seems incapable of forgiving himself for being human.

I brushed back the first tears, and kept reading. The short story, going on for a few dozen pages, mentioned colorful tales of Japanese samurai and Indian warriors and Marine Corps pilots, and even ancient cave people who were each part of tightly knit and rigidly defined social groups nonetheless heading off on their own to accomplish solo tasks, meeting up with the groups later. *Where did he find this stuff?* I wondered, curiously wishing for a good illustrator. This would indeed make a nifty young reader's book, since it was just offering a lesson about the wide wild world. I felt intrigued at the images of all these young warrior types, compensating for naivety with strong language, and marveled at how I'd dreamt quite recently about what might have been part of this story. Was that how in tune Dave and I had become, or was I just projecting coincidences, or whatever?

He explicitly mentioned in this tale that here was a species in which the group was necessary for the greatest chance of survival and for the opportunity to learn to work as a unit, offset by the emotional need to occasionally just be alone, or at least with just a smaller version of the group. Apparently his research (Dave actually included a little bibliography to show me) led him to conclude that this same species taught us how to be human: no other primate species cares for its young in groups, nor seems to learn to work together so cohesively as a group. Dave was arguing that wolves largely gave us the notion of group identities in the first place and inspired cooperation, even with the disputes that arose from it. I noted Leo Tolstoy in the references: his own masterpiece spoke also of this individual versus group dichotomy, and that same novel also included a graphic depiction of arrogant humans hunting wolves.

There were more margin notes, this time about agriculture. Dave described the advent of agriculture and the idea of staying put as the transition from seeing these animals as helpers to viewing them as rivals, so we tamed and later domesticated a few of them and left the rest to their own devices, often hunting them down as well. It was just like what Mariska had described as the "Great Divide."

Gods: no wonder he wanted to save that wolf! It wasn't just that notion of "Tat tvam asi" and that we're all connected. He also wanted to save it specifically because it was a wolf. When did wolves become such symbolic creatures?

And there was still more. Dave wanted to explain the justification for treating Alaska's wild creatures, particularly wolves, in a certain way. I read how on multiple occasions Alaskan voters had said there could be no policy allowing same-day land-shoot extermination of wolves, and how those voters were ignored by local politics each time. This so infuriated Dave that he turned to his old friend logic, and he'd written another little piece called "Philosophy of Wolves," this time with a specific hand-written request for me to consider somehow getting it into print, at least on the op-ed pages. It appeared as kind of a footnote for "Packs," so maybe that story wasn't such a kid's tale after all. He knew it was far more difficult to get something published in the mainstream venues of other periodicals and books, and I decided I'd see what I could do, even before reading it.

But I was nonetheless very interested by what else I soon read.

The phone rang again. Dad this time. It seemed he had a lovely time with Lila, and actually asked if he should wait another customary three days to call her again. I laughed. I told him to call her right away.

"Don't wait with love," I said to him, reminding him that Mom had been gone for a while now, and would likely approve of his mature taste in women. Under different circumstances, one of those endless "what-ifs," Mom and Lila might have become friends. Dad fell silent at that; I think he agreed, but I guess felt he couldn't say so. Love and sex and all that stuff do have a way of messing things up in our heads. More divided loyalties and group identities.

And yet Mom's not really gone, is she? Or at least it feels that way, and not just in that ghostly traditional religious "peeking over your shoulder" way, either.

I have to see Dave right away. My pack is waiting for me. I almost pick up the phone again to place the call when it rings yet again. Jack: "We're heading up to the Valley to get Armpit Boy out of the big house. Shall we pick you up?"

"Yes, of course. Thanks. And Jack?"

"Yeah?"

"The KWS plan would never work up here."

It takes his memory just a moment. "Oh, I know, Morgan. But I can dream. And even so, the logic is the same: they're all worth far more alive than dead. In many ways. Dead, we're all just protein for scavengers."

An hour later, we're all back at the new MatSu Valley Regional Hospital.

* * *

There's so much thick gauzy dressing beneath Dave's right armpit that he can't quite lower his arm all the way, something which Jack finds hilarious. He picks another movie example to lighten the mood, one with firefighters even: Robert de Niro in *Backdraft*, right after he saves a couple of folks from being dramatically blown up in a house fire but injures his arm in the process. He is next seen sitting upright in a hospital bed with his arm wrapped up and elevated against his will.

"'Sorry it took a while to find you," Mariska says. "We were unsure where this floor could be found, and the lobby in this place is amazing: better than most hotels I have seen."

"Yeah, I've dropped off a few patients up here, too, in a pinch," Dave says, thankfully in a better mood than de Niro was in that film.

It's what I expected, more or less: a sterile-feeling light grey room filled with relatively little equipment. This is some kind of observation floor, the Progressive Care Unit, if I read right, so the scary things like "crash carts" and drug trays and sterilely packed containers of who-knows-what kind of medical apparatus are nowhere to be seen. Dave even has a view, looking over the flatlands of the MatSu Valley. The other bed in the room is empty but obviously in use by someone; maybe the other patient is out for a stroll on the floor somewhere.

I think back to the piece I did for the *Daily News* about the Alaska Native Medical Center, wondering how much a hospital is based on a community message of care for the benefit of the group, and how much is based on the individual concern for the acquisition of money. It's weird: since reading Dave's items, left behind in my apartment, I've already started thinking more about that individual-versus-group dynamic. On this floor, it's mostly individual nurses or techs doing the patient care. Down in the ER where Dave came in yesterday, health care's more of a team sport.

Jack and Mariska have already approached our eager patient, while I'm still gazing about. There are the wall-mounted "plumbing units," as Dave's referred to them: plug-in sources of oxygen and vacuum suctioning. Here are the quirky bed controls, and I recall Jack once wondering aloud if you could really adjust these heavy beds to have such mechanical bends in them that you could "blow or eat yourself," if I remember his charming choice of words accurately.

But it's less funny this time. This room is just a holding area, another modern stopping point which witnesses the passing of individuals who never really get to know each other, some of whom are doing their jobs or pursuing their careers, the others of whom are having really shitty days and don't want to be in this emotionally cold environment in the first place. It's like a reminder of my own old teenaged depression, when I hated life and living and cut off most of my long red locks in some form of protest, which I later realized was why I've tended to choose "safe" decisions: safe jobs, safe men, a safe life. But intellectual safety in this sense leads to a stifling of creativity and thought, which is worse than mere death.

There are no real connections here in this room. That's it. This place has little to offer by way of the connections Dave keeps talking about. That's why I distrust it.

I run over and give him a quick smooch on the mouth. Warm and inviting, I want to pursue my racing thoughts. To their credit, Jack and Mariska smile at my action, but say nothing. Even Jack refrains from what could have easily been snotty and juvenile commentary.

"I've already signed the final paperwork, so I can head out of here, if you guys are ready."

"Ready?" Jack says. "Hell, Dave, I can't stand hospitals. Too many sick people. So let's get going."

"Remind me to not recommend you for paramedic training."

Jack and I do our best to repeat our maneuver from earlier, bracing Dave at the arms and slowly easing him so he can come up off the bed. He's mostly dressed, too, and the nurses must have cleaned him up a bit, even though these clothes have definitely seen tidier times. I don't mind the funky mix of smells coming from him: partly medicinal, partly grubby outdoors, partly male sweat.

He still has to get on his fleece vest and his pants. He's not embarrassed at all by standing before us with a hiking shirt, undershorts, and socks on. "I can get the rest myself," he maintains, though I could swear he winked at me. This is not the image I've often had of the "Double-P," as we've sometimes called him: the philosophical paramedic.

The vest proves easy. Dave has a bit of trouble with the hiking pants, but diligently manages the task, though his effects drop out. The wallet lands with a thud on the semi-clean floor, and I hear, then see, something bouncing and brittle sounding making its way under the electric bed.

"What was that?" Mariska says, reaching for it since she's the only one left with really free hands, as Jack and I are watching Dave to make sure he doesn't fall. I don't believe for an instant that he will, but I feel oddly helpless otherwise.

And Dave seems slightly flustered by this small revelation. "It's just a marble. I'll take it back, please, Iska."

She's picked it up and is now staring at it. "This is pretty."

He's got his pants on but not quite fastened. They nearly drop again while he almost but not quite grabs the marble from her. It's blue, I notice. But I don't know what the big deal is.

Jack jokes about Dave losing his marbles. Mariska and I find it amusing, but Dave's expression has yet to change.

"It's just a reminder," he exhales forcefully, as though he's just confessed to a family of congenital morons. For a moment I'm taken aback by how little I know of his family, other than Dennis and a woman who's no longer really family and who I'll likely never meet.

I hold out my hand and wait for him to drop it, like a parent who's caught a kid with his hand in the cookie jar. He finally offers it my way.

Dave finishes grabbing the rest of his things. Jack's already fetched his wallet. Studying the marble, I notice there's a map of the world painted on it, with the word "Peace" covering most of the Pacific basin.

It's worthless. And the paint is a bit scratched. Some is missing around Australia and Mexico, I notice. And Dave was obviously carrying it around for the whole trip, unless he just acquired it here in the hospital, which I doubt. And I recall seeing him play with it during the trip, too, yet as though he didn't want the rest of us to find out about it.

"What does it remind you of?" I say to him, handing it back. He seems fine to walk on his own, unassisted.

"Tat tvam asi, that's all," he says. "I think the 'peace' rendering is a little superficial and unrealistic, since the world and its inhabitants are never really at peace, and that's not always even a bad thing."

"Gotta eat to live, or are you talking about war?" Jack wonders, watching Dave while he moves.

"Gotta eat to live. War is only embarked upon by humans and ants, so far as we know. And ants are definitely not the most independent thinkers; they're always part of their own colonies."

More groups. "So it's just to remind you that we're all connected?"

"Well, yeah," he says, leading us out of the stark room, waving briefly to the three people at the PCU desk, each of whom is wearing playful and colorful work scrubs. They cheer Dave on quickly, admonishing him to take care, and for us to take care of him. He answers one of them by saying that being a patient sucks, and that it's more fun acting as the caregiver.

That's the closest I've seen him to upbeat about working in health care for months.

"Think of it," Dave says now, shuffling along towards the elevators, a noticeable stride in his step which is accentuated by heavy and filthy hiking boots. "This whole thing," he gestures to the hospital, but really means the entire world, "is just one little ball, a blue marble like this one, and even though it's tiny and rather insignificant in a cosmic sense, it's still all we have. But it doesn't care at all about our petty little agendas and our ego displays. It just keeps going on with its affairs, and all of us are part of it, with our own miniscule roles to play."

He punches the "down" button. A couple of other people on the floor who look as though they might have wanted to use the elevator as well have deliberately turned from us; no one wants to be near a philosopher in a hospital, it seems.

"I told you we're all immortal," he says at last. *Finally.* "It's easy, really: this planet itself is immortal, even though it began basically as a hiccup from our sun. You could say the nearest star just belched us into existence."

Jack loves the imagery at once. What a surprise. "And eventually things will wind down, and the Sun will consume us all again? Or will God light another fart and produce another big bang later?" I can't help grinning at the devilish way Jack has just combined theology and astrophysics with flatulence.

"Well, that's one option," Dave says, smiling at the joke as well. "But the clock's ticking for both the Sun and the Earth. And I eventually realized what delightfully entertaining news that is."

"Dave, what have they got you on?" Mariska says. The mechanical doors ding and slide open, revealing an elevator occupied by two official looking persons wearing white coats over less colorful scrubs: physicians, they must be. I'm oddly glad Dave doesn't seem to recognize them, since he usually only gets to know the emergency docs to whom he turns over transported patients.

"I'm not on anything other than simple gladness, Mariska," Dave boasts, leading us into the cramped chamber. We're all on our way down to the lobby now, I hope. His apparent embarrassment over us finding the little marble appears to be gone.

Dave looks at each of us in turn. "We each get reborn," he concludes. "And I don't necessarily mean reincarnation or salvation or any of the other religious explanations. I mean, really: if you want confirmation of life beyond death, you don't turn to religion, you look at science instead."

I steal a glance at the docs. They seem to be wondering what Dave may have had prescribed recently as well. I just shrug at them.

"How so?" Jack wants to know.

"Matter and energy are the same, Jack. There's not a genuine difference anymore, or if there is a difference, they're just two sides of the same metaphysical coin. That's been the trend with knowledge lately: things keep getting unified. The mind-body problem we already discussed, and that one's no longer an issue, once you get a grip on what I'm saying."

The elevator stops, letting us all off back into the spacious lobby that Mariska liked. She was right: it's cozier and cleaner and better decorated than my apartment. I'd not noticed so on the way in.

Dave keeps right on going. For someone recently wounded, he's got a lot of energy, though on the ride up here Jack and Mariska explained to me that they'd spoken to his nurse, who confirmed that the only things he was on included an antibiotic for the injury site and a narcotic for pain. Dave denied taking any of the latter so far; he hates being on drugs, but folks high on life can be even weirder, I'm learning. "And then there's space and time, and the philosophers and astronomers now talk of spacetime, one entity, one measurement. And then there's the old convention of past and future, but if you really think about it, we're conscious of a little bit of past, a tiny sliver of present, and a slight projection of future, at any given moment, so there's no need to worry about that one either. And there are also those little quanta, which sometimes act as particles and sometimes as waves, so they seem to be different things at different times but they're actually not. And finally, this notion of our seeing ourselves as separate from the rest of Nature is going away. Call it separation from God if you want, it amounts to the same thing just with different manifestations. At any rate, can any of you feel the molecules between us right now? Or the quanta, or even just the air itself?"

We stop by the main doors. Apparently Jack wants to wind this one up before we start driving back. That means he really wants to concentrate.

"You okay, old buddy?" Jack says, only half-joking.

"I promised you the answer about the immortality question. A while ago you were all excited about it; don't give up on me now!"

"Okay, then what is it?" Mariska this time.

"Iska, if there's no separation between matter and energy, if they're really essentially the same, and if we see ourselves as being made of some kind of matter, then isn't it safe to say that we're energized? In other words, we see this fleshy mass," and he pinches his right arm near the elbow, away from the injury site, "and it feels material, but so many of us believe in something spiritual also. That was part of the mind-body dichotomy, too, just with an older religious spin to it."

"Yeah," Jack says slowly, trying to take it all in.

"Yeah," Dave adds, "if energy and matter are the same, just manifested differently, and if energy can never be created nor destroyed," he pauses now, letting us all follow.

"Right," I say, gently prodding.

"Then where does the energy that makes us alive go when we die? Do you see now? This is the reason why there are no divisions, why the ancients got it right after all, some of them anyway. It's taken us this long to realize it!" Dave cheers as he says this, tossing the blue marble up into the air and catching it effortlessly. I have a brief image of God doing the same thing on a larger scale, then remember that I'm a religious agnostic.

"Wait, what about the 'molecules between us'?" Mariska wants to know.

"What? Oh, that was just an example. I remember, when I was a kid, just kind of intuitively feeling that whatever tiny things we're all made of, we're necessarily connected to everything else that exists. It's taken years for me to figure it out this clearly, though. At least, it seems clear to me, or it's starting to."

"Let's just head out to the car," I say, vaguely noticing that some other folks, the doctors not among them, gathering in the center of the lobby. Once upon a time, they might have become a mob at the sound of such potentially heretical thoughts given voice.

Dave is suddenly serious. "Guys, where does the energy go when we die?"

Shrugs all around. Maybe some security guards will show up soon.

"It must go somewhere. The energy animating these fleshy bodies must necessarily and literally go to another location when we cease to be alive. Otherwise, there's either no actual energy animating us, or energy can be destroyed after all, both of which are logically and demonstrably false."

Dawning light, I wonder now, feeling like I might be starting to get it. "Then if energy and matter aren't really separate things after all, that same energy has to be reformed somehow, in something we'd describe as physical?"

"I really love you, Morgan." That's the first time he's said it quite like that. I didn't quite picture that "first time" to turn out quite like this. "That's a gorgeous description. And it's true. All the atoms and quanta or whatever component parts make up this weirdly elusive 'Dave' will automatically become something else someday."

Leave it to Jack to add the joke to the logic: "So you're saying, in essence, that I might have once been, for instance, a tyrannosaur's colon?"

Mariska howls at that. I mean, her laughter really almost sounds like the howling we tried when we started hiking days ago, it's so high-pitched and nasally. "Jack the dinosaur's butthole," she says.

Dave's laughing, too, though not quite as animatedly; he's far too animated on ideas. "Sure. Why not? We began as spacedust, and we return to that state. And even the spacedust gets reformed eventually into other things. How cool is that?"

"You can't base a religion on this, you know," I tell him.

"Exactly, which makes it even better news. There's no way to use this as a form of power over others, so far as I know, nor any money to be made from it."

"Except maybe offering it as a story," I add, grinning. Dave glares at me mischievously. I can only imagine what the publishers for young readers might have to say if he added Jack's curious but logically intact imagery to "Packs." Dennis would probably love it, his mother likely hate it.

And then I wonder about my own mother again. Where is "she" now? All those component unimaginably small parts which made "her?" Hopefully not lining some huge animal's posterior, but she's still here, in a very literal sense. Maybe that's why I swear I can sometimes still feel her. She's everywhere, in another sense.

Also like the old descriptions of God. *Where do these thoughts keep coming from?* I wonder, hoping they're just part and parcel from my upbringing in a culture which often uses divine explanations for the grand mysteries.

"Come on," Dave says, trying to throw his one good arm around all of us at once, which of course doesn't work very well. "I starve. Feed me." And out the doors we go, leaving the curious onlookers wondering what they've possibly witnessed.

"You know, guys," Dave says a couple of minutes later, climbing gracelessly into the car but insisting that he doesn't need help maneuvering. "That bit about immortality is for you: not everyone's going to believe it. It's especially odd for Westerners, since we've been separating ourselves rationally from everything else since the presocratic Greeks. We can't handle the notion that we're all connected and that these supposed divisions are just illusory, but it has a price. It's what caused us to believe that we're better than everything else."

Jack rolls his eyes while pulling on his seatbelt. "Not the philosophers again."

"Don't worry, I won't take this anywhere. Just remember what I told you. We do go on, you know. The energy must go somewhere. It cannot just disappear."

Jack's about to start backing up while Mariska and I finish getting in together in the back, and then we're moving. "So where do you suppose the energy of those wolves we saw so recently took them? You know, that pack?" I deliberately emphasize the last word so the reference is unmistakable to Dave.

"I really have to wonder," Mariska says. "I hope they make it." I notice Mariska glued to the sight of some ravens flying overhead. She's always watching the birds, fascinated with the little mystery of where they go and what they do.

Gliding through the hospital parking lot and aiming for the nearby highway, all of us save for Jack stare northward, wondering the same thing about the wolves we saw.

"I love you guys," I say impulsively. "I really do. I wouldn't have missed this trip for the world, weird as that sounds." I reach over the passenger seat and massage Dave's shoulders. "And I'm just glad you're okay."

He takes my hand and kisses it while Jack steers onto the onramp. "Thanks. Let's go home."

The colors outside the car dazzle: brilliant gold and shining green, with a clear day offering an azure background for the mountains while we drive through the flatlands glimpsed from Dave's hospital window. "Tell me about your arguments," I say now.

Jack tries to see me in the rearview mirror, and Mariska I know is also curious. Arguments? "You mean from what I left in your apartment?" Dave says.

"Of course. Tell me why we have to preserve the wild things."

"Is this an extension of what you just said using your little planet model?" Mariska says. "Or are you back to our little talk on ethics from a while ago?"

He sighs, ready to practice on us, but it's difficult. It's exceedingly difficult to explain your words when they're private and important to you, even when you're sharing them with friends. And it's harder still to get them across when your audience is hostile, which is what I'm easily anticipating from the readership of something like "Packs," or the little story about what Jack told us regarding certain managerial practices in Kenya.

So Dave begins. "There are five premises for the necessary conclusion of preserving wildlife, as I see it. And none of this is based on violent passions either way, and none of it espouses any particular political agenda, and they're not based on ego or sentiment or that nauseatingly selfish notion of 'preserving things for future generations,' which is actually just another ego statement."

None of the rest of us encourage him. We just let him talk. We're passing the spot in the Valley where we noticed the mother moose with her calf when we were driving in the other direction recently. It feels like years ago.

"When we saw the wolves, I was just reminded of all this. It just came crashing back, and the wolves are such strong symbols, so I'll talk about them. I'm fascinated by them, and by how they represent so much up here, for good and bad. But whenever they get mentioned, most of what I hear is about egos and power and misinformation."

"Why power?" Jack says. He seems the father figure now in the car, as Dave was earlier when he was driving.

"When you forget those connections I've been talking about this whole trip, then you start clamoring for power, maybe because some part of you recognizes that you've already lost, at least once you've forgotten that those divisions are bullshit. But as pertaining to the wildlife, the concerns regarding this abuse of power and misinformation and the argument that I alluded to are as follows.

"The first premise is political: Alaskan voters have repeatedly indicated their refusal to permit airborne hunting of wolves, and continue to be ignored, so that when the ballot issue comes up a final time it's worded so strangely voters seem to either have trouble deciphering it or they just feel apathetic for being illegally overruled. The second premise is economic: Alaska is dependent on outside revenues, and many persons are willing to pay for the chance of seeing large species, including predators such as wolves, and are liable to spend their money elsewhere in protest. That's similar to what Jack told us a while back from his excursion to Africa." I see Jack nod in the front seat.

"Next comes the scientific premise: all ecosystems must have predators to remain healthy, and this has been demonstrated repeatedly around the world. Without them, there's all kinds of needless suffering with the skewed populations. And then fourth, there's the main logical point, in that blaming another species for decreases in prey populations that have actually been caused by combinations of weather and human intervention is irrational and fallacious. That's what really happened in the parts of Alaska where all this unnecessary and unjustifiable hunting and trapping has taken place: people refuse to take responsibility. We've turned irresponsibility into an art form in this country. Most of the lawyers and all of the talk-show hosts would be out of business if that wasn't true. We always have someone else to blame in this nation.

"And finally," Dave says, pausing for a deeper breath this time. I've already described the passion he gets when speaking. I'm going to try to see if he wants to pursue teaching after leaving emergency work, assuming he does want to leave, which I'm hardly questioning. "We come to the moral issue, one we've touched on so far but which needs clarification. And it's like this: taking false and unjustified revenge against anyone, including another species, is an action that can only be described as cowardly. Like what I said to those goddamned hunters. I'm not anti-hunting. I'm actually anti-unnecessary causing of suffering, and I'm particularly against the ego statements which often accompany hunting, like with that idiotically selfish pursuit of trophies. If you're going to use the animal, then use it all, but don't just waste so much of it so you can have a pelt or a rack or whatever else."

"And it's not based on just opinions, right, old friend?"

Dave laughs, recalling the talk from four days previously. "No, Jack. It's an argument, an actual argument, with five premises drawn from five key issues by which we live our modern lives: politics, economics, biology, logic, and ethics." He sounds pleased but not arrogant, like he knows how painfully slow people can be to change, while they can alter their behavior with alarming and dangerous speed when they're engaged by group-based passion. We call it "group think," but it's actually the absence of thought. Only individuals can think; that's the real difference. The groups are more about identity and survival.

Several minutes go by. We small talk a bit about where to go for some food, hoping Dave can hold out until Eagle River, where we know some great places in a variety of genres. And then Dave finishes.

"Wolves are ideas, too, you know. Just like all of us. They're as necessary to what I'm trying to say about interconnectivity as logical ideas are to philosophy. I mean, they interact, often violently. They strive for dominance amongst themselves, but also get regularly replaced by others. They seem to take nothing for granted. They require fresh input to avoid inbreeding, just as thought requires fresh input to avoid stagnation. They exist hierarchically, and they have to remain on regular vigilance, maybe just because they realize somehow that their time is temporary. Just like ours, and just like ideas. I'm so glad we saw them." I can feel him shudder slightly as he says that. Maybe it was just his shoulder bothering him a bit.

"They are also adaptable," Mariska says, getting in on this now. "Anything we domesticate, animal or plant, requires flexibility in diet, rapid growth, an ability to reproduce in captivity. In the case of animals specifically, they also have to have what we would call a pleasant disposition."

"They also need some resistance to fear," I contribute now, recalling our talk about that painful topic. "And they need to be able to alter their social arrangements, just like we do," and I knead Dave's neck and left shoulder a little firmer at that. "That's why we turned them into dogs. But we can't forget what the dogs really are."

"Like we cannot forget what we are, also," Mariska says quietly.

* * *

Scores of kilometers northward, near a river racing its endless way through tundra and taiga, two wolves sat staring at each other. There were no sharp territorial boundaries here, so it was safe: the Chelatna pack lands lay to the west, and the Fire Creek survivors were still marking out a tentative new territory roughly thirty kilometers south, where the tree cover proved thick and the hunting promising. The four of them had managed to feast on a yearling caribou that had carelessly strayed from its small herd.

With a buffer zone between the territories being established, these two individuals felt more secure in their approach.

Neither had known the other would be there, but both had the same idea. And with that timeless canid curiosity, each had wandered slowly and stealthily away from pack duties until they were once again adjacent to the Kahiltna River, though some twenty kilometers south of where they'd been disrupted by the noisy and smelly bipeds.

Dog-chaser recognized Rendezvous partly by sight and partly by scent when she appeared. He'd been lazily waiting there, not feeling rushed for the first time in more days than he cared to remember. And it was good to take a break from the pack, much as he cared about them all. There'd been very little picking on him as the *omega* during their ordeal, but it was still refreshing to venture off a bit.

The male wolf came to attention immediately upon Rendezvous' arrival. She noticed him quickly also, and sat on her haunches, panting lightly and savoring the breeze which blew her recognizable scent down towards Dog-chaser's alert nostrils.

They each sat, wondering about each other, until Dog-chaser, cautiously and anxiously, rose and began walking towards Rendezvous. There were no howls, no warnings, no threats, just two wolves who had the capacity to head off on their own and become a new pack: two current *omegas* who would automatically become their own *alphas* if they chose. Sometimes there were delicious options in the world of wolves.

Dog-chaser made eye contact with Rendezvous from a distance of just the few remaining meters, then brazenly closed the distance and licked her muzzle, receiving a surprisingly warm if sloppy greeting in return. There was no reason for the pair of them to be enemies. It was so simple, and yet not often easy. To them it simply felt good to be alive, right in that moment, temporarily without any other concerns.

For they are wolves. And this is their story as well as ours.

Afterword

This is of course a work of fiction, though the following souls have graciously contributed to the background information contained throughout this novel. Please understand that any and all technical and factual errors which might occur in the text are solely my own responsibility, not theirs, and that their mention here does not mean they always (or even often) agree with what I say. My thanks goes out to every one of these individuals, as they represent specialties as diverse as Alaskana, aviation, biology, canid and other wildlife research, dancing, education, emergency health care, history, literature, martial arts, parenting, philosophy, photography, and travel, all of which were topical necessities for "Packs"...

...Stephanie Bauer, Jon Bogart, Sam Bogart, Connie Brandel, Tom Buller, Mike Citti, Jayne Crupi, Caroline DeVorss, Jennifer Dow, Erin French, Francis French, Martyn Giles, Wendy Giles, Patricia Goodmann, Johnathon Green, Petra Grosskinsky, Henry Hedberg, Erik Hirschmann, Davin Holen, Stewart Iskow, William Jamison, Martin Jeckelmann, Siri Kavanaugh, Dorothy Keeler, Leo Keeler, Erich Klinghammer, Isabelle Lange, Michael Levy, James Liszka, Tom Meier, Willie Murry, Jon Nickles, Joan O'Leary, Todd Palmatier, Chris Rahe, Pat Russell, Tracey Scott, Bill Sherwonit, Asta Spurgis, Lori Stuart, Maria Talasz, Tom Talasz, Wade Turner, Vic van Ballenberghe, Sandra van Bork, Corinna Vehreschild, Henry Wilson, Rodger Withers, Dave Wollert, Kendra Wollert, Ken Zoll, and my various students, who remind me to never stop thinking, especially Lucas Becker, Seth Bowen, Sara Brock, Art Carney, Kim Doss, Ricky English, Casey Lark, David Leonard, Chris Lindgren, Breanna Maniaci, Bailey Orbeck, Chad Rancourt, Tiffany Ruby, Michelle Scott-Weber, Kira Singleton, Jamie Tuttle, Heather Wilson, and Lindsay Windel.